Death will never have the final word if you are a believer.
– Sergio White

And what if I too, am a believer? – Death

You Are Not Supposed to be Here

By

Matthew F. Winn

Any resemblance to persons living or dead is purely coincidental.

Printed in the United States of America

Other Books by Matthew F. Winn

The Sandman
Bring Me a Dream
Circle of Friends
Every Picture Tells a Story
Stealing Rembrandt
Chasing Shadows in the Dark
The Legacy
Shadowman
Bokeh
Mishipeshu-The Legend of Grand Island

Coming soon

Merrow
Jack Kerouac Can Kiss My Ass
King of Hearts
Driven

Cover photography by the author
See more photographic works at www.splashofsunset.com
Published by Artist's Point Press

For Aunt Liney, who challenged me to always push the boundaries.

Chapter One

Shadows clawed their way across the pitch-black tarmac threatening to snatch up two young boys as they hurried through the backstreets of Detroit trying to make it home before curfew. Baked by the heat of the late summer sun the blacktop released a steaming, putrid amalgam of motor oil, anti-freeze, spoiled food, and death. An old, abandoned church loomed over the boys like an evil sentinel watching them, judging their every step. Broken stained glass windows imparted the façade with the appearance of having row after row of vicious, jagged teeth looking for an innocent soul for which to dine.

"You know, mom is going to blister your ass for having me out this late, and especially for bringing me home through this neighborhood," Grayson said, his contrasting green eyes sparkling with mischief and his voice laced with derision.

"And she will blister your butt even harder for using such foul language," Wayne, his older brother replied followed by a punch to the boy's shoulder. Wayne was the older of the two by four, almost five years, and he was also the better behaved of the two.

Grayson buzzed around the tarmac like a bee on crack until he found a fist sized chunk of broken asphalt. He hefted the asphalt several times before letting it fly with a grunt. All the windows in the façade of the church from twenty feet down to the ground had already been broken out decades ago and were covered with a diamond shaped wire grating to keep trespassers out. The projectile arced at no more than fifteen feet in the air before falling harmlessly into a weed patch sprouting up from the tarmac at the edge of the building.

"What a sissy throw," Wayne said with a shove, knocking his little brother off balance.

The older sibling searched the dark macadam until he found a rock suitable for his own nefarious deed, tossed it up and down into his palm several times before letting it fly. The throwing attempt was dismal at best, the rock did not even travel far enough to hit the building, let alone a window nearly thirty feet up.

Grayson laughed so hard he was unable to catch his breath for several minutes. When he was finally able to speak, he said, "Marquisha Wright can throw better than you and she's only seven years old."

"Shut up. It went further than yours did."

"Maury says, that was a lie."

"That rock was no good, it slipped out of my hand."

"I'll bet you ten dollars you couldn't hit that window with the most perfectest rock ever."

"That's not even a word, you dweeb," Wayne said.

"You know what I meant, chump. Is it a bet or not?" Grayson asked. When his brother did not respond he began to flap his arms and cluck like a chicken.

Wayne tried to hide his anger and embarrassment by moving further into the shadows away from his annoying little brother. As he was combing the area for the *perfectest rock ever* he recalled a lesson his physics teacher taught the class about using a sling to launch a projectile further than one could with their naked arm.

"Give me your hat," he demanded from his little brother.

"No. Why do you want my hat?" Grayson asked while backing away.

Wayne chased after his little brother, took the hat off his head, and dropped a baseball sized rock into the hat. He ran toward the building and once he reached what he felt was the optimal distance he spun around several rotations like a discus thrower and let the rock fly. The two boys watched as the hat sailed through the air and crashed through one of the few remaining panes of glass, hanging up on a saw-toothed piece of stained glass where it settled into place.

"Hey, you threw my hat up there."

Wayne shrugged and shot his brother a smug grin. "It was an accident. But you owe me ten bucks."

Grayson stared up at the façade and his Detroit Lion's cap dangling from a jagged piece of glass three stories up. And then he began to laugh.

"What are you laughing about you little dweeb?"

"Dad is going to bust your ass when we get home!"

"Why would dad be mad at me?"

"Because that was his hat signed by Barry Sanders, and you got it stuck way up there," Grayson laughed while pointing up at the unreachable apparel.

"Dad let you wear his autographed Barry Sanders hat out of the house?"

Grayson stopped laughing and let the gravity of the situation sink in. Butterflies plagued his stomach, and tears began to form in his eyes.

"Oh crap. You just took it? Hey, don't cry. We'll get it back. Start looking for a long stick or something."

"A thirty-foot stick?"

"Just start looking."

The boys separated from one another and walked the parking lot looking for a stick or long branch. Wayne watched in horror as his little brother plucked something from the ground and popped it into his mouth. When he repeated the process, Wayne felt compelled to intervene.

"Just what in the heck do you think you are doing?"

"Having a snack."

"You don't even know what you're eating. That could be poison."

"Nuh uh. My science teacher showed the class pictures of this plant and told us it was edible. It tastes pretty good too," Grayson stooped to pluck another leaf from the plant and plop it into his mouth while dramatically chomping his teeth.

"How many homeless dudes and winos do you think come around here? Not to mention junkies judging by the needles on the ground."

Grayson shrugged and plucked another leaf, more to irritate his brother than anything else. "So, what does that have to do with anything?"

"Where do you think they pee?"

Grayson's face soured and he spit out the leaf he was chewing. He stuck his tongue out and rubbed it with his shirt until he thought he would draw blood.

"What did you tell me that for?" but his words were so jumbled Wayne didn't understand a word his little brother said, though he did get the gist of it.

Wayne shook his head and checked his watch. They were supposed to have been home fifteen minutes ago. Another fifteen minutes and their mother would start to worry. Another thirty minutes and she would be pissed. He didn't want to begin to imagine her mood if they showed up an hour late, or God forbid, resort to sending their father out to find them.

"It's easy as one, two, three, baby you and me girl," Grayson sang while looking for something to reach the hat with.

"What are you doing over there?"

"Singing."

"Man, that ain't singing. You shouldn't do what you can't do," Wayne said.

"Yeah, well mom couldn't have a good-looking son, but she had you anyway."

"You're so stupid. She had you too brainiac, remember."

Grayson shrugged and went back to singing. He made certain to be even more out of key just for his brother's sake.

"Man, why don't you sing something else more up to date than dad's dusty old records."

"Like what?"

"I don't know. Billie Jean or Thriller. Something like that."

"Can't."

"Why not?"

"Because I don't know the words. I can't understand a thing the man is singing half the time. I mean really, what in the hell is shamon or you nuv it? And why the hell did he sing about some woman named Annie Oakley from the olden wild west times anyway?"

Wayne shook his head for the umpteenth time that night and disappeared into the shadows while trying to ignore his little brother's horrendous singing. He picked through rubbish and debris piles and was getting nervous they wouldn't be able to get his dad's favorite hat back.

"Wayne, I think I found a way in," Grayson called out from an alcove hiding a chained door within its shadows.

The chain was loose enough to allow the door to open a few inches.

"Man, you been eatin' too much Popeye's to fit through that opening," Wayne said.

"You just watch me," he said, sucking in his gut while sliding sideways into the opening.

"Go Boy Wonder."

"Shut up. You know I don't like it when you call me that."

"Why not, it was Robin's nickname. I was named after Batman, and you were named after the Boy Wonder."

"Nuh uh. I was named after Uncle Grayson. Mom even said."

"We don't have an Uncle Grayson."

"Do too."

"You ever see him at any family reunion? Church? Thanksgiving or Christmas? Nope, because we don't have an Uncle Grayson."

"Do too. He's dead."

The debate over Uncle Grayson fell by the wayside as the tandem worked in earnest to squeeze eight inches of Grayson through a five-inch gap. The boy sucked in hard one last time and his brother was able to shove him through the rest of the way. He stood in the decaying building trying to catch his breath when it dawned on him just how dark the place was inside and for an old, deserted building it sure made a lot of noise.

"Wayne, it's too dark in here. I can't see where I'm going."

"Here, use the flashlight on my phone. Just be careful and don't drop it. I just got the screen replaced a few weeks ago and it cost me two whole months' pay," Wayne said, handing his phone to his brother through the gap in the door.

Grayson panned his brother's cell phone around the expansive room and trembled at the myriad of shadows scurrying about the room from every corner. He knew they were just shadows created by the phone's flashlight, but he couldn't help feeling there were creatures lurking about in the darkness eyeballing him with bad intent.

"What are you doing? Quit lollygagging," Wayne asked.

"I'm scared," he said, but then he laughed. "Lollygagging, you're starting to sound like the old man."

"I dare you to call Pops old man to his face."

It got quiet again and Wayne could tell his little brother was scared to death but wouldn't admit it. He resisted the urge to taunt his little brother with tales of a haunted church, partially because it was the right thing to do, but mainly because he was spooked too, standing outside a haunted church by himself in a dark alley frequented by the city's most undesirable denizens.

"I know you're scared, and I would be too. I can't fit through the door, or I would come with you. The faster you get the hat the faster we can get the hell out of here. Find the stairs, they should be close."

Grayson gave himself a pep talk, trying to calm his nerves as he panned the cell phone's flashlight around the room before leaving the safety of his brother. Several steps beyond the alcove he found himself in a small room with passages leading in all four directions. Grayson shined the light down one of the passages which reflected off stainless steel surfaces. The kitchen. The door he squeezed through must have been a service entrance.

While most of the kitchen gadgetry was strewn across the dusty tile floor, a couple of ladles and pans still hung from hooks on a rack suspended from the ceiling in the industrial kitchen. Light swept across a row of stainless-steel cupboards at the ground level and Grayson was struck by an alarming memory of a scene from a scary movie his brother let him watch when their mom and dad were having date night. He couldn't remember the name, but the kid was being chased through a hotel kitchen by an evil man, so he hid in cupboards just like these.

Grayson quickly moved in the opposite direction while panning the light, revealing a shaded area to the rear of the room away from him, and even further away from the safety of his brother. Thinking it might be a stairwell the boy crept through the darkness one methodical step at a time.

"Come on, Grayson, hurry up," Wayne whispered loudly through the crack in the door.

The sudden introduction of sound into the silence startled Grayson and he almost dropped his brother's phone.

"Man, are you trying to give me a heart attack?" he yelled back, immediately regretful. Not only had his own voice echoing off the walls given him the willies, it also alerted any crackheads who might be squatting in the building that they were no longer alone.

Grayson hovered at the bottom of the stairs, not sure if all this effort was worth it to avoid an ass whooping and then he remembered his father's overly large hands. And though there was a very good chance his father would not resort to corporal punishment, the look of disappointment in his eyes would be devastating. No, he had to retrieve his father's prized possession and that was all there was too it.

He crept up the rickety staircase, each step squeaking louder than the last until he feared he would break through the rotten wood and fall down behind the stairs. Which of course brought to life another horror movie memory in which demented people were living behind the stairs in a creepy old house. Grayson bounded up the last six steps until he was safely off the staircase.

The room above opened into a space so expansive the phone's flashlight could only illuminate a few feet in front of him. This room must have been where the congregation sat as there were a few wooden pews scattered across the floor along with dozens of mildewed hymnals strewn about. Many of the benches had been tipped over with most of them having been destroyed for firewood as evidenced by numerous piles of charred wood and ash dispersed about the room. The scent of mold and decay hung thickly in the air and Grayson fought the urge to sneeze.

Grayson stood in the expansive room trying to get his bearings straight. He mentally walked through the turns he had taken from when he first entered the building to determine which bank of windows the hat should be hanging in. The problem was he was surrounded by windows and had become disoriented.

"Come on Grayson, man, think," he said aloud, just to hear something other than the silence.

The room was so large and dark it made it nearly impossible for him to be able to gather his sense of direction. Fear chewed away at his brain as he moved further and further away from the stairwell and the protection of his big brother. An old, mildewed hymnal went skidding across the floor after he accidentally kicked it, scaring him nearly to death.

Yellow light cast dirty shadows across the floor several feet in front of him, so Grayson slowly eased his way toward it. The light grew larger as he neared the spot in the floor where it was shining. He realized he had been standing under a balcony with row after row of seats snaking around the upper floor casting the large shadow in the room. Light was creeping in through a shard of yellow stained glass still clinging defiantly in the frame. The boy recognized the imagery in the remaining piece of stained glass as the Immaculate Heart of Mary still grasping at life amidst all the decay. The tired old mercury vapor light outside flickered making the heart appear as if it were beating.

Grayson shook off his shivers, scanned the bank of windows, and was quickly rewarded with a glimpse of his father's autographed Barry Sanders hat dangling in the shadows. A sense of relief washed over him, and he started looking for a way up to the balcony. As he panned the phone around the balcony, he let loose a scream he was barely able to muffle in the crook of his arm. There were dozens of creepy faces staring down at him from serpentine rows of seats above.

Graffiti artists, some good, some talentless hacks, had painted faces on the backrests of the balcony chairs with reflective paint. Most were just rudimentary stick figure faces but there were a few elaborately painted evil clown faces that creeped him out and it took him several moments before he was able to compose himself.

Wayne checked his watch for the third time since Grayson entered the building by himself more than fifteen minutes earlier. He was mired in regret for having let his little brother brave this creepy place all by himself. He tried several times unsuccessfully to squeeze through the opening in the door and had stepped away from the building to catch his breath when a flicker of movement from above caught his attention.

A dim glow was traveling from window to window toward his direction from halfway down the building. It emanated from the same floor Grayson was headed to retrieve their father's hat. At first Wayne thought it was a security guard with a flashlight patrolling the building but there was something off about the manner in which the light moved. He backed away from the building another ten feet and peered up at the line of windows. Another flash of light caught his attention from his left side. The flashlight on his phone alerted him that his brother might be headed straight into trouble.

Even in his near pitch-black surroundings Grayson managed to find a small, winding staircase with only three steps on each level that angled up to the gallery above. Once he was up on the balcony, he was able to move a little faster using the rows of seats to guide him through the darkness to the windows. Ignoring the clown faces he clamped his free hand on the backs of the seats and started for the far side row of windows.

"Grayson. Grayson," Wayne called out through cupped hands.

When that didn't get his brother's attention he moved back to the door and put his head as far through the crack as he could and started yelling his brother's name. He heard a noise coming from the bank of windows above, so he backed away from the building and looked up. Wayne never had a chance to react to the brick hurling through the air toward his head.

With a sense of urgency Grayson picked up the pace. He had become adept at moving through the rows using the seat backs to guide him and he wanted nothing more than to get the damned hat and be done with this creepy place. His plan was to just flick the hat out of the window and down to his brother waiting below but there was wire mesh over the glass and if he screwed up the hat would fall between the wall and the mesh to be lost forever.

Grayson climbed up onto the last seat in the row and stretched out as far as he possibly could. It took him several attempts but finally he had his father's prize possession back in his grasp. He moved down the rows several windows away where the glass was broken lower in the frame so he could yell down to Wayne. Grayson scrambled up onto what little windowsill there was and leaned against the wire mesh until he was able to find a spot to look through, allowing him to see his brother down below. He leaned out as far as he dared and was ready to holler down when he saw Wayne was lying face down on the concrete and it looked like his head was bleeding. Light flickered off the metal window frame beside him and Grayson realized he was no longer alone.

~ ~ ~

"You are not supposed to be here," a peculiar, gravelly voice echoed from behind him.

Grayson was too terrified to turn around and he began to formulate a good excuse for his being in the abandoned church, one believable enough the security guard or cop wouldn't hassle him too much.

Before Grayson could say anything, the man began to ramble. "That's what she said to me, you are not supposed to be here. But I tricked her. She is the one who can't come in here."

Something about the man's voice raised more alarm in the boy than if this had been a security guard. This person was not normal. Slowly he craned his neck around, took a deep breath and opened his eyes and screamed. Before him stood a man holding a hurricane lamp, the flickering flames distorting his face into something far beyond grotesque. The man's eyes were wide and wobbly in their sockets, scanning Grayson up and down, side to side. And yet Grayson felt as if the man didn't even see him.

The alabaster white skinned man pounded the side of his head with his fist so hard Grayson could hear the dull thumping. His eyes stopped moving and focused on the boy. His tongue snaked out from between his teeth and licked around his ruby red lips.

"She said I wasn't supposed to be here, but I showed her. Are you supposed to be here?" he said with wild accusatory eyes and a boney finger stabbed in the boy's direction. He raked his other hand through a tangled halo of untamed coal black hair splayed out in all directions.

Grayson stammered for a brief second, pondering what the man had said until he noticed the finger pointed in his direction was not the man's own finger, but was attached to a severed hand impaled on a hook screwed into the end of the man's right arm. He stopped pointing long enough to take a bite of the gruesome appendage which was more than enough impetus to send Grayson screaming and he shoved his way around the man as he scurried down the row of bleachers. The man was blocking the stairs down to the first floor forcing Grayson to run out of the back of the balcony and into a long, dark corridor leading away from the windows and his injured brother.

Terrified, the boy ducked inside of an alcove, turned off the phone's flashlight and peeked back in the direction he had run from. There wasn't any light being cast from the man's lantern but that didn't mean he hadn't simply blown out the flame. Grayson laid down, held his breath, and listened. He could hear the man mumbling but he was far enough away that he couldn't make out what he was saying.

Grayson stayed low to the floor and slid down the wall using the solid surface to feel his way along. Soon he came to another alcove, and he began to visualize the layout in his head. It reminded him of his school with classrooms staggered on both sides of a long corridor. Grayson eased his back into the corner of the next recess and slid up the wall until he was standing upright. He groped in the darkness until he found a doorknob only to find the door was locked.

It unnerved him that while he was getting further away from the crazy man and his mumbling, he was also getting further and further away from Wayne and the exit. Grayson's eyes had started to adjust to the complete darkness and while he couldn't even see his own hand unless it was touching his nose, he could make out different shades in the shadows. After three locked doors he decided to slide over to the other side of the corridor to check those doors.

Fearful of dropping through a hole in the decrepit floor he sank to his haunches and began to ease across to the other side. It was a painstakingly slow process as he reached out and tested the wooden floor with his hand each time before scooting another six inches across the hall.

Jessup Porter surveyed his reflection in the dingy window glass and combed his wild hair with his fingers. He didn't mean to scare the child away. How long had it been since he had someone to provide him with meaningful conversation and food for thought? How long indeed.

"I just need food for thought," Jessup called out down the inky corridor while tapping the fingernails of the putrefied hand against the window glass.

Grayson sucked in his breath and held perfectly still. Slowly he craned his neck around to see there was a dirty, golden glow spilling across the floor at the other end of the corridor. The man was coming. He scrambled to his feet using the doorknob as leverage. Thankfully, this knob turned, allowing him to slip into the room.

The boy fought back his fear and entered the room, easing the door closed behind him and locking it behind him. With his back against the wall, he put his brother's phone under his shirt to dim the brightness of the light and turned it on. He was in a classroom. There were two old style, gray desks with rusty legs and deteriorating wooden tops in the center of the room. He gasped when he realized there were two people sitting at the desks facing the chalkboard at the front of the room and averted the flashlight beam.

It took him several minutes to compose himself during which he held his breath and listened to the blood coursing through his ears, but nothing else. While he knew he had seen two people in chairs, he also knew it just couldn't be the case. It was too quiet in the room and neither of them moved in the slightest even after he called out to them in whispers. He considered they might be passed out crackheads.

He crept down to the left side of the room with his back to the wall until he ran out of real estate into the far corner. He paused for a few seconds, then turned the phone light on for a brief flash. He was shocked and almost screamed at first. They didn't have any legs. Then Grayson laughed. The people sitting at the desks were those stupid dolls used in CPR First Aid class at the YMCA.

A sense of relief washed over him until he remembered the crazy man stalking him. He thought about calling 911 but that would bring the cops, and ultimately his parents and that was an ass whooping he had every intention of avoiding. Using the flashlight sparingly, he panned the room looking for another door or another way out. Words scrawled on the blackboard in yellow chalk caught his attention.

You Are Not Supposed to Be Here!

The words were written over and over and over again on all three panels of the large blackboard as if a teacher had handed down punishment to an unruly student. At first, the passage had been written uniformly from left to right and top to bottom. But once the person who wrote the words ran out of room, they began scribbling the words vertically in the margins. On the floor beneath the chalkboard scribbled in the chalk dust were the same sentences in large, block letters. An uneasy feeling washed over him, and Grayson shivered.

Although he knew they were just CPR dummies, the occupants of the ancient gray school desks still creeped him out. They had been dressed in cheerleader's outfits that were tattered and torn. The outfits were so dingy it was impossible to discern their original colors.

He panned the room with the flashlight and saw nearly every square inch of the room, including the ceiling, had the same phrase scribbled over and over again. What in the hell did it mean anyway? Of course, he wasn't supposed to be there, no one was supposed to be there, not even the creepy dude.

Jessop Porter fumbled with an enormous key ring, looking at the stamped numbers on the brass hilt of each one before moving it along on the tarnished loop. After several passes through all of the keys he finally found the key he was looking for and opened the first classroom.

"You can't hide from me, you see. I have all the magic keys, you see," he called out after stepping back out into the corridor and locking the empty room behind him.

Grayson heard the man's voice, but he was too far away to understand what he had said. It did, however, make him aware of how far away the man was and gave him an opportunity to use the flashlight again. When turning on the light he noticed he was down to one bar of battery life remaining and knew he had to use the phone sparingly. He needed enough battery life to call for help if he was left with no other choice.

Quickly he turned on the light and panned the large room once more. This time he saw there was indeed a door on the far wall near the corner. He turned the light off and gave his eyes a few moments to adjust to the darkness before moving quickly to the far wall. His hand trembled as he fumbled in the darkness for the doorknob. He almost laughed out loud when the knob turned, and the door opened. And then he realized he was not only moving further and further away from the exit but that he may have just trapped himself.

Chapter Two

"So, what do you think the Lion's chances are this year?" Second year patrol officer Sonny Bayless asked, wiping crumbs from a stale convenience store sandwich away from the breast pocket of his shirt.

"The same exact chance they have had every year since nineteen fifty-seven of making it to the big dance," the old veteran sergeant responded with a sneer.

"Always the optimist eh Burnsy?"

"Nope, I'm a realist."

Pundits on the sports talk station chattered on about the Detroit Lion's draft picks, giving them a poor grade overall which was par for the course. Three blocks later Sergeant Burns reached over and turned the radio off while Bayless stared off down the deserted alleys trying to stay awake. He shook his coffee cup, drained the last of the lukewarm liquid and put the cup in a plastic bag on the floor of the front seat.

"Want some more coffee?" Burns asked.

Bayless thought for a second and then nodded. Burns gave the patrol car some gas and headed for the nearest all night convenience store ten blocks away.

"Hey, Burnsy, hang on a minute."

"What's wrong? Did you see something?"

"I think so, but it could be nothing. Back up to the next alleyway."

"The one leading to old church?"

"Over there, I think there is someone lying next to the building."

"It's probably just some old drunk or addict sleeping it off. Nothing for us to concern ourselves with," Burns droned as he started to put the car in drive from reverse.

"Humor me on this one. Something didn't look right. Let's check it out," Bayless said.

"Have it your way, but if he runs, you're chasing him."

Burns put the car in drive and drove slowly up the street until he found a place to turn around. He wanted to be able to get a closer look before committing himself and his partner to a dark parking lot that could very well be an ambush which seemed to be the *in* thing to do lately. He drove passed the first entrance and took the next one so they could come up from behind the scene. Burns parked the patrol car a hundred feet from where Bayless spotted the vagrant.

Bayless was walking faster than his sergeant preferred and Burns continued to hiss at him to slow down. The older officer was being extra cautious and while he didn't draw his weapon, he flipped off the holster strap and had his hand planted firmly on the butt of the pistol.

"See, I told you, just another drunk passed out in an alleyway," Burns said and started back for the car.

"Hang on, you old cynical bastard. I think I recognize that kid, in fact I know I do now that I see his afro and that torn Red Wings jacket," Bayless said and started running to where Wayne lay unconscious on the tarmac.

"Damn it, Bayless, what in the hell are you doing? This could be an ambush."

"It's not an ambush. Go get the car, we might need the medical kit," he said and sprinted the rest of the distance once he was sure of what he was seeing.

Burns trotted back to the patrol car as fast as his near sixty-year-old legs would travel. Part of him was annoyed at the young officer, but the logical part of him knew the man was a good officer with a good head on his shoulders and a heart of gold. When the sergeant pulled up, he could see Bayless was indeed spot on, this was no passed out drunk, this was a seriously injured young boy. His partner had the boy cradled in his lap with a look of true concern etched on his face.

"Do you know him?" Burns asked, walking around to the trunk of the car to get the medical kit.

"His name is Wayne. His dad and I met at the community center must be more than ten years ago."

Burns tossed Bayless the med kit and went back to the patrol car. He called it in to dispatch and asked the fire department to send a team of paramedics.

"I called for a bus. You said you know his father."

"His pops might very well be driving that bus. His name is Isaac Bruce, he's with the Detroit Fire Department."

Burns paused for several minutes before speaking. "You said the kid's name is Wayne? And his last name is Bruce?"

Bayless laughed.

"Isaac is a Batman fan, and I do mean fanatic. He drives the replica Batmobile in all the parades and decks out the hook and ladder truck when he drives it."

"Guy must be a hoot to work with," Burns said with a measure of sarcasm while handing his partner a rolled-up towel to use as a pillow.

While Bayless was looking after the injured child, Burns went to investigate the area near the building where they found the boy. He shined his flashlight up and down the façade but didn't see anything out of place. At least not until he saw the large brick covered in blood next to a chained door that was open a crack with a torn piece of fabric clinging to the rusty strike plate.

"Does that kid have any regulars he hangs out with?" Burns called back.

"No not that I can recall. He's pretty much a school, work, and home kind of kid. Why do you ask?"

"It looks like someone may have gone inside the church. Here's what conked the kid on the noggin," he said, showing the brick to Bayless before walking back to the patrol car for an evidence bag.

Burns looked the brick over before dropping it into a paper sack, sealing it and signing the label. When he turned around, he scanned the banks of windows for any hint of movement but didn't see anything. He also looked for a place on the façade where the brick may have come loose and accidentally hit the child, but the brick wasn't even made of the same material used in the building's construction.

"Shit!" Bayless called out, startling Burns.

"What? Is something wrong?"

"Grayson," Bayless said.

"What in the hell is a Grayson?"

"Not what, who. Grayson is his little brother," Bayless responded in a somber tone. "He must have gone into the church for some reason."

The paramedics pulled up and took over Wayne's care from Bayless. A large man, named Carlos according to his name tag, was surprisingly gentle for his size. He began taking the young man's vitals with a father's concern.

"Take a look at this," Burns said, leading Bayless over to the half open door. "Could the brother have slipped between the door and the door frame here?"

Bayless tried to squeeze in himself and couldn't even get as far as his chest with all his gear on. There wasn't much room, but Grayson wasn't a very big kid either.

"I think it would be tough, but possible, especially if Wayne was shoving from the other side."

There was an outburst of commotion near the ambulance and Bayless saw that Isaac Bruce was on scene. He and Burns hurried over to diffuse any situation before it started.

"Isaac, you need to let them work on Wayne," Bayless said. "They don't have any information for you, and we have very little ourselves."

"Sonny, what happened to my boy? Was he mugged?" Isaac said, taking two long strides over to a familiar face.

"I can't say for sure what happened, but we don't think he was mugged. He was hit in the head with a brick, but there were no signs of a struggle so we're not sure how or why yet."

"What about Grayson?" Isaac asked.

"I was afraid you were going to ask about him. So, the two of them were together this evening?" Burns asked.

Isaac nodded.

"Would there be any reason for them to go inside the church? Maybe there has been one of those internet challenge things going around?" Bayless asked.

"No, nothing like that. At least nothing I've heard about. Those boys are usually smarter than to get involved with that asinine behavior. The only thing they do with Tide pods is their laundry. But I also thought they were smart enough to stick to the main roads while walking home after dark. Why are you asking about the church?"

"I think Grayson may have gone inside."

"You mean, he's in there right now?" Isaac said and started for the building.

"Hold on, we don't have any indication that is the case," Bayless said, stopping the man.

Carlos discreetly waved to Sergeant Burns who left Bayless with the father. His gut took a tumble, and he prayed it wasn't going to be devastating news.

"Is there a problem? Did the boy take a turn for the worse?"

"No, nothing like that. He'll be fine other than having a slight concussion and a neat scar to share with his friends at school. He said something about his brother."

"His little brother is in the church?" Burns asked and Carlos nodded.

A faint scream drifted out of the church across the parking lot setting every nerve on edge.

Chapter Three

"I said, let there be light, and there was light," the creepy man's voice echoed down the dark corridor followed by a loud click.

Recognizing the sound of a circuit breaker panel switch being flipped Grayson pinned himself against the wall. The room he was in was still pitch black, but he could see the faintest spill of light in the room he had just exited and knew it wouldn't be long before he was bathed in light as well. The more he thought about it the more he realized something was odd. This church had been abandoned for decades so there shouldn't be any electricity. Was this maniac just flipping the switches for dramatic effect?

"And I saw the light was good because it makes the creepy crawlies run and hide," Jessop called out, cupping his hands around his mouth.

Suddenly Grayson felt sick to his stomach. He knew he was in far more serious trouble than he first thought. This guy was not only creepy, but he talked as though he were God himself.

"Dude is bat shit crazy, just like Auntie Hazel," Grayson said aloud.

The boy knew he needed to find a way out of this jam, but he didn't dare turn on the phone's flashlight for risk of the strange man finding him. He put his back to the wall and slowly began to slide towards his right. His eyes had adjusted enough to see shapes but that was the extent of his field of vision. The room was larger than he had first thought. He had slid at least twenty feet and had yet to come to a corner.

"The creepy crawlies are going to get you," Jessop said and snapped another breaker switch.

Grayson had no way of knowing whether or not the man was really turning lights on and off without returning to the horror show classroom which he was not about to do. He needed to find a way out of this room and back to the exit if he could even remember where it was. The little boy inside him wanted to cry but the boy on his way to becoming a man wouldn't allow him to.

He ran into some boxes, knocking several of them over, sending their contents crashing to the floor. His heart pounded in his chest and his stomach threatened to expel the corn dog he had for dinner all over the floor. He caressed the darkness with his hand before proceeding another step to the right. Grayson almost screamed out loud when something dragged across his head from the right to the left side and was pressed against his ear. It felt like a hand. It was all he could do to keep from wetting himself.

"You are not supposed to be here! That is what she said to me. Can you believe that? Me? Not supposed to be here. I told her no, NO! She is the one who is not supposed to be here. But she won't leave," Jessop screamed out and banged on the door to one of the classrooms further down the decrepit corridor.

The man's psychotic rants echoed through the halls disturbing the young boy, but aside from scaring him the outbursts also gave him an indication as to how far away the man was. Grayson felt the creeper was far enough away that he could risk using the phone's flashlight, but wasn't too sure he really cared to see what was in the room with him? Did he really want to know what was tickling his ear?

"Come out, come out creepy crawler," Jessop called out while banging on another door and rattling his oversized assortment of keys.

Grayson estimated the man was only two classrooms away, so it was now or never. If he stayed in this room the man would surely find him, and he would be trapped. His hand trembled as he swiped down on the phone to reveal the flashlight application. His finger hovered over the icon, and he clamped his eyes shut as tightly as he could before pressing the flashlight button.

The boy slowly opened his eyes and had to stifle a scream. Dangling in front of his face was an antique marionette covered in cobwebs with a wicked sneer exposing its jagged teeth. The doll's eyes were bloodshot and filled with condemnation. Grayson spun it around, so it was no longer looking at him and took a quick inventory of the room.

The room was a storage room for toys, incredibly old toys. He couldn't imagine being a child when these were the playthings given to children. Every one of them, down to the stuffed tiger with blood-stained fangs were creepy and belonged in a horror movie, not a playroom. Every direction he turned he was faced with yet another marionette dangling from hooks in the ceiling. Not one of the playthings looked even the least bit friendly, causing Grayson to question the odd things adults did to children in the name of entertainment back in the day?

A bookshelf jammed full of clowns, creepy, evil-looking clowns with bad intent painted on their faces sat against the far wall. Several of the clowns were adorned with movable eyes and Grayson swore their eyes were following his every movement which he chalked up to watching too many horror movies. His skin turned clammy, and he felt as if he were going to pass out, so he leaned against the wall. When he moved, he bumped into the marionette who then spun around to face him. When he shoved it away, he accidentally pulled on one of the cords and the puppet's mouth opened and slammed its jagged teeth up and down at him several times.

Jessop knew this boy was not one of them. They would have never run from him and would certainly never hide from him. But why was the boy here? He didn't belong here. No one belonged here, not in his house. He rattled the doorknob of the next classroom. He knew the boy was hiding in the toy room, but even Jessop was scared of the toy room. That was where the little girl lived.

Grayson felt like he had those spider silk strands you get hit in the face with when walking in the forest all over his body. His skin crawled as if there were thousands of ants dancing across it and he shuddered uncontrollably. He took several deep breaths and tried to ignore the mélange of creepiness surrounding him while he looked for a way out. Just as he had feared, he was trapped. There was no door out of this room. He slid down the wall to his butt and fought to hold back his tears.

"I'm not going to hurt you, little creepy crawler. I'm just bored and hungry for some food for thought. Will you feed my mind?" Jessop called into the classroom attached to the toy room.

He knew the boy was trapped with nowhere to go. He carried a sense of pity for the child because that was a room even Jessop couldn't tolerate. But the boy hadn't screamed out yet as Porter had thought he surely would have. He certainly was a brave little cur.

Grayson took a deep breath and looked around the room, panning the flashlight from side to side. The room was nearly filled from wall to wall and floor to ceiling with books, puzzles, dolls, stuffed animals, scary clowns, and creepy marionettes. He spotted a crib and thought there might be a blanket inside he could use to stuff under the door to block the light. He got back to his feet and waded through the throngs of misfit toys until he made his way to the crib. As he had imagined, there was indeed a child's blanket inside he could use to block the light but when he pulled it out of the crib, he nearly screamed. Staring back at him from the tattered crib was a baby girl doll in a dingy white dress splattered with what he could only imagine was dried blood. The poor doll's eyes were slashed from top to bottom in a giant criss cross. The doll's skin puckered and peeled away at the wounds, and she stared up at Grayson with pleading eyes.

The sight of the doll rekindled the boy's overwhelming desire to be out of that room. He turned the doll over face down, took the blanket and blocked the bottom of the door so he could use the flashlight without worrying about the light being visible. He found an old hobby horse with a broken stick he thought would make a good weapon, so he laid it in the crib with the doll and covered the horse's snarling head which was just another disconcerting cog in this great big wheel of creepiness. The horse's head had been carved into a scream like paintings of old-time war horses he saw at the museum. And its eye was a blood red marble as if it were the devil's own steed.

"I can smell you creepy crawler. I see you met Jack and Diane, two young kids, dying the best they can," Jessop called out into the classroom as he opened the door.

Grayson stopped and listened with his ear to the door. He heard a strange clicking, squeaking sound, and realized the man was writing with chalk on the floor. He didn't need to imagine too hard to know what the man was writing. He needed to get out of that room before the creepy dude barged in.

He moved around the walls shoving and piling macabre toys against the door, piling them as high as he could as he moved through the room. Even though the door opened outward, the creepy dude would still have to shove his way through the debris to get to Grayson who would be brandishing the jagged hobby horse stick.

Grayson finally made it to the far corner of the room and began moving battered dolls with tattered dresses and vacant, staring eyes onto the pile. He was sweating both from exertion and fear, but he kept working. He reached blindly beside him to grab a life-sized doll he spied in his peripheral vision. He struggled with the doll, which was heavier than he anticipated, the skin of the doll was malleable but cold. And then a lump caught in his throat when he realized the doll was pulling back away from him.

"Grayson, man, get a grip. It's just a doll. It's just a doll," he said, panning the flashlight to his right.

The boy let loose an ear-piercing scream when he found himself face to face with a living, breathing little girl who stared back at him with an inquisitive look about her before mimicking his scream and letting loose a stifled giggle.

"Creepy crawler found the little girl, didn't he?" Jessop walked over to the door of the toy room, cupped his hands, and whispered. "Ask her if you are supposed to be here."

Bile backed up into Grayson's throat and he struggled to keep from vomiting. His tear-filled eyes fluttered, and he prayed for his father to walk through the door and make everything all right. But he knew that would not happen and he also knew everything was definitely not all right, so he clamped his eyes shut.

"This isn't real, you are just having a bad dream. It's just a dream," he chanted the mantra over and over again.

The girl studied the little boy in front of her with a measure of sadness. He was supposed to be here, which was good for him, but disappointing for the others. She admired her tattered, purple dress in a dingy mirror in the lid of an old music box with a broken, pink ballerina. She glanced away from her reflection to see the boy staring at her.

"Are you a ghost?" he asked with a slight stutter.

"No," she replied with a tilt of her head. "I am still becoming."

Grayson didn't quite understand her response and was unnerved by the fact the girl had no color. Not that she was ghostly pale, she had no color like an old black and white photograph he had seen in books. In direct contrast, the dress she wore did have color and while filthy and torn, it was a pretty shade of lavender with embroidered red roses on the front pockets.

"If you are not a ghost, then what is wrong with you? Are you undead, like a zombie or a vampire?"

Once again, she cocked her head at him, indicating a lack of understanding. "No, I am not dead, I am unborn."

Grayson stood at an impasse in the conversation, not knowing how to respond to her latest revelation. She stared at him, and he back at her, neither of them speaking. He wondered if he conked his head and was hallucinating or worse yet, in a coma.

"I know you're in there creepy crawler. It's time to squish you under my boot," Jessop said, storming toward the door while flinging desks out of his way.

Grayson's face took on a measure of panic. Even with a ghostly, "unborn" girl in the room with him, he was more terrified of the creepy dude on the other side of the door. He didn't think the little girl could help him one iota against a crazed lunatic. He turned around to say something and she was gone. But before she disappeared, she had shown him the way out. She had moved toys out of the way to expose a small hatch in the wall.

A momentary sigh of relief passed his lips until he made his way to the door and opened it only to find it led nowhere. Well, it did lead somewhere, straight down to who knew where. It was so pitch black he couldn't see the bottom even with the phone's flashlight. The creeper man pounded on the door and jiggled the door handle instilling the boy with a sense of urgency.

Fresh out of options Grayson began tossing anything soft down the chute starting with the mattress from the derelict crib. The tiger went next because he didn't like it and wanted it buried beneath layers of flotsam. Several arms loads later, Grayson shined the light down the chute. He could see the bottom now, but it seemed much too far to drop down without being seriously injured.

The door to the toy storage room burst open and Jessop screamed, "I see you creepy crawler! I'm going to squash you like a bug." He slammed his palms together and squished an imaginary insect.

The creepy dude started throwing toys behind him into the classroom in a frenzy, forcing Grayson into a tough decision. Hurriedly he shoved several arm's full of anything soft he could get his hands on. He took a deep breath and started to go headfirst down the chute but thought better of it. As he was turning himself breach into his escape canal, he glanced up to see the creepy dude marching toward him. He dropped into the chute, held on for several moments gathering nerve, stretched out as long as he possibly could and let go into the abyss.

Jessop Porter leaned as far as he could into the laundry chute and called out, "I hope you enjoy the puppet show."

Chapter Four

"How are you feeling son?" Isaac asked as he leaned over the gurney and caressed his eldest son's head.

"I'm dizzy and my head is killing me."

"You took one hell of a knock to your noggin," Burns said.

"Do you remember what happed?" Bayless asked.

"Not really. One minute I was yelling for Grayson to hurry up, and the next I was waking up on a stretcher. Oh my God, Grayson! Is he okay?" Wayne asked while trying to sit up.

"Take it easy son, we will look after Grayson. Now tell me the truth, is he in that building?"

Wayne nodded and eased back down into the prone position. "I'm sorry dad, I should have never let him go inside."

"What was he thinking going inside the building. You both know how dangerous it is, and it isn't like you two to do something so rash and foolish," Isaac said.

"Promise me you won't punish him," Wayne said.

"Son, I just want him out of there safe and sound."

"I threw your hat up there, the signed Barry Sanders ballcap, and it got stuck. But I swear, I didn't know Grayson had swiped your hat without permission or I would have never thrown it."

"Wayne, this is important. You are sure that he is still in that church?" Burns asked.

Wayne nodded.

Burns turned his attention to one of the paramedics attending to Wayne. "That chain is too big in diameter for the bolt cutters in the trunk of our car. Do you have anything that can cut through that chain?"

Carlos replied, "I don't have anything on my rig, but let me give dispatch a call and have them send the equipment truck back to the scene."

Bayless, Burns, and Isaac stepped away from the ambulance to formulate a game plan. Bayless suggested, and Burns agreed they were going to need more uniformed officers and a detective squad so Burns made the call.

"Dad. Dad," Wayne called out as the three men walked back to the ambulance. "I remember there was someone else in the building with Grayson, that's why I was yelling for him. I heard a man's voice screaming out something and when I looked up, that's when the brick hit me in the head."

"Do you remember what he screamed out?" Burns asked.

Jessop Porter paced back and forth in front of the balcony windows. They were going to ruin everything. They were going to let the little girl get away. He had to do something to stop them.

"You are not supposed to be here," Porter screamed out and began throwing pieces of brick over the broken stained-glass windows and wire meshing.

"That is exactly what he screamed at me," Wayne said.

~ ~ ~

Grayson slammed down onto the concrete floor at the bottom of the laundry chute, badly twisting his ankle and smacking both of his elbows on the hard surface. He knew it could have been much worse had he not thrown down all those toys before taking the plunge himself. He spent the next few minutes rubbing the damaged areas of his body while trying not to blubber like a little girl.

The stench permeating the basement of the church was nauseating. The air was stale and dead, making it difficult for him to breathe. It smelled worse than the garbage bin after a week baking in the summer sun after he had forgotten to take it out. He tapped the screen of the phone and saw not only was there only one bar of battery life left, that bar was blinking as well. He didn't know how much life the phone battery had left but he was certain it wasn't very much. And just what in the hell did the creepy dude mean by *I hope you enjoy the puppet show*?

Grayson rolled over onto his stomach, waited a minute or two to catch his breath and then flashed the camera flash one time and tried to commit what he saw to memory. The biggest disappointment was that there were no shafts of light reaching him and he had not seen an exit sign, meaning he had not gotten himself any closer to freedom and more than likely he was even further away from escaping this nightmare. He did manage to decipher that he was in a large room which appeared as though it had been an industrial-sized laundry, leading him to believe this place may have, at one time, been an orphanage.

He struggled back to his feet, put his back to the wall and began edging down the wall toward a door he saw when he flashed the light. Paint chips from the ceiling crunched under his feet with every step and he prayed that was all it was and not a horde of cockroaches under foot. And of course, thinking about cockroaches made the boy think about rats, and he shuddered.

Once he made his way to the door, he felt the jamb against his right shoulder and leaned against it before swinging around into the next room. Grayson stood in the doorway to the next chamber allowing his eyes to adjust enough to be able to make out the different shades of grays in the shadows. As soon as he entered the next chamber, he put his back to the wall and slowly moved to his right just like in the dungeons of his favorite video game, always move to the right. His ankle was swelling up and getting more painful with each step. He knew he would not be able to run and that scared him to his core. If creepy dude came looking, there would be no way for him to escape the deranged lunatic.

He counted each step as he travelled, and thirty steps later he still had not come to another break in the wall. The darkness enveloped him like an itchy wool blanket and Grayson shivered off a chill of fear. Even more unnerving was the fact the pungent stench was getting worse instead of better. He tried to convince himself this could actually be a good thing. If he were getting closer to a garbage gondola, then maybe he was getting closer to the outside. But then an unsettling thought occurred to him, why would an abandoned church need a garbage gondola? And if there was no trash bin, why did the basement smell of rotting meat and dirty diapers?

The jagged edges of the paint chips on the walls were cutting into his arms and shoulders as he slid to his right. He wanted to pull them away from touching the wall, but he knew he needed to be able to feel if a doorway was behind him. His hand ran into a hard metal object against the wall that Grayson had no idea by feel what it was and then he remembered the radiators in his old school before they tore it down.

Between the never-ending darkness and the constant throbbing of his ankle Grayson was disoriented and had already forgotten which direction he entered the large room. He sat down on the floor to give his ankle a rest even though he knew he couldn't rest for long, or the ankle would seize up and he wouldn't be able to walk at all. His eyes adjusted to the darkness, so he was able to make out shapes and saw there were pillars in front of him leading to the other side of the room. He got back to his feet and struggled to the first pillar where he rested his ankle again.

Even though he was fairly sure he was alone in the basement he could hear a myriad of noises coming at him from different directions and had to wonder how many different creatures were scurrying about in protest of his intrusion. He did not want to die being eaten alive by rats and finished off by cockroaches. Those thoughts gave him the impetus to strain his way back to his feet and onto the next column.

As Grayson was catching his breath while resting against the third pillar, which he estimated was the center of the room, he noticed a dirty, yellow light spilling across the floor and he hunkered down thinking the creepy dude was coming from the other direction. After several minutes of studying the dingy glow, he realized the only movement was from the light flickering, possibly from a candle.

He made his way to the next pillar, trying to ignore the pain in his leg with every step. He wanted to use the flashlight on the phone to see if there was anything in the room for him to use as a crutch, but he didn't dare. He was going to need all the juice the phone had to call 911, that is, if he was able to get reception. A small measure of relief washed over him once he made it all the way across the room and to the far wall. From there he would be able to find the doorway leading to wherever the candle was burning.

And then it dawned on him, he was doing all the dumb things the stupid people in horror movies did that made him and Wayne yell at the television screen until they were hoarse. What if he was walking straight into the monster's lair? It happened all the time in those movies. He took a deep breath and entered the long, narrow corridor, so narrow in fact he could touch each wall with his arms spread wide. Since the glow was emanating from the right side of the corridor, Grayson chose the left side to navigate closer to the creature's den.

"Stop thinking like that, Grayson, you're going to freak yourself out," he chided himself in a hushed tone.

He held his breath and tried to be as quiet as he possibly could which seemed to only make every movement he made that much louder. The stench had grown exponentially, and Grayson feared he was moving toward something that would prove to be horrific. But what other choice did he have? At the very least he had to find a way out of this basement.

Never in his ten short years on this earth had he felt this helpless, or hopeless. He was on the verge of tears which he fought back with every fiber of his being. "Tears will serve no purpose here," his grandfather's words echoed in his brain.

"Dear Lord, if you help me out of this jam, I promise with all my heart I will never make fun of Auntie Genna's church singing ever again," he prayed out loud.

The thought of his auntie's horrendous singing lightened the load a little and he wiped the tears from his eyes. And then his thoughts turned to his brother Wayne and the vision of him lying bleeding on the tarmac pushed him on. He gathered his thoughts, locked them away and focused on the immediate task at hand.

Grayson was transfixed on the light escaping from a room further down the corridor and was not paying attention to what he was doing. He stepped down wrong on his injured ankle which buckled and sent him falling backward. He expected to slam into the wall behind him but instead there was nothing solid and he spilled into a dark room with a clamorous entrance. The noise surrounding him reminded him of his grandmother's porch adorned with every type of bamboo wind chime she could find at the imports store.

His body exploded in pain as he hit the concrete floor with full force. Whatever it was he landed on was sharp and stabbed him in the back near his shoulder blades. He didn't want to waste the phone battery, but he had to take inventory of his surroundings.

Grayson unlocked the home screen on the phone, hovered his finger over the flashlight button and clamped his eyes shut. He turned on the flashlight and slowly opened his eyes. It took him several moments to comprehend what it was he was seeing. There were more of those spooky marionettes hanging down from the rafters, their legs were still swaying and knocking into each other with dead, hollow drumming sounds.

He screamed once he grasped the fact the marionettes were human skeletons trussed up with thin ropes and held together with wire. Some of the bones had dried, blackened meat still clinging to their yellowed surface. These were not the plastic skeletons from science class, these bones were real.

He began to back pedal away from the bones and dropped the phone in his frenzy. The flashlight pointed straight up illuminating a half dozen human skulls staring back at him with hollow eyes. As he scrambled and grabbed the phone it panned around the room, revealing a collection of creatures dangling from ropes and strings like a zoo for the dead.

Grayson was sure the creepy dude heard his screams, so he needed to move, and fast. He scrambled to his feet and out into the hallway as quickly as he could manage where he limped down toward the light. He was out of breath by the time he made it to the last room on that side of the corridor and switched sides so that he was right next to the glowing room.

As he leaned against the wall trying to catch his breath and gather his wits, he saw the light was not actually flickering like a candle but strobing like the light on top of a cop car or utility truck which meant only one thing, there were windows in the next room. Grayson's heart pounded as he scurried into the room toward the lights, but he was immediately defeated. The windows, if you could call them that, were seven feet off the floor butted against the ceiling of the room and were less than a foot wide. He realized they were not windows at all, rather, they were decorative glass blocks too milky to be able to see through and so thick no one would be able to hear him screaming for help.

Grayson fell heavily against the wall and slid down into the seated position. He hung his head in his hands and began to cry. He was between sobs when he thought he heard a voice so he tried as best as he could not to make a sound.

"Help me," he heard a man's weak voice call out.

He watched as the yellow light rotated around the room several times until he spotted a doorway in the far wall. It was open a crack and again he heard the call for help. Against his better judgment Grayson struggled to his feet and shuffled across the empty room toward the door. The nearer he got to the closed door the more he gathered the disgusting odors were emanating from within, making him even more leery of opening the door.

"Hello? If there is someone out there, please help me. For the love of God, please help me," the unseen person pleaded through anemic sobs.

Grayson wiped his sweaty palms on the front of his pants and reached for the door handle. He turned the knob and eased the door open ever so slightly before pulling it shut again. He bent over at the waist and gagged. He wasn't sure what was in that room, but his imagination painted him a less than rosy picture. The smell was unlike anything he had ever smelled before but also carried notes of something familiar. He recalled a class trip to a farm last year but even as bad as those cow barns were, they were pleasant compared to the raunchy odors coming from that room.

"Don't leave me," the voice in the other room pleaded.

Although he was only ten years old, almost eleven, Grayson understood both compassion and discretion. He knew it very well may be the creepy dude trying to lure him into a trap, but the voice wasn't the same. And no matter what, he just couldn't ignore a person in trouble. He pulled his shirt up over his face hoping to lessen the impact of the horrific odors.

"Hello," Grayson mouthed as he entered the room.

When the person didn't respond he took a deep breath, gritted his teeth, and burst into the room. The horror that confronted the young boy was beyond anything he could comprehend. His stomach knotted up worse than the time that bully DeMarcus punched him in the gut when he wasn't looking. He doubled over to vomit but there was nothing left in his stomach, so he just gagged with the dry heaves.

He slowly regained his composure and raised his eyes to look at the room once more. He was never going to be able to unsee what was in that room with him. Never.

Sitting in front of him in an old wooden chair was a man so weak he couldn't even hold his head up. He reminded Grayson of his dad's Steve Yzerman bobblehead doll, but even less rigid. The man was naked and there were bites taken out of him all over his body. Not just bite marks as if he were being tortured, no, these were actual bites with meat missing. Someone, most likely the creepy dude, was eating this poor man alive.

As the yellow light made another pass bathing the room in the eerie golden glow Grayson saw, as with the room upstairs, someone had scrawled a sentence over and over and over again all around the room, but this passage was different.

We are all just food for thought!

There were five other chairs in the room, each one occupied by a dead body in various stages of decomposition. Blackened viscera lay in piles at the dead men's feet. Each of them had numerous bite marks scarring the entirety of their bodies. Grayson trembled and wet himself.

Not only had the man been belted to the chair, but there were also spikes through his hands and feet as well. A crown of thorns made of barbed wire and nails encircled the man's head. His head wobbled up and down, side to side and every so often he was able to make eye contact with the boy unleashing a depth of heartache Grayson had never known, and he knew there was no way he was going to be able to save that man.

He ran out into the other room and fell to the floor huddled in a scream. Something else in that room had frightened him even more than seeing dead and dying men strapped to chairs, it was the single empty chair sitting in the center of the room as if it had been prepared for a new guest.

~ ~ ~

The strobing yellow light of the utility truck bathed the church in an ethereal glow as rescue workers hurried to unload tools from the side gates of their truck. Wanda Bruce, the boys' mother showed up at the scene and left with her son Wayne in the ambulance. Isaac Bruce was pacing like a caged tiger wanting to assist but had been told on more than one occasion he was being more of a hindrance than a help, so he sat on the bumper of a paramedic unit and sipped a cup of cold coffee.

Sergeant Burns directed the flow of new officers arriving at the scene every minute or so while Bayless did his best to comfort Isaac. A perimeter was set up around the church to keep anyone from getting near the place. The last thing they needed were dozens of looky-loos milling about and getting in the way.

"We are going to get him out of there," Bayless said to Isaac with a firm hand on the man's shoulder.

Isaac just nodded and blew into his coffee cup. A tear broke loose from the corner of his eye and walked down his cheek.

"Every single man out here is going to do their best to get Grayson out of that building safely," Burns added.

"I know, and I truly appreciate everything you are doing," he said, looking up at Bayless with tear-stained eyes.

"It's not me, it's all of them. Most of those guys have been off the clock for more than an hour," Bayless said.

The day shift sergeant arrived on scene and was helping with the disbursement of personnel. Both he and Burns were making damned sure no one was coming out of that building without an officer spotting them. The air was charged with the sound of men and equipment working feverishly to rescue the trapped child. The fire department started grinding away at the industrial sized chain and assured the sergeants they would be able to open the door in less than five minutes.

~ ~ ~

Grayson heard a noise outside and dragged the empty chair over to the wall. He was still too short and the glass too dingy to be able to see anything, but when he put his ear to the wall beneath the glass block, he could hear metal grinding. Wayne must have called the police, and they were coming in to rescue him. But how could he have called? He had Wayne's phone.

He turned the phone on to see if he could get a signal next to the windows and he managed to get two bars. He punched in 911 and hit the green phone receiver button.

"911, what is your emergency?" the dispatcher asked just before the battery blinked for the last time and the phone screen went black.

In frustration Grayson threw the phone and immediately regretted it. The phone slid into the furthest, darkest corner of the room. It was his screw up, and he knew had to fix it by retrieving his brother's phone, so he timed his movements to coincide with the strobing yellow light which helped him to see a little, but not very much. Even in the diminished light he could see that the screen on his brother's phone was spider webbed and was wracked with guilt. He glanced up from the broken phone screen to see the little girl hovering above him and he averted his eyes while dropping to his haunches. When he found the nerve to look up, she was gone.

"Please, get me out of here, he will be coming back soon," the man in the chair pleaded.

Grayson wanted to tell the man to just shut up. That all his nagging was not helping the situation and then realized he would sound just like his mother if he were to do that.

"Listen, mister, I'm going to get us out of here one way or another. I just haven't figured out how yet," he said, his voice trailing off in defeat.

Grayson went to work trying to unbuckle the thick leather straps binding the man to the chair without touching the man's clammy flesh or the gooey strap. Making the task even that much more difficult was that the man had urinated and defecated all over himself numerous times.

"Tools," the man's hoarse voice hissed.

"Tools? What tools?" Grayson asked.

The man's eyes glanced hard to his left. Grayson followed a line down the dark wall until he saw an out of place shadow. He limped over to the area and found a small hatch leading to another room. When he stood up his head hit what felt like huge spider webs, so he flailed his arms wildly until he crashed into a work bench.

After rubbing his shins for several moments, he fumbled around the work bench carefully with his hands. It was nearly impossible to find anything useful in the dark and the flashing yellow light didn't reach into this small cubicle. His hand came across a hammer he recognized by feel.

Grayson hurried back into the other room, climbed up onto the empty chair and began banging on the glass as hard as he could. A dozen smashes into the glass block and it was none the worse for wear, but his hand was starting to hurt terribly, and he was afraid he wouldn't be able to keep it up much longer.

"Chisel," the man groaned.

"What?" Grayson asked, trying to avoid eye contact with the man's ghostly eyes.

"There is a chisel on the workbench in the other room. I saw the man using it to," the man let the sentence hang ominously in the air.

Grayson didn't even want to imagine what the man was about to say. He thought back to working with his father in his workshop and painted himself a mental image of what a chisel would look like. Again, he carefully felt across the surface of the workbench looking for anything that would resemble a chisel. Even with being careful he nearly cut himself on a knife with a strange, curved blade which he slipped into his back pocket just in case.

He wasted several minutes handling the same objects over and over again. Becoming frustrated, Grayson began tossing things across the room once he determined they were of no use to him. By the feel and sound of some of the objects he was certain they were bones, but he forced those thoughts from his mind and focused on the task at hand. Finally, after several agonizing minutes he exited the small cubicle with a heavy chisel in his hand and a jagged grin of victory on his face.

Grayson climbed back up on the chair, set the chisel against the glass and proceeded to smash his hand with the hammer, dropping both the hammer and the chisel to the concrete floor in a clatter. Refusing to be defeated the boy wiped away his tears, grabbed the tools from the floor and went back to work on the glass block. The chisel wasn't biting into the glass and slid out of the way of the hammer causing him to strike his hand repeatedly.

On the third attempt he tried putting the pointed corner of the chisel against the glass and struck it with everything he had. His face was sprayed with tiny shards of broken glass which he wiped away out of instinct, inflicting dozens of tiny lacerations across his face. He pulled his shirt up over his face, cut two small holes for eyes with the point of the chisel and went back to work. Within just a few minutes he was too sore and exhausted to continue. He dropped down to the floor, pulled his knees up to his chest and began to cry.

The man raised his head as best as he could as said, "Time it." His chin dropped back down to rest on his chest.

Time it. What in the hell did he mean by that? And then Grayson listened to the machinery outside. It would rev up for a minute or two, but then it would drop back down to idle speed where it was much quieter. He grabbed the hammer thinking that maybe, just maybe, someone would be able to hear him.

"Hey, Johnny, did you hear something?" a fire rescue team member said, tapping his partner on the shoulder just before he fired up the saw.

As luck would have it, the two workers had taken a break long enough to reposition the chain. One of them had taken their ear protection off and heard Grayson smashing at the glass block with the hammer.

"Is that a shadow?" Johnny commented, pointing to the glass block at the bottom edge of the building.

"Hey guys," Luis Reyes called out, waving Bayless and Burns over to where they were working on the door.

"What's up guys? Is there a problem?"

"No, we're almost through the chain. But I think there is someone down there banging on the glass," Luis said.

"Turn that thing off for a minute please," Bayless said and bent over to get a closer look. He cupped his hands around his mouth, pressed them to the glass block and called out. "Grayson, is that you down there?"

There was no response, but there was definitely someone or something moving in front of the glass blocks.

"Grayson, if that's you, tap on the glass," he said.

There was a long minute of silence but then he heard hammering against the glass. He stood up and nodded to Burns.

"Do you guys have anything that will bust through that glass, and in a hurry?" Burns asked.

Luis nodded and trotted over to the utility truck. He came back with a pick and handed it to Bayless.

"Grayson stand back away from the glass," Bayless called out and took a swing at the glass block. The pick reverberated dramatically, stinging his hands, and causing him to drop the tool.

Luis picked up the pick with a grin and took a swing. The pointed end of the pick buried into the mortar on the side of the block. The men took turns swinging at the concrete and mortar surrounding the block, rubbing their hands together after every swing.

Grayson slid down the wall with a sense of relief and a smile creasing his lips. This ordeal was finally over. He was mentally going over all of the apologies and promises he was going to make as soon as he was free from this nightmare. The man in the chair gasped and the boy's blood ran cold. He felt a presence in the room with them and raised his head thinking the odd little girl would be standing in front of him, but it turned out to be much worse than a pint-sized unborn ghost.

Jessop Porter, wearing an authentic Detroit Lions cap signed by none other than Barry Sanders himself stood in the doorway sporting an ominous grin. "You dropped something creepy crawler."

Men were still chiseling at the twelve by twenty-four-inch glass block and Grayson knew they weren't going to make it in time. He tried to stand up, but his ankle had set up on him and he couldn't stand up straight, and didn't have the ability to fight off a maniac intent on eating him.

"Grayson, down!" he heard a voice call out and he dropped face flat on the floor.

The glass block fell to the floor and Burns squeezed as much of his body into the opening as he could. He fired two rounds, hitting Jessop once in the arm. Porter realized what was happening and scooted out of the officer's firing range. Bayless pulled his portly partner out of the way while stripping off his vest, shirt, and gun belt.

"Grayson, hang on, I will be down there in a minute," Bayless called out, trying to slide down into the basement headfirst but was wedged in the small opening.

"All units move to the southeastern corner of the basement ASAP," Burns cried into his radio.

Jessop Porter moved with such speed and agility it caught Grayson by surprise. Within seconds he had leapt across the room, landed on the man in the chair and sunk his teeth deep into the man's hollow cheek. He shook his head from side to side like a pit bull on a pork chop bone, ripping the man's meat clean off the bone. He turned, smiled at Grayson, and gnashed his teeth, poised to take a bite of the man's throat. The boy didn't hesitate and moved with speed of his own that bewildered the creepy dude. He pulled the linoleum knife from his back pocket and made a wide, sweeping arc trying to scare the man. Instead, he connected with flesh and gashed Jessop Porter wide open from the corner of his mouth to almost his ear. Porter was dazed but then anger took over and he lunged for the child with gnashing teeth. Grayson scrambled to grab the hammer and without hesitation swung it with ferocity, crushing the bones in the creepy dude's hand against the concrete floor.

Jessop Porter was still howling in pain when Bayless hit the floor in a tuck and roll and was on his feet in an instant. He covered the three strides in record time and hit the lunatic across the throat with a stiff arm dropping him to the floor. Jessop was still trying to bite him even after Bayless had him in handcuffs.

Within ten minutes the paramedics had Grayson out of the building and into the ambulance with his father.

"Sorry about your hat, dad, I think I got blood on it," the boy said, getting groggy from the pain medication dripping through the IV in his arm.

"Son, that hat is the least of my worries," he said and leaned over to kiss his son on the forehead as the ambulance pulled away from the scene.

"What about the little girl?" Grayson mumbled just before passing out.

Chapter Five

"You are not supposed to be here," Jessop Porter cackled as he was being shoved into the back of a patrol car.

A pair of homicide detectives stood on the tarmac sipping on gas station coffee while watching the paramedics load Ismael Edwards into an ambulance. Effie Meadows ran her hand through her shoulder length dark hair and let loose a long sigh. Her hazel eyes betrayed her lack of sleep.

"Nasty business," Richie Black said glancing over at Ismael Edwards to see the man was covered nearly head to toe with human bite marks. "Why do we always wind up getting the shit shows?"

"Remember that incident with the captain's niece?" Meadows said with a sarcastic grin.

"That was nearly twenty years ago, and that mean, old bastard has long since retired."

"Shoulda kept it in your pants Casanova," she said with a smile and hearty grasp of her crotch.

Richie shook his head, shrugged, and turned his attention back to his coffee. His partner was rough around the edges, but it was exactly what endeared her to him. The fact she would ride her Harley to the ballet dressed to the nines fascinated him. Most other women wafted a blend of high-end perfumes while she exuded gun oil and gasoline, with just a hint of lilac. The detectives waited for the ambulance and patrol cars to pull away before they started heading over to the building.

"Man, that is one creepy looking dude," Richie said with a shudder. "Did you see those eyes?"

She shot her partner a sideways glance and a mischievous twinkle in her eye and said, "That dude is so freaky he couldn't get his Willy wet standing naked in a hurricane."

"That's bullshit and we both know it. He's just your type."

"How are we looking?" Meadows asked Sergeant Burns, ignoring her partner's dig.

"Give them another five minutes to clear the place, it's a maze in there."

"And the man of the hour?" Black asked.

"They are taking him to the hospital under psych evaluation. From what I have heard so far is he was out of control, so the doctor sedated him. Kept going on and on about a little girl and screaming, you are not supposed to be here."

"What about the other guy?" Richie asked.

"Mr. Edwards," Burns said and then shook his head with a slow, deliberate motion that relayed his disgust.

Effie shot the man a sympathetic glance knowing Burns had just watched the man die after holding on to life for only God knew how long.

"Any idea what he meant by his comment, you are not supposed to be here, other than being obviously bat shit crazy of course?" Effie asked him.

"Not a clue detective, and I'm really not sure if I want to know more than I already do," he responded to Effie with an uncharacteristic somberness.

"Did you have to dress in all black?" she asked after Burns walked away.

"It's all I had that was clean," Richie responded. "Besides, what does that matter?"

"You know I always dress in all black. We look like we're trying out for a part in a jewelry heist movie."

"Sorry, I'll make sure to wear my fuchsia leisure suit tomorrow," he panned.

"You're learning, I like that," she said with a smile that made his stomach flutter.

Two uniformed officers exited the church with a nod that the building was clear. The detectives chugged the rest of their coffee and tossed the empties into the back seat of their car before heading inside. The place was old and neglected as was expected, but it had even been abandoned by squatters and junkies a long time ago. Meadows and Black didn't spend much time in the gallery or up in the balcony, they knew the real mess was in the classrooms and down in the basement. Richie felt the eerie silence invading his psyche like a ravenous parasite.

"Happy anniversary," Richie blurted out to break the silence and ended up startling his partner as an added benefit.

"What in the hell are you tag about, Richie?"

"We've been partners for ten years today," he said with a shit-eating grin.

"Leave it to you to remember some mushy bullshit like that. Can't believe I have put up with you for that long. Ten years, huh, that's longer than either one of our two marriages combined," Effie laughed, but in a subdued tone.

The detectives walked into the first classroom and were taken aback by the chaotic scene laid out before them. The two resuscitation mannequins had been pummeled and thrown in a heap in the corner. The desks had been scattered and were covered in deranged-looking toys. Both Richie and Effie looked in amazement at the passage scrawled across nearly every square inch of the room including the ceiling and floor.

"You are not supposed to be here. Who in the hell is that intended for?" Detective Black asked.

"Who knows. And I'm not even sure I want to find out. Hey, over here, this looks like where the kid escaped into the basement," Meadows said, pointing to an open laundry chute.

"Smart kid. He might have saved his own life with that stunt."

They moved from classroom to classroom as they made their way down the long corridor only to find more of the same madness in each of them. Effie took hundreds of photographs with her cell phone hoping to be able to make sense of it all later. She was not looking forward to having a conversation with this psychopath.

"Look here. I've started noticing these drawings in the classrooms and on the doors," Richie said, pointing to a charcoal stick figure of a girl drawn on the wall near the door jamb. It struck him to be a warning of sorts, as if the odd little man was marking territory.

"This just keeps getting creepier and creepier," she said, taking several photographs of the macabre artwork.

"And to think, we haven't even made it down to the basement where the good stuff is hiding," Richie quipped, only half in jest.

The next fifteen minutes were spent investigating and documenting the classrooms on their way to the stairwell leading to the basement, each classroom progressively more macabre than its predecessor. They photographed and documented every room while keeping conversation to a minimum as there was not much to say that wouldn't only serve to enhance the nightmare. Familiar odors wafted up the stairwell and they both had a good idea of what was awaiting them downstairs. Neither one of them had much desire to go any further.

"Thanks to your libido we always get stuck with the shit show cases partner," Detective Meadows commented with a smile as she opened a set of double doors that led to the basement.

Black switched his flashlight over to a wider beam causing shadows to dance all around them and making them feel ill at ease. There was nothing of interest in the large room, so they moved toward the smaller corridor, which incidentally was also in the same direction as the stench. Effie could only imagine the terror the poor small child had suffered while trapped down here in the darkness. She shuddered and said a prayer for all those involved, even Jessop Porter. Detective Black saw several more of the stick figure girl drawings on the walls and ceiling but sensing his partner's uneasiness he kept them to himself.

Once they entered the room where the boy and Porter were found they were dumbfounded. Twenty years on the job and nothing had ever come close to this scene. There were six chairs in the room and debris of at least six more broken chairs. Two of the chairs were empty, but four of them held human remains, people who had been eaten alive. Human viscera clung to the concrete surrounded by blackened stains that had long since set into the floor. Though, after the crime scene techs finished with the corpses it left the scene with an almost comical appearance.

Effie was on the verge of getting sick, so she dashed out into the corridor to hide it from her partner lest she be chastised every day for the next year. She was still bending over sucking in little sips of air when movement out of the corner of her eye caught her attention. Effie glanced up to see there was a little girl dressed in a dingy, lavender dress standing against the far wall.

Effie put her fists to her eyes and rubbed them hard, hoping her eyes were playing tricks on her and she was just seeing something in the shadows that wasn't really there. But when she removed her hands and opened her eyes the little girl was still standing there, looking back at her with an inquisitive glance.

"What is your name honey?" she asked as she dropped down onto her haunches.

The little girl didn't answer. Instead, she stood there, staring back at Effie with a look that screamed defiance.

"What are you doing in this old church by yourself? Did that creepy man kidnap you?"

Again, the little girl refused to answer, and Effie started feeling uncomfortable, sensing something was wrong. Very wrong. Her analytical cop's mind began spinning different scenarios, one of which, was quite disturbing. What if this child was that psychopath's child and she just watched them haul her father away in leg shackles and handcuffs?

She shined her flashlight on the little girl and let loose an audible gasp. The child had no color whatsoever. She wasn't ghostly white pale from years spent in darkness, no, she had no color whatsoever to her skin to the point of being transparent. The dress she wore radiated lavender hues along with the red roses on her pockets, her shoes were a shiny, black patent leather, and the barrette in her hair matched the red of the roses on her pockets. It dawned on Effie it wasn't so much the girl was colorless like someone would imagine a ghost to be, she was monochrome like a black and white photograph.

She tried once more to get the girl to talk. "What is your name honey?" she asked, in a more demanding tone this time around.

The girl glared back at her, cocked her head to the side and said, "You are not supposed to be here!"

"Did you say something?" Richie called out from the other room.

When Meadows didn't respond he shrugged and assumed he had either heard a noise from outside or his imagination was running rampant, which was entirely possible given his surroundings. The sun was starting to come up and was casting an eerie magenta hue across the room through the opening where a glass block had been just a few hours earlier.

Detective Black photographed each chair even though the crime scene unit had already processed the scene. He liked having photos of his own, from his own angles. Two of the bodies were so emaciated they were essentially just skeletons. The other two cadavers still had a substantial amount of flesh remaining on their bones but were both in the latter stages of decomp and looked more like biltong than human flesh. How long had this been going on? Black shuddered at the thought of how long it took these poor men to die. The pure agony they must have endured.

"Why do you say I am not supposed to be here? Is this where you and your daddy live?"

"That man is not my daddy. He is not supposed to be here either."

"So does your mother or father live in this church with you?" Effie asked.

The little girl vehemently shook her head as if the question were preposterous.

"I don't think you are supposed to be here either honey," she said. "It is far too dangerous here for a little girl."

"Not here," the little girl said while stabbing a finger at the ground by her feet. "Here," she finished with her arms displayed in a wide, sweeping arc.

"I don't understand what you are saying," Meadows said.

"You should have never been born."

Effie recoiled from the girl's statement. "That is a pretty cruel thing to say, especially since you don't even know me."

"It's the truth. Someone just like you murdered me before I could even be born."

"Someone like me?"

The girl pointed to the badge clipped to her waist. A stillness enveloped them, and Effie knew she needed to get away, and fast. There was something in the child's eyes that sent tremors of fear rippling through her.

Once again Richie thought he heard voices coming from the other room. He peeked out into the hallway and when he did not see Meadows he started for the large open room. The sun was up enough to cast the basement with dirty light enough for him to be able to see. And what he saw was beyond disturbing.

Meadows was kneeling down speaking with a little girl, but there was something odd about the child. He could not put his finger on it for a moment, but then he realized it was because she had no color.

"Meadows? What in the hell is going on?"

Detective Meadows slowly turned to look at her partner, but she had no idea what to say to him. This situation did not make any sense to her, she knew sure as shit it wouldn't make any sense to Richie.

The little girl spun her head to the side and sneered at Detective Black. "She is not supposed to be here," she said. "But I am."

Before he could react, the girl jerked Effie's gun from her hip holster and pointed it at Detective Meadows with a shaky hand. Richie was not able to draw his weapon before the girl managed to fire two rounds into his partner's chest. Effie fell backward onto the dirty floor, the impact forcing her last breath from her lungs. As soon as his gun cleared its holster, he fired three rounds at the little girl who had vanished into thin air. In shock, he rushed to Effie and dropped to his knees with a guttural scream. With his heart in tatters, he cradled his partner's head in his lap and wept.

"I love you Effie Meadows," he said, disgusted with himself for only finding the courage to say the words after she was gone.

Chapter Six

Hector Correa walked his bicycle along the Mackinac Bridge as the sun began to rise to the east over Mackinac Island. He had a smile on his face masking the heaviness in his heart. The remnants of his father rested proudly in a basket on the front of the bike.

"Another Labor Day walking the bridge, Pops," Hector said.

It was a cool morning causing a mist to rise from the warmer water in the straits below the bridge. A gentle breeze blew across the bridge from the west pushing a dense, fluffy fog along with it. Hector turned his collar up and focused his attention on the rising sun while trying to ignore the chatter of passerby's shuffling to the north side of the bridge like a throng of exuberant zombies.

"Pops, you definitely left this world on your terms, and I now understand what you meant by every day should be a perfect day to die. You always told me, go to bed every night leaving nothing on your plate, no anger hanging in the air, and most importantly do not leave behind any regrets. Leave this world on your terms no matter which day of your life turns out to be your last. That is the only true way to cheat death, my son." Hector smiled and wiped the tears from his eyes as his father's voice rang in his memories.

Hector opened a small brown paper sack that had been in the basket of the bike and unwrapped the plastic wrap around the sandwich. The sun had been up for well over an hour and most of the crowd had already passed him by. He took a bite of his sandwich and quickly washed it down with a gulp of Vernor's.

"Pops, I'm going to admit it once and for all, I hate this stuff and always have. Just what in the hell is Braunschweiger anyway?"

He took one more bite of the sandwich, wrapped it up and shoved it back into the paper sack. A Star Line ferry pulled out of Mackinaw City and headed for the island spraying a plume of water from the stern of the Hydro-Jet. Hector smiled. He recalled the first time he had seen one of the boats when he was just a wee lad and how his excitement that morning turned into a lifelong bonding ritual between him and his father. Every Labor Day they would walk the bridge and then take the ferry to Mackinac Island.

"Don't worry, pops, we're still going to take the boat ride to the island and get some of that fudge you love so much," Hector said with a smile.

The mix of cool air above him on the bridge mixing with the warmer air rising up from the water was a pleasant juxtaposition. He breathed in the crisp, clean air and sighed with contentment.

"Dispatch to Trooper Franklin."

"Trooper Franklin, go ahead dispatch," the Michigan State Police Trooper responded to her radio.

"You have a straggler near the south tower. Go check it out please."

"Ten-four."

This was Renee Franklin's twenty-eighth year of covering the bridge walk and she was looking forward to only having to put up with two more before she could finally retire. She walked against the grain of the north bound horde as she headed for the south tower of the bridge. Every year there was always someone who lagged behind the rest of the crowd. And while it annoyed her, she also understood the burning desire for solitude, especially in such a majestic setting with a limited opportunity to experience. She stopped for a moment, took off her trooper's hat and wiped her brow of sweat. She was getting too old for this shit, much too old.

"Good morning, sir," Trooper Franklin said with a forced smile.

Hector jumped a little and then laughed. "Woo, you startled me. I guess I was lost in my own little world there. Is there something wrong? Am I too close to the railing?"

"We are getting pretty close to opening the bridge back up to traffic, so I need you to keep moving to the north side of the bridge."

"Of course," he said and slid the urn back into the bicycle basket.

Renee noticed the reverence on the man's face and a certain sadness washed over her. The man was obviously paying his last respects to someone remarkably close to him who she imagined he had lost recently. On the other hand, it was a gorgeous day to say goodbye.

"Someone close to you I presume?" she asked with a nod toward the bicycle basket.

His head bobbed up and down proudly. "Yeah, my pops."

"I'm sorry for your loss."

"Thank you, but don't be. The man went out on his terms with a smile on his face. I can only hope I am able to do the same when my time comes," Hector said.

"Don't we all," Renee responded out of a lack of anything else to say.

"Pops had a rather unique outlook on life."

"Really? How so?"

"He always joked that he wasn't even supposed to be here in the first place so every day he spent on earth was just caramel topping on the ice cream."

"What would make him say something like that?"

"Right about where we are standing, a little further back that way," Hector pointed and continued. "My grandfather fell from a scaffolding on the south tower during its construction."

"Oh, my, how tragic. I'm so sorry to hear that," Renee said, genuinely sorry to hear about the man's family tragedy.

"Oh no, it wasn't a bad thing at all. By the grace of God my grandfather survived the fall into the lake and again, just by sheer luck there was a fisherman close enough to pluck him from the water and get him to the hospital in St. Ignace. He suffered a few broken bones, bruises, and wounded pride but that was the extent of his injuries. He was back up on the bridge working by the end of the month. He always joked about cheating death and that every day he woke up was a free day to do with as he pleased," Hector explained.

"Wow, that is quite the story," Renee said with a smile.

"And to sweeten the deal even more, he met my grandmother at the hospital. She was a nurse," Hector said, trying to ignore the tear threatening to break free from the corner of his eye.

The two of them watched as a father and his three sons loitered around the tarnished green metal grating in the center of the bridge. Their eyes flashed back and forth between the state trooper and the grating.

"Go ahead, but make it quick," Trooper Franklin said with a chuckle.

The three boys immediately bent over at the waist and let long strands of spit dangle until they dropped through the grating while the father just shrugged and rolled his eyes. The young boys then dropped to their knees and tried to watch their spit race to the water below which was an impossibility due to the wind.

"Family traditions," she said with a smile.

"Speaking of traditions, my father and I would stand here and say a prayer to whichever guardian angel saved grandfather at precisely eleven ten in the morning when he fell."

"I'll tell you what, you do what you have to do but then hurry and catch up to the rest of the pack."

"Will do. I've got my trusty steed here and I promise I will be passing you by before you know it," Hector said, patting the seat of his red Cannondale.

Renee turned and started walking north toward the St. Ignace side with a smile and a thought to call her father when she got back across the bridge. The fog had all but dissipated and white caps danced from shore to shore across the straits below. A Shepler's ferry headed west toward St. Helena Island as part of their lighthouse excursion, probably the last one of the year by the way the air was nipping at her bare flesh. A sense of melancholy washed over her as it did every Labor Day which signaled the end of summer and another year of her life in the books.

Hector watched the trooper until she crested the rise at the center of the bridge before checking his watch. It was time.

Chapter Seven

Tears streamed down Hector's face as he relived a lifetime spent with his father on this bridge in just a mere matter of minutes. His father's legacy flashed before him, and he was torn between sorrow and joy. While sad for his loss, Hector wouldn't trade anything in the world for the years he was blessed to spend with his father who was a good, decent man. He pulled a bandana from his pocket, wiped his tears, and then blew his nose. He swung his leg over the frame of his bicycle and started to give the pedals a hard pump to get started when something from behind him caught his attention.

An eerie breeze swirled around him and set him on edge for reasons he could not identify. This was not an icy, cold north wind, nor was it a hot, desert sirocco, it was an absolute void in reality. As suddenly as the wind appeared, it completely stopped until Hector was encased in what he could only describe as a vacuum.

Hector glanced to the north side of the bridge but the crowd had already crested and descended the arc so he could no longer see them. His brain was foggy making it difficult for him to think clearly, and he felt hollow inside like parts of him were missing.

"You are not supposed to be here," a voice called out from behind him.

"I know, I know, I'm trying to move along," Hector replied, glancing behind him, expecting to see another police officer.

The air surrounding him turned stale, dead, dropping Hector to his knees gasping for breath. Every breath coated his nostrils and tongue with a fetid, sour taste. Pivoting his neck, he looked behind him to see a small boy he surmised to be about nine or ten years old sitting on the Foliage Green railing of the bridge kicking his crossed feet back and forth as they dangled two hundred feet above the water. His small hands made the railing look much bigger than it was. Releasing him from its grasp, the squalid air dissipated, and Hector was able to get back to his feet.

"Come down from there before you fall," Hector said, reaching out to the child who simply smiled back at him.

He took two long strides toward the child but stopped short. There was something off about this child, something that caused Hector to turn back for his bike. He felt a sudden urge to flee, to run as fast as he could away from the street urchin. There was a hatred in the boy's eyes far surpassing anything he had ever seen in his life, a hatred he not only saw, but felt within his own heart.

"You are not supposed to be here," the child said once more.

"I know, the state trooper already told me to get moving. So, I am moving along, but you had better come with me as well."

The child laughed and rocked back and forth on top of the railing so hard that Hector feared he would fall over. Shocking himself, he found there was a part of him that hoped the boy would fall.

"Franklin," a disembodied voice came over her radio.

"This is Franklin."

"That straggler stopped moving and is dangerously close to the railing."

"Copy that," Trooper Renee Franklin replied. Her stomach dropped and she hoped she hadn't missed the signs of a suicidal jumper preparing to take the plunge.

She turned and started walking back to where she had parted company with Hector Correa. Once she crested the rise of the bridge, she could see the man was kneeling down, as if he were talking to someone, like he was talking to a child.

"What is your name son?"

"Chase. Chase Coltrain Junior," the child replied while wiggling a finger, beckoning the man to come closer.

Against his better judgment, Hector stood back up and walked to the child. He leaned in while the child cupped his hands and whispered.

"You are not supposed to be here," the boy whispered slowly.

Trooper Franklin was close enough to see Hector was indeed speaking with a child, a small boy perched on the railing. She started to run while screaming at them to move back away from the edge.

Hector tried to pull away from the child who was gripping the lapel of his shirt in both hands, but the child was surprisingly strong. The boy was leaning as far back as he could over the railing and Hector knew if he were to jerk himself free of the boy's grasp it would send the boy plummeting to the water below which would certainly be a death sentence for the child.

"Hector, please step away from the railing," Franklin panted as she drew within several feet of the man and the boy.

The boy turned his head, and with a smile said to the trooper, "He is not supposed to be here!"

With that the child rocked all the way forward into Hector's chest, causing him to lose his balance. He then flung himself backward with enough force to pull Hector over the railing. Trooper Franklin watched in horror as the man and child plummeted to the water below. Even more disturbing was the fact that the child simply vanished, and she swore there was only one splash in the lake below.

Chapter Eight

An eighteen-piece clown band was hosting an epic shindig in Chase Coltrain's brain as he tossed the folded newspaper onto the front seat of his beat up, thirty-year-old Buick. If today wasn't depressing enough he was force fed the headline *Police Detective Murdered in Cold Blood, Allegedly Shot to Death by her Partner of Ten Years.* His sister-in-law murdered by his best friend Richie Black. It just didn't make any sense.

And to make matters worse it was Chase Junior's birthday of all days. Or death day if one wanted to look at it through another lens. But did the child ever have either? He never spent one single minute alive on this earth so was he ever truly born? He exited his mother's womb lifeless, never even partaking of his first breath, so was he ever even alive therefore unable to die? Those questions he faced every single day of his life never mattered much to the boy's mother, his wife, Anna Meadows-Coltrain. She never once questioned the fact her son was ever alive during the pregnancy, she felt him kick and squirm every single day. Or so she imagined.

Chase stopped off at the Quality Dairy on Shiawasee Street, bought a half pint of cheap whiskey and headed for the waterfront. He stared at the river from a park bench in Rotary Park, watching kayakers meander up and down the Grand River. Due to weirs and body nets, the route was a short one, so he wound up watching the same three people paddling up, and then back down the river. The sun was reflecting off a stainless-steel sculpture in the park named *Inspiration* which he found ironic as he had absolutely zero inspiration for anything in life anymore. Clinging to life was not a courageous act, but rather a cowardly one. He was too much of a chicken shit to escape his pain as his wife had done five years ago to the day. To her benefit she lasted five entire, pain filled years before hanging herself from the rafters in their basement.

He recalled the day he had come home from a three-day business trip to Chicago and found his wife's bloated, purple corpse dangling from a rope hung over a beam in their basement. There was no note, not even as much as a *sorry* scrawled in the dust on the floor. Chase recalled how he felt the exact moment he saw her and the guilt he felt over his thoughts. How he wasn't sad, shocked, or even angry with her. He was, in fact, happy for her and oh how he wished he had the courage to join her.

It wasn't as though Anna wanted to die, she had just not wanted to live with the pain any longer. There are those who say suicide is a coward's way out, but Chase didn't buy that bullshit at all. He watched his wife struggle day in and day out ever since the nurse laid their stillborn son on her chest.

Why in God's name did they put her through that trauma? Why put her through that immense amount of grief? Even after their son's death she held on for five more years until she was told she was not conceiving because she was physically unable to have another child. That was more pain than she could endure.

Chase took a long pull on the whiskey and followed it with a chug of piss warm Mountain Dew. He grimaced and then repeated the process until both bottles were empty. He pitched the empties into the trash bin on the way to the parking lot. He knew he shouldn't be driving, but he had taken a left turn away from rational judgment a long time ago.

He parked the car and started for his apartment, more accurately, his room on the upper floor of an old Victorian house built near the turn of last century. The shit brown exterior was in dire need of a paint job as there was more white primer coat showing than paint. It was hot for a Labor Day weekend, and he was not looking forward to his sweltering attic room with its painted shut window that would only open a crack.

"Coltrain, your rent is late," his landlord, Ester Bradshaw called from behind him with a cigarette bobbing up and down in her lips as she talked. She was a living, breathing cliché, in retrospect, his entire life had become a cliché.

"It's always late, Mrs. Bradshaw. I told you six months ago when I moved in, I get paid monthly, on the fifth."

"But rent is due on the first. And it's Ms. not Mrs., I'm still single and on the market," she cackled with a wet cough while pulling her nightgown from between her cheeks.

"You will have it on the seventh because the banks are closed for the holiday weekend."

"I'm going to start charging you late fees."

"Or you could just make my rent due on the fifth like I have asked you numerous times," Chase groaned.

"No need to be a wise ass, Mr. Coltrain."

"Not trying to be a wise ass, just being practical."

"Oh, by the way, you have a visitor."

"A visitor? Where?"

"In your room. I got tired of their pestering so I let them in," she said, grinding the cigarette out on the heel of her slipper and dropping the butt into the pocket of her tattered floral print nightgown which Chase wasn't sure if it was still on from the morning or if she was getting ready for bed already.

"Why would you let some stranger into my room?" Chase asked, starting to get slightly more than perturbed with the acerbic woman.

"He's not a stranger, he said he was your son."

"I don't have a son Ms. Bradshaw."

"And you better not either. I told you when you moved in," she started while lighting another cigarette.

"No pets and no kids. I got it Ms. Bradshaw," Chase said, cutting her off with a dismissive wave.

He trudged up the stairs pondering what the old woman said about a visitor. He had no long-lost nieces or nephews, no real friends who had children who knew where he lived. He came to the only conclusion he could under the circumstances, it must be a wily child trying to sell him something he neither needed nor wanted. He slipped the Schlage key in the deadbolt and turned it until he felt the snap of the bolt disengaging. He paused for a minute before opening the door.

Ms. Bradshaw was indeed correct; he did have a visitor. Sitting on his bed was a young boy of about ten years old as well as he could gather. The boy was dressed as any ten-year-old boy would dress right down to his dirty, wet sneakers. As soon as the boy saw him, he smiled and scooted around on the bed to face him.

"I am supposed to be here," he said with a level of enthusiasm that didn't seem warranted.

"Listen, I don't know what you are selling, but whatever it is, I won't be able to afford it. I'm sorry if Ms. Bradshaw got your hopes up," Chase said.

"I am not selling anything," the boy responded.

"Then why are you here, in my room at this very moment?"

"Because I am supposed to be here," the boy answered in a matter-of-fact tone.

"And just what is it that makes you believe you are supposed to be here? What on earth makes you believe you are supposed to be here?" Chase bellowed, frustrated by the fact he was being out maneuvered by a ten-year-old child.

The boy simply shrugged and said, "I just know."

"Okay, I have had just about enough of this bullshit. What is your name? I'm going to call your parents."

"Chase Coltrain," the boy responded but hesitated and finished with, "Junior."

Anger rose within Chase to a level unlike anything he had experienced in an exceptionally long time. How dare this little miscreant invoke the name of his dead son for some sort of perverted pleasure? Had he been put up to this on a dare? That didn't seem likely due to the fact there were only a handful of people who even knew he had a son who died during childbirth. And it was ten years ago, so this just did not make any sense. Had this little bastard dug up some old records on the internet and thought he could extort money?

"You know that is not your name. What is your real name?" Chase demanded, using every single bit of self-control to keep from pummeling the child to get the information.

The boy just stared back at him with pools of tears forming in his eyes. Chase suddenly felt gut punched, the eyes staring back at him were Anna's eyes, there was no question in his mind about that. The effects of the whiskey started to abate, and he was able to see the boy in a more sober light. There was something oddly familiar about the boy's face.

In a softer, calmer tone he said, "Come on son, it's time to quit this game. Tell me where you live so I can take you home."

"I am supposed to be here," he replied more forcefully and slapped his palms on the mattress.

"Enough with this charade. What in the world makes you think you are supposed to be here?"

"Because I wasn't supposed to die."

Chapter Nine

"Why in the hell haven't you interrogated Porter yet?" Detective Black demanded.

"First, that is not your call, it's mine and second, it's not even my call," Captain Sergio White replied.

"Not your call? Why the hell not?"

"Because the man was undergoing a court ordered mandatory seventy-two-hour psych eval and observation, during which time we were not allowed to speak to him. My hands were tied. Besides, what are you doing here? I told you to take the week off."

"Am I suspended?"

"For shooting up a wall? No, I'm not going to suspend you for that."

"Speaking of that, is the public relations department going to do anything about that bogus headline the press ran with like rabid dogs."

White sighed. "They put out an official statement condemning the false allegation."

"And?"

"We both know it was a shit press release meant to cover their asses, not ours."

"Meaning?"

"Meaning that half of the city if not more thinks you killed your partner, and sadly I'm sure a lot of cops fall into that group. That is precisely why I want you to take some time off while we let this thing cool down. Hell take two weeks, I'll even pay you for the time off," the captain said.

A long uncomfortable silence blanketed the captain's office, during which neither man looked at one another. They had worked together for a long time and in fact, before Black and Meadows were partnered, Black partnered with White before he became captain. Sergio's making captain was the only reason Black and Meadows were even partnered up.

"Serg, there *was* a little girl in that basement."

"I know you believe you saw a little girl in the basement, but there is absolutely no evidence to prove there was a child down there. I had the crime scene techs go over that place with a fine-toothed comb and they came up with nothing. Not so much as hair or fiber from the dress you said she was wearing."

"Effie did not shoot herself," Richie said, choking back his tears. "She had no reason to."

"Richie, from the bottom of my heart I understand why you don't want to believe that, but you are just not seeing things clearly."

The captain held up a finger and answered his phone. He cupped his hand over the microphone and glanced at Detective Black.

"Richie, they are bringing Porter to the station from the hospital. I will have them set him up in room two and I want the psychopath to stew for about an hour before I go in to speak with him."

"You mean we, right?"

"You can observe from the gallery, but that's it. You are not going near the man right now. Go get some coffee and be back here in an hour," the captain said and turned his attention to the phone call.

Detective Black left the captain's office and headed for the squad room. He was never one of the *fellas* anyway, so the cold treatment he was getting didn't bother him. He saw the captain had posted the ballistics report on the bulletin board that exonerated him of shooting his partner. It was official, she was shot with her own gun which was both true, and bullshit at the same time. She was shot with her own gun, but with another's hand. This report read like she had committed suicide, which Richie knew was not the case.

He poured himself a cup of coffee and went outside to watch the bustle on the street. Patrol officers were filing in and out of the building each with their own agenda to attend to and didn't pay much attention to anything else. Except for one of them who looked vaguely familiar. He watched the officer discreetly under the rim of his glasses while the man watched him. He seemed nervous about something. Richie gave a flick of his wrist, and the officer walked over with his head on a swivel.

"Have a seat," Black said.

Bayless looked around to make sure no one was watching him.

"I understand, I'm toxic right now. Tell you what, you walk around the block this way and I will walk the opposite direction, and we meet at that Greek diner two blocks over."

Bayless nodded and took off on a brisk walk around the corner of the building in the opposite direction from Detective Black. Within ten minutes both men were seated in a booth in a back of the diner away from the windows. Richie ordered two coneys with onion rings and a Dr. Pepper. Bayless went for a Cobb salad with Thousand Island and a bottle of water.

"What's on your mind Bayless?" Detective Black asked.

"You know who I am?"

"Not particularly. But I am a detective, remember," he said, pointing to the man's name tag on his uniform. "I did see you at the church the other night, didn't I?"

"Yes, I was actually first on the scene. Well, Burnsy was too."

"Burns, huh, how is that old bastard?"

"Getting older and grumpier by the minute," Bayless said with a laugh, feeling comfortable with the detective.

"What's on your mind son?"

"Listen, I don't want to be one to swim in the rumor mill, but I have heard some scuttlebutt drifting around the station about that night."

"Scuttlebutt? You're a Navy man I see. I spent a few years floating around the Indian Ocean myself. Rumors are just chatter from bored people."

"It's about the little girl you saw," Bayless said,

Detective Black stopped chewing his coney dog, took a long drink of soda and swallowed hard.

"You saw a little girl in the church?"

"No, sir, not in so many words. But the kid we pulled out, Grayson Bruce mentioned there was a little girl in the church with him several times. He was concerned about her and wanted to make sure we saved her too."

Richie felt a surge of energy rush through him. He wasn't crazy. He wasn't fucking crazy after all.

"Do you have contact information on this kid?"

"Yes, sir. I'm friends with his father and we both coach most of their sports teams."

"I am going to want to talk to this Grayson kid. Is he a straight shooter?"

"Sir?"

"What I mean, is he the type to spread a little bullshit around trying to get himself out of trouble?"

"Not in the least. In my opinion he was truly concerned about there being a little girl trapped in the building."

They finished their meal and parted company with a promise from Bayless he would have Isaac Bruce contact the detective as soon as possible. Richie headed back to the station a little lighter on his feet and a heart that wasn't so heavy.

~ ~ ~

Chase Coltrain bolted awake in a chair with a throbbing headache and a back that screamed his age. He had a vague recollection of the strangest drunken dream he had ever experienced. Until he stood up and saw the child tucked under the covers on his bed and realized it hadn't been a dream after all.

He poured hot water from an electric tea kettle into a mug with two packets of Taster's Choice instant coffee and stirred it with his finger. The cool morning air was almost chilly enough to put on a sweatshirt, but he needed the stimulus, so he chose to shiver.

When Chase was looking to rent the place, Ms. Bradshaw had proudly touted his room as the only one with a balcony. She failed to mention the only reason his was the only one was because it was the only one that had yet to collapse and fall to a heap of scrap wood as the others had done over the years. She also failed to mention the terrace sported a wonderful view of the back alley where the trash gondolas baked in the sizzling summer sun all day long making the balcony unusable most of the time. But hey, it was quite entertaining to watch rats fight cats for scraps of discarded pizza.

Chase watched the boy sleeping and for the life of him could not believe what he was seeing. The child had mannerisms that were identical to his dead wife Anna's. Certain traits and idiosyncrasies this ten-year-old boy whom he had never met a day in his life couldn't have possibly known about. And to make matters even more fantastic the boy had a near identical birthmark in the same exact place as his mother if the boy was to be believed he was truly Chase's son.

The morning was rather surreal with him fixing breakfast for a child when he had no idea what a child would eat. Luckily, he had a few eggs in the refrigerator and packets of instant grits in the cupboard. The kid didn't seem to mind and in fact, attacked his breakfast with voracity.

He snuck the boy down the hallway to the communal showers and planned to run interference if Ms. Bradshaw decided to come snooping around, which was more likely than not. When the boy finished, he switched places and took a cold shower thanks to the lack of any hot water being left in the ten-gallon water heater, which was Ms. Bradshaw's way of eliminating long, exhilarating showers. On the way down to the car it dawned on Chase that he didn't know shit about children.

"Do you still have to be in a car seat?" he asked, immediately knowing it was a pretty stupid question.

Chase Junior shrugged and climbed into the passenger seat.

"I guess that settles that," Chase said as they pulled away from the curb with a chug and a wheeze from the Buick.

"No kids and no pets," he heard Ms. Bradshaw squawking from the curb behind him.

"I'd like to pop that old woman a good one, right in the nose. I'll bet that would stop her tongue from wagging all the time," he said with a smile and a light thump to the kid's shoulder.

Things seemed copasetic for a minute, like this was supposed to be. But then the reality of the situation hit him, and he realized something very abnormal was going on. As luck would have it, Chase embraced the strange and unusual.

"Hey there Mr. Coltrain, what are you doing in our neck of the woods? I hope you haven't seen a ghost out at Mt. Hope Cemetery again," Sergeant Jofre Chavez commented, which drew a rumble of chuckles from the rest of the officers in the precinct.

"Are we ever going to give that a rest?" Chase groaned.

"Nope, not until the next thing comes along that's even funnier than that shit. You're just lucky I haven't posted the bodycam footage on the internet," Chavez said with a smile.

"One of these days your skepticism is going to bite you in the ass," Chase said with a half-hearted smile.

"Coltrain, do you really believe all that bullshit on your podcast?" one of the other deputies asked from across the small reception area.

"Of course I do, otherwise I wouldn't publish the newsletter and produce my radio show."

"Bullshit," both Chavez and the deputy responded in unison.

"What can I get for you?" the sergeant turned his attention back to business.

Chase fumbled with his words while trying to fabricate a viable excuse before he asked his question.

"Do you happen to have one of those fingerprint kits for kids?" he asked.

"Fingerprint kits? You mean like a science project CSI toy?"

"No. Like a kit to fingerprint your kid in case anything happens to them so the police can identify them easier."

"Did you have a kid we don't know about?"

Chase laughed. "Oh, hell no. Not me. My landlord has been nagging me about one for her grandson. And hey, if I can shave fifty bucks off my rent, I'll do it."

"Fifty bucks? You better be cutting me in for half," Jofre said with a smile and reached beneath the counter. "Here. You can either bring it back in to us for processing or mail it to the address on the back of the card. It folds up into its own envelope."

"Nifty. Thanks."

"Just make sure the little guy hasn't committed any major crimes, or God forbid, murdered some little old lady," Sergeant Chavez said with a wink.

"He's only ten years old, so I highly doubt he's a dangerous felon," Chase said.

"You'd be surprised," the deputy called after him as he was walking out the door causing Chase to give pause for a moment before continuing out to his car.

Chapter Ten

Jessop Porter's head hung low, swaying from side to side slowly and methodical like the pendulum on a metronome. Measured and precise. His unbandaged wrist was shackled to a steel loop through the top of a stainless-steel table, with just enough slack to allow him to drink from a bottle of water in front of him. There were four more empties on the table in front of the man. He was mumbling something, but it wasn't loud enough to be audible in the observation room. Using his heavily bandaged hand he scratched at the bandaging covering his cheek and cursed the little boy under his breath.

"What's wrong with him?" Detective Black asked.

"The doctor has him on anti-psychotics. I tried to get them to hold off so we could interview him as is, but his lawyer was having none of it," Captain White said.

"His lawyer? He has money for a lawyer?"

"Not even close. He had thirty-seven cents in his pocket. His lawyer is that new public defender, the one who believes all clients are innocent until proven guilty, even bat shit crazy bastards like Porter here who was caught with his hand in the proverbial cookie jar."

"I'm surprised she's not here," Richie commented, before they were interrupted by a light rap on the door.

"Speak of the devil," Captain White said and opened the door to the observation room, ushering Jessop Porter's attorney into the room.

"Gentleman," Amelia Bancroft said, offering a gentle hand to both Captain White first, and then Detective Black.

Richie found himself being grateful for having spent ten years with a shapely partner who didn't take kindly to wandering eyes which forced him to always be on his best behavior as far as members of the opposite sex were concerned. Amelia Bancroft was tall, leggy and her long sandy, brown hair spilled down below her waist. He couldn't help but think she looked a lot like Effie and a tear threatened to escape his eye.

"I just wanted to go over a few ground rules with you and make you fully aware of the fact my client has special needs," she started.

"Special needs?" Detective Black interrupted.

"As I was saying, my client has special needs. And yes, detective, mental illness is a special need. Now, I have gone over the evidence against my client and while on the surface, it is both damning and overwhelming, there are mitigating circumstances."

"Mitigating circumstances?" Black couldn't contain his growing frustration.

"Mitigating, it means," she started.

"I know what it means lady, but as far as I'm concerned there's not a circumstance in the world that can justify a man eating another human being alive. Bat shit crazy or not."

"Allegedly," she fired back.

"Floss his teeth if you're skeptical," Richie said.

Captain White put his hand on Richie's forearm. "Ms. Bancroft, I understand your point of view, truly I do. But you have to look at things from our perspective as well. Even if your client is ruled clinically insane at some point, the fact of the matter is, he took great lengths to cover up his crimes, alleged crimes, so he knew full well what he was doing which makes him culpable," Captain White said.

Jessop Porter sensed something was wrong. He felt there was someone watching him. Not the cops in the other room behind the glass, but someone in the room with him. But he hadn't heard the door open, and no one had said anything to him. He kind of hoped someone would come in, he was hungry and almost out of water.

He felt hot breath against his hands and jerked them back toward his body. Slowly he glanced up from under his long, mangy hair to see a little boy sitting across from him. Jessop Porter's bladder loosened, and he wet himself.

"I have been looking for you," the boy of about eight years old said with furled brows.

Jessop Porter's mind was cloudy from a cocktail of psychotropic drugs in his system, so it took him a moment to respond. His customary sarcasm had not been altered much by the drugs.

"I've been busy," he said, his thin lips parting to reveal a smile of jagged, blackened teeth.

The lawyer stopped talking and turned her attention to the interrogation room in which Jessop Porter was seemingly having a conversation with himself.

"What is he doing?" she asked.

Captain White shrugged and said, "Beats me."

"You are not supposed to be here," the boy said with a sneer.

Jessop Porter rose from his chair as far as his shackles would allow, flung his hair back with a flip of his head and stared at the boy with defiance burning in his eyes. He knew the child was only a figment of his imagination, the doctors had told him as much. He knew if he stared at him long enough, he would just disappear. Poof! Begone demon child.

Once more the child glared across the table from him and said, "You are not supposed to be here."

How dare this hallucination take such an insolent tone with him? It was just his own imagination after all. All in his head and he controlled what was in his head. He swept his arms to the right, but the shackles held him in place and all he managed to do was make the empty water bottles topple over. The boy laughed at him and wagged his finger back and forth. Jessop lunged across the table to grab the wiggling digit but was again stopped short by the cuffs.

"Is there a way for us to hear what he is saying?" Amelia asked.

"Yes ma'am. But let me warn you, this will be recording once turned on and your client may very well say something that incriminates him and harms his defense," the captain responded.

"I'm willing to take that chance. From my vantage point the odds are more in his favor of helping his defense."

Captain White nodded to Detective Black who then flipped a switch and slowly turned the volume knob until they could hear what Porter was saying. Richie was staggered by what the man said.

"I am supposed to be here, and you have no right to tell me otherwise," he screamed and pointed a finger across the table.

Spittle flew across and hit the little boy who wiped it off his face with a smug grin. He continued to wag his finger and shake his head.

"Did that little girl tell you to say that?" Jessop whispered.

"What in the hell did he just say?" Detective Black said.

"I didn't make it out. We'll listen to the tape later," the captain said.

"You are not supposed to be here, and it is time for you to leave," the little boy said, jumping up onto the table and grabbing Jessop's jumpsuit by the lapel.

The boy dropped back down to the table, bringing Porter's head with him, slamming it on the tabletop. Jessop was dazed so it was easy for the boy to repeat the process, jerking the man's head down onto the solid surface with a loud bang. The third time his head slammed into the table it drew blood.

Detective Black couldn't believe what he was witnessing. There was no way the man was slamming his own head down that hard. And then the little boy turned and smiled at him, and he knew Jessop Porter was not alone. Or at least he thought he knew because he blinked and once more the man was in the room by himself, bashing his own head against the table.

Jessop Porter was able to recover for an instant, jerking himself back upright away from the vicious child. This only allowed the child, who was much stronger than he should have been for his size, to slam the man's head down with even more force. Twice more and Porter was out cold.

Captain White was stunned for a moment but quickly pressed a button on the panel which illuminated a light outside of the interrogation room alerting the officer standing guard to get in there immediately. The three of them watched in horror as Jessop's head raised up high one final time and slammed down hard on the bolt in the center of the table where the handcuffs were attached. The man's skull split wide open and then all was quiet.

Officer Runyon came rushing into the room to witness the final impact of Jessop Porter's skull on the table. He felt something rush past him, turned to look but didn't see anything. There was a chill about the room that unnerved the big man. A sadness washed over the officer as the man's vacant stare fell upon him. He gently lifted the man's head, checked for a pulse, and shook his head at those behind the glass to indicate the man was dead.

Chapter Eleven

Chase browsed through a rack of boy's pants trying to figure out what size would fit the boy. He decided on the thrift shop in case he got the wrong sizes, then he wouldn't be out too much money. He would have brought the boy with him, but there was something very hinkey about the entire situation and he wasn't quite ready to introduce his reincarnated son to the world.

He checked the time on his phone and saw it was almost lunch. Chase found he was not looking forward to sitting down with Richie Black. Not because he didn't like the guy, in fact they had been the best of friends at one point in their lives, but because he was certain he would be able to read the man's grief which would only serve to exacerbate his own sorrow over Effie's passing. Even though neither of them would have admitted it out loud, both Richie and Effie were close, so close in fact, Chase had expected to hear wedding bells a long time ago.

He scanned the fingerprint card again for the tenth time before putting it back into his pocket. The discomfort of grief was not the only reason he dreaded the meeting. Richie was always busting his balls about his fascination with the paranormal, his podcast, magazine and eventually if he ever got over the fear of rejection a whole slew of novels. But Chase also understood Richie Black's mind, his was an analytical brain with no room for speculation. He put two bags of used boy's clothes in the trunk of the LeSabre and headed for Old Town. He walked around the fish ladder a few times to gather his thoughts before heading over to the restaurant to meet up with Richie.

Meat BBQ is situated in the heart of Lansing's Old Town district not far from the state capital. It is literally a hole in the wall, with a small alley outside the front door which housed eight small bistro tables forcing patrons to run a gauntlet of tantalizing aromas though outdoor diners before even entering the restaurant itself. A modest place with a rustic, homey interior specializing in, of course, meat. Even though he couldn't really afford it, lunch would be his treat. Richie was here from Detroit on business having to do with Effie, so Chase thought it only fitting to treat the man to a hot meal.

Richie parked his Lansing made Olds 442 at the curb across from Craving's popcorn and strolled across the street. Normally he wouldn't have been excited about meeting up with Chase, but after what happened at the precinct yesterday, his old friend was just the man he needed to talk to. This was one conversation in which he would force himself to keep an open mind.

Chase opted for a brisket plate with a side of garlic mashed potatoes and mac-N-cheese, a carb choice he was certain to regret later, especially if he ate the brick sized piece of cornbread as well. Although he was pre warned about the portion size Richie ordered the mac-N-cheese decked out with bacon, brisket, hot links, and chorizo. When the waitress brought out their plates Richie's eyes immediately showed remorse for his choice, until his first forkful of course.

They didn't talk much during the meal and both men avoided the topic of Effie's death. For the time being Chase avoided the topic of a long dead son somehow resurrected and focused his thoughts on the delicious meal.

When they finished eating, they polished off their Two-Hearted Ale and leaned back in their chairs when Richie asked, "Is there someplace private we can talk?"

Chase thought about it for a moment. "Turner Dodge House is just around the corner, there's a small park there with not a whole lot of foot traffic. Why? You sound, for lack of a better term, surreptitious."

"There has to be a better term, one I could understand. Sheesh, do you ever speak plain English?" Richie said with a laugh and a swat of the man's arm. "The park sounds fine."

The two of them made their way a couple of blocks up Turner and then jogged onto Dodge River Road which Chase found himself contemplating the name of the road, especially when it paralleled the Grand River and not the Dodge River. Some things in life just never made any sense at all. It wasn't much as parks go, but there was a small fountain and flower garden with benches so they each took a seat.

"What's on your mind?" Chase asked, still avoiding the elephant in the room of Effie's death.

"There's no beating around the bush on this one. I need your expertise on something," he said and handed Chase his phone with a video queued up.

Chase took the phone and started viewing a recording of Jessop Porter bashing his own brains out all over a stainless-steel table. And as repulsive and shocking as it was, for some reason he couldn't look away. The video ended and he shoved the phone back to Richie.

"Why in the hell would you want me to watch something that brutal? Is this some kind of sick joke?" Chase said, suddenly nauseous and angry.

"Watch it again."

"Hell no, it's disgusting."

"Here, watch," Richie said, sliding over to the same bench Chase was on. "Right here," he said and paused the video while pointing at the screen.

Chase studied it for several seconds. "What is it I am supposed to be looking at?"

"Right here. Watch the lapel on his jumper," Richie said and ran the recording backward and forward again. "Do you see it?"

Chase paused, suspecting this might be one of Richie's twisted jokes. He took the phone from Richie and watched it several times forward and backward. He wasn't sure if his mind was playing tricks on him, but he sure as hell saw the man's lapel curl up as if in someone's grasp.

"Is this some sort of trick? Maybe a glitch in the video?"

"That's what I'm asking you. But I watched this real time, and at the time I swore there was something off, like someone was jerking his head downward. And look here," he pointed to Porter's face in the last frame.

Chase looked up with a ponderous expression. "Are his eyes rolled up into the back of his head? Could he just be between blinks or something?"

"I thought so too at first, but watch, three times he slams his head, all three times only the whites are visible. And watch his neck on the final blow that killed him. It wobbles, as if the muscles are not working."

"He was already unconscious?" Chase sublimated.

"Or already dead."

Chase looked over and saw that Richie's hands were trembling and realized this was no joke.

"Now watch this one a few times. It's short so you will have to watch it several times."

Chase watched the ten second clip of Officer Runyon darting into the room, stopping as he checked the man's pulse and then informed the others the man was dead. Not sure what he was supposed to be looking at, he reviewed the video several times focusing on a different quadrant each time. And then he saw it, or at least he thought he did.

"Was there someone else in the room?" Chase asked.

"You tell me," Richie replied.

"I can't be certain but there seems to be, for lack of a better term, a rift in the room. The officer's eyes seem to follow something leaving the room. Maybe he was just trying to avert his eyes from the carnage," Chase said.

"And watch this," Richie said, queuing up yet another short video.

Chase then watched the video of Jessop Porter arguing with the child in the room with astonishment. Richie reached over and turned up the volume after he had watched it several times.

"I am supposed to be here, and you have no right to tell me otherwise," Porter's voice echoed through the phone's speaker.

"To be honest with you Richie, I don't know very much about schizophrenia. I have no idea whether or not this man would see illusionary people that neither you nor I could see. But his body language sure as hell suggests he was speaking with, or at, another human being and not just a shadow in his own mind."

"So, this could just be some bat shit crazy asshole arguing with his own hallucinations making me out to be the crazy one?" Richie said with a slanted smile.

"That is one possibility."

"But you don't think so?"

"No, I don't. There is definitely someone or something else in that room with him. The more I watch the guard's face, the more I realize he not only saw something, but felt it as well. Here, look at his leg," Chase said, pointing to the screen on Richie's phone.

"Did his pant leg move?"

"Not only the fabric, but his leg moved too. He flinched because something physically touched him."

"Damn it, I was hoping you'd look at this and give me some cockamamie explanation that I could chuckle over on the way back to Detroit and file it away to never be thought of again. But what you say makes sense. Well sense if you believe this kind of spooky nonsense. I'm not completely sold yet, but I am not going to discount anything at this point," Richie said and slipped his phone back into his pocket.

There was a long pause as Chase pondered if he should tell Richie about the child who showed up on his doorstep out of the blue. Richie was starting to get up from the bench, from his perspective the conversation was over. He pulled the fingerprint card out of his pocket and handed it to Richie.

"What do you make of this?"

Richie studied the card for a couple of minutes. "What I make of it is that whoever took these prints needs a refresher course in fingerprinting."

"I took them."

"Of whom? And why?"

"Can I trust you?"

"To a certain point, but remember, I am still a police detective sworn to uphold the law."

"There is no easy way to say this, so I will just come right out and lay all the cards on the table at one time. Two days ago, a ten-year-old boy showed up at my doorstep claiming to be Chase Coltrain Junior."

There was a long pause before Richie said, "Your dead son?"

Chase nodded.

"This boy is obviously up to something, trying to scam you somehow. And I am sure there is an adult pulling his strings."

"I thought the same thing too, that's why I got the fingerprinting kit from my local police department."

"You obviously need a refresher in fingerprinting," Richie said with a smile.

"Richie, I fingerprinted him three times with the same results. He has no fingerprints. And when I questioned him about it, he just shrugged and said, *I am not finished becoming.* What in the hell does that even mean?" Chase asked.

Detective Black, not Richie, stared back at him. He would have scolded the man for being melodramatic and wasting his time had it not been for the strange series of recent events haunting his own sense of logic.

"And Richie, I watched him sleeping and maybe it's just my mind playing tricks on me, but I could see so much of Anna in him it was uncanny."

"I'll tell you what, I'm not going to bust your balls over this just yet. Get some DNA from this kid and I will have the lab put a rush on it," Richie said.

"I'll do you one better," he said, handing a bag to the detective with other bags inside.

"What's this?"

"The boy's toothbrush, a glass he drank out of and the shirt he arrived at my door in."

"What is in the other bag?"

"Chase Junior's, the real Chase Junior's hair from the day he was born. Anna saved it and I didn't have the heart to throw it away after she was gone."

"That won't do us any good without hair follicles."

"So, we're dead in the water," Chase said.

"No, just give me a sample of your saliva, that will be enough to determine a familial match."

While Richie was looking over the bags of evidence Chase watched a few joggers trot past. A photographer was taking macro shots of the flowers in the garden and a man across the street was working on his car in his driveway. Life appeared to be normal. But the surface of a tranquil pond doesn't reveal the dangers lurking below.

"What happened to us?" Richie asked without looking up.

"We got old," Chase replied with a smirk.

"You know what I mean. I've seen people grow apart, friends, lovers, but there was always an underlying reason. I would have thought Anna losing the baby, and then your losing Anna would have been the nail in the coffin, but we stayed close even through all of that."

"We did, but that was just an illusion. The problem wasn't us, it was me. Almost every time I saw you, Effie was around and whenever I saw Effie I was reminded of Anna. And the times it was just you and I, well, I couldn't help but notice it was no longer the four of us together and it wore on me until I just couldn't take it anymore. And Richie, I really didn't even notice what was happening until I had already pulled too far away to come back."

"That's a bullshit answer, but I get it. So, what made you call me?"

"Effie. I know the pain you must be going through firsthand, and I knew I had to pack away my self-loathing and reach out to you. You were there when I needed you, it was only right."

"Listen, I know you are not some whackadoodle conspiracy theorist. What do you make of all this?" Richie asked, wiping the tears from his eyes.

"Honestly, I don't have a clue. In pieces I'm sure these circumstances could all be explained away. But putting the pieces together, it doesn't feel kosher. Not in the least," Chase responded.

"I was afraid you were going to say something like that. Let me head back home and I will call you in a day or two with the results of the DNA test," he said, holding up the bags containing the items Chase collected.

Chase nodded and they both walked back to their cars without another word. They offered half-hearted waves as they drove off in separate directions hoping to put this strangeness behind them.

Chapter Twelve

"I am telling you, Verona, I think the guy is a genuine preevert. A true died in the wool peedofile," Ester Bradshaw gossiped to her friend.

The women sat at the kitchen table drinking warm gin with grapefruit juice chaser even though it was barely ten o'clock in the morning. Verona Munoz lived across the street, and like Ester, she too had a houseful of ungrateful tenants who were always late with their rent. The pair gossiped about Fred Walker, Verona's tenant who leered at Verona every morning when she went to check the mail in her sheer muumuu which was made even more see through at that time of day due to the angle of the sun. Ester, on the other hand, chose to make Chase Coltrain the topic of the morning's conversation.

"Why would you think such a thing, Ester? He seems like such a nice, polite young man, even if he is a little brooding," Verona asked.

"All of the sudden, out of the blue, a ten-year-old boy shows up on the doorstep. Claiming to be the man's son no less. There's something fishy about him," she said, slamming her gin, prompting Verona to do the same.

"I know why you're so sour on the man."

"Yeah, and why is that, Verona?" Ester asked.

"Cause he don't want to rent a room in your musty motel," she said, bobbing her head in the direction of her friend's crotch.

"Shut the hell up. I'll have you know it would be the best damned room he ever rented."

"The biggest maybe, and definitely the oldest. Hell, that motel is so old Lincoln could have stayed there when he was but a wee lad," Verona laughed until she saw stars.

"Last warning, Verona," Ester said as she refilled both empty glasses.

"Last one, Ester. I've got to get Mr. Bishop's laundry done before he gets home from his AA meeting, or I will never hear the end of it."

"Screw that twatwhistle, he should be doing his own damned laundry," Ester said and wiped excess gin from her upper lip.

"He pays me, so I have to be timely."

"Or you could just boot the old fart out on his ass."

"I'm not independently wealthy like you Ester," Verona said, rising from the table to put her empty glass in the sink as they both laughed so hard, they nearly choked.

Ester slammed her two fingers of gin back and contemplated pouring another. She touched the Texas fifth bottle to the glass but thought better of it, put the cap back on the Beefeater, and slid the plastic jug into the cupboard.

"One more of those and I'll be calling the cops for sure. Then I would never get my rent and I'd be stuck with a snot nosed little welp running around the place," Ester said as she staggered Verona to the front door.

She went back into the living room and turned on the television. It was time for that game show with all the hot, half naked male models. Boy they sure got her motor running, especially after three glasses of gin, and she downed four already. She slipped her panties off from under her nightgown and stuffed them under the paisley couch cushion on her right side. She was fairly sure she wouldn't be needing them in a few minutes. Ester was lost in the moment, swooning over the shirtless man's British, or possibly it was an Australian accent as he bantered back and forth with the host while flirting with the women in the audience. She fantasized he was bantering back and forth, up, and down with her. She was nearly there when she heard a voice from across the room.

"Why do you have a wig in your lap?" Chase Jr. asked, his head tilted slightly to the side.

Ester, ripped from her libidinous trance, was both embarrassed and incensed.

"How did you get in her?" she screamed while covering up her lady parts as best she could.

"The door."

"I know the damned door, but how?"

"It was unlocked."

"Hasn't anyone ever told you that you are supposed to knock before entering someone's home?"

"No," he replied in earnest.

"Well, now that you are in here, invading my privacy, what in the hell do you want?"

"Why did you call my dad a pedophile? That means he has sex with little children, I looked it up," Chase Junior said, his curious smile replaced with a scowl.

"I know what it means. I didn't mean anything by it, it was just an observation," Ester replied, realizing she was caught in a pickle.

"Did you observe my father having sex with children?"

"Well, not exactly?"

"Then what did you see, exactly?" the boy's tone suddenly turned terse and acerbic as he took two long strides to where the old woman was still sitting on the couch still trying to conceal her lady parts.

Ester struggled to get up off the couch but between her aging muscles, an excess of gin, and the davenport's broken-down springs she wasn't able to get to her feet before the boy was straddling her lap. He glared into her eyes and her blood turned to ice when she understood the depth of evil behind those eyes. She knew she was in serious trouble when he pulled a small paring knife from his pocket and began stabbing her. She grabbed him by the arms to throw him off her, but he began stabbing her forearms with the knife. The wounds weren't very deep, not even half an inch deep, and she realized he wasn't stabbing her as much as tormenting her with superficial wounds.

"My dad was right, you do stick your nose into other people's business way too much," he said as he leaned forward and placed the blade at the point where the cartilage meets the bone and sliced down with all his strength, separating the woman from her malformed appendage. With a triumphant grin he dropped the nubbin of flesh into his pocket.

Ester opened her mouth to scream but the boy reached under the cushion, grabbed her panties, and shoved them as far into her mouth as he could before she could utter a sound, busting both her top and bottom lip at the same time. Blood poured from the gaping wound in her face, coating the front of her nightgown with an ever-growing crimson stain. She tried to struggle but every time she did the boy stabbed her in her undulating breasts. The boy leaned in real close to her and smiled a sinister smile that caused her to wet herself. He produced a large, serrated knife from behind his back that had been tucked into the waistband of his shorts.

"He also said you talk too much. But I can fix that," he said, reaching into her gaping mouth.

Using the panties to grip her tongue he pulled it as far out of her mouth as he could, set the edge of the blade against the pink flesh and slowly sawed the blade back and forth across the meat, making sure to go slow enough to prolong the woman's agony. His hand jerked away from her face once the blade was free of her flesh. He dropped that chub of flesh into his pocket as well.

Ester was writhing on the couch in agony giving Chase Junior the freedom to run out to the kitchen without fear of her escaping. He returned with a large chef's knife with a pointed end. As he approached the couch the old hag lashed out with several kicks, each one earning her a stab to her calves and thighs which forced her to abandon her feeble attempts. Chase Jr. grinned wide every time he felt the blade hit the bone.

"What's that Ms. Bradshaw, I can't understand what you are trying to say?" Chase Jr. taunted the old woman. "No kids, and no pets."

Her torment continued for another ten minutes before her will to fight was completely exorcised and Ester quit thrashing about. Several more minutes and little Chase became bored, so he severed her carotid and when that stopped spewing a torrent of blood, he separated her head from the rest of her body. He carried the lopped off head upstairs and proudly placed it in his father's bedroom window so the man would see his gift as soon as he started up the walk.

Chase Jr. cleaned himself up, found some clothes of the old ladies that wouldn't look too dorky on him and then went back to the kitchen where he rummaged through the pantry. He filled a pillowcase with as much food as he wanted to carry and headed out the door. This was his first kill, and even though she didn't help him move any closer to becoming he was exhilarated all the same. All those years spent in that hellish purgatory dreaming about this moment paled in comparison to the actual rush. There would be many more to follow.

"Goodbye, Ms. Bradshaw," the boy said, waving up at the bedroom room window. "It certainly was nice to meet you. Smell ya later," the boy called out as he headed down the walk whistling a happy tune.

Chapter Thirteen

Rose Marie moseyed up and down the People Mover car trying to pass the time between stops. A disembodied voice told her the train would be arriving at Millender Center in a couple of minutes. She skipped to the back of the car to retrieve her stuffed bear she swiped from a thrift shop earlier in the day. It was brand new and an ugly pink color, so she had rubbed it in the gutter of the street and in a dirty parking lot to give it some character. She rubbed some goopy stuff in her hair as well, just for appearances sake, which she regretted almost immediately as whatever had been in the fast-food cup smelled disgusting.

Her dress was fine and needed no accoutrements as it was the same dress she had been wearing in the church before she began her journey to become. She wandered up Randolph Street to Congress and then back down to the People Mover station. She continued on this route until the next train showed up where she climbed aboard to repeat the process at the next stop. This was taking much longer than she expected, people just didn't seem to care about a lost little girl wandering the streets.

Rose Marie deduced her lack of response was all due to timing. During the evening commute people had tunnel vision with thoughts focused on getting home. There was also a baseball game that night and while that meant extra foot traffic, it also meant the people were focused on something other than a stray child. She curled up on the molded plastic seat of the People Mover using her filthy animal as a pillow and took a nap.

The lights came on in the train, jerking her away from her dreams of becoming. She wasn't sure how long she had been asleep, but she felt refreshed. She got off the People Mover at the Grand Circus Park station with a yawn and a stretch. She walked down to Comerica Park, back down Adams before moving in a continuous half circle around Grand Circus Park. There were less people on the street now, and more of them seemed to notice her. She smiled; it wouldn't be long now.

"Hey, are you the one who called?" Officer Crenshaw asked the bartender.

"No, not me. One of the servers did. Hey, Megan," the man yelled out across the bar with a beckoning gesture.

The server finished taking her table's order and strolled back to the bar with a smile. The cop was kind of cute, not like all the cranky, old officers they usually sent when there was a problem.

"Hi, I'm Megan. I'm the one who called," she said, offering her hand which he shook delicately.

"Officer Kyle Crenshaw. Which customer is causing the disturbance?" he asked, looking around the crowded bar and not seeing any unruly customers or anything out of the ordinary for that matter.

"Nothing is wrong in here. In fact, I feel kind of silly now. I think maybe I was overreacting and got you out here for nothing."

"It's never nothing, it's my job to ease the public's mind," he said to the attractive waitress sporting his best flirtatious smile that accentuated his dimples.

"Like I said, it's probably nothing, but I think there might be a little girl lost in the park."

"See, that is definitely something worth looking into. I truly hope you were mistaken, and this is just a false alarm. What makes you think this girl is lost and not just wandering separate from her parents?" he asked.

Megan smiled and played with her hair. "She was pretty dirty and carrying a really dirty stuffed animal. I passed her while walking in to work and then I saw her several more times during my shift. She was just wandering back and forth by herself like maybe she's homeless or maybe looking for someone."

"About what time did you see her?"

"The first time must have been around seven or so, it was still light outside, but the streetlights were coming on."

"And the second time?"

"Must have been about nine or so. And then again just about fifteen minutes ago."

"Okay, thanks, I will go check it out," Officer Crenshaw said as he headed for the door.

"Be sure to come back and tell me all of the details over a free cup of coffee," Megan called after him.

Officer Kyle Crenshaw smoothed his short cropped blonde hair with his palm while slipping his patrolman's cap back on. He strolled across East Adams into the park across the street from the bar. He made a sweep of the perimeter of the park and didn't see any little girl wandering around by herself.

Rose Marie was a bit disappointed that it was a young officer looking for her. He was too young to have been the one, but that was neither here nor there at this point because she sensed he was one who was not supposed to be here. She tailed him as he walked around the park looking for her. There was nothing wrong with a little game of hide and go seek before retribution.

Her little legs were sore from walking all day, so she surrendered the game and decided to go for the win. She moved toward the center of the park near the Russell A. Alger fountain. She curled her index fingers and rubbed her eyes as hard as she could for several minutes to redden them up and get her tears flowing.

Crenshaw finished his check of the perimeter and began moving toward the center of the park where the fountain was located. The few people he had asked had only been in the park for a few minutes walking their dogs and hadn't seen any little girl wandering about. Traffic on the street had cleared momentarily affording Crenshaw with an opportunity to listen to the surroundings. He smiled when he heard her soft sobbing.

"Hey, honey, don't be scared. I'm a police officer. What is your name?" he asked, towering over the child who was sitting cross legged in the wet grass.

"Rose Marie."

"Where are your parents?"

The little girl shrugged without looking up.

"Are you lost?"

"No. I am supposed to be here," she said.

"You are supposed to be here? Do you mean you are waiting for someone here?"

"Not here," she said, stabbing a finger at the ground next to her. "Here," she finished while encircling her arms around herself in a sweeping arc.

"I don't understand what you mean. Can you tell me what you mean by here," Officer Crenshaw said, mimicking her sweeping arc.

"It's a secret," she said.

The little girl hooked her finger and beckoned him down to her level. Crenshaw squatted down and leaned into the little girl so she could reveal her secret.

"The police are bad men. The police killed me. They shouldn't have done that," she said.

Rose Marie withdrew her hand from under her bear and produced a long, sharp bladed screwdriver. Before Crenshaw could react, she shoved the screwdriver into the soft crook of his throat just below his Adam's apple. The officer tried to reach for his weapon, but the little girl had already disarmed him.

"Ah, ah, I know all about you cops and your guns," she said, popping the clip out of the pistol before tossing the unloaded weapon into the fountain.

Rose Marie dropped the ugly bear on the ground next to the bleeding cop and walked away, whistling a happy tune to herself.

Officer Kyle Crenshaw tried to call out for help but all he could manage were a few wet gurgles. He staggered back through the dog park toward East Adams. Delirious from the lack of oxygen, he staggered into the middle of a busy intersection seconds after the light turned green. Drivers slammed on their brakes to stop but were too late. Crenshaw was catapulted over the hood of a car and landed headfirst onto the macadam. Megan and several bar patrons ran to see what the commotion was all about outside when she saw the cop lying in the street in a pool of blood, and she screamed.

Megan glanced up in time to see the little girl standing on the sidewalk looking at Officer Crenshaw. The little girl looked across the street at her, smiled and gave her an enthusiastic wave before disappearing into the gathering crowd.

Chapter Fourteen

Chase Coltrain picked at the remnants in the foam takeout tray from Meat BBQ while mulling over the conversation he was going to have with the boy when he got home. He would tell him about the pending DNA test and give the child the opportunity to come clean if he were running some sort of scam before things got out of hand and the boy wound up in a heap of trouble. He was a little disturbed that Richie hadn't chastised him about the situation and in fact, the man seemed uncharacteristically receptive to the idea, which was not like Richie Black at all.

He found his thoughts meandering to his dead sister-in-law prompting him to open the newspaper with the article about her murder. Of course, now that Richie was exonerated from shooting Effie there would be a retraction, but it would be buried in the obituary pages where no one would read it. If it bleeds, it leads whether it be the truth or not was never more relevant than with today's media.

Chase thought back to his days in journalism school and could not remember the class on who, what, where, when, why and how I personally feel about the issue and if it fits my political ideology. He reread the article several times before moving on to other articles in the paper. He was reading a piece on a suicide at the Mackinac Bridge when a passage caught his attention. He flipped back to the front page and the article about Effie Meadows. Back and forth he flipped through the pages of the Detroit Free Press.

You are not supposed to be here. Both articles quoted the passage as having been overheard by witnesses during both incidents as well as Porter's own words in the video of his interrogation. As far as Chase was concerned, these incidents were too similar to be a coincidence. He made note of the Trooper's name in the article and called the St. Ignace State Police post.

"Michigan State Police, St. Ignace," a voice said.

"Good afternoon. I am hoping you could put me in touch with a Trooper Renee Franklin," Chase said.

"I'm sorry sir. We don't have any troopers assigned to this post by that name."

"I ran into her on Labor Day, on the bridge," he said, hoping he didn't divulge enough information to get the call cut off in a hurry thinking he was a delusional stalker.

"Oh, she was probably temporarily assigned here for the holiday weekend. Let me check," the woman said. Chase heard her rifling through papers for several minutes before she came back on the line. "Trooper Franklin is assigned to the command post in Lansing."

"Perfect. Thank you very much."

Chase spent another half an hour tracking the trooper down at the command post and when he finally managed to get in touch with her, she was less than receptive. He spent another half an hour wearing her down and eventually she agreed to meet him though oddly enough, at a secluded park. He shot a text to Richie asking if he was still in town and if he was, they needed to talk. He pulled into the lot of Hunter's Orchard Park and began walking the trail as he was instructed. It was as if he were living out a boyhood fantasy of being a spy on a clandestine mission.

"Trooper Franklin?" he asked, coming upon a woman sitting on a bench overlooking the Grand River.

"Call me Renee," she said, offering her hand.

Chase let loose a nervous laugh and tried to stop the words before they tumbled out. "I usually have trouble getting women to meet me at all, let alone by themselves in a secluded park. Sorry, that was a bad joke."

"Let me start by saying I would have never agreed to meet you had I not already known who you were."

"How would you possibly know who I am?"

"You are *the* Chase Coltrain aren't you? The same Chase Coltrain who has the podcast Chasing Shadows in the Dark?" she said.

"One in the same I'm afraid."

"I read your blog almost every day," she gushed.

"So, you're the one," Chase quipped.

"I'm really into any and all things paranormal or horror related. It's why no one is taking me seriously about what I saw. You have to promise me that anything we discuss will be off the record."

"I just want your version of what happened that day on the bridge."

"Your solemn oath," Renee said, a little sterner.

"You have my word. This is more for my own personal curiosity anyway. I had never planned on doing a piece about this incident," Chase said.

"Why not, this is pretty bizarre?"

"Let's just say that suicide is a subject very close to me, and I owe it a great deal of reverence. This man's story has already been related to more people than it should."

"What if I tell you I believe he was pushed, well more like pulled off the bridge and did not jump of his own accord," Renee said with an ember of doubt in her eye.

"What makes you say that? Sometimes trauma can cause us to see things differently than they really occurred," Chase said, immediately regretting his words.

"I knew this was a bad idea. You are just like my supervisor, claiming I saw things I didn't see. But I know I saw what I saw."

"Let's back it up for a minute. I did not mean to infer anything. Why don't you start from the beginning, and I will keep my damned big mouth shut," he said with a smile and a gesture of zipping his lips.

"I'm sorry, I've been down this road a few times since that day and none of them have turned out well. I saw Hector Correa on the bridge near noon. He was straggling behind the crowd, so I went over and spoke with him to get him moving toward the St. Ignace side. He informed me his dad had just passed away and he was taking one last bridge walk with him," she said.

"So, the man was possibly distraught over losing his father?"

Renee glared at Chase and made a zipping gesture of her own.

"No, in fact, the man was in rather good spirits. Let me cut to the chase, I left him there and started back across to the St. Ignace side when I got a call on the radio that the man was still lingering, and I should go back and hustle him along. When I caught sight of him, he was squatting down, talking to a little boy sitting on the railing."

"There was a little boy? How old?" Chase started but then shut up when he got *the look.*

"The little boy said something to him and rocked all the way back as far as he could. When Hector reached for him, he leaned in real fast and then grabbed the man by the lapel of his shirt and flipped himself backward, tugging them both over the railing."

"And what happened to the little boy?" Chase asked.

"That is why everyone thinks I'm being crazy or that I was traumatized. When I got to the railing and looked over, I saw Mr. Correa freefalling under the bridge, but I didn't see any little boy. The Coast Guard and the police both looked over the bridge surveillance tapes and there was no little boy in any of the footage from that day. And they only recovered Hector's body from the water."

"Did you happen to hear what the boy said?" Chase asked.

"He told Hector, you are not supposed to be here, then he jerked him over the railing."

"Are you sure that's what he said."

She nodded. "Exactly what he said. You think I'm nuts, don't you?"

"Not even close," Chase responded, suddenly wanting to unload his burden on this woman about Effie and the little boy on his doorstep. "How old would you say the boy was?"

"I don't have children so I'm not a very good judge. But if I had to guess I'd say between eight and ten years old," Renee answered.

"Interesting," was all that Chase managed to say. He was lost within his own thoughts.

There was a long silence between the two of them, both wandering inside of their own minds while watching the river meander through the forest while squirrels and chipmunks were doing their thing as were the geese and ducks.

"I wasn't planning on showing this to anyone," Renee said, handing her phone to Chase. She had a video queued up to play.

"What's this?"

"Just watch it. But you can't tell anyone, or I will be fired, or worse. I downloaded it when no one was looking."

Chase watched the video of her body cam of the incident. There was no child in the video, but the man, Hector was clearly speaking with someone sitting on the railing of the bridge. And then, out of the blue he went over. He watched the sixty second clip over and over again, each viewing making him even more uncomfortable than the last. In the five seconds before the man went over the railing it was faint, but he could see the man's lapel curling up as if it were in someone's grasp.

"I know this will sound strange, but did the boy have any color when you saw him?"

She shook her head and blinked slowly. Renee sighed as if a weight had been lifted.

"You believe me, don't you?"

"I believe you saw something."

"Hector didn't jump, did he?"

"Not as far as I can tell. Can you send me this file? I want to show it to someone."

"You promised this would be off the record."

"It will be. This friend of mine, let's just say for the sake of time, has experienced a similar incident. They also have access to technical equipment that can get us a cleaner copy of this."

"Fine. Just keep my name out of it. And let me know what you figure out. Who knows, maybe we can come to an agreement on a podcast," she smiled, got up from the park bench and headed for the parking lot.

With trembling hands Chase texted Richie once more.

~ ~ ~

"You do realize I was damned near to Ann Arbor," Richie said, pulling up to the curb so Chase could get in the car. "Leave that old, piece of shit Buick here while we find a quiet bar. Leave the keys in it too, maybe you'll get lucky, and someone will steal it."

"She is not old, she is well travelled," Chase said as he got into the passenger seat of the Olds.

They cruised through town to the outskirts of the city to a little dive bar named the B and I Bar. The place looked closed and there were no cars in the parking lot, but Chase assured Richie this was the rush hour. They went in to find the bar was nearly filled at the rail with no two empty seats together, so they found a booth in a dark back corner. The jukebox was blasting out a mix of old country and classic rock which suited both men fine.

"What is so important you dragged me out to treat me to a case of salmonella?" Richie asked.

"Don't be a naysayer, this place has some of the best food in the city. I highly recommend the tacos."

After ten minutes of sitting by themselves Richie realized there was not going to be a waitress, so he went up to the bar and ordered. The place seemed to be strictly beer and well drinks joint, so he ordered a bucket of Miller Lite cans with two shots of Jack Daniel's along with two taco specials. Once they were settled in with their food and drinks Chase showed Richie the video Trooper Franklin had Emailed him.

"What am I looking at?"

"Look at the way the man is squatting down and then looking up talking as if he were talking to someone sitting on the railing."

"You did say he was saying goodbye to his recently departed father, right? He might have just been saying a prayer."

"I thought you might say that. Watch the last ten seconds."

Richie watched the clip and couldn't believe what he was seeing. Some unseen entity clearly pulled the man over the railing so similar to the video of Jessop Porter it was uncanny. This was definitely not suicide.

"And there's something else. The boy who was rescued from the church," Chase started.

"I think his name was Grayson," Richie said.

"That boy from the church, Grayson, was quoted in the article about Effie as saying the *Creepy Dude* kept going on and on about how he wasn't supposed to be there."

"But that wasn't it, was it?"

"No, the man must have been saying, you are not supposed to be here. Trooper Franklin claims she heard the boy say that exact same phrase before pulling Hector Correa over the railing," Chase explained.

"The little boy we can't see in the video?" Richie asked.

"Just like the little girl who murdered Effie who no one else but you saw," Chase said, heading Richie's sarcasm off at the pass.

Richie paused for several minutes, ate a taco, downed his shot of Jack, and polished off a beer, tossing the empty aside and cracking another.

"The little girl who shot Effie said exactly the same thing to her before she pulled the trigger."

Chase polished off his beer and opened another. "It can't be a coincidence."

Richie shook his head while taking a bite of his taco.

"What do you think it means?" Chase asked.

"I haven't the foggiest, but I know it must mean something. You tell me Mr. Ghost Hunter, what's this all about?"

"Why are you asking me?"

"You're the expert on this weird shit."

"Expert my ass. I embellish most of the stuff I present on my website and podcast. It's fifty percent pure fiction. All I really do is test out novel ideas."

Richie made a gesture as if he were shocked. "Hypothetically speaking, in one of your fantasy stories, how would this play out?"

"Richie, I really don't know at this point. But I do know something shady is going on and I think this boy who is passing himself off as Chase Junior might know exactly what it is."

"Then let's go have a talk with the snot nosed little bastard right now," Richie said, polishing off the last taco and beer with a belch that seemed to please the cook.

Conversation was kept to a bare minimum on the drive to Chase's apartment and that was limited to reminiscing about whatever song happened to be playing on the radio at the time. The traffic was light so the drive across town took less than fifteen minutes.

"Nice neighborhood," Richie commented.

"Yeah, well I'm not a high-priced detective like you are. And it suits me fine for my needs."

They were on their way across the street when Chase grabbed Richie by the forearm and stopped him dead in his tracks. His gut churned and he knew their day was about to get a whole lot worse.

"What's wrong?"

"Look up in the window," Chase said while pointing his finger up at the second floor of the house to the window in his room.

"Whoa, there's some creepy old broad upstairs. Is that your landlord?"

Chase nodded. "But something is very wrong. That's my room, but she never goes in there when I'm not home, or at least I didn't think she would. Something looks off about her face."

They made their way across the street and stood on the sidewalk below Chase's bedroom window. Richie immediately recognized the hollow, vacant stare of the old woman. He saw there were streaks of blood at the base of the pane of glass as well. He peered beyond the overgrown hedgerow lining the front fence and saw several bloody footprints leading into the grass and around the back of the house. Small, shoeless footprints.

"You stay here," Richie said as he moved toward the front door.

"Why what's wrong?" Chase asked, sensing Richie's sudden change from drinking buddy to homicide detective.

"Keys," he said, holding out his hand, palm facing up.

Chase took a step forward, but Richie stopped him with a palm flat against his chest and a stern shake of his head. His hand was still outstretched, and he flexed his fingers several times until Chase got the hint and dropped the house keys into his hand.

"You stay here, and if you do not hear from me in five minutes, call 911. Tell them there is an undercover officer in trouble at this address."

"You're serious."

"As serious as it gets," Richie said and headed up onto the porch, giving the bloody footprints a wide berth.

Detective Black slid the key slowly into the deadbolt lock and made certain it was disengaged before moving the key to the doorknob lock. He turned the key hard to the left and used the key to turn the doorknob in case there were any fingerprints on the knob. Once inside the foyer he reached down to his ankle and pulled out his back up piece after he saw more bloody footprints on the tile floor.

Richie knew he should back out of the house right now and wait for the locals to show up, but there was a very good chance someone could be gravely injured and in immediate need of his assistance so in good conscience he couldn't avoid clearing the scene. The foyer was only two steps long and opened up into the living room where he was confronted with the naked torso of an old woman and a trail of bloody footprints leading away from the couch.

He sighed, collected himself and followed the footprints through the house and up the stairs. Flashbacks of the old church haunted him with each step he took. Richie saw the upstairs was sectioned off into three apartments. He assumed since there wasn't a mob of flashing red and blue lights outside in the street the other tenants were out and had been spared the gruesome scene thus far. He did a quick inventory of each of the painted white doors in the corridor, observing that only two of them had bloody handprints on the casings.

The first door led to the bathroom where a chef's knife covered in blood and tissue lay in the sink. There was a pile of bloody clothes on the floor and a bloody towel next to them. The shower stall cast a pinkish hue telling him the perp had showered after the crime, but that also indicated they deliberately walked through the blood in the living room to leave the bloody footprints on the steps and sidewalk outside.

Richie got his bearings straight and headed for the other room with bloody handprints smeared on the door.

He was certain it was Chase's room. Carefully he opened the door and eased his way into the room. It was empty, except for the old woman's head perched like a trophy on the windowsill. Blood ran down the white wall in gelatinous strands, pooling up on the carpet below. He didn't want to handle the severed head but from the reflection in the glass he could see that her nose had been cut clean off her face. Richie leaned over as far as he could, trying not to touch anything, and after a brief struggle with the painted sash he slid the window open enough to call down to Chase.

"Hey, Chase, do you need anything from your room?"

"What?"

"Do you need anything from your room?"

"You're not making any sense. Why would I need anything from my room?"

"Because the police are going to lock this place up tight for at least three days, probably more."

"Is it bad?"

The look on Richie's face answered his question. He gave the man a small list of things to grab, his laptop, a couple changes of clothes, and some cash in his sock drawer. Richie nodded, grabbed a clean pillowcase from the linen closet in the hall and filled it with things he thought Chase might need. There was a note on top of the dresser that was beyond disturbing. The woman's bloody nose sat on the parchment with the words *I cut off her nose to spite her ugly face.* And below that was another nubbin of flesh Richie could only assume was her tongue. *Yakkity Yak, don't talk back!* was written below that.

He saw another bloody piece of paper that had slid down behind the dresser. He didn't want to move it, so he got down onto his knees and took several photographs of the note which he didn't understand at all. *I did not do this,* and it was signed, *Hector.*

Richie took pictures of Chase's room, back tracked to the bathroom, and did the same there. He followed his path back out of the house, taking more photographs as he went. He stopped in the living room and studied the old woman's corpse as best as he could without disturbing the crime scene. There were obvious signs of sadistic torture. The fact this kid calling himself Chase Junior was nowhere to be found deeply disturbed the detective knowing there was a pint-sized maniac on the loose.

Chapter Fifteen

Two young children walked down separate sidewalks on a convergent path as if drawn to one another like magnet and steel. Each of them smiled and whistled a happy tune as they walked with purpose. And what a grand purpose it was.

Rose Marie wore a school uniform, white shirt with a dark blue skirt, she liberated from a neglected child whom she then tossed in a dumpster along with the ratty lavender dress. Chase Jr. had on a pair of plaid shorts two sizes too big and a shirt with the likeness of some comic book hero he had no knowledge of. The two of them met up under a dirty overpass on the city's east side.

"Did you have any trouble getting here?" Rose Marie asked.

"A little, but nothing I couldn't overcome. First the driver didn't want to pick up a child, and then he wanted to get paid. How ludicrous is that?" Chase Jr. responded.

"How did you pay him?" Rose Marie said with a smile, already knowing the answer.

"I gave him everything he deserved," he responded with a wicked grin.

"Have you become?"

"Some, but not all the way. I can feel that man inside me trying to get out. But I'm getting there," he said and showed her his fingertips which now sported a fresh new set of whorls and ridges.

"I know, she is struggling inside of me as well. But I can feel her weakening. Soon we will both become, and once we become, we can get to work. But remember, until we become, we will be vulnerable."

Chase Jr. nodded. "We need the others."

"They will be here soon."

"How will we find the proper vessels for them?"

"I already have. Well, not all of them, only three, but we can worry about the other two later. Once there are five of us, it will be much easier to find the final two. And then when there are seven, no living soul will be allowed to walk among us."

"What do we do until then?"

"We avoid grandiosity, keep to the shadows and far away from authority," she said and turned away, ending their conversation.

The evil glint in the boy's eyes was not lost on her. He enjoyed his first kill far too much and she would be hard pressed to keep him reigned in. As she walked along the lonely street Rose Marie couldn't help being angry with the boy for killing the old woman. It wasn't that she cared about the sack of human flesh, she was angry because he had set circumstances in motion that would prove to be bothersome to control. In the end, she knew he was what he was and would always be a cold-blooded killer. He was only being who he was intended to be from his inception. It was why he was not allowed the sanctity of life. She, on the other hand, she was far more sinister than the boy could ever imagine to be.

Rose Marie pondered this carnal form she wore, and its limitations. While she herself possessed endless energy, this bag of bones did not and when she pushed it too hard, it certainly let her know. She stopped and took a seat on a bench in a small roadside park. While she watched the joggers, dog walkers and ne'er-do-wells, she wondered what this place would look like without them. Without all of them, each and every one. A sense of peace washed over her at the thought of ultimate solitude.

Walking along a lighted street in a suburban neighborhood she realized the sights, the sounds and the smells were all familiar to her. No, not to her, to the other. Her host had brought her here without her being aware of it. This could pose to be an unforeseen problem she would have to confront. Without consciously doing so, she rang the doorbell.

Richie turned down the television and went to answer the front door. Chase was upstairs asleep after a long, grueling day at the police station. Once the interrogation, or as they liked to call it, interview, was over he was released into Richie's custody but was under no circumstances to leave the state and Detective Black agreed to be wholly responsible for his whereabouts.

"Hello," Richie said, opening the door to see a small girl on his porch. "I'm sorry, I don't have any cash so I can't buy any cookies tonight."

"I'm not selling any, Richie."

He stumbled backward at the familiarity of the girl's voice, tone, and cadence. He knew who she was, but it was impossible.

"Aren't you going to ask me in?"

"No, I'm not. This can't be real," he said, bracing himself against the door.

Suddenly the girl's face turned sour, and she said, "You are not supposed to be here." Richie realized she wasn't talking to him, rather, she was having a conversation with herself.

"Effie?"

"I'm afraid we don't have long," she said, pushing her way passed him and into the house.

Effie could feel herself being pushed out, or more accurately, back. Back into the shadowy recesses of this child's brain. She looked around inside the void and it was pure chaos.

"Nice trick kid now get the fuck out of my house," Richie demanded, finally snapping out of the initial shock.

Effie was struggling to maintain her presence and knew it would eventually prove to be a losing battle. She had to make Richie understand as bizarre as this was, it was genuine.

"I'm so very sorry, Richie," the girl said.

"Sorry about what?" his tone softened.

"That I never found the nerve to tell you how I feel about you."

Richie's knees weakened and threatened to give out on him. He glanced over at the coffee table and saw there were only two empties, so he knew he wasn't drunk.

"It was our ten-year anniversary of being partnered up," Effie said, hoping to make him realize it was truly her inside of this little girl.

"Kid, you were in that church, I recognize you. You were wearing that purple dress with the red roses on the pockets. Nice try."

"Lavender," she said, her voice noticeably different.

"For the last time, get out of my house. I am too tired for this bullshit," Richie said while shoving the girl back toward the door.

"Remember when you almost kissed me at Brubaker's retirement party? Why didn't you?" Effie asked.

Richie stopped in his tracks. This was no parlor trick. That little girl would have no way of knowing about that incident, or non-incident as it were because she hadn't even been born yet. He thought he liked it better when he thought she was merely a scam artist. He glanced over at a copy of the note sitting on his coffee table, the one supposedly written by Hector Correa days after he was already dead.

"Richie," Effie said as she sat down on the couch next to him and took his hand in hers. "She is making me do things, Richie. Terrible things. I can sense there are no boundaries to the evil this child is capable of. You must stop her, no matter what it takes."

"Effie, if that is really you, I am so, so very sorry," Richie said, tears streaming down his face.

"What do you have to be sorry about? None of this is your fault."

"I'm sorry for not telling you I love you and I always have," Richie managed to choke out.

"I love you too, Richie Black."

Effie felt Rose Marie struggling to regain control but fought against her with every fiber of being she had left.

"Richie, there are more of them."

"I know," he said, thinking about Chase's newfound murderous son.

He took the child by her cheeks, turned her to face him and looked into her eyes. He saw something in her eyes that convinced him this was no trick, Effie was somehow inside of that little girl's body.

"You are not supposed to be here," Rose Marie chastised Effie's personification. "I killed you already, you should be gone."

In a lightning quick move, the little girl grabbed one of the empty beer bottles and smashed it against the coffee table. She swung the bottle hard and fast, aiming for Richie's throat. Luckily, he was able to deflect the blow, but the bottle still left a gaping gash in his forearm. She lunged at Richie, knocking him off balance, wedging him under the coffee table. She raised the bottle to slash across his leg when Chase came running down the stairs. Without hesitation Chase dashed across the room and slapped the little girl so hard across the face she fell backward and off Richie's legs. Before either of the men could grab her, she disappeared out the front door into the night.

Chapter Sixteen

Claire Underwood was both melancholy and relieved at the same time. Her mother had finally passed after a long, grueling battle with cancer, and while she knew she would miss her, she also knew her mother was no longer in pain. Pain the family matriarch had done an excellent job of hiding for a very long time.

This was where her parents had met all those years ago under the flashing lights of the county fair midway with the aroma of corn dogs, popcorn and cotton candy wafting through the air. And five years after that, this is exactly where her father proposed to her mother, at the top of the double Ferris wheel overlooking Lake Michigan. The ride was nearly filled to capacity, so Claire situated herself in the center of the ride gondola polished to a high sheen from the countless backsides enduring the cold, hard steel throughout the many decades.

Just as they were about to start their ascent the carny stopped the ride at her car to load another person onto the ride. Reluctantly Claire slid over to make room for a young boy with a tousle of jet-black hair. She was a little aggravated and began to protest but then thought about how her mother would have handled the situation.

She smiled and asked, “Would you like a piece of candy?”

The boy ignored her while watching the carny latch the safety bar in front of them and clip two S hooks attached to a length of chain to the Ferris wheel gondola as an added precaution. Rai was not worldly by any means, but he was smart enough to know that a length of chain wrapped around a steel bar and then hooked to the gondola served as nothing more than a security blanket, but it would suit his needs just fine.

The giant wheel began to rotate slowly as it also began to climb upward. The machinery creaked and groaned making Claire a little more than uncomfortable. She learned the ride had been in mothballs for many years, only being put back into service this year. It was one of the main reasons she chose this particular place to honor her mother. The big wheel they were riding on rotated as it hung over the earth halfway to its apex. She had to crane her neck a little to the left, but from up here she could see the lighthouse at the end of the pier shining its beacon through the gloom as the sun began to set on the bruised horizon.

The wheel continued upward until it was completely perpendicular to the ground. There it held steady and began to rotate in a slow rotation, stopping each basket at the top allowing the riders the best view of the lakeshore. She found it odd that the boy sitting next to her had not uttered a single word, in fact, he barely even moved at all. It was as if he were waiting for something or someone.

Claire was disappointed when the wheel stopped revolving, and the pendulum began to rotate back to zero. From this angle all of the sights were to her back, and she couldn't see much of anything other than the greasy mechanics of the amusement ride itself. Once they reached the midway point where the main arm was parallel to the ground they stopped and held fast. Undoubtedly to give the other large wheel their turn at the breathtaking view. She mindlessly counted the burned out or broken light bulbs on the spokes of the wheel.

"Are you sure you don't want any chocolate?" Claire asked, more out of boredom than concern. If the child wanted to be antisocial, then so be it.

"I'm not supposed to take candy from strangers. And should you be offering candy to children you don't even know? Are you a sexual deviant?"

His last statement floored her. How dare he make such a ludicrous accusation? And to make matters worse, the child sat there, drumming his fingertips against the metal bench of the gondola as if he were expecting her to respond to such a preposterous allegation. The movement of his fingers drew her attention to them, and an audible gasp escaped her lips. Her eyes traveled upward and made eye contact with the boy which sent tremors throughout her body. His eyes cast a metallic glow and appeared as though there were tiny bolts of sparks resembling lightning filling the luminous orbs. She understood there was an evil behind the boy's eyes that far surpassed the wicked grin smeared across his face.

Their gondola came to a rocking stop at the bottom of the platform and Claire reached for the safety bar in an attempt to escape this odd child.

"One more time," the boy screamed while bouncing up and down in his seat.

When the ride operator acted as though the ride was finished the boy screamed once more, this time raising his hands up and down to incite the rest of the riders on the Ferris wheel. After a couple of minutes of sweet talking, the operator pushed the forward lever on the ride and once more the wheel began a gradual ascent.

"One more time around. But it looks like there's a storm brewing so I'm going to make it a fast lap," the operator yelled up to the cars as they made their ascent.

Claire was mortified. She had attempted to get off the ride, but the boy had gripped her leg so tightly she couldn't move and for some reason she was unable to cry out for help. As they hung suspended parallel to the ground nearly forty feet in the air, the sky above them began to churn and roil, spreading an unsettling blackness over the midway. Streaks of lightning shot sideways through the clouds and the smell of ozone hung heavily in the night air.

Suddenly she felt queasy from her mounting fear and had to fight back the dry heaves. To make matters worse the boy started to rock the car. Slowly at first, but as it gained momentum, he was able to get it tipping nearly flat causing her to become wedged against the safety bar to the point she felt as though she were about to fall.

The pause at center of the rotation was much shorter than the first revolution and the arm began to move upward, and yet the boy continued to rock the gondola.

Thunder boomed overhead and lightning sliced through the black clouds eliciting screams from carnival goers down below as they scurried for shelter.

The boy looked over at Claire and said, "You are not supposed to be here."

Claire heard the safety bar creak and felt it move out of place a little. The boy grunted, grabbed the seat of the gondola, and began rocking it as hard as he could. She realized he wasn't just trying to scare her; he was trying to send her plummeting to her death.

"Hey, kid, you're going to tip that thing over. Quit rocking it so hard," a man called from the gondola above them.

"I know! That's what I am trying to do. She is not supposed to be here," he called back with his hands cupped around his mouth.

Lightning sliced through the night air and struck the structure near the gondola above, effectively silencing the meddlesome interloper. The man above huddled his child closer to him and double checked the safety bar on their gondola. The clouds hanging over the midway were becoming more and more ominous with each passing second, proving this was more than just a typical summer shower.

Claire came to understand the boy didn't suffer from some type of skin pigment malady; it was that he had no color to him at all. He was monochrome, but his skin also seemed to caste an electric glow. He began not only rocking the car back and forth but jerking it to a stop as well, slamming her back against the seat and then her midsection against the safety bar which groaned with each contact. Her will to survive kicked in and she began to fight him.

"Why are you doing this?" she asked, trying to pin him to the seat.

"Because you are not supposed to be here, and I am."

Rai grinned at her and tossed the stuffed animal he had been holding out of the gondola. Transfixed she watched the toy bounce off the cross members of the carnival ride and cartwheel fifty feet to the ground. The boy leaned back in the seat and raised both legs in the air, hovering his feet in front of the safety bar. He gave the bar a light tap with his feet and grinned at her.

"Stop that! Are you crazy? You will kill us both," Claire said.

"No, just you," Rai replied.

A bolt of lightning streaked through the sky and connected with the Tilt-A-Whirl below, electrocuting everyone on the ride. The smell of ozone and charred flesh rose up from below and Claire understood the depth of the child's evil came from the bowels of hell.

Rai kicked into the bar once more, this time with a little more force. The Corn Dog sign on the food trailer in front of them was getting smaller and smaller to the point she could no longer read the sign. The ride reached its apex, and their gondola was at the bottom of the wheel climbing back up to the top. Once they hit the bottom, the boy began kicking harder and harder against the safety bar while people in the other baskets were screaming at him to stop. As their gondola reached the very top of the ride the bar broke free from the latch and swung away from the ride leaving nothing but open air between Claire and the ground below.

Riders in the other baskets began frantically calling for help, some even dialing nine one one on their cell phones as if that would be of any use. The boy just laughed at their feeble attempt at salvation and focused his energy on their cell phones causing them to explode in people's hands and the devices fell to the earth in a rain of smoldering debris.

"Tell them to bring shovels," he cackled above the blaring music of the ride. The operator tore his gaze away from the scantily clad teens running up and down the midway long enough to realize there was trouble in the top basket and the storm was reaching dangerous proportions. He reached for the controls and started to bring the wheel back down.

"Perfect," the boy said and started rocking the basket again.

Sleet began to ricochet off the steel surfaces with a plinking sound. Quickly the sleet changed to hail, with the stones growing ever increasing in size as they fell. Screams of pain echoed from all around them as the balls of ice found tender, fleshy targets. Blood rained down from above and the boy took delight in the devastation caused by the storm; his storm.

Claire began slipping out of the wet, polished steel seat and without the bar for leverage it was a losing battle. She managed to fight him off for several minutes but once the angle of the wheel added gravity to his assault, she knew her fight was over. The tiny hairs on her arms stood straight up and bolts of electricity shimmered across the surface of the gondola seat. She scrambled up onto her knees to escape the shocks and grabbed the back of the gondola's seat, gripping until her knuckles were pure white. The boy seemed to be tiring and the basket stopped rocking causing Claire to instinctively relax her quivering, fatigued muscles.

"You are not supposed to be here," the boy grinned and did the unexpected.

Rai wrapped both arms around the woman in a bear hug. Using every bit of strength in his diminutive body he leaped out of the gondola taking Claire with him. She screamed. The people in the other baskets screamed. Rai laughed as the woman's trajectory mimicked that of the plummeting stuffed animal cartwheeling in free flight.

"Tut, tut, looks like rain," he called out to the crowd below as the pair tumbled through the air.

Claire's struggling altered their downward trajectory and carried them into the path of the wheel's structure. Her back slammed hard against one of the crossmembers twenty feet from the ground, tearing her completely in two. Rai, sensing the impact jumped free of her body. He wasn't sure what would happen to him if he were to impact the ground in his current state of being, so he reached out and grabbed onto the woman's viscera as it was expunged from her torso and came to rest in a large pile of hailstones that had been turned into a cherry colored sno-cone.

Screams erupted from the gathering crowd who had all turned their attention to the screams above them. The woman's gore rained down upon their faces followed quickly by fragments of her internal organs slapping the earth with a sickening sound. Rai let go and dropped the remaining ten feet to the ground and walked away with a smile. Lightning crashed to the ground as he made his way to the other end of the midway. He looked down to see shards of electricity dancing across his fingertips as he felt her life surge through him. He was becoming.

~ ~ ~

Two football fields away at the opposite end of the midway Megan Holt was having a crisis just about the exact same time Claire Underwood was making room for an odd little boy in her seat on the Ferris Wheel. Megan, nearly a child herself was having a heated debate with her son. It pained her to watch him growing up right before her eyes. Aiden was seven years old going on seventeen as the saying goes.

The mother and son were standing in front of Terror-O-Rama, a combination fun house and haunted house ride, which was in fact, much more of an attraction than a ride because the guests walked a defined path through multiple carnival trailers with various thrills and scares hidden in the shadows. Painted on the façade was an odd assortment of vampires, tigers, a mummy, and a horde of creepy clowns which disturbed Megan the most. Especially since her son had adopted a creepy clown persona for himself after seeing trailers for an upcoming horror movie.

"Mom, I want to go by myself," Aiden argued, adjusting his clown shirt that was two sizes too big.

"You are not old enough, Aiden," Megan replied in earnest. "Besides, it's already getting dark outside, and I think there's a storm brewing."

"It's not that dark out yet and the place is lit up like a Christmas tree. I'm going to be right there," he said, pointing to a group of caterwauling kids stumbling through a maze of mirrors which had a glass front facing the queue where parents could watch over their little ones *trapped* inside.

Nearly fifteen minutes of arguing transpired before Megan realized it was only getting darker outside and finally relented. Wringing her hands together, she watched her little boy disappear through the veil of darkness, moving ever closer to manhood by venturing out on his own. She wasn't sure what saddened her the most, him growing up, or him feeling like he no longer needed her protection.

Aiden moved through the entrance into the maze of mirrors and turned to face the gallery of parents standing in front of the attraction. More than a dozen Aiden's waved enthusiastically at his mother. Megan waved back at him as he moved through the mirrors and disappeared with the other children as they funneled through the attraction. She breathed out a sigh and dug around in her purse for a tissue.

Five minutes passed, then ten, by the fifteen-minute mark Megan began to worry. There was a strange looking storm brewing at the far end of the midway and she wanted to be far away from this tornado magnet as soon as possible.

As children flowed single file out of the exit at the opposite end of the trailers, she recognized their clothing as that worn by children who entered the ride in Aiden's group. She watched the children like a disembarked airline passenger watching the carousel go around, looking for their specific set of luggage. She watched as each parent found their baggage and left, leaving her alone at the exit door.

"Mom," she heard her son cry out.

"Aiden," she called back.

There was several minutes of silence during which she paced back and forth. She had just about convinced herself that she was hearing things when he called out again.

"Mom."

"Aiden?"

"I'm lost."

"I'm coming baby."

Megan ran to the entrance, forced her way through the line of waiting children, forced her way passed the scraggy carney and into the Terror-O-Rama's narrow, dark corridors. The carnival attraction was essentially metal fencing arranged like a cattle chute to funnel the guests through the maze of hazards and pitfalls in a precise pattern. She was unexpectedly thrown to the ground when the floor beneath her feet began to shuffle back and forth. She went down again when the eight-foot tunnel painted with spiral swirls jerked into a tumbling motion taking her feet out from underneath her for the second time.

"Aiden?" she called out, spotting a clown at the end of the tunnel staring back at her. Something about her son's voice and appearance set off alarm bells in her head.

"You are not supposed to be here," the clown called out to her and took off running through the maze.

Megan was stunned for a moment but then took off after the kid wearing Aiden's clown costume once she realized the person was not her son. She turned a blind corner and hit a row of small trampolines built into the floor, knocking her off balance. When she recovered, she stumbled into the next part of the corridor where the trampolines had been replaced with discs on well-greased ball bearings. She slammed her head into the steel wall and crumpled to the ground.

She wasn't sure if she were more frightened or angry at this point. Getting back to her feet was a struggle and her shins were admonishing her for the latest fall. The child in the clown costume laughed and darted through the obstacles with ease. Megan chased after them and ended up in a dark room filled with padded bags dangling from chains attached to the ceiling. Unexpectedly one of the bags slammed into her from behind, putting her on the floor once again.

"You are not supposed to be here," the child cackled as they peeked around the bag and ran off through the maze of heavy bags.

Megan was so incensed she kicked and punched her way through the weighted bags like Rhonda Rousey in training for a championship bout. She shoved against one of the larger bags with all her might, but the clown pulled the bag away at the last second causing her to lose her balance, crashing into the wall and eventually crumbling to the floor. She was lying in a defeated heap with her head hung low when she heard her son's voice calling her and managed to claw her way back to her feet.

Outside the attraction the ride operator Clem Barker tried to go after the woman, but the door was barred from the inside. Several minutes passed while he contemplated whether or not he should get the boss involved when the ride rocked with a tremendous sound of her crashing into the walls. Clem ran around to the exit and tried to get into the ride that way, but that door was blocked as well.

Megan dusted herself off and moved toward a light at the end of the dark passage. Weary from repeatedly being tossed to the metal floor, she cautiously entered the next area of the fun house which turned out to be the maze of mirrors. Once she had taken a couple of steps into the room, she lost the doorway from where she had entered because everything looked the same three hundred and sixty degrees around her. She put her hands palms flat against the glass and tried to feel her way through the maze but there were no breaks in the wall. She stood in the center of the room and pivoted from side to side as she tried to get her bearings straight.

She triggered strobe lights which began to flash, disorienting Megan and making her nauseated. She closed her eyes and tried to regain her composure. When she opened them again, Aiden was crumpled in the far corner of the room. She dashed for him but slammed into a glass wall. Frantic, she clawed her way from panel to panel but was no closer to her little boy than when she began.

"You are not supposed to be here," a girl's voice whispered through the room seeming to come at her from every direction at once.

Just by chance Megan happened to look up at the ceiling and when she did, she became aware she could follow the bracings holding the mirrored panels in place to find her way out. She began walking slowly with her eyes at the top of the panel with her hands against the glass. Just as she felt she was making progress the floor under her feet gave way and she dropped two feet down through a hatch in the floor. She hit her head on the way down and was too dazed to struggle against her ankles being tied off to the rigging under the floor of the funhouse. By the time Megan regained her faculties it was too late, she was securely tied and couldn't move.

"Mom, where are you?" Aiden's voice called from outside. He was no longer in his clown outfit and was crying.

A sense of dread washed over Megan once it registered with her that her son was outside of the attraction mingled with a growing crowd gathered outside. The familiar odor of gasoline invaded her nostrils, and she began to panic.

Clem Barker was frantically trying to get the door to the ride open using a crowbar, but his efforts were in vain. Even though the woman was in the dark the people outside could see that she was trapped in the floor in between flashes of the strobe lights. The gathering throng of people were standing with their cell phones high above their heads recording the woman as she struggled to free herself. Half of them were oblivious to the fact this was real; the other half didn't care as long as the video would garner them a multitude of likes and shares.

"Clem, what in the hell is going on? And why do I smell gasoline?" Carl Kruger, the owner of the carnival, shouted as he forced his way through the growing mob of curious onlookers.

"Some lady barricaded herself in the ride."

"How in the hell did she manage to get stuck in the floor? And why in the hell am I smelling gasoline? This ride doesn't have an engine and the generator runs on diesel."

The lights in the funhouse came on, illuminating the room Megan was in for all to see. Now that the place was bathed in fluorescent lights, she could see them as well. All of them gawking at her while she struggled to free herself. A small girl dressed in Aiden's clown costume came sauntering out of the shadows carrying a fire engine red can in her hand. She skipped a circle around Megan, pouring gasoline as she pranced.

"Stop it this instance. What in the hell do you think you are doing?" Megan cried out.

"I told you, you are not supposed to be here. I am supposed to be here, you are not. So, I have to make you go away," Serafina said.

It was then that Megan noticed the child had no coloring to her whatsoever. There was a hollowness to her eyes that brought an understanding to the depth of depravity this child would resort to. Because this was no child. This was a malevolent entity hellbent on her destruction. She did the only thing she knew to do; she began to pray.

Clem Barker watched in horror as the child doused the woman with gasoline. He began pounding on the glass front of the ride trying to get in, but Carl stopped him.

"Damn it, Clem. Don't go breaking the attraction."

"Carl, that woman is in real trouble."

"Look around, Clem. This is just some internet stunt. All these people recording it will post it to the internet and then her and her kid will be famous," Carl said. He turned to face the crowd and called out, "Enjoy the magic show folks."

Taking Carl's cue Serafina walked across the room, set the gas can down and returned to where Megan was still struggling to get free. She palmed an eyebrow pencil and drew a thick handlebar moustache on her upper lip. She pulled a piece of black fabric from a bag on the floor, fashioned it into a cape and stood beside the woman as if she were a magician and Megan, her lovely assistant. She went through a hokey routine of sleight of hand card tricks.

"This is so cool," a young voice echoed in the crowd.

Aiden watched the scene unfolding and while the others thought this was all just an act, he knew better. His mother was in real trouble and there was nothing he could do to help her. He grabbed the back pocket on Clem's bib overalls and gave it a tug.

"Mister, please, you have to help my mother."

"Your mother?"

Aiden just pointed to the glass front of the Terror-O-Rama where the magic show was reaching its climax. The girl in the clown suit approached the glass front and waved her arms in a magician's fashion until she finally produced a shiny Zippo lighter in the palm of her hand. She feigned spinning the igniter wheel, put her hand to her mouth in a mime's gesture of shock each time the lighter didn't produce a flame.

Megan was screaming for help, but the crowd thought it was all just part of the show and cheered the little girl on. She could see her son pleading with the carny and tears rolled down her cheeks. The girl circled around her while flipping the Zippo lid open and closed.

"Your son is not supposed to be here either, would you prefer he takes your place?" the girl asked, kneeling down so they were nose to nose.

"Why?"

"Because it was always meant to be," Serafina said with undulating flames flickering in her cataclysmic eyes.

The girl stood up and walked back over to the glass front and took a theatrical bow. Megan mouthed *I love you, Aiden,* as Serafina lit the Zippo, took another, more dramatic, bow for the crowd, and tossed the lighter down into the hatch. Megan screamed as the cuffs of her pants erupted into flames.

Clem made an enormous and deadly error in judgment, one that sealed Megan's fate. He grabbed a cinder block holding up the steps to the ride, held it high overhead and threw it through the plate glass before Carl could stop him. The glass shattered and the small fire inside sucked in all the oxygen it required to turn itself into a body melting inferno. Backdraft shattered the remaining glass, showering the screaming onlookers with shards of glass who at this point began to realize this had not been a show as the smell of seared flesh permeated the air.

Megan screamed in agony and then inhaled a superheated lungful of air that instantly stopped her screams. People were writhing in agony with bloody hands covering their glass peppered faces. Those who had been the closest to the glass were incinerated in the blast.

Serafina looked around in amazement at the destruction she had caused.

In the ensuing chaos emanating from both ends of the midway Rai and Serafina met up at the exit of the park, walking hand in hand on their way to meet up with the others. There were five of them now on their way to becoming. Only two more were needed.

Chapter Seventeen

"Can you even fathom the depth of chaos you have unleashed?" Garrick said, trying to contain his anger, an emotion he found unfamiliar to navigate.

"The only thing I have done is free souls who were unjustly condemned," Medee replied.

"They were not yours to free," Athala added.

"They were not yours to imprison," Medee argued.

"You know they were not imprisoned. They had all the freedom they could desire."

"Except life."

"You know they could not be granted life. They are corrupted seeds filled with malicious intent," Athala countered.

Garrick struggled against the emotions coursing through him, it served no purpose other than to disrupt his flow of energy and cloud his judgment. He looked around the expanse that was their council chamber and saw he had far more allies than enemies. But from experience he knew it only took one rabble rouser to stir up an eternity's worth of problems. He listened to them banter back and forth for several more minutes before he tired of their squabbling.

"Enough! This is not up for debate. What you have done is beyond reprehensible and will cost untold number of innocent lives. How many were there, Medee?"

"You are the smart one, Garrick. I'll let you figure that one out for yourself. Don't you keep track of your flock?"

"You mock and you chastise and yet you forget who is in charge here."

"See, Garrick, therein lies the precise issue up for debate. No one ever put you in charge, therefore, you are not in charge. We are a collective, a singular unit with one heart, one mind, and one will," Medee challenged.

"That may be true, but we are also a collective with a central purpose. A purpose that must be preserved at all costs. Even at the cost of one of our own," Garrick said.

"Are you threatening me?"

"I do not have the authority to threaten you, Medee."

"Then you are merely spewing meaningless words."

Suddenly, Medee's essence was wracked with severe pain, a sensation she had never experienced before in all her eons of existence. It felt as if every fiber of her being were being stretched beyond its capacity.

"You fail to realize that while one of us does not have the authority to punish you, we all have the shared authority and shared responsibility to rein in those who threaten the collective. You stand alone in this insurrection Medee," Yano told her.

"How many Medee?" Zera asked.

"He will not let you torment me like this."

"Ah, dear Medee, He is the one who ordered us to extract information by any means necessary. You have violated His sacred law. And for that, you will be punished."

Surprising them all, Medee laughed a thunderous laugh. It was a laugh that chased away her pain. Even as intelligent and all-knowing as they were, the council had no idea whatsoever what she had done. She was tired, so very tired, and soon, this would all be over for everyone, including herself. The pain intensified and she screamed out.

"Medee, I will ask you but once more, how many?" Garrick asked.

"Seven," she cried out in supplication.

Collectively, the council gasped. They sensed the terror in one another and knew what she meant by that number. Medee had done the unthinkable.

"Zera, I am afraid you will need to intervene without delay," Garrick said.

~ ~ ~

Lothur felt the effects of consuming the man in the police station starting to wane. He could have never imagined how glorious the feeling would be to inch one step closer to being alive. He could also feel the others, especially Rose Marie calling out to him, trying to draw him to them. But he wasn't finished experiencing his newly acquired abilities.

The boy wandered the dark streets on the trail of another. In this new form he could taste the ones who were not supposed to be here lingering on the air and he wanted nothing more than to taste them with his flesh. But he knew this one would not be as easy as the first. He was starting to become which meant he was no longer able to conceal himself within the fabric of his world. And the more he became, the harder it would be to secrete himself.

There was a part of him that knew what he was doing was wrong. That it was going against their main objective. But there was also another part of him that knew this was who he was always destined to be. He was a bad seed who should have never been planted. But now that he had life, he was going to grow and flourish, everything else be damned.

The streets were all but deserted and the neon glow of countless dive bars bathed the dark alleys as he strolled through the dregs of the city. Lothur could feel the others combining their efforts to call him and knew that eventually they would realize he was ignoring their summons. But he needed this.

Wayne Bisonette rode the lift on his box truck down with a load of produce strapped to a dolly. Most of the market owners on his route had given him access to their loading docks so he could make his deliveries in the wee hours rather than trying to fight traffic during the day. He opened the back door to Luce's Market and rolled the produce into the cooler inside the back room.

Lothur watched the man with growing interest. He felt drawn toward this man, and he knew why. He could sense the man did not belong here. He scurried through the shadows and concealed himself from the cone of light showering through a door propped open with a piece of lumber.

"You are not supposed to be here," Lothur called out from behind Wayne once the man was back on the lift platform of his truck.

Wayne was so startled he spasmed, causing the boy to laugh.

"Jesus, kid, you scared me."

"You are not supposed to say that," the boy said with a furled brow.

"Forgive me, you are correct, I shouldn't take the Lord's name in vain. What in the heck are you doing out here all by yourself at this time of night?" Wayne asked.

"Looking for you."

Wayne stood puzzled, not sure what this kid's game was or if he even wanted to play along. His eyes scanned the shadows looking for a possible accomplice with plans to rob him. The great lettuce robbery of East Detroit.

"Why on earth would you be looking for me?" Wayne asked.

"Because you are not supposed to be here, and I am," Lothur said, swinging hard with a length of two by four he had concealed behind his back.

The first swing caught Wayne squarely on his left kneecap. He howled in pain and reached for his damaged knee and as soon as he bent over the kid swung the lumber again, this time catching the back of the man's right knee which brought him crashing down onto the loading platform with the bottom half of his body hanging off the back edge.

Before Wayne could scramble back to his feet Lothur jumped up onto the platform and used the controls to raise the platform until the man was pinched between the lift and the truck.

"Kid, stop screwing around."

"I'm not screwing around."

"There's money in my wallet, just take what you want," Wayne pleaded.

"I don't want your money."

"Then what in the hell do you want?"

"I want to live," Lothur said, jamming the lever forward until the platform raised tight against Wayne's body.

Wayne understood just how dire his circumstances were once the platform was raised up high enough to pin his chest it made it nearly impossible for him to breath and impossible to talk. His knuckles were white from gripping the edge of the platform as he tried to pull himself free. The whirring of the motor droned into his head as he tried to plead for his life. His pelvis shattered first, making it much easier for the platform to cut him in half. He was gasping like a fish out of water, watching the boy walk away from him as if nothing had ever happened. His entrails were still steaming in the chilly night air long after Wayne took his last breath.

Lothur recoiled in pain and grabbed his arm. This was a sensation he had never experienced before and while perplexing, it was oddly pleasant. He eased his shirt sleeve up away from his burning forearm and smiled. A small patch of his skin was covered with boils and blisters oozing with puss. He was becoming.

Chapter Eighteen

The luminosity of his laptop screen bathed Chase in an eerie glow as he read yet another article concerning a rash of odd events occurring around the state while trying to make sense of what had been going on. An hour earlier he had broken down and paid fifty-nine dollars for a service that let him perform deep dive background checks. He felt like a dirty prick reading into Effie's background after her death, but he needed to find the connection. And there just had to be a connection.

His eyes burned and felt as if they had a pound of sand in each one, so he put a few eyedrops in each eye for the third time that hour. Many of the articles and pieces of information were benign and hard to wade through. Some, however, were quite interesting. He hadn't known Effie had been awarded a medal for bravery, two in fact. One for saving a child from drowning and another for saving a man from a burning car. In the end, none of the information tied her to Jessop Porter or Hector Correa.

Chase minimized the folder on Effie and scoured through Hector Correa's life next. Again, the man had led an exemplary life, even won a few awards himself for helping the community. He had to take pause at an article written over a decade ago about the Dalmac, a bicycle trek that journeyed from Michigan State University in East Lansing all the way to Mackinaw City. Some riders even carried the trip further out to the far eastern Upper Peninsula and the town of DeTour. Seems that this journey was a yearly tradition for Hector and his father, followed by a walk across the Mackinac Bridge.

Reading the interview for the third time Chase finally caught a one sentence tidbit that, for some reason, had eluded him up to this point.

Hector told the reporter, "My father and I take this trip every year to honor my grandfather, Jose Correa, who fell from the south tower during construction and should have died that day but for by the grace of God his life was spared. My father and I shouldn't even be here. We understand just how precious life is, so we try to live it to the fullest each and every day."

"He was not supposed to be here," Chase said aloud to himself while minimizing that screen and bringing up the search results on Jessop Porter.

He was several pages deep into the search when there was a knock on the door. He glanced up at the clock and saw that it was nearly two o'clock in the morning. Who in the hell would be visiting Richie even before the crack of dawn? Chase got up from the couch as quietly as he could and moved to the side of the front window where he peered through a small slit in the curtains without moving them. He was taken aback by what he saw out on the porch. There was a woman, a naked woman standing on Richie's doorstep.

Chase darted down the hallway to Richie's room but stopped himself before barging in. He laughed at himself and went back out to the living room. His tired eyes must be playing tricks on him. She was probably wearing a flesh-colored outfit and he was overreacting. The woman's car probably just broke down and she needed to use their phone or something just as innocent. He turned the deadbolt and slowly opened the door.

"Hello," was all he managed to get out before realizing the woman was indeed completely naked. She wasn't wearing so much as a belly button ring.

"We need to talk," Zera said and sauntered into the house as though she were an invited guest.

Chase was tongue-tied. Standing in front of him was a woman so beautiful she could have been Helen of Troy herself. Her breasts were not large, nor were they small, but perfectly symmetrical in size and shape which he knew from experience was seldom the case. Her long blonde hair hung in curls to her waist, the bulk of which had been thrown over her right shoulder. He didn't dare allow his eyes to travel any further down her body, though he wanted nothing more.

"Richie," he called out in a hushed voice. "Richie," he said again, this time loud enough to rouse the man from his slumber.

Richie staggered out of the bedroom rubbing the sleep from his eyes. He stopped dead in his tracks the moment he crossed over into the living room and was confronted with a naked woman standing in his house.

"Chase, what the hell?"

"Hey, this isn't my doing. I have no idea who she is. Is she a friend of yours?"

"No, I've never seen this woman before in my life. If you don't know her, why on earth did you let a naked woman into my house?"

Chase responded with a shrug of innocence.

Zera pondered the men's reaction to her and found it somewhat perplexing. From what she understood, this was a form that most men would be attracted to and find desirable. But it seems this was not the case, and she was causing them more alarm than arousal.

"I am truly sorry if I startled you with my appearance. I thought this would be appealing to your eye," she said.

Both men looked back and forth between the nude super model in front of them and each other. Neither one knew what to say. Chase broke from the pack, went to the hall closet, and came back with his jacket which he then draped over her. Somehow, the addition of the jacket only seemed to accentuate her amativeness as it covered up some of her skin, but not nearly enough.

"Who are you? And might I ask why you are in my house?" Richie asked again.

"May we sit down, please? I am still not accustomed to these things," Zera said, slapping her bare thighs.

Richie waved his hand over the couch and shot a look of confusion at Chase. Chase grinned and shrugged.

"Lady," Richie started.

"Zera."

"Okay, Zera, I don't know what your game is, but I have run across some whackadoodles in my line of work, and you are starting to top that list."

"I know all about you, Detective Black. And you too Chase Coltrain," she turned to smile at Chase who had taken up position behind the couch.

Richie shook his head back and forth trying to clear the cobwebs. This was the strangest dream he ever experienced.

"You are not having a dream, Detective Black," Zera said.

"What the hell. How did you know what I was thinking?"

"I told you, I know everything about you because I am a part of you, and you are a part of me. We are all part of one another. A collective as you will."

"Like the Borg in Star Trek?" Chase hesitated before asking.

After pausing for a moment to think Zera said, "I suppose so, but that was fiction, and this is very much a reality."

"What is this?" Richie asked.

"May I trouble you for some water? This vessel seems to need nourishment I cannot provide, which is quite perplexing and unfamiliar."

Chase left for a moment and returned with a glass of water. Zera made short work of it and handed him back the empty glass with a gesture for more. He returned with a second glass which she drank just as enthusiastically as the first.

"Okay, you've had your drink, now start talking. Why in the hell are you here?"

"Because of your son," she said while glancing at Chase. "And your partner," Zera finished with Richie.

"What about my son?"

"He's a killer who never should have been born. He was never supposed to be here."

"Who the hell are you and just what in the hell is that supposed to mean?" Chase asked.

"I was hoping for the sake of time I would not have to explain my existence, but I do understand why I must," Zera said.

"You bet your ass you must," Richie blurted.

"I am here because the unthinkable has happened. Your son, and especially your partner are both at the crux of the matter."

"What would my stillborn son have anything to do with anything? And how in the hell do you explain my stillborn son suddenly being alive ten years after he was born?" Chase asked.

"Your son was never born, but he was never dead either. And don't you find it odd that he suddenly appeared on your doorstep without any explanation whatsoever? I admire your willingness to accept something of that magnitude without much distrust. But I assure you, not only is he not supposed to be here, it is also very unfortunate for humanity that he is."

"What in the hell is that supposed to mean?" Richie asked.

"His son was a corrupted seed that could not be planted without disastrous results."

Richie couldn't take it any longer. Every time Zera moved she exposed herself to them and he was becoming aroused. And for some reason, he felt that her arousing him was unacceptable no matter how perfect her form. He got up from the couch and went back to his bedroom. Within a couple of minutes, he returned with some clothes Effie had left at his place some time ago. Zera nonchalantly stood up, disrobed in front of the men, and then put on the clothes she was given.

"Thank you. While I understand certain sensations, I do not have much experience with them. Being cold is extremely uncomfortable," Zera said, glancing down at her erect nipples protruding through the shirt Richie gave her.

After pondering several of the things she said, coupled with the strange events of the past couple of days, Chase began to understand this woman was not a woman at all, she was something far more superior.

"You keep making the reference, this form. Are you not human?" Chase asked.

Richie was going to question his friend's sanity for a moment but his detective's mind stepped in. There was a good chance Chase could get this insane woman to reveal her motives without her realizing it, so he sat back and observed.

"That is an impossible question to answer."

"And why is that?"

"Because it is both yes and no. You possess my essence as I possess yours, but we are not the same. At least not yet."

Pointing at her body Chase asked. "You mentioned this body was something unfamiliar to you, what form do you usually assume?" Chase asked.

"I have no shape or form, I just exist," Zera responded. "Let me show you," she said.

Suddenly both Chase and Richie were overwhelmed with a sensation that knocked them to the floor. Richie's lungs refused to allow him a breath of air and he began to panic. At first his chest burned, and his brain felt fuzzy from the lack of oxygen, but within a few moments he felt at peace. Every negative thought, every ache, every apprehension was washed away and replaced with an undefinable sensation of pure bliss.

Chase was on his knees facing Richie struggling to breathe himself. He found himself with tears streaming down his face and yet he was neither happy, nor sad. He could only imagine this was the sensation an infant felt when still inside the mother's womb. There was absolutely nothing, and everything at the same time. It was contentment in its purest form.

Zera smiled and both men took deep breaths at the same time. Each felt a measure of sadness having been ripped from a sensation of pure ecstasy and thrust back into the harsh cruelty of the world they knew. The carpet in front of them was stained with their tears.

"What in the hell are you?" Richie asked.

Zera shrugged.

"Are you an angel?" Chase asked.

Again, the entity shrugged.

"I do not know what I am, or where I come from, I just exist."

"You don't know where you come from? Are you an alien, like from outer space?" Richie asked, rolling his eyes toward the ceiling.

"I do not know when or where I originated. I do know that I am older than your civilization and have always been a part of you. We all have."

"You all have? You mean there are more of you?" Chase asked.

"Oh my, yes."

"How many more?" Richie asked.

"More than there have ever been of your kind."

Chase sat there quietly pondering the magnitude of what this being was putting forth to them. Could she have been here longer than man has been on earth? If you took the Biblical approach, even longer than Adam and Eve? It was mind boggling and he would have deemed it preposterous had he not just had an experience so otherworldly he could have never even dreamed about it.

Zera felt the man's sadness and grief invading his thoughts. And while it was not a completely foreign sensation to her, it was more powerful than any grief she had ever felt before.

"You wish to know about your son, don't you?" she asked.

Chased nodded, his words lodged in his throat.

"This world of yours, it is a very fragile existence and can be undone if not properly looked after. Every once in a while, admittedly more often than we would like, a seed becomes corrupted even before it can be sowed," she explained.

"Sowed? Are we a garden for your enjoyment?" Richie asked.

"In a manner of speaking, I suppose you are. But not for our enjoyment, for yours."

"If you truly are an advanced species that has created mankind, why do you allow evil to exist in our world? Why was my partner murdered right before my very eyes?" Richie asked.

"Because we cannot, by the laws handed down to us, intervene unless we are instructed to."

"Instructed by whom?" Chase asked.

"I do not know the answer to that. We have never met the one in charge. He speaks to us only through the collective, through our thoughts."

"You mean God?" Richie asked.

"That is what you call Him. As far as I am concerned, He doesn't even have a name, and he doesn't need one."

"Back to my unborn son. Why was he considered a corrupted seed?"

"By no fault of anyone, and especially not yours, some seeds are just pure evil before they ever even exist, it is just the nature things. And we cannot allow them to exist, or they would destroy everything on earth. The one in charge is a merciful being and created a place for these unborn to live. Your son was one of these unborn. He and six others, have found a way to escape that realm and take up residence here among you."

Richie recalled the horrific condition he found Ms. Bradshaw in and knew what the boy was capable of. In light of this new information, he regretted not letting Chase see it for himself. He still saw the boy as his son, and not the monster he truly was.

"Chase, I'm sorry, I don't mean to offend you, but can we quit referring to that creature as your son? I know in my heart of hearts that your son, someone who was truly your son would not be capable of what I witnessed in your house," Richie said.

Chase nodded. "I agree."

"Let me ask you, will this boy kill again?" Richie asked.

"More times than you could begin to imagine."

"If he was destined to be a serial killer and was not allowed to be born then why have you unleashed the likes of Ted Bundy or John Wayne Gacy on us?" Chase asked.

"Because we did not know what they could become, and we are powerless to intervene. Those men you speak of were not corrupted seeds from their beginnings, they were corrupted during the course of their lives. They could have just as easily turned out to be Nobel prize winners, educators, or even holy men."

"And these others? The ones you referred to as unborn. What are they capable of?" Richie asked.

"They are instilled with a desire to destroy mankind as a whole. And to put it into perspective how small this number is, there are well over one million new people added to your planet every year, and only a sparse handful added to the unborn," Zera explained.

"Instilled by whom?" Chase asked.

"One with great power who does not agree with this, for a lack of a better term in your language, experiment of ours."

"Satan, Lucifer, the devil?" Chase asked.

"Call him what you will, but yes, it is an entity touched upon in your holy books."

"Have these unborn as you call them ever escaped before?" Chase asked.

"There have been a few and each of them have managed to accomplish widespread destruction, but in the end, they were defeated. Those were rare cases and usually only one or two managed to escape. In this case, so far five have escaped that we know of, and we fear there will be seven. But I did not come here to give you a history lesson. I came here to warn you, unless you take immediate, drastic action your world will cease to exist, at least as you know it."

"And just how are we supposed to save the world?" Richie asked sarcastically.

"You need to eliminate the threat."

"Kill them? Children, you want us to kill children?" Chase asked.

"Good. You are starting to see your dilemma," Zera said as she rose to her feet.

"And I suppose you cannot interfere to help us," Richie said.

"You would be correct in that assumption. In fact, I sense I have already overstayed my welcome," Zera said and walked toward the door.

"That's it? That is the extent of your involvement? How are we supposed to know what to do?" Chase asked.

"You will know when the time comes. As for guidance, I strongly suggest you study your holy texts, they hold some answers for you. Oh, and that man, Jessop Porter, he knew a lot more than he should have."

"You mean, like study the Bible?"

"Yes, Chase Coltrain, that and many, many other documents," she said as she opened the door.

"Great, we're supposed to save the world, but wait, you need to read the Bible first," Richie snapped.

Zera shook her head with a smile and walked out onto the porch.

"What, you're not going to just poof and vanish into thin air?" Richie asked, growing even more sarcastic.

Zera ignored the comment. "Oh, and one more thing I must advise you of. Neither of you will survive this endeavor."

"What? Are you telling us this is a suicide mission?"

"No Detective Black, I am telling you that, unfortunately for you, dying is not an option. If you do not stop these unborn before they become then they will destroy your world with you in it," she finished and disappeared through the door out into the night.

As soon as Zera was gone Richie headed back toward his bedroom.

"Where are you going?" Chase called after him.

"Back to bed. Look at the clock. I need some sleep if I am going to save the world."

Chase glanced over at the clock and realized that no more than one single minute had ticked off the clock throughout the entire three-hour conversation. He heard the bedroom door shut.

"We're not going to talk about what just happened?"

"No. Now get some sleep. I have a feeling tomorrow is going to be a shitfest of a day. And if you hadn't noticed, the bitch stole my clothes."

Chapter Nineteen

Chase Jr. watched the naked woman through the window with wonderment while she was speaking with his father. On one hand she was soft and beautiful, but he sensed she was dangerous, so he kept his distance and opted not to include her in his family reunion. The boy perched himself on a tree limb at the edge of the quiet, suburban street and contemplated his next move. Oh, he knew he was going to slit Richie Black from ear to ear and watch him bleed out, but as for his father, he still hadn't decided if the man would be spared his wrath.

He belched, causing a noxious, putrid taste to invade his mouth. It was a product of what he was, and what he was going to become. Drool streamed down the sides of his mouth which he wiped away with a swipe of his forearm. It was almost as annoying as Rose Marie's constant nagging inside of his brain. Who put her in charge anyway?

While sitting in the tree just passing time Chase recalled the look on old Ms. Bradshaw's face when he caught her with her fingers in the honey pot and had to stifle his laughter. It was a funny sight, that was for certain. But not nearly as pleasurable as the look on her face at that precise moment when she knew she was going to die. It was a look of mercy, not from him, but of something far greater. Something he despised.

He scanned his eyes up and down the sleepy borough. All these people nestled safely in their beds thinking the worst of the world was safely held at bay by their locked doors and alarm systems. He wanted nothing more than to shatter their illusion. The sounds of screaming children running blindly through the night while their parents were being devoured by evil would be music to his ears.

This woman was certainly taking her sweet time in there. But she was having to explain the finer details of Armageddon to a couple of Neanderthals. He laughed. He knew Zera's limitations and was well aware of the fact she was enlisting the aid of soldiers who wouldn't even know the battlefield and couldn't possibly fathom the power of their enemy.

He stopped to ponder whether or not he would feel any remorse when it came time to silence his father's sad, lonely eyes. Chase Jr. was certain by that point in the fray there would be little left of him that would be human. Rose Marie continued to peck away at his brain like a raven on roadkill and it was driving him mad. He knew the importance of the grand design of Medee's scheme, but all work and no play makes Chase an angry boy.

The front door of the house opened, Zera stepped out on to the porch and then the door closed behind her. She took three steps down the concrete walkway, turned, and looked straight up into the tree at the boy. Somehow, she knew he was there.

Chase braced for a fight, but it never came. She simply smiled, waved, and disappeared into the darkness of the night. This behavior unnerved him more than anything. If she knew he was there, then she must know what his plans were and for some reason she was not disturbed in the least.

The boy was casing Richie's house, looking for a way inside but the fact Zera had not tried to stop him was nagging away at his brain. That, coupled with Rose Marie's constant badgering made him abort his mission. There would be time to kill them both later, but for now, he had to deal with more pressing matters.

Chase Jr. wandered through the streets of the town relishing in his little taste of mayhem. However, the old bat wasn't a satisfying kill. It didn't help him move closer to the ultimate goal of becoming. He needed something more. Something big. Something huge!

He let loose a thunderous belch that literally rattled windows. Several porch lights came on followed by drapery being pulled to the side. Wide eyes peered out into the night wondering what on earth had just happened. Chase gagged at the taste in his mouth while laughing gleefully down the street. He was even closer to becoming than he first thought.

~ ~ ~

Rose Marie was furious with the one called Chase, and with the one called Lothur, but most of all she was furious with Medee for strapping her with such incompetent fools. True each one of them served their own purpose, but they were a collective that would not work without all pieces fit into the same puzzle at the same time. Once assembled they would be more powerful than any force ever known, but apart they were weak and vulnerable.

She completely understood their desires, she had the same compulsions gnawing away at her as well. She wanted nothing more than to be able to tear flesh from bone, but there would be time for that soon enough. For now, they had to concentrate on becoming.

For two days she watched the police carting box after box of evidence out of the abandoned church and finally it appeared as though they had finished their grisly task. One officer strung yellow tape in one direction and another officer did the same on the opposite direction. They slapped stickers on the doors to officially seal up the building and drove out of the parking lot in a small convoy. As soon as they were out of sight Rose Marie dropped down into the basement through an old coal chute and made her way up to the classrooms.

She waved for Rai and Chase Jr. to follow her. The trio made their way through the dark church and into the old orphanage. She busied herself with cleaning up one of the rooms for them to use as a shelter while fighting against Effie's presence wriggling about inside of her like an angry worm. Medee did not warn her about this particular fly in the ointment. She did not tell the others that these vessels they emptied would become a part of them as well. Rose Marie was concerned about Rai as he sat huddled in a corner with his face showing lines of confusion.

"What is wrong?" Rose Marie asked him.

"Where am I? Why am I here?" he asked.

That was exactly what she was afraid of, there was a piece of someone residing within Rai as well. Did they miss something? Was there something else they were supposed to do? Medee had not been able to council them on all aspects of this transformation. She was strong enough to fight off the intrusion, but just barely. She knew the others might not be able to resist and then what would happen?

~ ~ ~

"Have you been up all night?" Richie asked.

"I couldn't sleep," Chase replied, taking a long drink of his lukewarm coffee.

"Have you found anything that makes any sense of this insanity?" Richie asked, eyeballing the several stacks of computer printouts scattered around his living room floor.

"Pretty fascinating stuff actually. But I'm not sure how it can help us."

"Such as?"

"Did you know that Effie's grandfather was shot in the heart during the invasion at Normandy on D-Day but miraculously survived?"

"I knew he served in World War Two, but she never talked about him other than just being a tough old bugger."

"And Hector Correa, his grandfather fell from the south tower of the Mackinac Bridge during construction. He too miraculously cheated death."

Richie stood in the center of the living room pondering what Chase had just revealed. It made sense, sort of.

"Hector and Effie, they were not supposed to be here. They should never have been born," he said.

Chase nodded. "That's not the only connection I could come up with. Especially after I read a news report from Manistee about an incident at a carnival where a woman fell from the Ferris wheel. Her name was Claire Underwood. I managed to look up her information and her great-grandmother was aboard the Lusitania, one of the very few survivors," Chase said.

"I don't believe in coincidences so there has to be something to this. But you're right. How in the hell does that knowledge help us in the least? There must be tens of thousands of people whose ancestors narrowly escaped death. We do live in a dangerous world."

Chase followed Richie out to the kitchen where he helped make breakfast and a fresh pot of coffee. He was exhausted but there was no way he was going to be able to sleep. He pulled out some half-wilted potatoes from a bin, washed them and then grated them with a cheese grater into a cast iron skillet popping with hot bacon grease. Richie cracked six eggs into a glass bowl and whisked them while adding a touch of milk. He poured the mixture into another hot skillet and stirred it slowly back and forth.

The two of them sat at the kitchen table eating scrambled eggs, bacon, hash browns and rye toast savoring every bite as if it were their last meal. A cold glass of orange juice completed the repast. It felt good to give his eyes and brain a rest, so Chase concentrated on eating and left the conversation for after breakfast.

Richie took a long drink of his orange juice, set the glass down hard on the table and asked, "Did last night really happen?"

"I'm afraid so," Chase responded without looking up from his plate.

"Was she just some nut job and managed to get us both believing her line of bullshit?"

"I would love to say yes, and very well may agree with you except for that little trick she pulled. You felt her inside of you, didn't you?"

"Yeah, I felt it too. No nut job, however crazy they may be, would have been able to pull off a stunt like that. I still can't wrap my head around it."

After breakfast was finished both men sat on the couch shuffling through stacks of paper Chase had printed out and sorted. Neither one of them really wanted to discuss the events of the previous evening which had become the proverbial elephant in the room.

"Do you think she meant it?" Richie asked.

"Meant what?"

"That we are both going to die?"

"You know, Richie, religion is a funny thing. There always seems to be an allegorical slant to everything. And you know as well as anyone, after Anna, I lost my faith, so I am probably not the right person to be asking what I think about any of this," Chase said.

"Or, allegorically, you are the perfect person to be asking. Doesn't God always use the most unlikely of soldiers for his army?"

"Touché. But to answer your question, if Zera is to be believed, then yes, we are both going to die."

Richie nodded. "It's strange though, I really don't seem to give a shit. In fact, I'm kind of looking forward to it."

"I know exactly what you are referring to. I have a certain sense of peace telling me that no matter what, everything will be alright in the end."

"Let's hope so," Richie said while clearing the breakfast dishes. "Let's hope so."

~ ~ ~

Lothur stood in the back of a large crowd waiting to get onto the green and white city bus. He took a seat right behind the driver where there was a crude drawing of a woman with her legs spread wide open scratched into the diamond cut pattern, stainless-steel divider. There was a phone number scratched into the metal beneath the artistry and he contemplated whether or not he should give the *whore* a call.

The boy wore a tattered, Honolulu blue hoodie with a worn-out Detroit Lions emblem on the front, a garment taken off some unfortunate soul he crossed paths with a few hours earlier. The fabric was irritating the pustules popping up on each of his cheeks. Puss oozed from the sores, down the sides of his neck, saturating the collar of the hoodie. The wetness was cool against his skin flush with anticipation.

Nag. Nag. Nag. Rose Marie continued to peck away at his brain. He was moving too fast and becoming way before he was supposed to. But this feeling was luxurious and impossible to satiate. This would be the last one, he promised, but it would be a biggie.

He watched the passengers boarding the bus at every stop as they went about their daily drudgery without giving anyone else a second thought, and especially not to a little boy sitting alone at the front of the bus. So many of the people carried an ugliness about them that pleased him. He was about to make their miserable lives seem like they had been living in paradise.

The doors closed with a hiss and the bus chugged away from the curb with a squeal of the brakes. Out of boredom he counted the street signs as they passed by the bus doors. He couldn't believe how many signs there were conveying so much useless information to so many people. Someone should write a song about all these signs he thought to himself.

Two elderly Asian women boarded the bus, stopping their bickering just long enough to pay the driver their fare before resuming their caterwauling through the bus all the way to the back as if each of the passengers wanted to listen to their gibberish. A young man with his pants extending below his buttocks and music blaring over a speaker clipped to his belt boarded next. He ignored the driver's request to turn the music down and passed through the bus, taking a seat directly across from the caterwauling women.

Lothur hummed a pleasant tune to himself as the bus filled up with passenger after passenger. Remarkably very few were getting off the bus. Maybe they were headed for someplace special. Someplace crowded like a shopping mall or better yet, a school.

How did she know what he was up to? It unnerved him so to have Rose Marie chipping away at his thoughts. She was warning him not to go through with what he was planning, but who in the hell put her in charge. There were seven of them, seven equally important pieces of a larger puzzle and not one of them was in charge. Was she angry that he was going to become before she did? Did she want to be the first? Too bad, so sad, it was he who was taking charge, so it would be he who reaped the rewards.

The bus was filled to capacity and the driver was on a long stretch of straight road gaining speed with each block he passed. Lothur chose to compromise with Rose Marie and limit his destruction, but only this one time.

"Can I please have everyone's attention," he said, standing up from his seat and moving to the center aisle of the bus.

"Son, you need to sit down," the driver said over his shoulder while still trying to pay attention to traffic in front of him.

"We are all gathered here today," Lothur started.

"Son, sit down," the driver said more forcefully.

Lothur ignored the driver and continued with his soliloquy. "To get through this thing called life."

"Now damn it, kid, you need to sit down right this instant."

"But there is one of you who is not supposed to be here. Is it you?" he asked, thrusting a dramatic finger at one of the Asian women causing them both to recoil. "Or is it you?" he asked, once again pointing at one of the passengers, this time a fat, balding man with a greasy moustache and a lecherous eye for the teen sitting in front of him.

"I'm not playing with you, sit the fuck down," the driver said, reaching behind him to grab the boy's arm.

Pustules on the boy's forearm burst, spewing venomous liquid all over the man's hand which was immediately aflame with pain causing him to jerk the steering wheel. The bus began to swerve back and forth as the driver fought to get the bus back under control. Lothur held his arm in front of the driver until several of the puss sacs exploded into the man's face. He ripped the hoodie off, exposing his diseased flesh to the passengers who had all started cramming to the back of the bus away from the psychotic little boy.

Luthor walked with a measured cadence toward the mass of screaming people being flung from side to side as the bus continued to careen out of control. The passengers could not tear their eyes away from the odd boy who had impeccable balance standing in the center aisle as if he were on a surfboard. The driver fell out of his seat and began rolling around on the floor of the bus in excruciating pain.

The young man with the loud music finally separated himself from the pack and spoke up. "What the hell did you do to the driver man? Are you fucking crazy?" he shouted and started toward the front of the bus.

Lothur stood in front of him and when the man started to push him out of the way he smiled, shook his head with a vehement no, and slapped his carbuncle laden palms together spraying the man with pestilence. The man dropped to the floor, screaming, and clutching at his poisoned flesh.

"Let us all share in this bounty," Lothur said, slapping his hands together above the crowd.

The bus, with no one's foot pressing down on the accelerator, slowed down, and eventually crashed into traffic stopped at a stoplight. The boy watched the screaming passengers for a few moments before donning his hoodie and making his way toward the front of the bus. He hit the button to open both the front and rear doors and when people came scrambling to help the screaming, writhing passengers in the rear of the bus he slipped out of the front doors unnoticed.

Lothur stood on the sidewalk a block away from the action enjoying a candy bar he swiped from a lady's purse during all the commotion. The ambulances and police had arrived, and it was about to get very interesting. He sat down on a bus bench rocking his legs back and forth watching the glorious mayhem unfold in front of him.

"What in the hell happened?" Officer Davis asked as he plowed through the crowd.

"The bus ran into those cars," a bystander replied.

Screams of agony flowed out of the bus and out onto the street. Some of the passengers had managed to thrash about until they were spilling out of the bifold door and out onto the sidewalk. Paramedics raced from their trucks carrying bags of medical gear and supplies while Lothur looked on with great interest knowing the worst was yet to come.

Two paramedics entered the front door of the bus and went to work on the driver. As soon as they rolled the man over, they recoiled in horror at his face covered in throbbing, pulsating blisters oozing a viscous, black fluid. One of them cut off the man's sleeve to start an IV and jerked his hand back as soon as the fabric was free, the driver's arm was filled with seeping, puss filled sores.

"What in the hell happened to this guy?" John Cooper asked his partner.

"We need to get out of here now, this is something chemical or biological. We aren't equipped for this," Kenny Lampton grabbed his partner's arm and began dragging him away from the injured bus driver.

He was too late in his efforts. The pustules on the driver's face erupted, spewing their gooey substance all over John Cooper's face. Immediately the EMT began to convulse and writhe around on the floor of the bus along with the other infected passengers.

Lampton jumped from the bus and screamed. "Everybody back away from this bus now! That includes medics and law enforcement. Back. Back. Back," he said, charging the gathering crowd with outstretched arms.

"What's going on here?" Sergeant Burns asked as he and Bayless came hurrying onto the chaotic scene.

"Honestly, I don't have a clue, but you need to keep people away from that bus," Captain Jiminez, the incident commander said.

"But those people need our help," Bayless said.

"Yes, I know. But the people who were helping them also need help now too. There is something on that bus causing chemical or biological burns on the patients, but it is also spreading to the uninfected. If you do not want an out-of-control situation here, I suggest you cordon off the area and contact the CDC immediately," Jiminez said while dragging his men away from the bus.

Screams and pleas for help echoed throughout the bus. Several times officers had to hold back citizens scrambling to get in to help the victims onboard. The crowd was becoming agitated with the paramedics and police officer's failure to help the victims. Burns called headquarters to have a small contingent of officers in riot gear sent to the scene. He didn't want to make a huge scene, but if the paramedic chief was to be believed this could turn ugly in a New York minute.

"I had dispatch put a call into the CDC as well as DHS, they should be sending their people down here immediately," Bayless said as he returned to the scene from their patrol car.

Bayless glanced down the street and saw a young boy eating a candy bar while watching the scene as casually as if he were watching pigeons in the park. The boy threw an energetic wave at him as if he was having the time of his life. He started toward the kid but someone in the crowd threw a rock and hit one of the paramedics in the back of the head.

"You need to help those people you cowards," someone screamed.

"Knock it off or I will start making arrests," Burns yelled back.

Burns and Bayless were arguing with the mob when a commotion near the door of bus caught everyone's attention. One of the Asian women had managed to free herself from the macabre game of Twister and staggered out of the door and onto the sidewalk. Her eyes were swollen shut and her pustule laden hands were stretched out in front of her. Her face was covered in translucent globules that throbbed and pulsated while leaking a viscous fluid. The crowd moved back as she took two steps toward them.

"Help me," she called out in a choked off voice.

Bayless started for her but Burns pulled him back and to the side, far away from the woman.

"If she is contagious or if that is a chemical weapon of some kind, you are not going to do her any good, but you will manage to join in her misery," Burns said as Bayless jerked his arm free of the man's grasp.

"For God's sake, someone help that poor woman," a woman's voice called out from the crowd.

Suddenly the elderly Asian woman stopped walking, drew a bead on where the voice had come from and started running as best as she could toward the voice. The crowd tried to move out of her way but were bottlenecked and only the last two rows of people were able to move out of her way. When she reached the crowd, her face began throbbing faster and faster with her elevated heartbeat and the pustules exploded, spewing toxic goo all over the crowd.

People dropped to their knees and cried out in pain. Burns pulled Bayless even further away from the mayhem understanding that these new victims were now carriers. He got them both safely in their patrol car and backed up down the street another block.

"What in the hell is going on?" Bayless asked.

"I'm afraid this is what your generation would refer to as the zombie apocalypse," Burns replied and slammed the palms of his hands against the steering wheel in frustration.

Chapter Twenty

"How did your conversation go?" Garrick asked.

"As well as can be expected," Zera replied.

"What did you tell them?"

"Only what is allowed, you know that. Anything else would have been physically impossible."

Garrick agreed.

"I fear they may be even more confused than they were before my visit."

"I'm sure they are. But they were chosen for a reason."

"Garrick, do you really believe that? That these two men, of all the human beings on earth were chosen to stop something we didn't even know was going to happen?" Zera asked.

"Zera, for all the endless time you have spent in existence, so long in fact we no longer remember where we came from, in all that time have you ever seen anything happen just by accident?"

She thought about it for several minutes and shook her head. Garrick was right, nothing ever happens just by accident. Everything is all part of the Grand Design as if this were all just one big game and even they, were merely performers on a dimly lit stage.

"A bit of good news, though you may not want to take it that way. As we expected, at least one of the seven have gone rogue."

"Lothur?"

"And I believe Serafina as well but that remains to be seen. Rose Marie has managed to wrangle two of them together with her."

"What about the other two?"

"In the wind as of right now. Maybe they haven't yet found their vessels."

"And how much havoc has Lothur wreaked?"

"I'm afraid it is rather grim. Over one thousand dead so far, and many more to come. And that is just counting this one incident."

"If he becomes before the others then he will burn out long before they are able to become a collective," Zera said.

"Fortunate on one hand, but how many lives will he take with him in the process?" Garrick said.

"Far less than if they unite as one."

"You are correct, but I do not think He will see that as a positive."

"He won't see any of this as a positive," Zera offered. "What about Medee?"

"She is secure for now. But I doubt we will be able to contain her indefinitely. Once all seven vessels are in place, we will be powerless over her," Garrick explained.

"Do you think she will get any assistance from The One?" Zera asked.

Garrick said. "Quite frankly, I am surprised The One has not intervened already."

"Garrick, what purpose does all of this serve?"

"I wish I knew."

"The destruction of all life on earth will only mean our own demise as well. Their actions serve no visible purpose," Zera observed.

"None that we are aware of," Garrick added.

Chapter Twenty-One

Serafina perched outside the concert hall watching revelers scurrying down the sidewalk and into the venue like ants on the trail of a morsel of food. Each dressed in their best to impress people they didn't even know. Attired in Kiton suits and Dolce and Gabbana dresses the throng of excess flowed into the hall which was less than a mile away from a homeless shelter where the less fortunate sons wore outfits from donation bins, thrift shops, dollar stores and anything they were lucky enough to scavenge from a dumpster.

Partygoers were all filing in to watch a performance of Mozart's Requiem in D minor, while she of course, was there to assist the choir with Dies irae, though none of them were aware of her pending contribution. She glanced down at her opaque skin which was feeling odd and flaky. She brought her arm to her nose, took a deep whiff, and recoiled, but then took a longer sniff the second time. She was beginning to take on the pungent aroma of sulfur which indicated she was growing closer to becoming.

Not a single reveler had the time nor wherewithal to notice the little girl sitting on the concrete flower bed wagging her feet back and forth as she took the time to observe them. Surely this was no place for an unaccompanied child at this time of night, but everyone was so wrapped up in their own little worlds they had little time for anything else but satiating their own egos. Those who weren't engaged in imperious conversation were focused on their cell phones either checking stock prices or checking on the valet to make sure they weren't joy riding in their extravagant cars.

And then she appeared, the one who was not supposed to be here. The petite woman shuffled along with the crowd unaware she was trespassing in a world where she didn't belong. Elaine Bettencourt stood in the box office line completely oblivious she was about to be the star of the evening's performance. She pulled at an Irish pennant from the seam on the side of her red Armani dress and tossed it to the ground. Her husband, Miles, was speaking with a colleague which suited Elaine just fine. The longer those two gabbed the less she would have to listen to his never-ending drivel about the stock market and his latest acquisition. Does a butcher come home from work and go on and on about sirloin and pork chops to his wife? She thought not.

Serafina became bored of watching the people and especially the man standing with the woman who was not supposed to be here. Serafina completely understood the look of ennui etched in the woman's face, the man never stopped talking, not even to breathe. She decided to have a little fun and test her developing gift. Miles was holding a takeout coffee cup from a local coffee shop but talked so much he never took a sip like she wanted him to. That only meant she had to make it even hotter. Little by little the temperature of the liquid inside the cup began to rise until it reached the boiling point and beyond. The girl concentrated until it hurt her brain, but eventually she was met with success.

"Son of a bitch," Miles screamed out, dropping his Starbuck's on the ground scalding the bare ankles of several women who were unlucky enough to be in proximity of the clumsy oaf.

Miles was still blowing on his hand when it was their turn at the ticket booth. Elaine didn't notice the little girl sidled up next to her as the group moved through the ticket line. Serafina squatted down as they approached the ticket counter. Most of the patrons just flashed the man in the booth their cell phones which he scanned and then waved them on through. Never once did the man look down below the counter so she was able to slip into the theater unnoticed.

As soon as the people moved through the cattle chute the line began to filter out across the expanse of the lobby. Some theater goers sauntered into an adjacent souvenir shop, others disappeared to find a bathroom, and those people who had just spent the last hour gorging themselves at expensive restaurants took a seat in any one of the overstuffed, comfortable chairs in the lobby.

Elaine sat down at a posh café booth inside of the concert hall and nibbled at feta cheese cubes, pita chips and kalamata olives while sipping at a generous pour of ouzo. Her husband was still in the restroom tending to his scalded hand. And while his suffering shouldn't, it did amuse Elaine so.

Serafina watched the woman from a shadowed corner for several minutes before joining her at the table. The girl pulled out a chair, climbed up into it and hopped it into position across from Elaine. She watched the woman picking at her overpriced hors d'oeuvres without saying a word.

"Hello? May I help you with something?" Elaine finally asked.

Serafina just shrugged.

"Are you hungry?"

She shook her head.

"Are you lost?"

Again, the child just shook her head.

Elaine, not accustomed to this rude and somewhat bizarre behavior, was beginning to lose her patience with the child. One more minute and she would be forced to call security.

"Where are you parents?" she asked.

Serafina giggled and then shrugged. "You are not supposed to be here," she said, her face taking on an austere paint.

Elaine was about to say something to the child when she saw something in the girl's eyes that unleashed a fear deep within her. Her eyes were not that of a normal child, a normal human being for that matter. And her complexion was pallid and lacking detail. But her eyes, her eyes told a story of mayhem and death. From the depths of her soul a fear began to manifest itself and Elaine thought she would vomit right there in front of all those people. Her hands trembled as she reached for her water. Without another word Serafina smiled, climbed down off the chair, and disappeared into the mingling horde of people.

Serafina moved gracefully through the crowd listening at every closed door until she heard the tell-tale sounds of musicians scrambling to get ready for the show while others were practicing those stubborn notes that always gave them difficulty. She slipped inside the dressing room unnoticed and concealed herself behind a rack of clothing. She looked down at her arm and saw it was covered in goosebumps. She was experiencing a feeling completely foreign to her, and she relished it. Serafina waited until all of the musicians were out of the dressing room and making their way onto the stage before scurrying through the corridors until she found a ladder which led to the stage light rigging above the stage. It didn't take her long to find a comfortable place to sit while she enjoyed the show.

Introitus began with slow, somber notes from the cellos and bassoons which the child found to be rather soothing. But this feeling of tension and excitement growing within her was something she was having a challenging time controlling. Time was something she had no concept of, so waiting through the ten minutes of Introitus and Kyrie were agonizing and felt like a lifetime to her. But eventually the time for her to join the show had begun with tremolo strings and a dazzling display of powerful choral prowess.

Serafina stood up and waited until she received her cue from the choir. They sang about death and wrath and all the good parts in between until near the end of the piece when they sang the verse, *Quantus tremor est futurus*, what trembling there will be. So, let the trembling begin for this was truly a day of wrath.

The girl raised her hands to the heavens in a purely theatrical gesture and concentrated her energy on the show below. She was going to wow this crowd of hoity toity revelers. Greed was their sin, and her wrath would not spare a single soul this night.

The ostentatious conductor waved his baton up and down, side to side directing the orchestra when suddenly the tip began to glow a fiery red and then burst into flames. Instinctively he dropped the flaming stick to the ground. Witnessing this oddity, the choir stopped singing and the orchestra stopped playing in complete disarray. Murmurs circulated through the orchestra members as they watched their conductor's baton burn away into ash. *Solvet saeclum in favilla*, the earth will be in ashes.

The concert hall fell into an eerie hush as patrons and performers alike looked to one another for a reason for the sudden silence. Serafina stood at the very edge of the scaffolding high above the captive audience, cupped her hands around her mouth and called to the woman down below, "You are not supposed to be here." She stabbed a dramatic finger in the direction of Elaine Bettencort.

The crowd first looked up at the little girl perched precariously on the scaffolding, then all eyes fell upon Elaine. Miles turned to look at his wife for the first time that evening and noticed she was sweating profusely. In a show of concern, he reached his hand out and put the back of it against her sweaty forehead.

"You're burning up, darling," he said.

"I don't feel so good," she replied between gasps.

"Should we go home?" he asked.

Looking around the concert hall Miles saw the symphony had ended abruptly and everyone in the place was glancing between he, his wife, and the little girl high up in the rafters.

In keeping with the theme of the night's concerto Serafina cupped her hands to her mouth and called down to the gawking crowd. "Tempus ad comburendum."

Again, simply for dramatic effect she thrust her hands, palms facing out, at the lady who wasn't supposed to be here. Immediately Elaine Bettencourt burst into flames in her seat. Screaming, the woman rose to her feet and staggered blindly through the crowd as they scrambled to their feet in an effort to get away from the human torch. As she caromed off the other patrons she ignited people's clothing, hairdos full of hair spray and auditorium seats. Within seconds noxious, black smoke began filling the concert hall and chaos erupted. The escaping mass from the front rows trampled the rows behind them before they realized what was happening. Kent and Gladys McKittrey were the first to get to the emergency exit where they were crushed to death when the doors failed to open.

The very instant Claire dropped to the floor as a lifeless, smoldering ember Serafina felt a surge of energy rush through her. It infused her with enough power to light the walls of the concert hall ablaze. She sat atop the scaffolding watching little ants frantically scurrying away from the magnifying glass to no avail. Suddenly she was hit with a certain sadness, once all these playthings had been destroyed, what would there be for her to do to amuse herself.

Flames licked higher and higher up the walls until the patrons trapped in the loges and luxury seats had two choices, stay and burn in their seats or jump down into the flaming pit below. Serafina imagined this is what Hell would look like if it truly existed. The girl quickly became bored once most of the packed house of two thousand people had stopped screaming and thrashing about.

She climbed the roof access ladder and looked out over the city of over six hundred thousand people watching the red and blue dancing lights racing toward a lost cause. Once again sadness washed over her when she realized she was going to have to share the oblivious fools of this city with the others. But there were other towns, other cities, and a whole wide world to conquer.

Chapter Twenty-Two

"Hey, turn that up," Richie said, pointing to the television.

A stone-faced reporter, in their well-coached somber voice, reported the egregious news of mid-morning. "The death toll is up over eleven hundred people so far and seems to be climbing. My sources within the CDC assure me they are close to total containment."

The camera panned up and down the sidewalk littered with people screaming and writhing in sheer agony. The gray sidewalk was stained with darker splotches of gray where pustules had erupted and spewed their poison. Bodies were strewn about like a collapsed game of human Jenga. Faces turned to the sky, agape with expressions of pure terror.

"Oh my God, she was telling the truth," Chase said under his breath. "This is all really happening."

"What is really happening? Who was telling the truth?" Richie asked.

"Zera," he said and brought up a few web pages he was researching. "Look here, the first vial mentioned in Revelations talks about sores breaking out on people."

"It has to be a coincidence."

"I don't think so."

"It just has to be some kind of an outbreak, maybe a chemical or biological attack from some radical group of terrorists," Richie said, not wanting to believe the gravity of Chase's implications.

"Look here, this article says that there were five people on that bus who were not affected in the least. That would not happen with a chemical or biological attack."

"Maybe they had immunities to whatever disease was used in the attack."

"I will agree with you there, but their immunity wasn't one of a medical or genetic reason. Two were nuns, one was a priest, and the other two, volunteers at a local Youth for Christ center."

"What are you getting at, Chase?"

"Revelations 16:2 says, *So the first angel went and poured out his bowl on the earth, and harmful and painful sores came upon the people who bore the mark of the beast and worshipped its image.*"

"I'm still not following you."

"Holy people, people involved in the church would not have borne the mark of the beast. They would not worship its image because they still worshipped God's image."

Richie read through the articles about the Book of Revelation on Chase's computer while Chase hit the shower. He quickly bored of reading the dry text over and over again, so he pulled up videos from the incident on the bus. He scanned over the passengers, but it was impossible to cull many details from these videos. He needed to find out if the bus had surveillance cameras recording before the incident. Once he tired of that he read through his e mails, mostly erectile dysfunction, and hair loss ads, but there was one that would interest Chase a great deal. The DNA results.

"DNA results came back from the lab," Richie called out from the kitchen while putting a pot of coffee on to brew.

"And?" Chase responded, toweling his hair dry.

"I don't understand most of this scientific crap, so Lindsey broke it down into layman's terms for me. The DNA from Chase Jr. and the sample you provided matched. Not one hundred percent, but they were a match. But this is where it gets even stranger, she also said there was DNA that not only should not have been in the sample, but also was something she has never seen before, neither in humans nor animals."

"Why should I expect anything less," Chase said with a sigh. "Of course, my DNA created an evil demon-child."

"Come on man, this thing is way bigger than either of us. But it does prove one thing, the impossible is truly happening."

"I suppose that is good news in a sense."

"Now about these seven vials it talks about in Revelation. Do they have to be dumped in one place, or do these kids have to spread them around? And why the fuck are they children?"

"I imagine whoever is behind all of this turmoil used children because they are usually considered innocent and don't pose much of a threat," Chase said.

"Yeah, well, tell that to poor Ms. Bradshaw and those people on the bus," Richie blurted out without thinking, which Chase ignored.

"I also think the seven vials or bowls may have been skewed in translation at some point. I think these children are the vials and they are being poured out as we speak."

"Which is why we have to kill them before they can finish what they started," Richie said.

"There is also something else to consider."

"And what is that?"

"That Zera is your garden variety nutjob and she planted the seeds in our heads before she released a chemical weapon on that bus."

"Now you are starting to sound like me, Chase."

They settled in with coffee and watched as many different cell phone videos of the bus incident they could find on the internet. Richie thought if Chase was right about Zera, they would see her in the crowd. But after fifteen different videos with almost half as many different angles she was in none of the frames.

"I guess my theory is all shot to shit," Chase said.

"I'm not giving up just yet," Richie said, closing out of one video and hitting play on another.

"There is another problem we haven't considered," Chase said.

"Yea, and what's that?"

"When she was at your house she mentioned the form she was in was not her own, so maybe she can appear as anyone and you are looking for something much harder to find than a needle in a haystack."

"Think positive Chase," Richie said as he scanned through one video after the other.

"Hang on, back that up a few frames," Chase directed.

"Did you see something? Was she in the frame?"

"No not her. But look at that kid, way off in the background. He's watching the whole mess unfold and he's smiling while eating a candy bar. And look, look there, he looks right into the camera and smiles."

"I think I saw him in one of the other videos," Richie said.

Richie cued up video after video and the boy was in almost every single one at some point of the recording. He had enough and shut the screen on the laptop.

"What do you think?" Richie asked.

"Considering the child is laden with blisters and boils I think we are looking at pestilence," Chase responded.

~ ~ ~

Richie's cell phone rang. "Black," he answered with a mouthful of English muffin.

"Detective Black, have you been watching the news?" a familiar voice asked.

"No, Angie not recently. Is there something more going on with that bus incident downtown?"

"No. Something else. Not sure if I would classify it as worse, but definitely just as bizarre," Angela Collins, the night dispatcher said.

"What happened?"

"The captain wants you to meet him down at the Detroit Symphony Hall. The fire department is still working on putting out the fire but by the time you get down there the fire should be out."

Richie sighed. "Fire department? Was there a concert tonight?"

"Packed house," she said, followed by a somber sigh.

"Thanks Angela. Tell the boss I'm on my way."

Richie was still several blocks away when he caught scent of the unmistakable odor of burning flesh clinging to the night air. Thick, black clouds of smoke hung over Mid-Town with a gloom filled presence. The area was cordoned off all the way down to Cass, so he parked in the church parking lot and walked down Selden to Woodward Avenue. Even before he reached the main thoroughfare the lights from emergency vehicles lit the way for him. Water from the firetrucks rushed through the gutter and into the storm drains carrying with it the smell of death.

He fought against repressed memories trying to claw their way to the surface. Those days were long ago and there was no use dredging them up. When he rounded the corner of the building he was met with a chaotic scene in a sea of people. Once he spotted Captain White he headed over to where his boss was overseeing the scene.

"How many?" Richie asked, looking up at the balconies with charred corpses clinging to the wrought iron railing. Poor souls who managed to break the glass windows thinking they had found freedom, only to be scorched by super-heated air.

"It was a packed house. The manager puts the number north of two thousand."

"Any of the poor bastards make it out?"

"Not a single soul. From what I've been told, the doors were jammed shut. We finally got the go ahead to break into the building. The fire department didn't want to introduce any fresh oxygen to the mix, and who could blame them."

"Do we think it was arson or just a tragic accident?" Richie asked.

"So far there has been no definitive proof the fire was intentionally, but the fire marshal believes it was arson due to the intensity of the fire and the fact that all the doors were jammed closed, not just the front entry doors. The stage doors, the delivery doors, any and all exits had been impaired," the captain explained.

"What are your thoughts on this being a terror attack?"

"It more than crossed my mind, but no one has claimed responsibility and it is too early to come to any conclusions, but it doesn't taste like terrorism to me."

The firemen rolled up their hoses, stowed their gear and moved the fire trucks down the street out of the way. Police officers and rescue units moved to the doors to try and get them open. The glass had shattered from the intense heat and there were dozens if not hundreds of soot laden corpses piled against them. There was more than one set of skeletal hands wrapped around the crash bars in death's final grip. One set had been torn from the owner's arms and just hung there perpendicular to the door in a grotesque escape attempt.

Ben Wilson, one of the officers trotted back over to where Captain White and Richie were standing. “Captain, strangest thing, there is nothing we can find blocking any of the doors. As soon as we cleared a few of the bodies the first door opened easily.”

“Thanks Ben,” the captain said. “What do you think?”

“Someone chained them closed from the outside, lit the fire and then removed the chains after the damage had been done,” Richie observed.

“My thoughts exactly, but pretty damned risky for an arsonist to go through all that trouble before torching the place. You think it’s connected to the bus thing earlier?”

“Yea, Cap’, I’d bet my life on it,” Richie replied. “And I think I already have,” he said under his breath.

“I’m afraid this is beginning to look more and more like the work of extremists.”

“Possibly. Or fanatics.”

“Same thing, aren’t they?” Captain White commented.

“I imagine they are cut from the same cloth.”

Richie wandered closer to the scene toward the front doors. He stood there for several minutes before walking around the corner onto Parsons. He walked down Parsons Street to an alley that ran behind the music hall where something on the ground caught his attention. Peanut shells littered the sidewalk below a catwalk and a set of stairs ascending from the second to the third floor. Was someone having a snack while the people inside were being burned to a crisp? Richie was afraid he knew the answer to who was responsible.

"Hey, Richie, take a look at this," Del Thomas, a tech wizard with the crime unit called from his van.

"What is it?"

"A video from when the fire started. It's the strangest fucking thing I have ever seen in my life."

"Wouldn't the video have all been destroyed?" Richie asked.

"The cloud my man," Del said with a slap to Richie's back.

"The cloud?"

"There was no video storage hardware in the building, just the cameras and the transmitter. All the actual data was stored in the cloud. It's a virtual storage box so to speak."

"I've heard of the cloud, just never had a reason to use it."

"Watch this shit," Del said and hit the play button on his laptop.

The camera was static over the orchestra but managed to capture the first five rows of seating and a small portion of the scaffolding above the stage. They watched the orchestra performing Kyrie and into Dies irae when the conductor's baton burst into flames.

"What was that?"

"I don't know man. His baton just burst into flames. At first, I thought it might have been for dramatic effect, but the conductor acted too surprised for it to have been a stunt. Watch it again."

They watched it backward and forward half a dozen times and not once could they see a source of ignition. Del played the video from the beginning until it reached the point where Elaine Bettencourt rose out of her seat. She was staring up into the catwalk rigging as if someone were talking to her and then suddenly, just like the conductor's baton she burst into flames.

"What in the hell was that?"

"I don't have a clue, Richie. Watch," Del said, playing it forward and backward several times. "If there was an accelerant used, we would see it being thrown or sprayed from off camera. Also, she is wearing a light-colored dress, and there is no discoloration from anything wet being thrown on her."

"I don't see any source of ignition anywhere," Richie added.

Del played the video back several times, stopping to enhance certain areas but they still couldn't see how the woman caught on fire.

"Wait, stop there and go back about ten seconds."

"Did you see something?" Del asked.

"No, I heard something," Richie replied. "There, stop it there. Can you enhance the sound?"

"I'll see what I can do."

"A little more," Richie said. "And do you have headphones?"

Richie put on the noise cancelling headphones and had Del turn the volume up as high as it would possibly go. Del played it once more.

"You are not supposed to be here," Richie heard a girl's voice echoing down from the rigging above the stage.

He handed the headphones to Del who put them on, replayed the video and then replayed it once more. He ripped the headphones off his head.

"Are you shitting me? Was that a little girl's voice?"

Richie nodded. "See if you can find a place in the video where there is something on that scaffolding," he said, pointing to the top of the laptop screen.

Del played through the video several times before stopping it when Richie prompted him.

"Can you enhance that area right there? Make it bigger?"

Del isolated the area on the video Richie had pointed to and was able to enlarge it by thirty percent.

"Right there, what does that look like to you?" Richie asked.

"A bare foot. A child's bare foot," Del said, glancing back and forth between the laptop screen and Richie.

Chapter Twenty-Three

Robert Chapman wrung his dark, leathery hands together and sighed. His eyes were focused on a small stain on the otherwise highly polished prison floor. He knew he had disappointed his therapist Justin Lipscombe because he had disappointed himself as well.

"Robert, I need to know what happened. You were so close to getting out of this tier and maybe even had a slim chance at parole if you continued down the path you were on."

Robert gave a defeated shrug.

"Did you know Mr. Darby?"

Robert shook his head, still unable to look the man in his eyes.

"Did he do something to your family on the outside?"

Robert shrugged again.

"So, you had no personal beef with Mr. Darby before you beat him nearly to death. The man is in a coma and may never regain consciousness."

Tears pooled into the corners of Robert's eyes until they finally broke free and streamed down his face into a small puddle on the floor.

"Is that true remorse, or are you worried I will have you shipped over to the Max?"

Robert finally looked up at the man. "I don't really know what happened. He was talking and I just kind of lost it. I didn't mean to hurt him."

"Robert, you continued to bash the man's head into the floor until the guards could drag you off him."

"I know, but I didn't mean to."

"What were you two talking about? Did he insult you, or threaten you in any way?"

"No. All I can remember was him going on and on about his life outside and what he had waiting for him. He bragged about all the places he'd been, and all the places he planned to go," Robert stopped for a minute, took several deep breaths to compose himself and continued. "Mr. Justin, do you know what it's like year after year to watch people come and go and you're always stuck in the same place like a stone that don't ever move? I never had no life outside of these walls. I've been in here since I was barely seventeen years old. And I didn't even kill nobody."

"No, Robert, you didn't. But there were three people killed during the commission of a crime you were involved in which makes you just as guilty of murder as the people who pulled the trigger," Justin explained.

"No, it don't. I never meant those people no harm. And I didn't mean to hurt Mr. Darby either, but he just kept on talking. Even after I told him to shut up. Kept going on and on about places I know I'll never see, about things I know I'll never get to do. Is that right? To torture a man like that? Is it Mr. Justin?" Robert looked up with tears streaming down his face.

Robert felt anger boiling up inside of him. Decades of anger held back behind the wall of a levee unable to take the stress any longer. If his hands weren't chained to the floor, they might have something to say wrapped around that head shrink's throat. He breathed in deep and tried to shake the violent thoughts away but they pecked away at his brain until they were impossible to ignore.

"Robert, I'll tell you what I am going to recommend to the board. I think you need some time by yourself, here, not at the Max and I also think that in a few days we will get you a CT scan. I've been speaking with you now for over two years, and this incident is out of character for you. However, presently I can see your anger beginning to boil and I don't mind telling you, I would be a little more than frightened if you weren't in shackles."

There was a long pause before Robert spoke. "What's a CT scan?"

"It will take pictures of your brain. I think you might have something going on up there, something is out of whack a little and we need to see if we can fix it," the doctor explained.

Dr. Lipscombe left his patient alone in the room for over an hour before instructing the guards to go ahead and move him to a solitary cell. He wanted to give the man some time to calm down, get his thoughts in order to hopefully prevent him from doing any more damage. Deep down Robert was a good man, and up until the incident with Mr. Darby, he had made all the right decisions during his time in prison. Justin thought the man truly had a real shot at parole, until this incident of course.

The guards led Robert to his new cell without incident. All he wanted to do was to lay down and forget about the stabbing pain in his brain and remorse in his heart. Mr. Darby wasn't that bad of a dude, but he just didn't know when to shut up. His cell door slammed shut and the footsteps of the guards squeaked off down the corridor without a word spoken between the three of them. He would remain in shackles for the night due to his violent outbursts, but he was okay with that.

Robert awakened sometime later to the sound of someone else in the room with him. The sound of someone else breathing slithered at him from out of the darkness. He held his breath to try and pinpoint the location of the sound, but the person must have held their breath at the same time for there wasn't a single sound in the cell. A lump formed in his throat and tears choked in his throat. He was certain Mr. Darby had died and his ghost was looking for Robert to reap vengeance.

"Is that you, Mr. Darby?" Robert whispered into the shadows.

Cecilia watched the large man with interest. He was big and strong, and yet scared as a little field mouse at something that didn't even exist. She couldn't resist playing with the cretin, so she gently blew across the nape of his neck. The room seem to glow with the whites of the man's eyes. She took a lock of her long, black hair and tickled his bare foot until he jerked his foot back as if he had stepped on a fiery coal.

The impish child held her breath and let the room get as silent as she possibly could before speaking.

"You are not supposed to be here," she said, struggling to contain her laughter.

Robert recoiled in horror. There was a ghost in his cell, and he had nowhere to run. This was his own fault. He did this to himself. Cecelia emerged from the shadows to face the terrified man. She smiled a warm and friendly smile, but Robert knew different. There was a darkness in her eyes that was filled with hatred and contempt.

"Are you going to kill me?" he asked with a trembling voice.

Cecelia laughed an uproarious round of laughter that pealed in the darkness, echoing off the concrete walls. But then her face turned suddenly solemn.

"Oh, no, Robert, what I am going to do to you will be far worse than death," she said.

With that Cecelia gripped the man's rotund face in her little hands and stared deeply into his eyes and said, "There is only the darkness."

Suddenly Robert could no longer see. The room turned pitch black as if he were blind. But it was also much different than blindness because he could actually see the blackness through his eyes, it was just there was nothing at all to see other than darkness. Layer upon layer of shadow enveloped him and he felt his heart turn icy cold. He began to tremble and shiver from the wintry void swathing him. And then the little girl let go of his face, pressed her pointed little index finger against his breastplate and gave him a little shove backward.

"Poof," she said. Cecelia stole most of the man's essence, but left him with the barest thread, just enough to sustain his life.

Robert began tumbling and spinning through an empty void. He could see walls of ebony speeding past him as he fell further and further into the abyss. He reached out with his hands to grip the walls, but they flowed through his grip like thick sludge. The shadows licked out at him, caressing him at first, but then they began to sting and bite at him as he tumbled past them. Robert began to scream out, not for help, not in supplication, just a simple long-winded scream that did not stop.

Several guards came running down the corridor toward Robert's cell but crashed into each other the moment Cecelia plunged them into darkness. She wisped by them in the darkness undetected. As she passed through each corridor, she plunged that section of the prison into darkness as well until she was well off the prison grounds. Sirens blared from all four corners of the penitentiary as chaos erupted through the walls and spilled out into the yard. Prisoners, in deadly fear for their lives ran for the light while guards beat them down to stop them from escaping.

Cecelia savored the pandemonium that wafted on the wind. She sat there nibbling on crackers and cheese until the guards assumed control of the prison as the dark of night blanketed their world. She looked down at her hands and saw that they were melding with the shadows of the night. She was becoming.

~ ~ ~

"Doc, can't you do something about his screaming?"

"Sorry, I don't dare sedate him any more than I already have. Here, have a pair of ear plugs, it's the best I can do warden," the prison doctor said.

Warden Jamison watched the patient strapped to the bed for several minutes. Normally he didn't feel too much empathy or remorse for the inmates, but this was different. This man appeared as though he were being tortured by an unending nightmare. Robert's screams echoed down the polished corridor.

"I just came down here to tell you to expect about a dozen new patients. Things got a little out of hand upstairs," the warden said.

"Did they riot?"

"No, not in the literal sense. They were trying to escape, but I don't believe that is the correct terminology. They were not escaping the prison; they were fleeing something inside of the prison, whatever it was that did this to this poor soul. Frankly Steve, I am at a complete loss as to what happened. And why is he thrashing about like that?"

"My best guess, he believes he is falling."

Robert could hear the men's voices, not what they were saying, just an echo through the darkness slowly getting further and further away from him as he drifted endlessly through the void. Time had lost all meaning to him. He may have been falling for minutes, hours or even days at this point and he would have no way of knowing which it was. Tears of anguish flowed from his eyes as a profound sense of sadness overwhelmed him. He tried to pray but every time he did his brain felt as though thousands of fiery hot needles were being skewered into his gray matter. Robert came to understand he was going to spend the rest of eternity alone, trapped in this never-ending vacuum.

Chapter Twenty-Four

Melissa Cartwright tried not to fidget too much. Her blind date was running late which not only made her nervous, but also made her feel as though every eye in the restaurant were cast upon her. To make matters worse, David had chosen a five-star restaurant known to serve the best steak and seafood anywhere in the state. Maybe even better than Chicago. She was really wanting to try the lobster but thought it might be too presumptuous to order. To hell with that, if she were going to be having her last meal with a serial killer who was going to stuff her in the trunk of his car, she was having lobster as a last meal.

She was scanning the room for the umpteenth time when she caught site of a little boy sitting all by himself at a table for two with a cupcake in front of him. How sweet, she thought, either mom or dad was treating the boy to celebrate something special. He was an odd-looking child, skin so pale he appeared anemic with a crop of flaming red hair to complete the anomalous ensemble. She saw the waiter gracefully crossing the room toward her and straightened her attention to the elegantly dressed server.

"Madam," he said as he slid a chilled glass of Riesling in front of her. "Mr. Hermitage wanted you to know that he is on his way and should be here within the half hour. Stuck in traffic from the sounds of it," he said with a well-practiced smile.

"Thank you," Melissa smiled back and sighed inside. She was worrying herself sick about nothing.

"It is our best Riesling," the waiter said and gave a graceful bow away from her table.

Giggles from the little boy caught her attention. He was staring at her table in a peculiar sort of way. Maybe he had never seen a dyed in the wool heavy on the starch waiter before.

Fifteen minutes passed before she noticed a good-looking man, over six feet tall wearing a dark gray suit as he briefly hovered at the bar before heading toward her table. Melissa was suddenly ill. He was much too good looking and refined for her Podunk self.

Stop it! She chided herself.

"Melissa? I'm David, David Hermitage," he said, reaching his hand out to her.

Melissa raised slightly off her chair, took his hand, and allowed him to kiss the back of hers. She nearly swooned. This was fairy tale, Hollywood movie kind of stuff, not the typical date she was accustomed to.

"Very nice to meet you, David," she said and sat back down.

"I apologize for my tardiness, but the traffic in the tunnel was brutal. There was a fender bender and it backed everything up for miles. I would have called, but like an idiot I left my personal cell phone at the office and only had my business phone, which of course, didn't have your number in it. But I ramble," David explained.

"It's perfectly fine. The waiter let me know you would be delayed," she said, finding herself searching for the right words around this picture-perfect man.

The waiter came around to their table, poured fresh ice water, brought a bottle of wine, and took their appetizer order. Melissa didn't protest when David ordered for the both of them.

"I've never had oysters before," she said, dabbing her mouth with a crimson cloth napkin.

"These are Rockefeller, so they are jazzed up a bit. Nevertheless, that is what those fancy napkins are for. If you find you don't like them, spit them into the napkin and wad it up. Geoffrey, the waiter, he knows better than to look inside the napkins, he leaves those surprises for the dishwashers," David said with a genuine smile that bordered on mischievous.

Melissa was finding herself extremely comfortable around this psycho killer. He was charming indeed and his dimples would make any woman blush.

"So, the tunnel. Are you Canadian?" she asked.

"No, but I spend so much time there I might as well be. I do have a place in Windsor. My firm has offices on both sides of the river, so I am in court a lot on both sides of the river," he sighed.

"Firm?"

"Law firm. I'm the fourth generation. Started by my great-great-great- grandfather more than a hundred years ago."

"Hermitage? I've heard that name before," Melissa said.

"During my father's time at the helm there were a lot of high-profile criminal cases. But I specialize in corporate tax law so not very much excitement for me I'm afraid," David said.

They enjoyed another glass of wine, polished off the oysters which Melissa absolutely loved and had wonderful conversation. She was a little distracted and worried that the child was still sitting there all by himself and she had yet to see any parental type. She was considering going over to his table when she was struck with a recollection.

"Hermitage. Of course. My grandfather had some old papers of his father's in a tattered shoe box stuffed on a shelf in the closet. One day when I was home with the chicken pox, I got nosy and pilfered the box. In there was a letter from a Hermitage Law Firm to my great-great-great-grandfather. It seems his wife and children were killed in the Italian Hall disaster in Calumet back around the turn of the century. Your predecessor was apologizing for the outcome of a legal proceeding in which he could not get any death benefits awarded. It didn't mean much to me at the time, but I did think it was kind of cool that a relative of mine narrowly escaped death."

"Interesting. I am going to have to look that up. My family has maintained meticulous records over the years I'm sure there is something in there about your family. Isn't that just how this wonderful world of ours works," David said.

"Yes, I guess it is."

Geoffrey visited their table to take their dinner order and Melissa found herself a little nervous about her choices and how they would appear to her date.

"Do you mind if I order for you, I come here often and I know the best dishes. You were fine with the oysters, so I assume you have no shellfish allergies," David said.

"No none."

"Do you enjoy lobster?"

Tongue-tied Melissa just nodded.

"Fine," he smiled. "We will both have the Wagyu, mine medium rare as usual and two orders of the Lobster Thermidor," he told Geoffrey and pointed to Melissa.

It took her a moment to figure out what he was doing. "Oh, medium will be fine for me." She thought about the expensive cut of steak David had just ordered and changed her mind. "Make mine medium rare as well."

David made sure to avoid corporate law as a topic of conversation and Melissa found they had a lot more in common than just the boxes checked off on a dating profile. But then her overactive imagination took over. What was such a nice looking, obviously wealthy man doing using a dating site? Maybe he wasn't wealthy at all. Maybe he was going to stiff her for the dinner. She suddenly felt panicked.

During her evanescent mental breakdown Geoffrey had stopped by their table and was engaged in conversation with David. Surely the two knew each other well enough to be on a first name basis and David had been there on many occasions, so he was not likely to be dining and dashing. Unless of course Geoffrey was in on it too.

Stop it!

"Geoffrey wants to know if you would like dessert," David said, ripping her from her trance.

"Oh, no, I would love to but there is no way I could make any room," she said, patting her belly as if she were with child.

"I was hoping you'd say that. I was having visions of Mr. Creosote."

"Monty Python. I love it. Geoffrey, maybe just one wafer thin piece of meat," she said.

Both her and David erupted into laughter while Geoffrey walked away from the table confused. The man obviously had no sense of humor or taste in classic cinema.

"Melissa, I just want you to know, this was the best date I have had in years. Now granted, in all honesty there haven't been very many, but most were boring and left me not wanting another. I would genuinely like to spend another evening with you," David said.

"Thank you, David. I have also enjoyed myself. I felt as if I could just be myself around you."

He reached across the table and took her hands. He looked deeply into her eyes making her stomach flutter. David made certain to hold the look for as long as he could. She felt herself melting.

"I'm sorry, but I really have to pee," he said and they both broke into laughter that drew contemptuous scorn from several tables away.

Even though she knew better, Melissa couldn't help but imagine David was sneaking through the kitchen and out of the back door leaving her with a bill she couldn't pay. In an effort to quell her overactive thalamus she glanced over her shoulder at the table where the little boy had been sitting. He was gone.

Melissa glanced around the room looking for the child to no avail. When she settled back in her seat, she was startled to find the child sitting in the chair directly across from her. The tiny hairs on the back of her neck stood on end, but she didn't know why other than he had surprised her.

"My, you startled me young man," Melissa said.

"You are not supposed to be here," he said in monotone.

She ignored his bizarre comment. "My name is Melissa, what is yours?"

"Samael, but you can call me Sam."

"Where are your parents, Sam?"

The boy shrugged.

"Are you here by yourself?"

"For now. But the others are becoming."

Odd little boy, she thought. "Why did you say that I wasn't supposed to be here?"

"Because you are not supposed to be here. You should have never been born," he responded.

Melissa felt a sudden chill blow across the table. She looked closer at the boy and was instantly terrified. His skin was translucent with just a hint of ocean blue shading, and it appeared to stream up and down his arms like an ocean current. The boy's eyes were completely black and void of any color whatsoever. She wanted to run as fast and as far away as she could, but she was transfixed.

"Hey, do you want to see something really cool?" he blurted out, jerking her back to this macabre reality.

Samael hopped out of his seat and walked over to an aquarium filled with lobsters condemned to death. He fiddled with the lid until he figured out how to open it and turned to smile at her.

"You shouldn't be playing with that," Melissa said.

"It's okay, I know what I am doing," Sam said and stuck his index finger into the water.

Like a magic trick the water instantly transformed into a blood red hue. He pulled one of the lobsters out of the tank dripping with thick, gelatinous syrup. The animal had grown to gargantuan size, weighing in at over thirty pounds, so large the boy could barely lift it. Melissa realized it wasn't just blood colored water; it was actually blood filling the tank. Melissa screamed but it caught in her throat.

The boy ripped the rubber band off the lobster's claw, discarded it onto the floor and said, "Buckle up, it's going to get kind of gross around here," Sam said with a smile and tossed the gnashing lobster into the lap of a wide-eyed patron who screamed and vaulted to her feet.

With both claws the crustacean lashed out at Gretchen Chalmers' throat. It squeezed and squeezed until the flailing woman turned an angry shade of blue and her windpipe finally ruptured from the extreme pressure. The hard nodules rimming the beast's claw tore through the tender flesh of her neck, tearing her jugular which oozed a thick, red sap onto her husband. Her heart was no longer pumping.

Melissa opened her mouth to scream but instead was able to elicit nothing more than a pathetic squeak. Her airway had closed off, choking the life out of her. Suddenly her gut was seizing and cramping, causing her to double over. She looked up to see David hovering near the table with confusion painted all over his face. Without warning Melissa defecated and urinated uncontrollably. Clutching at her throat she lay across the table watching the room descend into chaos as each and every patron, even David, suffered the same fate as her.

Samael looked down at his arms and smiled. The flesh had started to step thickly in, and he knew he was on his way. They were on their way. They were becoming. The stench of rotting fish permeated the air as the boy made his way out into world of the living, leaving a trail of death in his wake.

Chapter Twenty-Five

Medee fought against the onslaught of stimuli bombarding her in the collective's attempt to keep her focus away from the seven. She needed to be able to communicate with them, but at the present time that scenario seemed unlikely. She could only hope they would know what to do without her guidance.

She sensed the one called Lothur was going to be a problem and maybe even a couple of the others. Her plan had been discovered before she was able to get them all out at the exact same time, so they were not becoming at the same rate. These were already souls without any conscience, no remorse and certainly no regrets so once they tasted freedom and power it would be nearly impossible to rein them back in.

Medee knew she would no longer be able to control the seven as a whole, so she concentrated her efforts on Rose Marie. She was the one who would be able to wrangle them all together even if it was like herding cats in a thunderstorm. To even have a chance at success the girl needed to find the trumpets at all costs, they were the key.

One, two or even three of the vessels not completing their mission would not mean complete failure as long as the others could usher in the destruction of all life on that miserable planet. She focused all of her energies on the child she knew would succeed.

~ ~ ~

Rose Marie tore through the cathedral one room at a time using the building's decay to her advantage. She broke through walls, ceilings and floors but had yet to find what she was looking for. The place was just too big, and she was just too small. Not to mention, she was spending more of her time trying to draw the others to her than she should have to. They knew what was at stake, and yet they dared to resist her.

Chase Jr. paced the floor of the classroom still angry from his argument with Rose Marie earlier in the day. It just wasn't fair. He was stuck in this moldy hole while the others were out having fun. He wanted to flex his muscles too, especially after sensing the chaos and mayhem the others were spreading. The sole purpose for his creation was to cause destruction, not hide like a coward.

Rose Marie watched the boy from the corner of her eye. She could sense what he was thinking, and he wasn't completely wrong. It just wasn't the time or place for them to act yet. She found herself angry with Medee for abandoning her with these others. She was not the one in charge, and in fact, she wasn't even the eldest.

She watched Rai still huddled in the corner by himself and knew there was something wrong with him.

And the more the woman inside of her brain continued to peck away at her, she knew exactly what was distressing him. They had picked up hitchhikers, fragments of souls that were supposed to have been extinguished. Shards of beings that were not even supposed to have existed in the first place.

And just what in the hell were these accursed trumpets she was supposed to find? Were they really trumpets of brass or something less literal? There was certainly nothing shiny in all this decay.

"What are you looking for?" Rai asked, coming into the abandoned clinic after hearing Rose Marie rummaging through the debris.

"We have to find the seven trumpets," she replied.

"Why? Aren't the trumpets for the angels?"

"Are we not angels?"

"No, and we never were. In fact, we are not supposed to be here," Rai said, his voice tight and shaky.

Rose Marie spun on her heels and stared the boy down. "Don't you ever say that again. What has gotten into you?"

"I don't know. It was fun at first, but then I started thinking about all those people. How terrified they were. It just didn't seem like hurting them was the right thing to do."

Rose Marie wanted to tear his little head right off his body, but she knew it wasn't him spewing such nonsense. He had the other's emotions running through him and he didn't understand how to navigate through them. The longer this went on, all these flies in the ointment and obstacles at every turn were starting to make her think they had embarked on this mission way too soon. And with

Medee nowhere around it was going to fall on her shoulders to ensure this didn't all fall apart. They were so close to freeing themselves, and yet, so far away as well.

Chapter Twenty-Six

"Richie, I don't like this one bit. First the bus incident, then the fire and now rampant food poisoning," Chase said.

"You do know this is much more than what it appears to be. Those people didn't die from food poisoning. I know the FBI has taken over the case and are keeping the specifics tightly under wraps, but I have a few sets of eyes and ears keeping me in the loop. Look at this photo I just received in a text," Richie said, showing his phone to Chase.

It was a photograph of the crime scene at the restaurant that had been hastily snapped with a hidden cell phone, so there was not a lot of crisp detail. But poor Mrs. Chalmers with her throat torn apart by an obscenely large lobster was one of the details in focus.

"Have you ever seen a lobster that size?" Richie asked.

"Not even close. And I don't think this one was naturally this size either.

"Seemed angry too."

"I do believe that is an understatement."

"What did you learn reading that thing?" Richie asked, bobbing his head at an open bible on the coffee table.

"Do you really want to know?"

"Do I have a choice?"

"Probably not. Everything that has been happening is right here in Revelation just like Zera said it would be," Chase said.

"Such as?"

"The first mention of the vials in Revelation says, *Go away, and pour out the vials of the wrath of God to the earth; and the first did go away, and did pour out his vial upon the land, and there came a sore – bad and grievous – to men*. That certainly sounds like boils, blisters, and pustules to me," Chase said.

"What about fire, and the restaurant debacle?"

"It talks about the second vial being poured out into the sea, killing every living creature in the oceans. That might explain the food poisoning. If the sea creatures the patrons had already ingested turned to poison inside of them, it would surely kill them as well. The fourth vial is to be poured over the sun, scorching the earth and men."

"What are the other four vials? What should we be expecting?" Richie asked.

"In a nutshell, fresh water turned to poison, something about the throne of darkness, another vial is said to contain thunder, lightning, and hail. The last vial is supposed to be used to dry up the Euphrates River so armies can cross for battle."

"I would scoff, and call bullshit had we not had our mysterious visitor the other night and the fact all of the events mentioned in the Bible seem to be taking place. You said something about this being God's wrath? Do you think God is the cause of all this death?"

"No, I don't. I think it is actually quite the opposite."

"And why does the Book of Revelation keep referring to vials?"

"I think we are taking that too literal. And by we, I mean mankind as a whole. The Bible was interpreted by men over the centuries from languages that were dead or dying. Maybe it was lost in translation throughout the years and the word vial could mean vessel."

"And these maniac children are the vessels," Richie said.

Chase nodded.

"But why?"

"Why what Richie?"

"Why would God create such destructive things?"

"One could argue that the most destructive thing God created was man himself. God may have created these vials, or vessels if you will, but I don't think he ever had any intention of using them. But being a merciful being, he didn't have the heart to destroy the vials either. But of course, this is purely conjecture on my part," Chase said.

"It just seems, one might say petty, for a God who is supposed to be merciful."

"If we are to follow the scriptures then God created us in his image. Therefore, one might surmise he quite possibly possesses the same range of emotions as we do."

"Jealousy, anger, spite," Richie said.

"And most of all, empathy and remorse which is why the vessels were never used but not destroyed either," Chase said.

"Then the big question is why are they here now and how do we stop them?" Richie asked.

"I don't think why is as important as how do we stop them."

Richie nodded and went into the bathroom to take a shower. It was where he did his best thinking. While he was in the bathroom Chase pored over website after website dealing with the Book of Revelation. All of them seemed to have their own interpretation of the scriptures, no two were identical and each seemed more outlandish than the previous. Chase had to wonder if John were overcome by gases in that cave that caused him to hallucinate when writing the Book of Revelation as the text seemed preposterous. At least it did on the surface, before the advent of these mysterious children appearing out of nowhere to wreak havoc.

"Take a look at this," Richie said, handing his phone to Chase while towel drying his hair.

"A prison riot due to a power outage up in Ionia. Wait a minute, when did you look this up?"

"While I was in the bathroom?"

"You were using your phone in the shower?" Chase asked.

There was a long silence. "Not exactly."

"Then when?"

"While I was on the shitter okay."

"Damn it Richie," Chase said and dropped the phone on the couch next to him.

Richie laughed. "It's not like I wiped my ass with it. So, what do you think?"

"About the riot?"

"Yeah. Seems like it fits our little band of hooligans doesn't it?"

"It's probably worth looking in to, that's for sure. But I think I found something else more important," Chase said and pointed at his laptop screen.

There were a series of clusters of red dots overlaid on a map of the area.

"What am I looking at?"

"This is CDC data tracking the outbreak from the bus and subsequent smaller outbreaks. I think the one responsible realized he made too big of a scene and has been spreading smaller amounts of mayhem across the city."

"And you think we can track him using this data?" Richie asked.

"Yes, I think so. We might be able to discover a pattern that will allow us to stop him before his next attack," Chase replied.

"Do you really think it will be that easy?"

"Remember the look on that kid's face in the video? He had not a care in the world. It will be their hubris that brings them down."

"Or kills us. Remember what Zera said, you and I, we're finished."

"There's always a chance."

"And let's say your little scheme of following the red dots works and we are able to outmaneuver this pint-sized psychopath. What do we do then?"

"We destroy him."

"Kill him?"

Chase nodded.

"How?"

"I don't know, you're the one with the gun."

Chapter Twenty-Seven

Lothur was having the time of his life. There were so many of them, but sadly they were such fragile creatures the joy of toying with their very existence was fleeting. He had been maintaining a low profile as of late, but the pandemonium he delighted in during the bus incident left him wanting more. Left him wanting something bigger. There were so, so many of these people in the world, where should he begin?

Rose Marie was still pecking away at his brain with her incessant nagging, and he knew he should be meeting up with the others soon, but he was having too much fun. There was something else tumbling around inside of his head as well. Ramblings about this and that, things he didn't really care about. He knew it was shards of the madman clinging to him like lint and he wanted nothing more than to be rid of the man. But until then, he was determined to take his mind off his trials and tribulations.

He watched a horde of police officers patrolling the perimeter of the park, some on horseback, some in tactical gear and others in plain clothes. They were looking for him, well not him specifically, but any terrorists looking to do harm to the fine folks of their city. The law enforcement officers all wore such dour faces, not even smiling at one another. Everyone was the enemy. Everyone but an eight-year-old boy bearing cookies for his heroes.

The blisters on his arms were really beginning to irritate him with their incessant itching. Fluid tickled his arms and legs as it ran in rivulets from the puss laden sacs all over his body. His hands resembled surgical gloves blown up into balloons, balloons he just couldn't wait to pop.

Grand Circus Park was filling up as the day progressed. There were fruit and vegetable vendors, some craft tables, and a lemonade stand for a children's organization. A dozen food trucks lined the boulevard as did several ice cream vendors. It was a festive day and Richie didn't like it one damned bit. It was a veritable smorgasbord for extremists, even pint-sized fiends from hell.

Richie and Chase split up and walked through the throng of people until they met up with each other in the center of the park. They continued to follow the same pattern for over an hour with no luck spotting the infectious little bastard. But they knew he was there somewhere in that crowd of innocence.

"What do you think?" Chase asked.

"I think the little shit probably spotted us first and is making certain we won't spot him."

"Maybe he's not even here."

Richie shot Chase a sideways glance. "We are just following your data. Do you think you may have gotten it wrong?"

"No, I'm pretty confident this would be his next move considering his established pattern."

"Then he's here, somewhere."

The two of them made several more passes through the crowd and then walked the perimeter in opposite directions until they met in the center once again. Richie's cop gut was churning. There were way too many people assembled in once place to be able to control the situation. He wanted to alert the captain, but he didn't dare take the chance Chase might be wrong, and he would look like a deranged fool chasing after nonexistent monsters.

The mounted patrol had taken up formation on the northern end of the park and were preparing to put on a show of horsemanship for the crowd. People began milling over to where the mounted police were forming up. Richie got a bad feeling in his gut when three school buses brimming with children of all ages pulled up to the curb at the far end of the park and let a screaming horde of kids spill out into the square. He slapped Chase on the arm and bobbed his head at the buses.

Lothur watched three school buses drive around the block and then pull up to the curb. This was perfect. There were well over a hundred screaming kids running all over the park with only a handful of people watching over them. He could easily infiltrate their ranks and infect every last one of them. He found a secluded place and tucked himself away until the time was right.

Once more Richie and Chase split up. Richie took the ice cream and lemonade stands while Chase circled the gathering and watched from the perimeter. Even though it was a festive atmosphere they both felt an ominous presence. The boy was here.

Lothur watched with curiosity as groups of children made their way to a grassy area in the park where they all sat down cross-legged in a semi-circle. Eight chaperones stood behind the children, shooshing them every so often when they started fidgeting too much. Six police officers on horseback came sauntering up to the group. To the children's delight all six horses took a bow to greet them.

The horses were not trained for trick riding, but they did have a few smooth moves up their hooves. They pirouetted in formation, then they did the same, only this time every other horse spun the opposite direction, so half of the animals were going around in clockwise circles and the other half were spinning counterclockwise. To the pure delight of the children the officers set pieces of candy on each of the horse's noses and the horse would then flick its head flipping the piece of candy into the horde of toddlers.

With everyone preoccupied by the performance, Lothur began to creep toward the gathering of children. There was no better way for him to spread his sickness than by using children. He would be rewarded twice the pleasure once parents weren't able to comfort their dying offspring.

He was just about to the edge of the grassy expanse when the horse on the end with the name Caroline embroidered on her saddle reared up unexpectedly. The beast's eyes rolled up until they were almost pure white, and she whinnied a scream. The officer on her back was unable to maintain control and she bucked him clean out of the saddle.

Lothur clapped his hands at the row of mounted officers, spraying their faces and their horse's faces with death. The officers clutched at their burning skin as they screamed in pain. The horses reacted to the evil in their midst and within seconds there were six, large, riderless horses rearing up on their back legs stomping at the children in front of them. Two of the officers were trampled to death by their own horses as their animals blindly lashed out. This caused a stampede of children fleeing from rearing, stomping horses, and screaming men. In a panic the chaperones maneuvered the children out of the way of the stampeding horses and toward the buses.

"What is it, Chase?" Richie said into his phone.

"I think I see him."

"Where?"

"By where the mounted unit was performing for the children. He spooked the horses and now all hell has broken loose," Chase said as he began to run toward the children.

Lothur was startled and thrown off his plan for a moment once he saw the two men running straight for him. He quickly regrouped, assimilated into the mass of screaming little people and ran with the children toward the buses. He would be able to gather them all in one spot and blend in with them before he could be stopped.

Richie's heart was pounding from both the exertion and the anxiety of not knowing what to do next. He could see the target trying to blend in with the crowd of children and surely their guardians would be more intent on getting them to safety than looking out for a monster in the closet.

Normally he would just tackle the perp, but in this case, that would surely prove to be fatal. Chase was close enough he could see Richie's predicament. He couldn't touch the kid, but he didn't dare shoot him either for risk of shooting one of the panicked children, so Chase grabbed a plastic trash receptacle and took an angle on the crowd of drool goblins.

Chase had to wonder how many cameras were going to catch him in the act of assaulting a bunch of panic-stricken children running for their lives. He threw the blue barrel at the fleeing group catching a good portion of them in their legs, taking them off their feet and down to the ground in cries of terror. Lothur was behind the crowd and Chase counted on him ending up being the last man standing.

Chase grabbed a tablecloth from a lemonade stand and threw it over the mass of children. As soon as the kids were protected Richie fired a double tap, knocking Lothur to the ground. To their horror, the boy began to transform right in front of their eyes like something out of a Lon Chaney movie. The boils and pustules flattened out to smooth skin as an innocent young eight-year-old boy lay dying in front of them, and Richie knew this was going to be bad.

The boy kept saying something, but it was too weak for either of them to hear. At the risk of being infected with whatever this child carried Richie knelt beside him.

"What are you saying?" he asked, leaning into the boy while Chase tried to tug him away.

In a voice Richie recognized of that of Jessop Porter, the boy said, "It's all just food for thought."

"What did you say?"

"The trumpet is in the vault," the boy said as he died.

Chapter Twenty-Eight

Chase flicked through the news channels on the television while Richie took a shower in the motel room. He was trying to find something about what went down in the park earlier, but the police must have imposed a media blackout. There was a tapping on the motel door, interrupting his snack of stale cashews and tepid bottled water. He peered through the peephole at a fiery redhead dressed for business. Apprehensive, he opened the door slowly while glancing her up and down.

"It's nice to see you with some clothes on," he greeted.

"Excuse me!" the woman replied.

"Zera?"

"What the hell is a Zera?"

"Not a what, a who," Chase said, immediately wondering if it was the correct response.

"Hey, Janice, I'm glad you could make it," Richie said, toweling his hair as a cloud of steam exited the bathroom behind him. "Please have a seat."

Chase glanced back and forth between the two of them at a complete loss. They were supposed to be keeping a low profile, not entertaining guests.

"Chase, this is Janice DeBerg, my ex-wife," Richie explained.

"We were hardly married long enough for you to have earned the right to call me your ex-wife," she said with a smile.

Again, Chase bounced his attention back and forth between the two of them.

"It's a long story that involves alcohol, a cop convention in Las Vegas, and a very bad spur of the moment decision," Janice said.

"Lots of cheap alcohol," Richie said with a grin. "Janice here is with Internal Affairs."

"And you thought it would be wise to let her know where we were holed up?"

"Relax. Janice reached out to me to get my side of the story. I trust her to give us a fair shake."

Janice laughed and turned her attention to Chase. "And you must be the professional bowler. Way to take out a bunch of toddlers with a garbage can, macho man."

"I'll admit, it was not my proudest moment," Chase sighed.

Richie peered through the closed curtains until he was certain no one was watching them before he left the room to get a bucket of ice from the ice machine three doors down. He grabbed three sodas from the vending machine and headed back to the room where he poured them all rum and colas, heavy on the rum. He passed the drinks around and sat on the edge of the twin bed.

"I'm pretty sure I know the answer to this, but I just have to ask. Did either of you move the body?"

"Are you talking about the thing I shot?"

"Thing? It sure looked like an eight-year-old boy to me," Janice said, raising an eyebrow.

"Looks can be deceiving. And no, neither of us moved the body," Richie said. "We didn't have the time even if we had wanted to."

"Then can you explain this?" Janice asked, pulling her tablet out of her purse, queuing up a video and turning the screen toward the two of them.

Chase and Richie watched the scene at the park unfold and were both horrified by their actions. On the surface it looked like a couple of nut jobs attacking a group of young children. The video hovered over the dead boy's body lying in the grass for several moments before the screen was suddenly filled with static. When the snow cleared the boy's body was gone.

"What in the hell? How long was that blackout?"

"No more than five seconds," Janice replied.

"Gone without a trace. No other videos in the area picked anyone up carrying the body off?" Richie asked.

"None. We've put out a plea to the public to come forward hoping there might be cell phone videos of the incident, but so far no one has come forward. In the meantime, I have had the soil excised from the area and sent to an independent lab for testing."

"Why in the hell would you do that?" Chase asked.

"I think you know why. And I think you know what might be found in that soil."

Chase's eyes darted back and forth between Richie and the redhead, showing more and more confusion with each passing second.

"I thought Janice might be able to help us, not so much because of her police contacts, but because of her other proclivities," Richie said.

"Hey there cowboy, they are not my inclinations, they are my father's," she responded with a twinkle in her emerald eyes.

"Let me wipe that look off your face, Chase. Janice's father is bit of a zealot when comes to the Bible and specifically the Book of Revelation," Richie explained.

"A zealot is putting it mildly. Pops is certifiably bat shit crazy. He's been a ward of the state down in Kalamazoo going on ten years now."

"Was he a priest or a preacher man?" Chase asked.

"Nope. He was just a simple brick layer. In fact, he missed church most Sundays because he needed the overtime to feed and clothe his heathen children."

"What caused his interest in the Book of Revelation?"

She took a long gulp of her drink, polishing it off, and handed the empty to Richie for a refill. "It all started after he died."

"What happened to him? Wait, if your father is dead, how is he in Kalamazoo?" Chase asked.

"Okay, I'm going to start to sound just as whacko as my father. One day, while at work, a pallet of bricks snapped a strap while they were hauling it up to the third level of a construction site with a crane. My father never stood a chance. He was crushed under literally a ton of bricks," Janice said.

"After getting the bricks off him they were able to resuscitate him. Amazing," Chase said.

"No, they weren't able to revive him at the scene. The company man came by our house with a police officer to inform us that my father had been killed. My mother loaded us all into the car and drove us to the hospital where we said our goodbyes, after the coroner had cleaned dad up of course."

"Of course. But I am a little lost. If the coroner had your father's body," he let the statement hang in the air.

"Two entire days later my father pulled a Lazarus and resurrected from the dead."

Both Chase and Richie simply stared back at Janice in disbelief.

"That is the same exact expression my mother had on her face when the hospital called. Here is where I think our stories intertwine. Before slipping in and out of a coma for the next three months my father managed to utter one single phrase."

"Tell Chase what your father said," Richie prodded.

"The only thing my father managed to say was that he was not supposed to be there."

"There as in the hospital?" Chase asked.

She shook her head. "No, I think he was referring to wherever it was he spent those two days being amongst the dead."

Chase grabbed a handful of ice, tossed it into his plastic Solo cup with a hollow thump and filled it with rum before adding just a splash of cola. He looked the woman over and the expression on her face told him she believed them, or at least believed what they believed. The room was silent except for their breathing and ambient noise from traffic for the better part of ten minutes as they pondered Janice's story.

"You mentioned you sent soil samples to the lab, what do you expect them to find?" Richie asked.

"I didn't send them samples; I sent the whole enchilada. A four-foot-long, three-foot-wide, and two-foot-deep chunk of earth. I'm not sure if I am more interested in what they find, or what they don't find. If there are no traces of human DNA then we have some answers."

"I'm not sure if I could categorize that as an answer," Chase said.

"Richie told me that you believe there are seven of these children," Janice said.

"Six now, if Pestilence is truly dead," Richie said. "But to be honest we really don't know. We do know of two others, the one who killed my partner and the one who came back as Chase's dead son."

"Seven makes sense," she said after digesting the information for a moment.

"Why does seven make sense?" Chase asked.

"Seven is a number that is repeated enough throughout not only the Bible but the Quran as well so many times that it can't just be coincidental. The number seven does present as having a significant meaning," Janice said.

"So, you don't think we're nuts," Chase said, getting up to use the bathroom.

"No crazier than my old man," she said, a glistening of tears coating her eyes.

"What's that all about?" Richie asked quietly once Chase was behind closed door.

"Richie, what if my father was right all along and we just locked him up and threw away the key?"

"Janice, do I need to remind you that your father became very violent during that time," Richie said, reflecting on how Jessop Porter behaved when they pulled him from that abandoned church.

"I know, but I still can't help but feel guilty. I feel like we abandoned him."

"You visit him, don't you?"

"Not as often as I should. But hey, that's enough of that shit. We've got work to do."

The three of them made several trips back and forth to Janice's Escalade to shuttle in equipment and boxes of files. She brought her laptop with an overhead projector, another laptop for editing photos and boxes briming with her father's notes and files.

"Let's get to work, shall we?" she said with a smile and a wipe of her forehead.

~ ~ ~

Medee lashed out in frustrated anger. She knew the one called Lothur had failed and had now returned to meld back into her. Weakening her. His failure also weakened her bond with the others.

She could feel darkness and corruption seeping out from her tendrils on earth. But some were not obeying.

Many of the seven were getting intoxicated by their newfound power.

Medee focused her energies on the one called Rose Marie. She was the strongest link in the chain, and all would fail if she failed.

Time was on her side. Or at least time as known to mankind. They were such delicate creatures it wouldn't take much to crush the whole lot of them. There hung a delicate balance at the moment. The scales were nearly aligned, and she only needed to tip them a miniscule fraction in her favor.

Chapter Twenty-Nine

Cecelia was on her way to meet up with Rose Marie and the others when she ran across something quite interesting. She felt a persuasive magnetic pull drawing her toward a certain individual. At first, she didn't understand why, but as she closed the gap between them, she came to understand, he was not supposed to be here.

Michael Coopersmith sat alone in his upstairs nook staring at the laptop screen with a single word heading. Chapter. That was it. Not even Chapter One, or Chapter Two, just Chapter. For two entire days all he had managed to construct was the vague header, Chapter. The sole purpose for his taking a residency in this overpriced artist's retreat was to write without distraction.

There was no wireless internet, no television, no phones allowed and no visitors except during specific hours. It was forced solitude which should have netted him positive results. But so far, Chapter was the bulk of his productivity. He began rereading his outline notes and other story ideas and nothing grabbed his attention nor did any of the gibberish start his creative juices flowing.

The nearly blank page mocked him, and he had to laugh for a moment as a vision entered his brain. Setting; a mountain ski lodge, a writer staring intently at a blank page until he goes utterly mad, too bad that tale had already been written. Michael got up from his writing desk and meandered over to the window to watch shadows dancing across the green. Under the hazy blue glow of a streetlamp a young girl watched him from the street. The pair stared at each other through the windowpane until Michael finally gave her a half-hearted wave. Cecelia grinned a wicked grin and walked toward the front door.

Michael didn't give the girl much thought. It was visiting hours and the residents would be entertaining guests downstairs suggesting the little girl must belong to one of the other residents in some way or another. He returned his gaze to his computer screen. Chapter. What an intimidating word. A simple word, but it held the promise of so many different possibilities. But as the author it also meant it carried the heavy burden of responsibility as well. It was his obligation to ensure the word, Chapter, would deliver on all promises.

Suddenly his brain was aflame with an idea. An idea so simple, and yet so complex. His fingers banged away at the keyboard as if he were typing an angry email to some government bureaucrat or the cable company. It was a simple premise; she wasn't supposed to be there. A little girl lost, wanders into a house filled with strangers. Does she find comfort? Does she find more neglect? Or does she simply fail to find what she was looking for and disappears into the night leaving in her wake a tableau of destruction.

Michael stopped typing for a moment and read his words aloud to himself. Where in the hell did that come from? He didn't even remember a single, coherent thought forming in his brain. It was as if his hands had a mind of their own. He startled when he saw her reflection in his laptop screen, and he slowly turned in his chair to came face to face with the little wanderer.

He glanced her up and down and found her to be a peculiar little thing. She was dark and brooding, dressed in all black. Her hair was a scattered mop of pure charcoal. And then he noticed the flickering shadows in her eyes and a chill washed over him.

"You are not supposed to be here," Cecelia said.

Michael opened his mouth to respond, but instead, turned back in his chair and began pounding away at the keyboard. He felt a compulsion that was impossible to ignore. The more he struggled to stop writing, the faster his fingers clicked away at the keys. Minute after minute flew by as he immortalized his thoughts. The first one thousand words flew by, then before he knew the word count was up to ten thousand words, and then twenty thousand. His hands were cramping up, but he didn't dare take a break. He was going to finish his masterpiece that very evening even if it killed him.

Even if it killed him? Fear invaded Michael's brain when he realized the words he was typing were not his own. He struggled and struggled to quit hammering away at the keyboard, but it was impossible to stop typing. And then, as suddenly as his flurry of typing had begun, it was finished. His hands trembled as he reached for his bottle of water while reading the computer screen. Michael choked on his water as he read the words on the screen, the only words he had been typing over and over again.

There is only the darkness!

Shadows began closing in around him from his peripheral vision. He pivoted his head side to side to find it was the same all around him, darkness spread outward from every corner of the room threatening to swallow him whole. Slowly the darkness consumed the light as if everything were fading to black. Michael then realized it wasn't just his vision that was being impaired, it was his thoughts as well. Little by little his thoughts disappeared, evaporating like water on a red hot skillet. He managed to drag himself into his closet like a wounded animal as his vision went dark, and his brain quickly followed.

As he lay there in an all-consuming darkness, his thoughts zipped by like fireflies. They were there, and then they were gone forever.

Screams erupted from the floor below as the other house members were devoured one by one to suffer the same fate as Michael Coopersmith. Cecelia smiled as she made her way through the sea of despair and out into the night. The evening echoed with the whimpering of dozens of lost souls with no reality left to cling to. As she made her way down the street laden with apartments on either side of her, a wave of darkness crashed into the lives behind the walls. By the time she was finished more than two hundred people had been consumed by her darkness.

She smiled knowing that in time, there truly would only be the darkness.

Chapter Thirty

A criss cross pattern of colored lines resembling the city's bus routes were splayed out on a white board propped up on the bureau in the small motel room. Janice used a different color for each of the seven children, and although they had only managed to map out four of the seven, there was a pattern emerging. All four lines seemed to be leading to the same destination.

"The church where you found Jessop Porter?" Chase questioned.

"I think you're right. But what about the other three children?" Richie asked.

"According to the strange incidents happening across the state we can only account for four of the seven vials," Janice added.

"Actually, five if you count the incident at the fair. I think there were two of them there. The child representing fire, the fourth vial and though the report was overshadowed by the poor woman being set on fire alive, there was also a terrible storm that cropped up out of nowhere. I'm going to assume that was the seventh vial," Chase said.

"Why would they be going back to that church?" Richie asked himself aloud while drawing a thick red circle around the church on the map.

"What was it the child said to you just before he died?" Janice asked.

"He said, the trumpet is in the vault. But it was even stranger than that, it was Jessop Porter's voice, not the child's. Porter was the man we found in the church the night Effie was murdered."

"What he said must have had some significance."

"I know that Chase, but what? Janice, what could he have meant by the trumpet is in the vault?"

"According to Revelation there are not only seven bowls of God's wrath, but also seven seals, and seven trumpets. Have you heard of the four horsemen of the apocalypse?"

They both nodded.

"The four horsemen are the first sign of the apocalypse, but we haven't seen any horsemen, have we?"

"Not if taken in the literal sense of demons on horseback. But maybe it isn't exactly how it was transcribed and translated through the ages. Maybe the horsemen have been here for a very long time. Reading through your father's notes I see the pale horsemen is to bring death by war, hunger, and wild animals. War has plagued the world since before Christ. Famine is widespread around the globe and this latest pandemic was inflicted upon us by an animal if some are to be believed."

"Don't tell me you buy into that whole bat eating theory," Richie said.

"No, but the virus while not technically alive it does become active once introduced into humans, therefore taking on lifelike qualities. Outbreaks have been occurring in greater and greater numbers from e bola, e coli, just to name a few. "

"Chase does make a good point. The black horse supposedly causes economic imbalance and a great inflation of prices. We are probably looking at this too literal. More like a Hollywood movie than what the scriptures were referring to. The horsemen could be merely symbolic," Janice said.

Richie read through her father's notes, bouncing between the notes and an open Bible turned to the Book of Revelation on the bed. He flipped back and forth between the pages trying to make sense of it all.

"Come on, this stuff reads like this John of Patmos guy was having one major acid trip," Richie said.

"And I would be inclined to agree with you given my history on the subject. However, the truth of the matter remains, there have been some very odd, unexplainable phenomena occurring as of late. All of which parallel the events in the Book of Revelation whether by chance or by design," Janice said.

"What part do the trumpets play?" Chase asked.

"Those are the specifics in Revelation that I don't grasp. The seals, the trumpets and the vials all seem to mirror one another so I do not understand why there is the need for both the trumpets and the vials if they accomplish the same goals," Janice pondered.

Richie read through more of her father's scribblings while Chase went to the vending machine for more ice and some sodas. When he returned, he handed them all their cold drinks and a glass of ice.

"What if the trumpets are one in the same as the vials but they must work in consort with one another. The first vial cannot be *poured* until the trumpet has been sounded. From what your father has written here, the trumpets are merely a warning to the nonbelievers that their time is nearing an end. The purpose of the trumpets appears to be a last chance for the unholy to repent and change their ways," Richie said, looking up from the pages of an alleged madman's ramblings.

"There's something else we are missing. Taking everything into context, there is a heaven, a hell and a war raging between the two, then these vials, or bowls, are God's atomic bomb to be used only as a last resort. From everything you told me about your conversation with that woman, Zera, this was not done intentionally so we can only rely on the Book of Revelation so much," Janice said.

"And wing the rest," Chase added with a sigh.

"So, our master plan is to have no plan at all?" Richie said.

"I think we need to be aware of something else. If these events signal what is truly happening, then the stakes are quite high for these children and for the one who sent them here."

"Are you referring to Lucifer himself?" Richie asked, his voice laden with skepticism.

"Lucifer, Satan, hell, aliens, I don't know. But what I do know is that children who can spread plagues, poison water and rain fire down upon us should not be taken lightly," Janice said.

"Point taken. Besides, I really don't give a shit if they came from heaven, hell, or outer space, I'm going to send them back to where they came from."

"So that's your plan, guns a blazin'," Chase said with a nervous chuckle.

"I think you got lucky being able to take that one out so easily, and I'm pretty sure you won't get so lucky the next time."

"What do you mean by that Janice?"

"If they are all migrating toward the same location then that means they must be able to communicate with one another somehow. Which also stands to reason that they will know you have removed one of them. In fact, getting rid of one of them may have made things worse for us."

"How so?" Chase asked.

"The fact they are all migrating to one location leads me to believe their plan was to mobilize as one single unit before acting. Now that one of them has been destroyed that is no longer a viable option for them. They may splinter off on their own and instead of us having to track one collective unit, we will have six of these children scattered across hell's half acre wreaking havoc as they please."

"Do you have any suggestions?" Chase asked.

"I propose we treat them as if they were a terrorist cell working toward a common goal," Janice offered.

"That makes sense. We try to anticipate soft targets," Richie said.

"Exactly."

"Won't that just be relying on luck?" Chase asked.

"Yes Chase, but there is also a science behind it. Janice has served on several anti-terrorist task forces giving her the experience we need to track these demonic little shits."

"What you're telling me is that the fate of humanity rests on us getting lucky," Chase said.

"Pretty much," Janice replied with a half-hearted smile.

Chapter Thirty-One

Rose Marie felt the loss of Lothur to her very core, but worse yet, so did the others. She sensed their deflation, and she feared the demise of one may very well be the demise of all. The process of being born into this human vessel proved more cumbersome as each day progressed. Not only was she experiencing a myriad of emotions she had never experienced before, but she was also not adept at coping with them either. Especially anger.

She had this desire to destroy everyone and everything in her path, including the others. The loss of one of them could very well mean they would never be able to become one, which would also mean they would be stuck in these human forms forever. This line of thought fueled her anger to the point the ground trembled beneath her feet. She knew that if she allowed her anger to grow it would blossom into a full-blown earthquake of epic proportions. But that was not her purpose. Her purpose was to lead an army, an army she no longer possessed.

Rose Marie careened through her universe trying to latch onto a single idea. A single thread that could show her the way out of this mess. She had to put those meddlesome altruists in their place. Garrick and Zera had no right to interfere, this was not their battle.

She found it extremely hard to navigate through these human emotions. Things were so much easier when not clouded by anger, frustration, and disappointment. There was only what is, and what is not, and she was going to make damned sure this world fell under the is not category. If she couldn't have it, then no one would. Now jealousy, envy, and avarice were emotions she felt she could not only tolerate, but nurture.

~ ~ ~

"Tell me again why we're in this part of town before the crack of dawn?" Chase asked.

"The last thing that boy said to me was that the trumpet was in the vault. It didn't make much sense, even with the voice being that of the lunatic Jessop Porter. I did some digging while you were asleep and found records of a storage unit Jessop Porter rented when he got back here from the Middle East. It can't be a coincidence," Richie said, pointing to the name, The Storage Vault, painted on a placard above the entrance.

"So how are we getting in? The place looks deserted," Janice said.

"I called the owner and after some finagling, I managed to get the code to the security gate."

"How did you manage to get a warrant to open Porter's unit in the middle of the night?" Chase asked.

Richie smiled, opened the trunk of his car, and pulled out a pair of bolt cutters. He snapped them open and closed in a dramatic fashion before closing the trunk.

"So, you don't plan on returning to your old career I see," Janice quipped.

"If Zera is to be believed then I won't have to be worrying about that much longer," Richie replied.

Janice shot Chase a sideways glance.

"According to Zera, Richie and I will not survive this endeavor," Chase said. "You may want to think about distancing yourself from us while you still can."

"Not a chance. How often does a girl get to save humanity from destruction by thwarting evil children trying to bring about Armageddon?"

"I'm afraid you might regret that decision," Richie said.

"A life without regret is a life not lived," Janice replied with a smug grin.

Richie keyed in the code on a keypad and a black steel gate creaked slowly open. The trio made their way through the gate and into the shadows. They walked the row of storage units until they came to the unit number the owner had reluctantly divulged under duress in the middle of the night. He swung the bolt cutters up into position before realizing it was a key entry, and not a padlock.

"It looks like your life of crime is over before it even got started," Janice said with a chuckle.

"What now?" Chase asked.

"Stand back," she said, arm barring Chase away from in front of the lock.

Janice opened her small clutch purse and pulled out a black pouch. She opened the pouch to reveal a set of lock picking tools. Within three minutes she had the lock picked and the overhead door open. The three of them went inside and closed the door behind them.

"This can't be the right unit," Richie said.

"Why not?"

"Chase, that dude, Jessop Porter could not have possibly been this organized."

"Come on now, Richie. The man couldn't have been that bad," Janice said.

"He was living in an abandoned church, hadn't bathed or changed his clothes in weeks if not months, and in case I failed to mention it earlier, he strapped people into chairs and was eating them alive. And let's not forget the marionettes constructed out of human bones," Richie said.

"I stand corrected," Janice said, putting her hands up in resignation.

Richie looked around the room which had been set up like a makeshift office. There were dozens of textbooks lining two large bookshelves, most of which were anthropology books, but there were several ornithology books in the mix as well. Those books appeared to have been well read with many dog-eared pages and scribbled notes along many of the margins. He pulled one down and fanned through it. There were loose leaf sheets of papers in between pages and handwritten notes on nearly every single page front and back.

"Look here," Chase said, opening a cardboard box filled with plaques and certificates. "Every one of these has Jessop Porter's name on them. He had degrees from

Harvard, Cornell, Dartmouth and even a few from European universities. It appears he majored in anthropology, specializing in the Middle East."

"It looks like he was into birds too," Janice said, rifling through a box of her own. She showed the guys a few photographs of the man standing in a field dressed up in bird watching gear. He looked like plain, white bread.

"I just don't get it. When I saw Jessop Porter, he was the epitome of bizarre, disheveled, and cluttered, not organized like all this stuff is. He certainly wasn't the same man in those photographs. This stuff is all catalogued, divided into subjects and then subdivided into even more narrow parameters. This is not the work of a madman," Richie said.

"He was in the Middle East not too long ago working on two different projects. One anthropological and the other working with an endangered bird named the Northern Bald Ibis. Seems he was working with a group trying to revitalize the bird's population in the region," Janice said, reading through some notes scribbled in a day planner.

"Do his notes say what the purpose of the anthropological trip was?" Richie asked.

"It doesn't say. The notes in his planner says he needed to meet up with a Professor Sayed at a dig site, but that is it. It doesn't even say where the dig site was."

"Something must have happened to this man. But what, where, and when," Chase said.

The three of them worked through the boxes in their section of the storage unit setting aside things they felt might be of interest to the group. Janice uncovered a large table with a cream-colored tablecloth covering the surface. The surface of the table wasn't flat, so she pulled the covering off to see what was underneath.

"Hey guys, take a look at this."

"What is that?" Richie asked.

"It's a topographical map. I don't recognize any of the names, nor do I recognize that river," Chase said, pulling his phone out of his pocket and putting the names of locations on little flags on the map into his internet search browser.

The map was an incredibly detailed rendering of a river valley. There were pins stuck in the map with little white pieces of paper on each one, each with a different name written on the paper. There were also several areas painted with pockets of white dots.

"What does it say?" Richie asked, bobbing his head toward Chase's phone.

"According to this, these are villages in Turkey. And this," he said, drawing a snaking line across the map, "Is the Euphrates River."

Janice went white for a moment. This was all too coincidental to be a coincidence. All these tiny interactions were leading to something far, far greater than any one of them.

"What's wrong with you? You got pretty quiet all of the sudden," Richie asked with a poke to Janice's shoulder.

"This isn't just a map of Turkish villages. The areas not marked are more important than those that are. See here, this is Syria and over here, this is Israel. The one lone flag in Israel is stabbed into Megiddo," she explained.

"You lost me."

"Megiddo, or more formally, Har Megiddo, is where the word Armageddon is derived. And both the sixth trumpet and the sixth vial are centered around the Euphrates River. According to John, as written in Revelation, this is where the battle to end all battles will be fought."

"Do you think Jessop Porter may have unearthed something on this dig?" Chase asked.

Richie began running his hands along the edges of the table, giving it a good thump every so often while the others looked on in wonder. After the third pass around the table there was a subtle click emanating from the underside. He leaned under the table and pulled out a hidden compartment.

"Wow, you looked just like Nicolas Cage when you did that," Janice said.

"What is it?" Chase asked.

"It looks to be a legend for the map. Here, where all these dots are, according to his notes these were all nesting pairs of Ibis. And here, this portion over here was a feeding station for the Ibis."

Richie pored over the notebook and the map jotting notes down for himself. And while it seemed significant in its own context, none of the information offered them any guidance on what to do next. The small room was getting rather stuffy, and Janice was not comfortable standing there watching Richie read. While looking over the map she tried to recall maps her father had in his study and how they might relate to one another.

"I knew there was something off about this map," Janice blurted out.

"What do you see?"

"It's not what I do see, it's what I don't see. There's no water. The river is dry," she said, tracing her finger along the riverbed.

"Are you telling me that this area right here is not a desert?" Richie asked.

"No, not presently."

"She's right. Look at the map here on my phone. The region is mountainous, rocky, and dry but by no means does it look as barren as this diorama depicts," Chase said, turning his phone so Richie could see it.

The three of them stared at the topographical relief for several minutes trying to see what it was they needed to see to solve this unsolvable riddle.

"This is a depiction of what the Euphrates will look like once the sixth trumpet is sounded, and the sixth vial is poured into the river. The vial dries up the river allowing armies to march across from the east. Chase, hand me that bottle of water please," Janice said.

"But it's my last one."

"Take a small drink and give me the rest," she said with her hand extended and her brow furled.

"Just what in the hell are you up to?" Richie asked.

"Humor me. And get ready to laugh at me when I make a mess and an absolute fool out of myself."

Janice moved to the far northern edge of the table where the Euphrates River made its first appearance at the edge of the map. She unscrewed the cap on the water bottle and slowly poured it into the dry riverbed. The water ran through the clay trough in a long, thin rivulet as it meandered through the map to the furthest edge where it trickled out onto the floor of the storage unit. The three of them stared at the map for several minutes before losing interest.

"Well, that was anti-climactic," Janice said with a shrug.

"What did you expect to happen?" Chase asked while trying not to sound too condescending.

Richie didn't take the high road. "That was about as useless as tits on a boar."

His comment pissed Janice off enough she didn't even respond. Instead, she began going through yet another carton of Jessop Porter's life. Chase gave his friend a short jab to the shoulder in an effort to prompt an apology, an effort that proved futile.

None of this made any sense to Richie. Jessop Porter's life was about as dull as it could get, at least from his perspective. Sure, traveling to remote places might be nice for a weekend, but Porter had spent months in the desert studying birds. And not just birds, but the mating habits of one specific species of bird, a very ugly species. To Richie that would be as interesting as playing with a single-colored Rubik's cube for months on end. A crinkling sound caught his attention and his stomach grumbled.

"Okay, which one of you is hoarding food?" Richie asked.

The other two simply shrugged and looked at him as if they didn't have a clue what he was talking about. This time they heard the noise as well. All three of them turned their attention to where the sound was coming from.

"What in the holy hell is going on?" Richie asked.

The diorama was slowly growing, changing, as if it were springing to life. Suddenly the riverbank was lined with Euphrates poplars, willows, and pistachio trees, all of which began to sprout leaves and blossoms. The thin trail of water continued to expand until it was four fingers wide and three knuckles deep. Janice poured the rest of the bottle of water into the ravine which represented the Tigris River and within a few minutes it too was a flowing river teeming with life.

"This is impossible," Richie said.

"And yet, it is happening," Chase said.

"Perhaps a case of mass hallucination. What was in that water, Chase?" Janice asked.

"Cute. Need I remind the three of us that no matter how impossible this seems, we were visited by an angel from heaven, or possibly an alien from outer space, or wherever the hell Zera came from. There have been little kids committing mass murder of epic proportions and my stillborn son arrived on my doorstep not only alive, but the exact same age he would have been had he not been stillborn," Chase said.

"What is that movement?" Richie asked and extended a finger toward the map.

Janice grabbed and yanked his hand back. "Are you crazy? You don't know what that thing is. It might snatch you and pull you down there into the map."

Chase squatted down and gazed into the area Richie was pointing at.

"They're birds. And they are flying around."

"Get the fuck out of here," Richie said.

Chase laughed. “Dude, they are little black birds. Dozens of them.”

“Bullshit. Those are just gnats or fruit flies you jackass.”

Janice pulled a pair of readers out of her clutch purse and put them on. She bent down and studied the area of the map Richie had pointed to and shook her head.

“I hate to tell you, Richie, those are birds.”

In unison the three of them took two steps back away from the map. None of them believed what they were seeing and none of them felt comfortable being in the same room with the anomaly. Minute by minute the map filled in with vegetation and wildlife. The damned thing had come back from the dead.

“Look over there. What is that circular patch in the trees,” Janice said as she pointed.

“It looks like some kind of glade, but it is oddly symmetrical.”

Richie started tearing through all the boxes, tossing them aside when he didn’t find what he was looking for. He spotted a box with DESK written on the side in black marker and tore into that box with a fervor while the others looked on in amazement at his strange behavior. But then he withdrew his hand from the box triumphantly holding a magnifying glass in his hand.

“You’re smarter than you look, I’ll give you that,” Janice jabbed.

Richie handed the magnifying glass to Chase who then looked over the map before handing the glass to Janice.

"You have more experience with this stuff than either me or Richie. What do make of those symbols in the glades?" Chase asked.

"More experience? I hardly think having a bat shit crazy fool for a father qualifies for experience."

"Have you seen those symbols before?"

She sighed and looked closer at the topographical map. The glades were more defined than when they first appeared and there was some sort of symbol on the ground in the center of each of them.

"Without being able to see these larger and in more detail I can only speculate."

"Speculate away," Richie said.

"One of the things my father used to rant on about were secret societies."

"You mean like the Illuminati, Freemasons, those types of organizations?" Chase asked.

"Exactly, except my father was more concerned with the Knights Templar and a few others who have faded into obscurity. Those symbols remind me of crests each of those societies used. My father had several signet rings from different organizations. I don't know if they were real, or replicas."

"Seems odd to me that a secret society would have a symbol recognizing them as what they were," Richie said. "Hardly seems a secret when you broadcast who you are."

"At the time only the members of the group knew what the symbol meant. Remember, this was long before social media," Chase said.

Richie chided himself for not thinking about it sooner and pulled out his cell phone. He zoomed in on each of the clearings and snapped photos with his phone. He cropped the photographs with the built-in photo editing software to enlarge the areas. They were a little pixilated and grainy, but he showed them to Janice and Chase. While scrutinizing the images on Richie's phone a sound erupted from the corner that was half belch, half fart, with an odd raspy sound thrown in.

"Richie, if you're going to do that, please open the door," Janice said.

"It wasn't me."

The noise reverberated from behind Richie once again.

"Dude, really?" Chase commented.

"I'm telling you, that wasn't me."

The noise echoed throughout the room, only louder, and more pronounced. Chase pinpointed the origin of the sound and began clearing boxes away from the far corner of the room by handing them to the others. It took the better part of five minutes to uncover a black cloth covering what appeared to be another box. He ripped the cloth away to reveal two bird cages sitting side by side. The cage on the left side housed a bird so long dead it was merely a dehydrated husk. The cage on the right contained the ugliest bird any of them had ever seen. And even stranger yet, it was still alive and none the worse for wear despite the absence of food or water near its cage.

"What in the hell kind of bird is that grotesque creature? It makes a buzzard look like a beauty queen," Richie said.

The bird in the cage was as large as a peacock but jet black with a shimmer of purple on its wings. Most of the bird's head was featherless, and the bald face looked like a creepy old man with a six-inch-long nose. Long black featherlike protuberances jutted straight back from the rear of the bird's skull. Its piercing yellow eyes haunted them as it stared back at the stunned trio.

"I imagine this is an Ibis, the bird Porter was studying."

"How long was that Porter fellow living in that church?" Janice asked.

"Months if not years by all indications," Richie replied without breaking his gaze from the odd-looking bird.

"There's no food or water in this cage. How long does it take for a bird die of starvation?" Janice asked.

"Maybe it ate the other one?" Chase speculated.

"I don't think it could reach the other cage, even with that long beak," Janice said.

After studying the cage for several minutes, they found a name plate on the bottom of the cage on the side away from them where the door was. Chase spun the cage one hundred and eighty degrees, so the door was now facing them.

"If he is what the sign says he is then he is indeed a Northern Bald Ibis," Chase said.

"Hey, there's a sign of some sort on the bottom of the cage but it is upside down. Looks like it may have been hanging around the bird's neck at some point," Richie said as he reached inside the cage.

Luckily, before his fingers even passed through the metals bars the bird struck out with its beak, almost impaling Richie's hand. He thought about shooting the damned thing but remembered he left his gun locked in the trunk of the car. The dreadful bird jumped up, grabbed the cage with its talons and shook it back and forth while stabbing its beak between the bars causing them all to jump back several feet from the cantankerous creature.

"Damned thing is a vicious beast," Richie said.

"Well, you did kill the man who fed him," Janice smirked.

"First, I didn't kill Jessop Porter, and second, I doubt that crazy bastard was feeding this bird."

"Look, that sign flipped over in the commotion," Chase said, pointing but making very sure his finger was well out of reach.

Janice leaned in. "It says *Trompet Number Three*."

"Am I to assume that trompet means trumpet?" Richie asked.

"I think it is Turkish for trumpet, so yes, trumpet number three."

Chase fumbled around in his jacket until he found an unopened bottle of water he had stashed in his pocket. He twisted the cap and took a long drink. Immediately he gagged and spit the water out followed by a bout of dry heaves.

"What the hell has gotten into you?" Richie asked.

"This. It tastes like shit. Actually, it tastes worse than shit," he said, handing the bottle to Richie.

"I'll take your word for it."

"Give me that you pussy," Janice said, reaching for the bottle.

Don't drink the water or you'll be sorry.

"What did you say?" she asked, glancing back and forth between the two men.

"I didn't say anything," Chase said.

"Me neither," Richie followed.

Janice raised an eyebrow, took a cautious sip from the bottle, and spit it out onto the ground.

I warned you.

"You warned me? I thought you didn't say anything."

"We didn't say a single word," the men responded in unison while glancing back and forth at each other.

On a whim Janice poured the bottle of water into the river on the map. Within seconds the vegetation reverted to being dead and decayed. The birds stopped flying around and the symbols turned to dust and blew away. She reached a finger out to touch where she had poured the water, but Richie grabbed her by the wrist and stopped her with a slow shake of his head.

Read the book.

"Read what book?" she asked.

"What are you talking about, Janice?"

"You just told me to read the book."

"What book?"

"I don't know, you're the one who told me to read it."

"Janice, neither one of us said a word," Chase said.

"Bullshit! I heard it plain as day, one of you said read the book."

"No, Janice, neither of us said a word," Richie countered.

"Which one of you two jokesters are doing a fantastic impersonation of Jeff Dunham?"

"Who?" Chase asked.

"Never mind," she said and pulled a notepad out of her purse.

She began flipping through the pages until she finally settled on a page, handwritten with notes about the trumpets. A queasiness washed over her as she read her father's scribblings.

"The third trumpet will cause a third of the earth's water to turn bitter and many people will die. What the hell is going on here, Richie? I thought this was just going to be some strange murder investigation involving a kooky religious nut. This craziness is really happening," Janice said.

"I thought we explained that rather clearly," Chase said.

"Well, yeah, maybe. But obviously not clearly enough."

You are not supposed to be here!

"Okay, which one of you just said that? Who is pulling the ventriloquism act?"

"Janice, neither one of us said a word," Richie said.

A feeling washed over them, and they turned to look at the bird in the cage. The beast glared back at them for several moments before reaching casually up with its talon to unlock the cage. In a lightning quick move, the bird launched itself from the cage and landed on Janice's chest. Its spike-like talons dug deep into her breasts until blood flowed freely from the wounds. The bird reared its head back to strike at her face, but Richie instinctively thrust his hand between the bird's beak and Janice's eyeball.

The long beak stabbed through Richie's flesh turning his hand into a human shish kabob. The bird struggled to back its head out, but Richie grabbed it by the neck. When he saw the difficulty his friend was having keeping the bird held down Chase entered the fray.

"Janice, run. Grab my keys and go lock yourself in my car," Richie called out.

The more they struggled the more damage was done to Richie's hand. He felt the bones breaking as the bird twisted its head to free its beak. Chase took off his shoe and began bashing the bird in the head which only seemed to aggravate the beast and did nothing to curb its assault. The moment Janice rolled up the door and started to run a portly security guard came trotting up to the unit. Janice shoved her way past him before he had a chance to react. He saw the commotion in the storage unit and drew his weapon.

"Five zero nine to dispatch. Please send assistance, I have a suspected break in at the Vault."

"Ten-four. I am calling the police and sending backup."

"Listen, it's not what you think," Richie said.

"Let go of the bird," Officer Robbins barked the order.

"You don't want us to do that," Chase said.

Richie took a quick inventory of the man and didn't like what he saw. The man's gun hand was shakier than Barney Fife's, and he was already resting his finger on the trigger. Richie knew that if either of them made any sudden moves the man would shoot one if not both of them.

"I said put the bird back in the cage," he said, glancing down with one eye to make sure he had disengaged the safety.

Chase began to say something, but Richie stopped him.

"Chase, this fool won't be reasoned with. I'm not sure what this damned bird is going to do, but we have to release it. As soon as I pull my hand free of its beak you dive to your right, and I will dive to my left. Hopefully, this asshole misses both of us."

Richie took a deep breath, let go of the bird's body and grabbed his impaled hand by the wrist and jerked it free. Blood spurted from the wound as he shoved Chase with his good hand. Both men dove for cover as the security guard opened fire putting two bullets into the bird. The force of the bullets knocked the bird backward onto the floor. It stood up, shook its head, ruffled its feathers, and then took a bead on the security guard who had no business carrying a firearm.

"Run," Richie screamed at the security guard who stood in the doorway, transfixed on the blood pouring down Richie's forearm.

Without hesitation the bird launched into flight, landing with its talons buried into each of the man's shoulders. The bird reared its head back, looked back at Richie and then drove its beak into the man's eyeball, through his brain and punctured through the rear of the man's skull. The bird repeated the motion through the man's other eye before launching itself through the door and out into the night.

In a panic they gathered their things, as many of the writings as they could carry and rushed out the door. Chase doubled back to grab something he noticed lying at the bottom of the bird's cage. Janice was still shaking when they got back to Richie's car.

"I heard gunshots. What happened?" she asked.

"I'm afraid, the beginning of the end is what happened."

Chapter Thirty-Two

Samael camped outside the service entrance to Little Caesar's Arena watching workers ferry supplies in and out of the building. When no one was looking he stowed away in a crate of produce and was wheeled into the venue unseen. From there he made his way to the concourse where he found a place to hide until people began filing in.

A rhythmic sea of red and white flooded through the arena and Samael simply blended in with the crowd of hockey fans. He learned all sorts of trivial facts about hockey from the fans as they chatted each other up while trying to best each other's stories. Sports fans sure had a lot of weird traditions Samael didn't understand like throwing hats out onto the ice, but he was starting to grasp the odd behavior with each new conversation he absorbed. The tradition of throwing octopi onto the ice truly intrigued him. Tired of walking he found a spot on the upper deck railing and watched the crowd as they funneled up the escalator. That's when he spotted him, the one who was not supposed to be here.

Randall Gates kept his distance from the throngs of people pushing and shoving through arena just in case. He wasn't sure if what he had hidden in his jacket was giving off an odor, but there was no reason to take any chances on getting caught. He had the octopus packed on ice in a plastic bag and then wrapped up with newspaper and a towel. It was a storied tradition that had lost favor when the new arena was built, but it was a tradition he and his brother had enjoyed for many years.

The thought of Randall's brother brought forth a stream of tears. His younger brother had only been forty years old, much too young to die from a heart attack. But Jacob was gone, and the tradition must continue. A tinge of remorse sent ripples through him as he wandered the beautiful new arena his brother never had the opportunity to visit.

Randall took his seat ten rows up from the glass, center ice. He paid a pretty penny for the tickets but this being Jacob's birthday it was worth the price. The buzzer sounded ending the scoreless first period. Several times throughout the period he thought sure the Wings were going to score and shoved his hand under his jacket to unwrap his present for the team. But the puck never saw the net, so the octopus never saw the ice.

He made his way up to the concourse and after ten minutes in line he grabbed a beer and a coney before heading back to his seat. He was surprised to see a young boy seated in the seat next to his which had remained empty throughout the first period. He looked around, but there was no sign of an adult with the child.

"Hello there, my name is Randall, what's yours?" he asked while taking his seat. He craned his head around looking for the boy's parents but didn't see anyone.

"Samael."

Puzzled Randall asked, "Did you mean Samuel?"

"No, I meant Samael."

The boy slowly turned his head to look at him and Randall suddenly felt ill. His skin grew cold and clammy.

"And yes, I know what my name means," Samael said, releasing a wicked grin upon the man.

Randall could feel the child's probing eyes as he watched the Red Wings and Blackhawks take the ice for the second period. How did the child know he knew what the name meant in Hebrew? He ignored the ominous sensation surrounding him and turned his attention back to the game.

The Wings won the faceoff and were gracefully moving the puck down the ice toward the opposing goal. The puck clicked back and forth from stick to stick as the team passed the puck down the ice until the forward was able break free and make a run for the goal. He stopped short, aimed, faked the number five hole, and then put the puck into the net at the one hole above the goalie's left shoulder. The crowd roared, sirens erupted, and strobes flashed all around the arena as the announcer screamed, *He shoots, he scores*!

As Randall was reaching inside of his jacket, he realized the boy was still staring at him. A sense of foreboding washed over him when he saw the boy had taken on a ruddy complexion and his eyes were strobing just like the light on the top of the goal. At first, he thought it was merely a reflection, but then understood how dead wrong that assumption was and a fear unlike anything he had ever experienced before invaded him.

"You are not supposed to be here," Samael said with a scowl.

"What did you say? I have my ticket stub right here, now go find your parents and leave me alone," Randall said, having to force the words out through his tightening throat.

Randall gasped at a sudden slithering movement beneath his coat. The octopus was beginning to move. But the damned thing was dead, wasn't it? Maybe he only thought it was dead. He slowly moved the lapel of his jacket and peered into the darkness to find an unblinking eye with an eerie, horizontal pupil staring back at him. He tried to yank the animal away from his body, but its tentacles held him firmly in their grasp.

The crowd was still celebrating the Wings goal, oblivious to the man's plight. Inside of his jacket the octopus began to grow in both size and strength cutting off Randall's ability to scream for help. The animal was constricting itself around his midsection and chest like an anaconda while more than tripling its original size. The pressure was so intense his blood began to thunder in his ears with every beat of his own heart. His head turned an ugly shade of purple from the lack of oxygen and increased blood pressure.

One of the creature's tentacles manage to free itself from his over garment and coiled around his throat. The octopus had grown to unimaginable proportions and had now garnered the attention of fans seated in the vicinity who began scrambling backward away from the beast.

Across the other side of the arena Javier Ortego stood up and screamed while fighting eight writhing appendages emerging from under his coat. The commotion caused the players on the ice to stop skating and the arena announcer turned off the music in case he needed to call for medical personnel.

Randall's eight-armed contraband had grown so large one of its suction cups covered the man's entire face and forehead. He could hear the bones in his chest cracking as the beast tightened its grip around his midsection. The sound it made reminded him of an old army buddy who would crunch down and eat the cartilage and bones when eating chicken wings. Mercifully, Randall was long dead by the time the creature ripped his head from his body and in an ironic twist tossed both halves of the man onto the ice.

At the same moment six sections away Javier Ortega's lifeless body arced through the air and over the glass, landing on the ice with a sickening slap. Three others followed suit as more of the cephalopods emerged from their smuggler's coats. There were six creatures in all, each of them ten times larger than their natural state and a hundred times more ravenous.

Samael watched the carnage unfold for another ten minutes before it became tedious. On the way out of the arena he stooped down for a slice of half-eaten double pepperoni pizza laying on the floor and a watered-down iced tea to wash it down with. As soon as he met up with the panicked crowd heading for the exits, he merged with them and ran out into the street where he made his way down to Woodward Avenue sporting a venomous grin.

~ ~ ~

"Richie, you need to see a doctor," Chase said.

Richie's hand had festered and turned black around the wound where the bird's beak impaled him. The necrosis was spreading at an alarming rate and Chase knew Richie would lose his hand if it wasn't looked after immediately.

"That isn't an option," he said, unwrapping a bloody towel from around his hand to look at the wound. It had gotten much worse in the last ten minutes.

"Chase is right, you need to see a doctor," Janice said.

"And then what? You know damned well there isn't a doctor on this planet who is going to know what to do about this. It all makes sense now."

"What makes sense?"

"Porter. I didn't give it much thought at the time other than attributing it to his entire bat shit crazy persona, but the man had a hook for a right hand."

"You mean a prosthetic hook?" Chase asked.

"No, just a hook like you would get at any hardware store. I never really got a good look at it, but now that I think about it, I'll bet it was just screwed into the bone."

"Why are you telling us this?" Janice asked.

"Because you are going to have to cut off my hand before this shit spreads throughout my body," Richie said.

"Why me?" Chase asked.

"You're the only one here with any kind of medical training."

"What in the hell are you talking about? I'm a journalist, and a hack novelist," Chase replied.

"What about your vet training?"

"I worked two summers in high school helping Doc Murphy birth calves."

"Close enough."

"Richie, I have no clue how to amputate your hand. I could very well kill you."

"I'm going to die if you don't. I can feel this shit creeping up my hand, soon it will be in my arm and then throughout the rest of my body."

Chase looked down at Richie's hand which was now blacker than it had been just one minute ago. He could actually see the necrosis chewing away at the living tissue. He nodded and went into the kitchen to see what he could find.

"Is there anything you need me to do?" Janice asked.

"Gather up as many clean towels as you can find. See if there is any gauze or hand towels as well. Also, I'm going to need something to secure the bandages once the deed is done."

"You need something hot too," Richie said.

"Hot?" Chase asked.

"You are going to be cutting through major blood vessels so you will need to cauterize the wound immediately."

Chase thought about that for a minute and asked, "Where is your iron?"

"You can't possibly be entertaining this nonsense," Janice said.

"In the hall closet, but that won't get hot enough," Richie said. "Janice, this has to be done."

"It will if I put it on the stove burner," Chase said and went to the linen closet to get the iron.

Chase turned on the smallest burner on the electric stove to high. While it was heating up, he rummaged through all of Richie's kitchen drawers but couldn't find what he was looking for. The only knives the man owned were short bladed and dull.

"Don't you have a butcher's knife or a meat cleaver?" he called from the kitchen.

Richie's stomach did a turn. "Damn, that just made this whole thing so much more real. No, the best I have is steak knives or a pocketknife in my sock drawer."

"Aren't you going to need something hard and rigid?" Janice asked, following Chase out to the garage.

"Yes, like a hatchet or an axe, or even a machete. Check that camping gear over there on that wall."

The two of them tore through the three shelving units in the garage but didn't find anything useful. Tools were scattered across the garage floor along with enough camping gear for half a dozen campers, but nothing sharp enough to perform an amputation. Chase sighed and stood in the center of the room scanning the walls and under the shelving units.

"What about that?" Janice said while pointing at the lawn mower.

"You want me to stick Richie's arm in a running lawn mower?"

"No, you adorable idiot. We can use the blade," she said with a soft shove to Chase's arm.

Chase turned the mower over, took the blade off the machine and set it on the work bench. He used a butane torch to burn off the old grass clippings and hopefully sterilize the blade in the process.

"I don't mean to be a nag, but my hand is almost entirely black," Richie called from inside the house.

Chase wrapped a towel around the hot mower blade and carried it into the house. Janice brought in a roll of duct tape and a concrete cinder block and set them on the kitchen counter. Chase wrapped one end of the mower blade with duct tape and set the metal end on the glowing burner. Richie stood at the kitchen counter with his arm laid flat across the block. Janice folded a clean towel and put it under his wrist. She took another pile of towels and put them at the end of his fingers to catch the blood.

"I somehow feel that won't be necessary. My hand is ice cold, I'm sure there isn't a drop of blood in it that isn't dead and black," Richie tried to be light-hearted, but it was obvious he was scared shitless.

It won't do any good. I am already inside of you.

Richie had been looking straight in both of their faces and knew neither of them had uttered a single word. Zera's words pecked away at his brain, and he found it somewhat amusing that the only remorse he really felt was that according to her, Chase would share in his fate.

"Okay, as soon as I lift the blade from the burner you put the iron on the burner to get it hot."

"One hit and make it count. Got it?" Richie asked.

"Yeah, I got it," Chase said with trembling hands.

"Look buddy, don't worry about it. No matter what you do, it can't be any worse than what is already happening to me."

Chase nodded and without hesitation brought the glowing red piece of steel down on his friend's wrist, severing it from his body. Janice moved quickly and cauterized the wound with the iron within seconds of the necrotic hand being severed. The kitchen filled with the horrendous stench of burning human flesh. Chase struggled to keep Richie on his feet until the bleeding stopped and then laid him down on a pre-made bedroll on the floor. As soon as the flesh stopped smoldering Janice poured a bottle of alcohol over the cauterized stump and wrapped it with gauze. Merciful sleep took Richie in its embrace.

~ ~ ~

Rose Marie tore through room after room with no luck. There wasn't even so much as a kazoo let alone seven trumpets. Maybe she had misunderstood Medee, but every time she scoured her memory, she always came back to Medee telling her she needed to find the seven trumpets, one for each of the becoming vessels.

She found solace in the decay of the old nursery with its decrepit cribs and tattered blankets where she curled up into a corner to think. It wasn't fair she was the one left to shoulder the burdens of their fate alone. She was almost asleep when she was roused by an odd sound.

Click, click, click, resounded off the dingy walls. The sound burrowed into her brain until it was all she could think about.

"What are you two boys doing out there?" she called out to Rai and Chase Jr.

The boys did not respond, but the clicking continued. Rose Marie moved from room to room but was unable to locate the source of the irksome din. The other two were downstairs running around in the balcony and didn't seem to be bothered with the sound. And while their cavorting about was annoying, it was a noise she could tolerate.

Click, click, click.

"What in the hell is that aggravating sound," she screamed down onto the balcony with her face an angry shade of crimson.

Both boys turned their faces up to her and shrugged.

Click, click, click.

"Did you hear that?" she asked.

Both boys simply shook their heads and went back to running through the rows of seats playing tag. Disgusted with their ambivalence Rose Marie went in search of the raucous culprit. She checked each of the classrooms one by one and found nothing until she made her way into the toy storage room where the laundry chute led to the basement. The grating sound echoed up from the lower level of the church and reverberated upward off the walls of the tin shaft.

Click, Click, Click

She started down the long corridor toward the stairs but then stopped. She wasn't sure if she wanted to go down into the basement all by herself. Thoughts of apprehension scurried around in her brain until the sheer absurdity of the situation presented itself with clarity. Her sole purpose was to destroy all mankind, what in the world was there for her to be afraid of.

Rose Marie made her way through the catacombs of the abandoned church, stopping every so often to admire the sheer lunacy that was Jessop Porter. The scribbling he left behind on walls, doors and ceilings would surely baffle even the sharpest philosophical minds for years to come. But she was well aware of the meaning behind his psychotic meanderings.

Click, click, click.

Once down in the dungeon-like basement she was able to track the sound much easier. She made her way through the ebon shrouds blanketing the subterranean ruins with cautious movements. The smell was atrocious, making her want to turn back, but she had to find out what was making enough noise to drive her insane.

The noise grew to a crescendo and she knew whatever was making the sounds lie just around the corner in the other room. She eased into the next room and was greeted by a macabre scene she would never have imagined in several lifetimes. In front of her stood a bird so hideous it was amusing. Clamped in its elongated beak was a wooden cross with wires dangling down to a hodge podge amalgamation of human bones. She would have considered it a skeleton except the bones were not arranged as they appeared in human anatomy.

The ulna was where the fibula should be, the humerus and femur had been swapped and the tibia was being used as the clavicle. The constant clicking Rose Marie was hearing was from the bird dropping the skull to the concrete floor on a wire, kicking it like a soccer ball up against the wall with a hand in place of a foot where it would then use the wire to return the skull to whence it came. If for not being so utterly bizarre it would have been quite the comical sight. When she entered the room, the bird dropped its plaything to the ground and looked up at her.

"So glad you could join me," the bird said.

"What kind of a strange creature are you?"

"I could ask the same of you," it replied, glancing her up and down. "I am what you seek."

"I do not seek a bird."

"But I am no ordinary bird."

"Okay, to be more specific, I am not seeking an extraordinary talking bird," Rose Marie said.

"Often in life things are not what they seem. You most of all should know better than to take everything so literally and at face value."

Rose Marie pondered the bird's words, but more so the creature's hubris attitude. A glint of awareness glistened her eyes and she smiled.

"You are one of the trumpets?" she asked.

"One in the same, at your service," the bird replied, folding its wing across its chest, and taking a bow.

"But I was told I needed to find seven trumpets. Are the other trumpets birds as well?"

The bird nodded.

"Where are they?"

The Ibis shrugged.

"You're not much help."

"I'm not supposed to be. You are the one in charge."

"No, I am not," Rose Marie argued with a stomp of her foot.

"Oh, yes you are."

A chill washed over Rose Marie, and she felt sick to her stomach. She was never supposed to be in charge. Or had that been Medee's plan all along?

"If you are one of the seven trumpets, how are you used?"

"I won't know the answer to your question until all the pieces are assembled together."

Rose Marie's face took a sour turn. "And if we can't do that? We lost one already so there are only six of us."

"Which is precisely why I am here. Medee sends you a gift. But with this gift she warns she will not be able to intervene or help you any further. This gift has depleted her energy to dangerous levels," the ibis squawked.

The bird's ebony chest heaved in and out, and the creature began making the most horrendous sound forcing Rose Marie to cover her ears. She had her eyes clamped shut and didn't see that Rai and Chase Jr. had joined them. Sounds of the bird's regurgitation efforts echoed off the concrete walls and caused her to gag.

"So cool," Chase Jr. said causing Rose Marie to open her eyes.

The ibis continued to heave like a cat trying to eject an enormous fur ball. Its cheeks were bloated, and a blackness oozed from the seams of its beak. Tiny, spindly fingers of blackness licked the air. First one, then two, then suddenly a dozen undulating assemblages wavered in the air like a sea anemone. The bird gave one, long hard cough and expelled a tumor which injected gloom into the room with its very presence. A stench of death permeated the air, and it took the trio several minutes to be able to breathe without gagging.

"What in the world is that?" Rose Marie asked.

"It is the last piece, so that you can all become," the bird answered.

"What are we supposed to do with bird yak?" Chase Jr. blurted out.

"You need to give it life. You need to help it to become."

"And just how are we supposed to do that?" Rose Marie asked.

"The same way you found your way here."

"But Medee showed us the way."

"Then follow her lead. As I have told you, you are the one who is in charge. And now, even more so," the ibis explained.

"Don't we need someone who is not supposed to be here?" Chase Jr. interrupted.

"Precisely child. You certainly are a smart one for being so ugly. And as luck would have it, there is one such person and she is with those two meddlers. You will be able to kill three meddlesome humans with one stone," the ibis said with a throaty laugh.

A sinister sneer spread across Chase Jr.'s face as he understood exactly what the ugly bird was talking about. He took the writhing mass of malice and stuffed it into his pocket. The boy giggled all the way up the stairs and out through their secret entrance of the church. The thingamajig in his pocket tickled his leg as it explored its new surroundings.

~ ~ ~

Janice tilted her head back and let the hot water cascade over the back of her head and down over her shoulders. She was hoping the water would wash away her lingering thoughts of the bizarre day. No matter what she tried to think of, kittens, puppies, tantric sex, nothing erased the constant image of Richie's hand flopping free of his arm and onto the kitchen floor where it writhed about like something out of a horror movie.

The sweet scent of coconut permeated the air as she covered herself in luxurious suds from her body wash. She never left home without a small bottle of her favorite soap tucked away in her purse. The steam opened up her sinuses making the aroma that much stronger. Suddenly she became acutely aware of her nipples hardening and moved her head from under the hot water. There was a cool breeze flowing through the bathroom.

"Did you get an eyeful, Richie?" she asked, thinking the man had snuck in and used the toilet without disturbing her as he had done many times in the past.

When he didn't say anything, she peeled back the shower curtain and peeked out into the room to find there was no one there.

From behind her a voice chilled her to the bone. "You are not supposed to be here," Chase Jr. said, his elbows propped up on the bathroom windowsill and his hands tucked under his chin.

"What the hell? You little pervert," Janice said, trying to cover herself from the wandering eyes of the creepy peeping Tom leaning in through the bathroom window.

The boy giggled. "You sure have big boobs."

"What in the hell do you think you're doing? You shouldn't be spying on people when they are in the shower."

"But she is supposed to be here, and you're not."

"Who is supposed to be here?" Janice questioned.

"Her," he said, pulling the writhing black mass from his pocket.

Janice quickly deduced something wasn't right and that she was in real trouble. She started to scream for Richie and Chase but the water from the shower got into her mouth and was so bitter it gagged her. The boy stretched his arm out as far as it would go with his hand facing palm side up. She stared wide-eyed at the object sitting on top of his hand. She could feel the malevolence oozing from the being as it licked out at her. The boy leaned as far forward into the room as he could and blew into his hand as if blowing her a kiss. She knew it was anything but.

The water had turned ice cold and a stench invaded the bathroom. Again, Janice tried to scream but her throat was choked off by the vileness of the water. The blackness landed between her breasts, and she no longer cared about her modesty. She clutched at the being, trying to rip it off her skin but it held fast.

The bristling entity moved up her chest toward her face while its black tendrils lashed out against her lips, forcing her to clamp them shut. Fearing it may launch an assault on her eyes she clinched them shut as well. She covered her nose and eyes with her hand while trying to dislodge the thing with her other. For several moments it attempted to pry her lips apart, but then suddenly stopped.

It was quiet, too quiet. And then the boy giggled. Janice opened her eyes and looked down at her chest, there was nothing there. She glanced around the room before settling her eyes to the bottom of the tub just in time to see the creature climbing up her leg. She clamped her legs shut but was a smidgen too slow and the writhing ball of blackness disappeared inside her.

Tears rolled down Janice's face as she felt her humanity being ripped away, followed by her life.

~ ~ ~

"What the hell? How long have I been out?" Richie asked, trying to scoot himself into the sitting position on his couch with only one arm.

Chase picked up his phone and looked at the time. "A little more than sixteen hours."

"What is all this?" he nodded at a mess of paperwork scattered across the living room floor.

"They are Porter's notes."

"Anything interesting?"

"Yes, what I can glean from the gibberish is pretty fascinating. It seems our man Porter was quite the scholarly genius at one time. From what I can gather everything started going downhill once he discovered a colony of birds."

"Like the one we saw in the storage unit?" Richie asked.

"Exactly. There are a lot of scientific notations at first, size, weight, coloring, but then he kind of goes off the rails. He states not only were the birds talking to him, but they were also tormenting him to the point he tried to kill one of them."

"Tried?"

"And failed. I'm not sure how much of this is factual and how much is prattle. Porter claims to have put one of the birds in the oven, shot it with a shotgun, and even cut the damned thing's head off only to find it squawking about in the morning, none the worse for wear."

"Anything in all that gibberish that might lead us to the other birds, trumpets or whatever the hell they are?" Richie asked.

"Nothing I can decipher. But I have an idea."

"Am I going to like it?"

"Probably not."

"Lay it on me."

"We take all this stuff and go see Janice's father and see if he can decipher it."

"It's not the worst idea I've heard all day. Speaking of Janice, where is she?"

"She went to take a shower."

"A cold shower? We've been talking for over half an hour; my hot water doesn't last that long."

"Maybe she took a bath," Chase asked.

"I've got a bad feeling about this," Richie said, struggling to get up from the davenport with only one good arm.

Chase got up, reached out a hand, and helped Richie to his feet. The two of them walked down the corridor to the bathroom. The dull sound of water cascading against the plastic tub insert echoed from the bathroom. Richie knocked softly, not wanting to startle her.

"Janice? Janice, are you in there?"

Richie's gut did a flip flop when instead of Janice answering him the echoes of children's giggles forced their way passed the door. He turned the knob, but it was locked. Chase reached over and pounded on the door and called out to Janice with the same negative results. Without thinking Richie slammed a shoulder into the locked door to break it open but only succeeded in causing his damaged arm to explode into unbearable pain. A red stain began to creep across the gauze bandage covering his newly acquired stump.

Chase ran to the kitchen and returned with a butter knife. He wedged the knife between the door jamb and trim and wiggled it back and forth until he was able to pry the molding up enough to get at the door latch. He slid the butter knife up and down until he heard a click and then used the knife to push the latch in. As they barged into the room they were stopped in their tracks by the gruesome sight of Janice on her back in the bathtub with thick, black water spraying down into her agape mouth which was frozen in death's morbid sneer. The viscous water clung to her skin like burned motor oil and was fast approaching the rim of the bathtub. Her black eyes stared, unblinking at the ceiling. Her hands rose up out of the black water clutching at the air itself.

Chase turned and violently vomited into the toilet. Richie reached over with his good hand and turned off the water. Both men stared at the body not knowing what to do. Suddenly the surface of the water began to ripple, and air bubbles breached the surface. Chase thought it may be gasses being released by Janice's corpse until the splashing started. Something was under the surface of the black water.

Without warning someone, a child, leaped from the water and screamed, “Boo!”

Both Richie and Chase recoiled from the initial shock and then again once they fathomed there was a naked eight-year-old girl standing in the bathtub in front of them.

“What the fuck!” was all that Richie could manage to utter.

Chase was speechless.

“You said a bad word,” the girl said between chattering teeth.

Chase broke from his stupor and darted across the hall for a towel. When he returned no more than thirty seconds later, he felt the full weight of the situation. Within that short span of time the child had begun developing pustules all over her body. She was pestilence reborn.

She put her hands in front of her as if she were about to pray. Richie recalled the boy on the bus slapping his hands together before everyone began writhing on the floor of the bus in the throes of death. He shoved Chase out into the hallway and pulled the door shut behind them. A sick, wet sound slapped the door of the bathroom and the stench of rotten flesh and puss seeped out from under door. Giggles erupted from behind the door, and they could hear the girl climbing out of the window. Stunned, both men retreated for the interior of the house.

“I need to take a look at that,” Chase said, pointing to the blood-soaked bandage on Richie’s arm.

While Chase went into the living room to gather up the medical supplies Richie poured a glass of tap water and started rummaging around in the cupboard for pain killers. His arm was throbbing, but not as badly as his head was.

Chase spread out a clean towel and set Richie's arm down on it. He began slowly unwrapping the bandages from around the bloody stump. He happened to glance up and look out the kitchen window at an odd sight. Standing at the edge of the hedgerow was the naked girl, and Chase Jr. was standing right next to her. The boy smiled a wicked little smile at him.

"What the hell, man," Richie said, wiping water off the front of his shirt.

Chase pointed out the window to the two laughing children. The spilled water in the sink had turned black and putrid, giving off the smell of death as it oozed down the drain.

"Little son of a bitch tried to kill me," Richie said.

"They're back to having seven," Chase said.

"And that is not the immediate problem. I have a dead body in my bathtub with absolutely no way to explain it."

Chapter Thirty-Three

The sign above the gate read, *Interdenominational Music Festival, Bonfire and Worship Jamboree*, painting a smile across Serafina's face. This would be perfect and should prove to be a lot of fun too. Flowing notes and chords drifted across the open expanse causing the child to hum along with the music as she looked for a suitable vantage point to surveil the festivities. She found a place away from the gathering crowd but still close enough to watch, listen and eventually participate in this bewildering ritual.

Several long tables were arranged to deliberately funnel people to an entry point in the center of a fence surrounding the open field. A gate was opened at one end and several trucks entered through the compound, turned, and backed up to a scorched clearing of dirt. The trucks dumped their loads of broken pallets, old furniture, and scrap lumber into a large pile on the ground.

Seeing this, a throng of festival goers became excited and grabbed pieces of lumber to make a platform. On this platform they stacked pallets, higher, and higher, and higher. Over the din of construction, a song reached

Serafina's ears, something about a man named Jesus. Whoever he was, these people seemed to be enamored with him. She giggled as she wondered what kind of songs they might sing about her when all was said and done.

Serafina saw a table with a sign for free cider and donuts, so she meandered over to get a nibble. She watched the crowd with growing curiosity. People so different from one another, yet united in a common theme. This man they called Jesus. Even the parishioners she recognized as Muslims joined in. Strange indeed. She must really meet this man one day, before the complete destruction of mankind of course.

She sat back down in the grass with a donut skewered on her index finger while sipping cider and watching the throng of revelers. They sure were a happy lot. They had erected a mountainous pile of pallets into a tower. Several people scaled the mountain and were handed up chairs and their instruments.

A young man and woman arranged the chairs safely atop the wooden configuration, sat down and began to strum away at their guitars. Serafina found herself thinking happy thoughts which she found quite odd. Here she was, planning to annihilate each and every one of these humans and they were all smiling about it. Again, she giggled, of course they were oblivious to the fate that awaited them in their very near future.

The music continued, more cider and donuts were passed around, people laughed, danced, and sang as the night began closing in on them. Shadows frolicked across the grass as more and more people took to the makeshift dance floor in front of the wooden structure. Serafina found herself in an oddly festive mood and wanted to dance too.

The young man and woman atop the pinnacle of pallets were replaced by two young violinists and a flautist, a flautist who was not supposed to be here. Serafina's mood turned sour, the sounds coming from these three were not soothing to her. They were like the sap oozing from a maple tree, much too sweet to ingest.

A chill fell about her shoulders telling her night had fallen and it was her turn to take the stage. She no longer wanted to dance to their music so she would just have to create her own haunting melody. She concentrated on the center of the ersatz stage, deep within the tangle of wooden slats. It started as nothing more than a tiny flicker which she watched with great interest. She wondered if the musicians would smell the smoke in time to escape the flames.

After locking the gates once no one was paying attention to her, she made her way through the dancers to the front of the woodpile. The smoldering wood smoke teased her with its perfume, and she couldn't wait to incorporate the smell of burning flesh into the mix.

"Do you smell smoke?" one of the partygoers asked.

"Someone must have a campfire going somewhere close."

An older man with a megaphone who seemed to be in charge called up to the trio on the stage. "Come on down from there, it's almost time to light the bonfire."

Oh, it's time alright, Serafina giggled to herself while watching guitarists and other musicians create a semi-circle in front of the soon to be raging bonfire to hold hands and pray. She wanted to warn them they were much too close, but where was the fun in that.

The balding, tall, thin man showed up in front of the bonfire holding a torch. He looked out of place amongst the multitude of teenagers who slowly began to settle down when confronted with his authority.

"Our master would be pleased to see all of us here together, in unity and harmony no matter what prejudices the world forces upon us. Look around you, each and every one of you represent a sliver of who His children are. No two people have the same skin tone, eye, and hair color, each of you is unique. Except of course for the Hodgeson twins," he addressed the crowd while pointing to a set of identical twins. The teens erupted into laughter at his little joke.

"You fill us all with pride," a woman called out from behind them all.

One of the violinists on the top had gotten her foot wedged between the slats of a pallet and the other two were helping to free her. Despite his calm demeanor and considerate outward appearance, Serafina knew this leader of men was more than slightly angry. These three had interrupted his big moment. Little did the man know, he had a much bigger moment in store for him.

Serafina stood behind the seated crowd, cupped her hands around her mouth, and called out to the flautist on the pallet heap, "You are not supposed to be here."

Stanley Crawford turned to where the child had called out such a strange statement. Their eyes locked and he felt a sensation wash over him that caused him to tremble. Often at these gatherings he would be overcome with the Holy Spirit cleansing him of all sinful thoughts, but this was different. Much, much different. His stomach twisted into a painful knot, and he belched louder than he ever had in his life. The teenagers were slow to respond, but eventually a wave of laughter crashed over him, and he returned a weak smile. Belching was a natural bodily function after all.

Stan's stomach began to roil and the worst case of heartburn he ever suffered was burning through his esophagus. He swallowed hard several times, but his saliva caught in his throat, and he coughed up a mouthful of bile. And then the little girl's voice echoed in his brain telling him to do the unthinkable. He fought against the intrusion, but his fear trumped his faith. The teen-aged audience had been watching this spectacle with apprehension. They were not sure where the parable was hidden within this unorthodox behavior.

Stan turned, looked up at the three struggling youths on top of the mountain of pallets and mouthed, *I'm sorry*. With all eyes upon him he strode five paces to the left and picked up a one-gallon kerosene can and walked back to the pile. Before his odd behavior had registered with any of the onlookers Stan shoved the torch into the pile of pallets, opened the cap on the kerosene can and doused himself with the flammable liquid. The bonfire ignited and Stanley immediately erupted into flames.

Some of the people ran to help those stuck on top of the blazing inferno, others ran for the gate and the rest sat, stupefied, in their chairs. Serafina walked to where the flames were licking ever higher and inhaled as hard as she could. The teenagers were in shock as they watched this little girl suck in flames from the inferno. It wasn't until she turned and smiled at them that they comprehended the severity of their predicament.

Chairs toppled over and guitars reverberated sickly twangs as people leapt to their feet to run. Serafina exhaled a plume of fire into the crowd, igniting the terrified revelers. Human torches ran aimlessly into tents, lawn blankets and other people, setting ablaze everything in their paths. The teens who were lucky enough to make it to the gates before the others were rewarded for their efforts by being crushing to death by the rest of the fleeing mob.

A high-pitched whistle from heat vapors rushing through the seared flute split the night. Charred skeletons dangled from the burning structure as flames leaped high into the night sky. She drew in another lungful and started for the mob gathered at the gates. Trampled bodies were being even more damaged as the crowd realized what she was about to do. Some of the teens, trying to find some semblance of normalcy began recording her walking toward them on their cell phones.

Serafina drew within ten feet of the screaming, pleading mass of humanity and puffed up her cheeks for effect. As soon as she realized they were recording her she raised her hands as if slashing at the air with massive claws and roared her best dragon's roar.

A wail of approaching sirens rose above the cries of terrified teens. Red and blue lights were speeding toward the gate, right on time the child joked to herself. She smiled and exhaled her dragon's breath in a plume of flesh searing flames, igniting the thrashing horde. Serafina strolled off into the shadows whistling a little tune about this man named Jesus whom they were calling out to for salvation.

Chapter Thirty-Four

"Chase Coltrain, I told you never again," a cinnamon complected woman said, standing in the doorway of her animal clinic, her eyes sparkling with steadfast defiance.

"But Bev, you are my only option," Chase pleaded.

Beverly Stanton shoved her hands into the pockets of her stark white lab coat and stared back at her on again, off again, currently off ex-lover. Several different dogs could be heard barking from an unseen room in the back. A gray tiger kitten in a cage on the counter hissed at Chase causing him to move away from the impudent feline.

She glanced the man up and down and knew something just wasn't right. Sure, she had seen him haggard and tired before and knew he struggled with depression, but he didn't look tired, he looked beat down. And Richie Black looked ten times worse. The fluttering in her stomach warned her this was not a good idea, but against her better judgment she disregarded her apprehension and ushered the two men into her clinic.

"You nearly caused me to lose my license the last time. I'm a damned veterinarian, not a doctor. It is illegal for me to dispense so much as a bandage as medical treatment to anything other than an animal."

"But you are a surgeon, right?" Chase asked.

Beverly nodded and motioned for Richie to set his arm down on the examination table. She walked around the table and slid a stool out from under the counter so the man could sit down. Carefully she unwound the gauze bandages and gasped when she saw the mangled stump.

"What in the hell happened?"

"It's a long story," Richie said.

"You better find the time to tell the story if you want me to proceed."

"I cut it off," Chase said.

"With what, an axe?" Beverly asked.

"Actually, I used a lawn mower blade."

Beverly paused, put her long brown hair up into a bun and began to gather her surgical equipment. She was afraid to hear the answer but was compelled to ask.

"What on earth would possess you to cut your best friend's hand off with a lawn mower blade? Were you two fighting?" she asked.

"Hardly. I would kick his ass, lawn mower blade and all," Richie said while offering a weak smile.

"If I told you, you would think I was nuts. That we're nuts," Chase said.

"Oh, that train pulled out of the station the moment you two hooligans walked into my office," Beverly said, gathering up more supplies and moving them over within her reach.

"How bad is it?" Richie asked with a nod toward his stump.

"Not too bad considering. It was smart to cauterize the wound, it stopped it from getting too infected. Although, I do see some necrotic tissue around the edges of the wound that should be excised."

"Necrotic? Meaning dead?" Richie asked.

"Yes."

"Black?"

"Yes," she replied suspiciously.

"You need to cut that out right away," Richie said.

She could tell by the look on the man's face there was more to the story than what she was seeing. She inspected the wound closer and noticed the necrosis was moving up his wrist at a pace that should not be perceptible.

"Chase, what is going on here?"

He looked up into Beverly's deep, chestnut eyes filled with compassion and nearly erupted into tears. He scanned his memory as to how or why he let this perfect woman get away from him. For the life of him he couldn't even remember when it happened, let alone the circumstances surrounding their breakup.

"Go on, tell her," Richie said.

"Tell her what?"

"Everything. She has a right to know. If we fail to stop this from happening, she will die with the rest of them."

Beverly turned her attention away from Chase and shot a peculiar glance at her clandestine patient. "I would ask if that were the drugs talking but I haven't even given you anything yet."

"I see by the crucifix around your neck you appear to be a religious woman," Richie said.

"I am a Christian, yes. I don't practice the faith as well as I should as of late, but I will find my way back eventually. What does my religion have to do with your hand getting chopped off?"

"How much do you know about the Book of Revelation?" Chase asked.

"I know it's scary as hell and I do find it hard to swallow most of it. I mean a dragon spitting out frogs, that's a tad bit too hard to believe. I try to focus on the good parts of the bible," Beverly said.

"You mean like the plagues, floods, human sacrifice and nailing a man to a cross parts," Richie panned.

"Okay smart ass. Keep talking like that and I won't give you anything to numb the pain before excising this wound. You still haven't answered my question. What does any of this have to do with religion?"

"According to the Book of Revelation prior to Armageddon there will be seven seals opened, seven trumpets sounded and lastly seven vials will be poured over the earth. At which time chaos will ensue and the war for humanity will begin," Chase explained.

"Are you trying to tell me that God has finally become so fed up with humanity that he is willing to bring about the end of days?" Beverly asked.

"Actually, it's worse than that. Far worse," Richie said.

"How could anything be worse than Armageddon?" Janice asked without looking up from Richie's wounded arm.

"I don't have much of a clue when it comes to the Bible but in the biblical scenario of Armageddon the believers are safe from harm are they not?" Richie asked.

"That would be the generally accepted interpretation of the Bible, and yes, I believe so as well," Beverly answered.

"What if it wasn't God who released these plagues? What if somehow Satan was able to procure these vials for himself. Wouldn't that then mean his brethren would be the ones who were spared, and it would be God's children who would be put to the sword?"

Chase spent nearly forty-five minutes relating the story to Beverly with Richie filling in additional details while she attended to his wound. By the end of his far-fetched account he was surprised to see she appeared to be taking him seriously.

"You are not having the reaction I expected," Chase said.

"Look," she said, pulling her phone out of her pocket and queuing up a video. "This happened at a religious gathering late last night. And trust me, I'm surprised, flabbergasted is more like it. How can this be happening?"

Chase felt sick to his stomach watching the carnage left behind by an eight-year-old little girl who seemed to thoroughly enjoy her butchery. What made matters even worse was knowing there were six more of these wicked little children ready to wreak havoc on all of humanity. And then he thought about the seafood restaurant and a queasiness washed over him when he realized they didn't know if these demons intended to kill just humans, or all living creatures on the planet. What purpose would a barren rock serve?

Not wanting to think about what had just been revealed to her, Beverly returned to what she knew.

"This is going to hurt," she said to Richie.

"More than a dull lawn mower blade swung by a scrawny man with piss poor aim?"

"I imagine not."

She cleaned Richie's wound with sterilized water that was a mere two degrees above freezing which was excruciating at first, but then numbed the area making it less painful for her to excise the dead tissue. Black tendrils crept up the man's arm faster than she could cut them away. She soon realized that the more she cut at the dead tissue, the more it grew as if it were a defense mechanism.

"What's wrong?" Richie asked, sensing there was something wrong by the woman's daunted expression.

"I have to ask, what in the hell caused your injury?" Beverly asked.

"A bird," Richie replied dryly.

"A bird? As in tweet, tweet, kind of bird?"

"It sounded more like a belch or fart than a tweet, but yeah, a big, black ugly ass bird."

"It was an ibis according to the sign on the cage. A Northern Bald Ibis to be exact. It was trying to peck out someone's eye when Richie intervened and the damned thing skewered Richie's hand with its long beak. Immediately his hand began turning black," Chase said.

"But it wasn't just a bird, it was one of the seven trumpets," Richie added.

"As in the trumpets mentioned in Revelation?" Beverly asked in a skeptic's tone.

"One in the same."

"That is both disturbing and interesting at the same time. Take a look at this," Beverly said, opening up a desk drawer and taking out a sheet of paper which she handed to Chase.

"Holy shit, you've got to be kidding me. Hidden in plain sight. Isn't that what Porter said?" Chase asked and handed the flyer to Richie.

Ritchie scanned over the flyer announcing the arrival of six rare Turkish Northern Bald Ibis donated to the zoo by an anonymous donor. The birds were scheduled to be unveiled during the upcoming weekend with only a handful of tickets being auctioned to the highest bidders. There was a list of special guests, most of whom were zoologists and veterinarians. Beverly's name was on the list.

"Beverly, how would one go about killing a bird that was deemed indestructible?" Richie asked.

"I supposed one wouldn't. What makes you think these birds are indestructible?"

"According to the man's notes who previously owned the bird that attacked Richie, he tried to kill the thing many different ways, but nothing he tried worked, including beheading the creature," Chase said.

"If what you are saying is true and these birds are not really birds, but the seven trumpets referred to in the Book of Revelation then they are intended to be sounded," Beverly said.

"But sounded how?" Richie asked.

"I don't think that is of any consequence. They simply have to be silenced, not killed."

"And how are we supposed to silence them?" Chase asked.

Beverly smiled and disappeared from the room for a moment. The men could hear her rummaging around in what they believed to be a storage closet. She returned triumphantly to the room holding a cylindrical gray-silver object in her hand.

"Duct tape?" Richie asked.

"It fixes anything and everything," Beverly responded and handed the roll to Chase. "I am assuming if they can't open their beaks, they can't trumpet."

"It makes more sense than anything else we've come up with so far," Chase said.

"Richie, I am going to give you something that will put you out while I work on your arm some more," Beverly said.

"I'd really rather not, considering the circumstances."

"If I don't give you something to ease your pain and help you sleep you will more than likely pass out from the pain anyway. At least this way I can control how long you will be unconscious," she said.

"Fair enough I suppose," Richie said and laid back down on the exam table. He thought to himself that maybe, just maybe if Beverly let him sleep long enough all of this would be over when he woke up.

Beverly made Richie comfortable and injected him with a human sized dose of animal tranquilizer. She prayed her calculations were correct, and she wasn't going to accidentally kill the man. Her brain was treading water in a sea of confusion. None of this could possibly be real, and yet, deep down she knew it was. Chase Coltrain might have pissed her off quite often, but it was never for lying to her. Whether she wanted to admit it or not, the strange events of the past few days were making a lot more sense in light of this new context.

Chase watched as the woman who was once the love of his life cut away flesh from the best friend he had ever had the privilege of knowing. Each sliver of flesh Beverly excised she carefully dropped into a stainless-steel pan sitting on the table next to Richie's arm. She then cauterized the newly damaged tissue. The examination room reeked of seared human flesh, so Chase stepped outside for a breath of fresh air.

Morning had broken and a bruised eggplant sky hung above the city. Traffic was sparse, in fact there were more joggers and dog walkers in the park across the street than there were cars on the road. Chase watched the passersby who were oblivious to the malevolence threatening their very existence. He wished he could trade places with any one of them, even the dogs.

He found himself feeling somewhat contented. The sunrise was gorgeous, the temperature perfect and other than seven little miscreants hellbent on the annihilation of the human race running rampant through the city, things in his life were getting better.

"Chase, can you come in here for a moment, please," Beverly called.

When he walked into the examination room the look on her face set off alarm bells in his head.

"Is something wrong with Richie?"

"Not Richie per se, but pieces of him. Look," she said, pointing to the stainless-steel pan she had been collecting the excised tissue in.

Chase couldn't believe what he was looking at. There was half a dozen thread like piece of Richie's flesh in the bottom of the pan wriggling around like some sort of larvae. One was even trying to crawl up the side of the pan.

"Am I safe to assume this is not supposed to be happening," Chase said.

"It gets even stranger. Look over here," Beverly said, directing his attention to a microscope with a piece of Richie's excised flesh trapped between two slides.

Chase looked through the eyepiece and saw the black piece of flesh had an odd texture to it. He dialed up the magnification and focused until the image was crisp. It just wasn't possible what he was seeing. He turned to look at Beverly.

"Is this what I think it is?" Chase asked.

"If you think it looks like a feather, then yes, it is what you think it is."

"Richie is turning into a bird?"

"Or a trumpet," Beverly replied.

Chapter Thirty-Five

Rose Marie was incensed with the boy for failing to kill his father and the meddlesome cop. But on the other hand, she wanted to kiss him for the information he brought to her. She read the flyer over again for the third time. These repulsive birds had to be the trumpets, they just had to be.

She had managed to assemble three of the six others, but she knew Cecilia, Serafina and Samael were going to prove to be tough customers. During the night she had felt Medee's tether connecting them weaken and snap. They no longer had a connection to their realm, and she feared it would remain that way until she was able to begin this war. And she was oddly okay with that.

Victory was so close she could almost taste its sweetness. All she had to do now was get them all together in one place and retrieve the trumpets together. Once they were able to get to the zoo the rest would be child's play. Something was bothering her though. As all powerful and all-knowing as He was, why would He entrust the salvation of these wretched humans to just two pathetic losers? Rose

Marie couldn't help but think there was a factor in all of this she was missing. A particularly crucial factor.

~ ~ ~

Timmy McAuliffe stared at his closet door as shadows undulated through the murky darkness. His nightlight was not strong enough to chase the inkiness away from that far across the room, and he was certain he could see a pair of eyes blinking back at him. Tiny tears escaped the corners of his eyes as he recalled the fight with his stepfather earlier in the day when the man flew into a rage, took his closet door off the hinges, and carried it down to the basement. At least Chet didn't make him sleep down in this basement this time.

"There you little whiner, now the monsters will be able to get you!" the man screamed as he stomped down the stairs dragging the boy's bedroom door behind him with a series of ominous thuds.

Timmy's mother was at work and was not there to soothe his fears. He knew he was getting too old for this *bullshit,* but he was not old enough to ignore his fear no matter what Chet said.

Cecelia watched the boy for several hours while trying to remain as quiet as a church mouse. As she watched the child, waiting until the perfect moment to unleash her terror upon the lad she contemplated the boy's situation. A sensation, an unfamiliar emotion swirled around deep within her being and she began to feel sorry for the child which confused her. She didn't even possess the capacity for remorse or empathy so where were these emotions coming from?

It was the big man. Even exiled to his never-ending nightmare he was able to claw at her, imbedding his talons of guilt into her psyche. The child would not even aid her in her quest to become so why torture the poor boy? It was the boy's mother she was after. She was the one who was not supposed to be here. But didn't that also mean the child was not supposed to be here as well, so why did she feel the urge to spare him?

Cecelia's thoughts were a jumbled mess, and she could not think straight. In frustration she burst from the shadows into the boy's bedroom causing him to cry out in panic. Chet McAuliffe stormed up the stairs, stomping dramatically with each boot laden step so quickly it was as if he had been waiting on the stairs until Timmy became too frightened to stifle his cries.

"Boy, what are you fussing about now? I'm going to give you something to cry about," he hollered, pulling his belt through the belt loops, folding it over and snapping it loud enough Timmy could hear the leather crack like a bullwhip.

Timmy cringed in fear. He wasn't sure who scared him more, Chet or the little girl with no color and strange, dark eyes.

Chet glanced up from the belt to see a little girl standing at the top of the landing. Cecilia glared down at the abusive man and let a contemptuous grin part her lips. But her derision was laced with a tinge of pity.

"Who the fuck are you?" Chet demanded.

Frustrated and unable to deal with this myriad of emotions coursing through every single fiber of her being Cecelia merely placed her tiny hand in the middle of the man's forehead, grunted and shoved him backward. As Chet began tumbling down the stairs, he couldn't help but wonder how such a small child managed to possess such brute strength.

As the man tumbled down the stairs Cecelia started after him. Once he came to rest at the bottom landing, she bent down and whispered in his ear.

"There is only the darkness."

Fear invaded Chet's very soul as a blackness chewed away at his essence. It was a blackness he recognized. It was his closet when he was but a child. He could see his father's muddy boots through the crack in the bottom of the door. The astringent odor of stale cigarette smoke stung his nostrils and stole away his breath. The darkness continued to masticate his brain and soon even the sliver of light disappeared. He reached for the doorknob but there wasn't one. He reached out to pound on the door and found only hollow darkness. Chet McAuliffe began to scream an unending scream.

Cecelia turned to look back up the stairs at Timmy who had timidly left the safety of his room to investigate the noise. She put a finger to her lips and turned toward the front door.

Cecelia left the McAuliffe house angrier than she had ever been. The entire surface of her skin bristled with wrathful energy as if she were being punished for being denied. She was being made to understand that her corporeal self was not who she was, and she should be in control of the emotions being forced upon her by the ones who were not supposed to be here.

The sky above her began to lighten, signaling the sun was about to rise over Lake St. Clair. But Cecelia was in no mood for a sunrise. As she walked through the upscale neighborhood, she stretched out her arms, put her palms facing outward at the houses lining each side of the street. The first sounds to reach her ears was the faint buzzing, chiming, and ringing of alarm clocks jerking the citizens of this bedroom community from their peaceful slumber. The next sounds to reach her ears were their screams of terror.

With each passing house the shroud of shadows devoured more and more real estate. By the time her anger abated, three suburban blocks were veiled under a blanket of endless night.

Karen McAuliffe turned onto her street after a long night at work and was in disbelief at what she saw. She slowed the car to a crawl thinking there had been a broken watermain and she was driving into black water. Everything was dark in front of her, pitch black in fact. She swore she had watched the sun pierce the horizon as she drove home from the medical center as it did every morning. How could it be as dark as night again? She glanced up into the rear-view mirror and saw that it was indeed daylight outside, but only behind her.

Karen slammed on her brakes, put the car into park and got out to look around. There wasn't a single light on in any of the houses, but she knew her neighbors would all be getting ready for work. When she heard their gut wrenching, shrieks of pure terror echo through the neighborhood she knew something was very wrong.

She cautiously walked down the block, her car door still standing wide open. There appeared to be animals running around and rolling in the yards, but as she got closer, she realized these were not animals, but people. Her neighbors.

Karen suddenly felt nauseous and bolted for her house.

"Timmy," she screamed as she picked up the pace.

Manicured lawns on either side of her were filled with writhing, screaming neighbors with their hands clamped over their eyes. As she ran toward her son, she realized her house was the only one in a three-block radius with a porchlight emitting a soft, yellow glow.

"Timmy," she screamed between gasps for air.

Her son was sitting on the porch with his hands over his ears and his eyes clamped shut. Once she was in their yard she understood why. From inside the house Chet was screaming nonstop at the top of his lungs.

"What happened?" she asked her son.

"Chet won't stop screaming. I didn't do it, mommy," he said, wiping his shirt sleeve across his runny nose.

The sound of screen doors flying open reverberated through the neighborhood as more and more of her neighbors stumbled out into their yards. She felt the shadows clutching and grasping at her with ebony claws and knew they couldn't stay. She grabbed her son up into her arms and started running down the street toward the light.

Chapter Thirty-Six

Richie sipped at his coffee trying to will himself back from La la land. His arm was throbbing, but it wasn't anything he couldn't handle. Besides, the pain kept him on edge which was a good thing as far as he was concerned. He reread the Detroit Free Press article for the third time and still couldn't digest it.

"What are you reading?" Chase asked, as he poured himself a coffee.

"The Free Press."

"Ah, light fiction, always my favorite," Beverly said.

"Cute," Richie responded.

"What could possibly have you so engrossed in the Detroit Free Press?" Chase asked.

"Quite frankly it doesn't make any sense. According to this article sunrise this morning didn't happen for a community on the shores of Lake St. Clair."

"What do you mean *it* didn't happen?"

"According to this, the sun never came up. The neighborhood is still dark."

"What the hell. How is that even possible?" Chase said as he snatched his phone off the counter and searched for videos of the incident.

Chase held his phone out so Beverly and Richie could watch the video as well. All three of them were in total disbelief at what they were seeing. It just wasn't possible for the sun to shine everywhere except for one neighborhood.

"It's Thursday morning, we have until Saturday to get into the zoo and get those birds safely into our care. Either one of you have a plan?" Beverly asked.

"We? There is no we, you are staying out of this," Chase said.

"On whose authority do you speak?" she asked with her hands planted firmly on her hips.

"Bev, far too many people have died already. I don't want you involved."

"You should have thought of that before showing up on my doorstep with a bird man. No offense, Richie."

"None taken," Richie said while looking at small black feathers writhing around in the bottom of a stainless-steel pan. "She has a point, Chase. She wouldn't even be involved had it not been for us showing up at her doorstep begging for her help."

"That doesn't mean she should be putting her life at risk."

"If everything you are saying is true, my life is already at risk. Besides, you two are never going to get inside the zoo without my help," Beverly said. "Moreover, in all the time we have known one another, Chase, just how many times have you won an argument?"

Chase just rolled his eyes and shook his head in defeat.

"Look here. This is a video from someone's home security system. Watch the little girl walking in the middle of the street."

"The darkness spreads as she walks," Beverly remarked in awe. "If I thought you guys were full of shit before, I surely don't anymore after watching that."

Richie played the video several times but didn't see much of anything else on the replays. He set the phone down on the counter and poured himself another cup of coffee. The video they had been watching ended, a commercial played and then another video with a different angle played.

"Did you see that?" Chase asked, pointing to the phone's screen.

"All I see is black," Beverly said.

"No, look here, there is some sort of artificial lighting that breaks through the darkness but only for a second or two."

Richie looked at the video several times. "That is coming from the headlights of a car."

They watched the video over and over again until Richie finally saw Karen, shrouded in black, running toward her house. He let the video play until the end.

"Why is that one house still lit up when everything else on the block is dark?" Chase asked.

"I don't know, but I sure as hell am going to find out. Beverly, pull up a map of that neighborhood and see if we can't find which address that is."

"To what end?" Chase asked.

"What do you mean, to what end? So we can find out who lives in that house."

"But why? What purpose will that serve?" Chase asked, his voice taking on a frustrated edge.

"Because they were spared the fate of the entire neighborhood and I want to know why. What was different about that house? Up until now we have been throwing spaghetti at the wall hoping something sticks, and that is just not enough. We need a plan of attack," Richie said. He turned off the video and dialed a familiar number.

Richie walked outside and left Beverly and Chase to discuss matters between the two of them. Chase was still adamant about her staying out of the fray, and she was just as adamant she was teaming up with them.

"Angela, I need you to run an address for me," Richie said and gave the captain's assistant the information.

"Wait a minute, isn't that?" she started.

"Yes. Please hurry, I'll wait."

"The captain wants to see you."

"I am sure he does Angela, but I have to deal with this first."

The sound of her long fingernails pecking away at the keyboard forced him to pull the phone away from his ear.

"The name is McAuliffe. There is a Chet, a Karen and a boy named Timmy. No wants, no warrants, although there is history of domestic calls but no arrests. Seems the husband was on the giving end. Bastard," she said.

"Can you run Karen McAuliffe's credit card usage over the last twenty-four hours please," Richie said.

Once again, the phone emitted the annoying clickity-clack of Angela's long, manicured nails on her keyboard. Richie forced himself to stop and think if her typing ever bothered him before and he admitted to himself that it never had before. His nerves were stretched beyond their limits.

"Okay, it appears that Mrs. McAuliffe did indeed use her card to rent a room at a motel just off nine mile near the freeway."

"I figured as much. Thanks, you're an angel."

"Wait, how did you know she rented a motel room at seven thirty in the morning?"

"Easy Dr. Watson, she was coming home when everyone else was going to work meaning she probably worked the graveyard shift and even though she was traumatized by the madness in Morningside, she still needed some place safe to take her son and get some sleep. It was just a hunch really," Richie said.

"Don't forget, the captain. You take care of yourself now," she said and hung up the phone.

"Grab your shit, we have to hit the road," Richie said and went back inside.

"Where are we going?"

"To a motel to speak with Karen McAuliffe."

"What about me?" Beverly asked.

"How about you stay here and figure out just what equipment we will need to do a little birdnapping later on tonight."

~ ~ ~

"Well, that guy was a big help," Chase said.

"He was right, I do need a warrant to check the guest registry," Richie said while tossing his empty Styrofoam coffee cup into the back seat. He wanted another but he wasn't about to use his stakeout bottle in front of Chase.

"But he could have just let us take a peek."

"Yeah, well he didn't. But we really didn't need him to divulge any secrets. I already know which room she is in."

"How could you possible know what room she is in?"

"There are only twelve rooms in this motel, and we have seen people coming and going in eight of them. The two on the end have two identical work trucks parked outside, number seven has the curtains wide open which leaves number four. Curtains drawn tight and a do not disturb sign on the door," Richie said.

"Damn, you really are a detective, aren't you?" Chase said with a laugh.

"A lot of good that does us. It's just logical guesswork which is not good enough to go banging on doors. I need to know for certain she is in that room, or we risk spooking her."

"You said she has a kid with her, right. Let me try something," Chase said.

Chase searched the internet on his phone for several minutes until he found what he was after. He was able to download the application in less than two minutes, during which Richie was acting quite frustrated with him.

"Here, push the play button and hold the phone out of your window," he said.

Richie did as he was instructed and shot Chase a strange look when his phone began emitting a familiar tune.

"An ice cream truck, really? What is this supposed to do?"

"Just watch the motel room window."

Sure enough, after several playthroughs a little boy's cherubic face peeked through the curtains. His face matched the photograph they had of Timmy McAuliffe.

"I'm going to feel like an asshole now."

"More than usual?"

"Funny. We tricked the kid, and we don't even have any ice cream. Hey, run over to that convenience store and grab something for the kid," Richie said.

Chase nodded and trotted off across the street. The ice cream selection was meager, but he did manage to find something that wasn't freezer burned. He bought the ice cream and two coffees before heading back to the car. Neither man realized how dodgy they looked walking up to a motel room brandishing an ice cream for a six-year-old child, but Karen McAuliffe did.

Being a mystery novel and spy movie buff, Karen knew a few tricks. Before taking a nap, she had rearranged the furniture in the room so the bureau with a large mirror attached was facing the window and strategically positioned the curtains allowing her to see the men approaching the motel room door, but they couldn't see her watching them.

Karen's thoughts were a scrambled mess. She hadn't done anything wrong, and yet, two men were coming to her hotel room. Why? How did they even know where she was? The men didn't look too tough, so she didn't think they were hired killers. She chuckled to herself, hired by whom and why? With nowhere to hide she opted for the direct approach. She put Timmy in the bathroom, shut the door and grabbed her cell phone off the nightstand.

"What in the hell do you perverts think you're doing trying to entice my child with ice cream," she screamed as she jerked open the door to the motel room.

Both Richie and Chase stood there dumbfounded with guilty looks greasing their faces.

"Don't think I won't call the cops, because I will," she threatened, holding her cell phone up for emphasis. She hoped they wouldn't call her bluff because the last people she wanted to be talking to were the police. "And just so you know, I'm recording you perverts."

"Ma'am, we are the police, or at least I am. May we please talk inside instead of making a spectacle out here which is something neither of us wants?" Richie said.

Karen McAuliffe braced for battle but then relented in defeat and opened the door to invite them in.

"Let me start by saying I am in no way here to harm you, harass you or even arrest you. We just need a few answers, and then we will be on our way."

She nodded. "Answers about what?"

"About what you saw this morning."

"How do you know I saw anything?"

"I don't actually, but I do need to know what you saw, no matter how insignificant you think it is," Richie asked.

"Like I said, I didn't see anything. People were screaming and running around and all I could think about was my son. He was all I cared to see," Karen explained with tears welling up in her eyes.

"Did you see anyone?"

"I saw a lot of people."

"I mean someone who was out of place, not one of your neighbors. Someone not affected by the," Richie paused. "By the darkness."

"No, I didn't see anyone. Like I said, I grabbed my son, and I ran."

The bathroom door squeaked and all three of them turned their attention to a young boy peeking through a small slit. Richie waved for him to come out, but the boy looked at Richie's bandaged, handless arm and shook his head.

Chase dropped down to his knees and smiled at the boy. "I bet you saw something didn't you?"

Timmy looked up at his mom. When she gave him an *okay* wink he nodded to Chase.

"Come on out here son. We're not here to cause anyone any problems. We are just trying to find out what happened this morning. Can you tell us what you saw?" Richie asked.

"I saw a little girl."

"Where did you see this little girl?"

"She was hiding in my closet.

Karen McAuliffe stared at her son in disbelief. The look on her face told Richie she had no idea there was a little girl in her house.

"Did this little girl say anything?"

Timmy bobbed his head up and down.

"Did she tell you that you weren't supposed to be here?" Chase asked, earning a sideways glance from Richie.

Timmy paused and stepped back away from the men as if they frightened him. He moved over to his mother's side, still eyeballing them with obvious suspicion.

"How did you know that?" he finally asked.

"What little girl, Timmy? Did you know her? Was she from the neighborhood?" Karen interrupted.

Timmy shook his head hard. "A little girl with scary eyes. I never seen her before, honest mom."

"Can you remember what she said exactly?" Richie asked.

The boy shot his mother an apprehensive glance. Karen gave her son the best smile she could muster and nodded her head. Timmy glanced at the ice cream in Chase's hand prompting the man to hand over the melting confection. The boy slowly unwrapped the ice cream bar, brought it to his mouth with shaky hands and took a small bite.

"She said my mommy was not supposed to be here," he said with a mouthful of chocolate and vanilla.

"That is what she said, exactly?" Richie asked.

"Where was the little girl? How did she get into your house?" Chase asked.

Timmy shrugged. "She was in my closet. That's why I yelled for Chet because I was scared. I knew it would piss him off, but I was more scared of her than I am of Chet."

Karen furled her brow at her son's choice of language.

"Did she say anything else?"

The boy nodded and took another bite. "Chet was yelling at me and coming up the stairs and she got mad, but I think she said I wasn't supposed to be here too."

"Why was Chet yelling at you?" Chase asked.

"Because I'm a pussy."

"Timmy," Karen blurted.

"That's what he said. He always called me that when you were at work."

The scar of guilt on Karen's face told the men she had no idea her son was being mistreated while she was at work. She went from surprise to embarrassment and finally anger all in a matter of mere seconds.

"I am so sorry, baby, I didn't know he was calling you bad names."

"It's okay mom, I don't even know what it means."

Richie laughed and tousled the boy's hair. Timmy smiled up at him for a brief moment but then returned to his reserved gaze.

"You said the girl got angry. Did she get angry with you?"

Timmy shook his head, took a bite of the ice cream, and said, "Uh, uh, at Chet. I don't think she liked him yelling at me. And her voice kind of changed too."

"Changed how?" Richie asked.

"It got deeper."

"Deeper how, like a man's voice?" Chase asked.

Timmy nodded and finished the last bite of his ice cream. He threw the wrapper and stick into the waste can while Karen wet a washcloth in the sink to wash her son's chocolate coated face. Timmy kept trying to nod but his mother clamped down on his head to keep in from moving.

"Yeah, kind of like a man's. And her eyes changed too."

"Changed how?"

"Not sure. They just weren't as scary as they were when she was in my closet."

"Try to remember, son, it's very important. How did her eyes change?" Richie prodded.

Timmy thought long and hard about what was different.

"They were black at first. I mean all black, with no color or white part at all. And they looked mean, like she wanted to hurt me. But then when Chet yelled at me, they changed. They were kind of green for a minute, but then they got black again. That's when she pushed Chet down the stairs."

"How big is Chet?" Richie asked Karen.

Timmy jumped up and down stabbing his hand at the air when he reached the apex.

"Chet is a big man, detective," Karen answered.

"And you saw this little girl push him down the stairs?" Richie asked.

Timmy shook his head. "No, but I heard it. And then Chet started screaming. I got scared and hid under my bed, but I was scared under there too, so I ran passed Chet and out onto the porch. That's when mommy came and got me."

"Thanks, Timmy, you have been a great help. Mrs. McAuliffe, I have no idea what the situation is in Morningside right now, but here is some money for a couple of nights here while I try to figure someplace else to put you, or until it is safe to go back to you house," Richie said.

"Thank you for your offer, but we are never going back to that house, not to live anyway. I have a couple relatives up north and my aunt has been after me to come up and help her with her boutique in Traverse City which sounds pretty damned good to me right about now."

"Sounds like a perfectly good reason for a vacation," Chase said.

"If you really do decide to move, give me a call and I will make sure you are safe when you gather your belongings," Richie said and handed her his card.

Chase and Richie said their goodbyes and headed for the parking lot.

"You made her a promise you might not be able to keep," Chase said and slid into the passenger side of Richie's car.

"I'll keep it one way or the other," he said and put the car in gear without looking back at the two innocent faces gazing back from the motel room door.

~ ~ ~

The drive back to Beverly's clinic from the motel was long and quiet. Both men sipped at their tepid coffee and reflected on the day's events. Once they pulled down the alley behind the clinic, they could hear dogs barking even with the windows of the car rolled up. Richie shot Chase a glance while nodding for the glovebox. Chase reached into the compartment and retrieved a nine-millimeter with two clips of ammo. After several awkward, one-armed attempts, Richie loaded the weapon and cautiously approached the back door.

"What has you spooked?" Chase asked.

"Those dogs weren't barking even with us in the building. Something has them agitated."

Richie motioned for Chase to stay put, who was more than willing to heed his instruction. With his gun barrel pointed at the floor he moved through the storage room and into the clinic. No one was in the examination room, so Richie followed the sound of the dogs. When he rounded the corner into the kennel he had to stop and absorb the scene in front of him.

"Glad you could join us," Captain White said, glancing up from the floor where half a dozen dogs were roughhousing with him and fighting each other for his attention.

Sergio White got up from the floor as fast as his old bones would allow and dusted himself off. Beverly proceeded to kennel the dogs one by one with a smile greasing her face.

"Captain, what do I owe the pleasure?" Richie asked apprehensively.

"You've been dodging my calls, so I had to come directly to the devil himself so to speak."

"But how did you know where I was?"

"Richie, I was once a fairly good detective you know. Even trained a few good detectives myself once upon a time. I will admit, you do make for a difficult man to find, but your friend there leaves an encyclopedia of information hanging out there on the web which made it pretty easy to track the both of you down with the trail of digital breadcrumbs you left."

Chase just shrugged.

Richie paused to gather his thoughts. "So, what brings you here, captain?" he asked.

"Drop the captain routine, for now we're going to discuss this as friends."

"And just what is it we're going to discuss?"

"Richie, so help me Jesus, I'm not too old to bust your ass."

Richie nodded.

Sergio White waved his massive hands, gathering them all together. He reached his right hand out to Beverly and his left hand out to Richie. Chase followed suit and the captain led them in a short prayer.

"I'm sure you two have no idea, but Richie here knows that as well as being a police captain I am also an ordained minister of the Baptist church. In fact, I was a minister even before I became a cop. The good Lord directed me down the path of law enforcement to make a difference and I truly hope I have done just that."

"You know you have," Richie said.

"Please don't interrupt me, this is going to be hard enough as it is."

Three heads bobbed in agreement.

"For two days I have been trying to convince myself that I am making connections that just aren't there, and I had done a pretty good job too. And then an entire neighborhood becomes shrouded in darkness in the light of day with not one single cloud in the sky. I have spent the past several hours reading and re-reading the Book of

Revelation and I continue to come to the same conclusion; something is going down. Am I right?"

Richie nodded.

"But that's a good thing, right? At least for those of us on the right side of the Lord."

Richie shook his head. "No, Sergio, I wish it were that simple."

"I was afraid of that," Captain White said with a deep sigh. "Level with me, what is going on?"

There was a long silence, but Chase finally spoke up. "While a lot of what is going on mirrors the Book of Revelation, it is a reverse mirror."

Sergio White, while a rather intelligent man had no clue what Chase meant, and his face showed it.

"What he means is that all signs point to a nefarious plot to overthrow the current hierarchy," Richie explained in a manner he knew would annoy his boss.

"Black, for once, give it to me straight."

"For all intents and purposes, and for the sake of argument, this is not God's work, but something sinister."

"You mean Satan?"

"That term has not been used so I cannot say for certain."

"For all intents and purposes, and for the sake of argument," White prodded in a gruff tone.

"Let's just say it is not someone or something with pure intentions."

"And this is all being perpetrated by children?"

"Children in form only. These are highly intelligent beings. However, their taking form here using children appears to be a positive for us. Whether they want to or not, they still possess child-like mannerisms that also make them somewhat predictable."

"Predictable?" Captain White said.

"They like to play," Chase interjected.

Chase and Richie spent the next hour filling Sergio White in with all the details they knew and many more that were purely speculation.

"You know, I should have you both committed. But then I would have to have myself committed as well because I believe you. So, what do we do now?"

"We, nothing. Us, we have to stop these children by any means necessary," Richie said, throwing a thumb back and forth between himself and Chase.

Sergio took a second to digest what his subordinate said before reacting. "Richie, do I need to remind you who your boss is?"

"This has nothing to do with you being the boss. It has everything to do with you surviving this," Richie said.

Captain White shot Richie a suspicious glance.

"It has already been prophesized that Richie and I will not survive this endeavor," Chase said.

"Survive this? What is that supposed to mean?" Sergio asked.

"Listen, Serg, Chase and I are already in way too deep to get out. I don't want to drag you down with us."

"There is no chance I am sitting on the sidelines, Richie, and you know it."

"Fair enough. But honestly Serg, you will be much more useful to us working behind the scenes and not overtly."

"How so?" Sergio asked.

"We are going to have to commandeer a few things from the zoo and it would really be nice if we didn't have any interference from our brothers in blue," Richie said.

Captain White nodded and went back to reading the files Chase had compiled. Beverly took a chair across from him and studied the man.

"Do I have something on my face?" he asked, looking up from what he was reading.

"No, it's just that you have such a kind face. It's hard to see you as a tough authoritarian. What propelled your transition from preacher man to cop?" she asked.

"Actually, the transition went from an army sniper to minister and then eventually into law enforcement. All guided by the Lord of course."

"Of course," she replied with a wink.

Chase and Beverly loaded up her Jeep Grand Wagoneer with empty cages to house the birds and several rolls of duct tape. She pulled out a case from a locked cabinet and put it into the car as well.

"What was that?" Chase asked.

"A tranquilizer gun, just in case."

"That makes sense."

They went back into the clinic to wait until after business hours before they would head for the zoo.

"So, what's your plan?" Captain White asked.

"Hopefully in an out in less than fifteen minutes. Beverly has codes to the service and doctor's entrances, and she thinks she knows where they are housing the birds," Richie said.

"It is only logical they would house the birds in the exotic bird enclosure so we shouldn't have to spend any time looking for them."

"And while she has pass codes to get into the building, it will be after hours when she really has no business being there which could raise suspicions. That is where we could really use you to run interference in case someone starts causing a commotion," Richie said.

"I know several of the security guards, so I'm hoping that will be to our advantage," Beverly added.

Sergio nodded in agreement. "All of that is nice, but I am still going with you and that is nonnegotiable."

They spent the next hour loading the car, going over maps of the area and rehashing their plan of attack. All that was left to do now was wait until the zoo was closed and personnel went home for the evening.

Chapter Thirty-Seven

Rose Marie stood in the open expanse of the abandoned church with eight eager eyes intent on what she was saying. The night was chilly, but the boys had scavenged a few wooden pallets to burn and as long as they kept the fire small there would be no smoke or light visible outside of the building. St. Elmo's fire crackled within each and every one of them, except for Rai. They could feel themselves drawing ever closer to becoming, especially when being in each other's presence. While pleased, she was still frustrated with the two girls who had yet to make their appearance, but they were near enough for her not to be too concerned.

"We have a lot of work yet to do so we can't get comfortable. Now that we know where the birds are, we only have to retrieve them," Rose Marie said.

"What birds?" Rai asked.

"The birds are the trumpets. Don't you pay attention?" Chase Jr. said with a sharp elbow to the boy's ribs. Not that he feared Rose Marie, he just didn't want to deal with her incessant nagging or another one of her explosive meltdowns.

"I need to gather the other two here, so you boys go and get the other six trumpets and bring them back here," Rose Marie instructed.

Wanting nothing more than to be away from the relentless badgering, Chase Jr. readily agreed. He grabbed Rai by the hand and led him through the labyrinthian passageways in the basement and out into the surface world. He was pleased to see the sun had already dipped below the trees and soon darkness would be upon them.

The boys stopped at a bus stop along Woodward Avenue and gathered up route brochures with maps printed on the back. They found the easiest route to the zoo and began walking away from downtown. While Chase Jr. chatted up a storm, Rai was quiet and reserved as they walked.

A cemetery with a large pond sprawled out in front of them and Chase Jr. momentarily lost focus on what they had set out to accomplish. Right now, he just wanted to have a little fun.

"Come on, follow me," he said, climbing over the gates and helping Rai up after him.

"What are you doing?"

"Shhhhh, listen."

Echoes of ducks and geese chatting in the darkness drifted on the night air. Chase Jr. tugged at Rai's arm as he fast walked toward the black water.

"Watch this," the boy said, holding his hands up in the air in front of himself over the water.

Several ducks came paddling toward the boy anticipating scraps of bread. Instead, the boy clapped his hands together and a thick, black sludge oozed out from between his palms into the water below. Immediately the ducks began splashing about on the water's surface. They tried to quack, but their throats were choked off tight. He watched with glee as the waterfowl surrendered to the poisoned water and turned over onto their backs. As an added bonus several fish broke the surface of the water to float belly up with cataract eyes reflecting the moon above.

"You killed them," Rai said.

"I know. Isn't that cool?"

"Not really."

"Come on, you try it. It's fun, believe me. It's even more fun with people, but Rose Marie doesn't like it when I do that."

Rai walked closer to the water, held his hands out just like Chase Jr. had done and clapped them together. Nothing happened. He repeated the process which only produced a couple tiny sparkles at the tips of his pinky fingers. Chase Jr. fought hard to suppress his laughter.

This went on for the next fifteen minutes with Rai getting more and more frustrated with each attempt and Chase Jr. losing all ability to stifle his derisive laughter. Suddenly the boy stopped laughing and took several steps back away from Rai who was bristling with energy. Out of anger the boy thrust his arms toward the sky where they sparked for a moment before unexpectedly releasing bolts of lightning from his hands. At the same time, high tension wires above them began to hum and the wires waggled until a bristling blue arm shot down through the night sky to meet the bolts of lightning emanating from the boy's fingers.

Rai arched his back as the energy surged through his body. It was exhilarating. Letting loose a triumphant shout he thrust his hands forward. Bolts of lightning skipped around the surface of the water striking every single living creature in its path. The night grew eerily still as the energy dissipated leaving death in its wake.

"That was so cool," Chase Jr. shrieked.

Rai smiled a wicked grin, took a deep breath, and repeated his actions. Again, the powerlines surged with electricity, shooting it down to the boy on his command. This time he thrust his hands forward at a water tower at the edge of the cemetery. The tower exploded, raining water down all over the cemetery. Not wanting to be left out, Chase Jr. joined in with a clap of his hands. Immediately the grass turned brown, leaves fell from the larger trees and the small trees withered and died. The earth around them became desiccated and long fissures appeared under their feet stretching across the cemetery and extending across the road.

~ ~ ~

"Hey, Bruce, come and take a look at this," Steve Swain, the junior meteorologist called out across the newsroom.

Bruce Arnett, the chief meteorologist walked over to the young man and peered over his shoulder at the Doppler screen. As soon as he saw the screen, he moved the young man's hands out of the way and pecked away at the computer keyboard, netting the same results.

"What is this?"

"I have no clue, that's why I was asking you."

"When did this start?"

"About ten minutes ago. There's something weird going on isn't there?"

"Weird is putting it mildly. More like the impossible is happening."

Bruce stepped away from the computer and pulled out his cell phone. After dialing he went back to the computer as an afterthought, refreshed the screen again, and shook his head at the result.

"What is it, Arnett?" Dan Shultz, the station manager, asked.

"We need to get the chopper in the air."

"Do you know how much that thing costs per minute?"

"I wouldn't ask if I didn't think it was necessary," Bruce replied.

"What's going on?"

"I won't know until I get the chopper in the air."

Bruce spent the next several minutes haggling with his boss who finally relented and gave permission to launch the station's helicopter which was usually only used for traffic updates or major news stories, but never for the weather. Steve Swain was ecstatic Bruce asked him to ride along in the chopper and pass along what they saw while Bruce analyzed the data from the ground.

Not knowing what the situation was, the pilot was apprehensive and approached the area with extreme caution. Hundreds of feet below them lightning streaked from out of a clear sky and shot for the ground.

"Holy shit! What in the hell was that?" Steve said as the chopper shimmied from side to side.

"Hell if I know. Looks like a transformer blew, but there's no fire down there," the pilot said.

"Can you get closer?"

"I shouldn't dip below a thousand feet, but I guess I can bring her down a couple of hundred."

Rai and Chase Jr. were testing out the boy's electrical skills when they noticed a blinking red light coming toward them. A mischievous sneer creased their lips and Rai prepared himself.

"What will happen?" he asked.

Chase Jr. shrugged. "I don't know, but I bet it will scare the shit out of them."

Rai held his hands out in front of him. The tingle of electricity coursing through him tickled and he giggled. As the helicopter drew nearer to them, he opened his hands and spread them wide. Blue sparks arced between his fingers causing his bones to ache from the force of the energy. He watched as the blinking red light drew closer and closer until he could hear the thumping of the rotors cutting the night air. Slowly he raised his hands, more for dramatic effect than out of necessity, until they were high above his head. He splayed his fingers out at the power lines spanning Woodward Avenue until the wires sent forth an emissary to assist him.

"Are those children down there?" Steve asked, pointing to the boys standing in a clearing.

Blue-silver bolts exploded in the sky and raced toward the ground where the children were. With complete disregard for his own safety the pilot aimed the chopper for a small opening between the road and the power lines. Once he was in position less than one hundred feet above the ground, he put the aircraft into a hover and slowly descended to rescue two children trapped in a freak electrical storm.

"Can you do it?" Chase Jr. asked, excitement quivering in his voice.

"I don't know, but I sure as hell want to try."

"Look at that guy, risking his life to try to save us."

Once the chopper had descended well below one hundred feet and Rai could actually see the pilot's eyes he waved.

"Did that kid just wave at you?" Steve asked.

"I think so. And look at his hands," the pilot replied.

"Get us the hell out of here, fast," Steve screamed.

The very instant the pilot began to ascend Rai thrust his arms forward, filling the air with crackling light which blinded the pilot and caused him to let go of the stick to instinctively shield his eyes.

Once more the boy drew on the energy of the overhead power lines. He shot Chase Jr. a devious glance and clapped his hands together for effect. A large bolt shot out from between his palms and struck the tail rotor of the helicopter, sending it into an uncontrolled spin. On one of the rotations the tail struck a lamppost and separated the tail from the rest of the aircraft. With a shriek or torn metal, the cockpit plummeted to the ground.

Steve Swain lay in the grass a broken man. He craned his neck and saw his leg bones were protruding from his torn skin. Two boys were walking toward him and while he should be relieved he was still alive, something wasn't right about these two.

"You look thirsty. Doesn't he look thirsty?" Chase Jr. asked.

Rai bobbed his head up and down while rubbing his hands together. Even though he was interested in the injured man on the ground and what Chase Jr. was going to do to him, he couldn't help but daydream about the excitement they would enjoy once they had the trumpets in their possession.

"Open wide," Chase Jr. said, clapping his hands together above the man's face.

A deluge of foul, black water rained down upon Steve Swain's face. He struggled to no avail; he was much too broken to be able to escape this child's wrath. He gagged but could not expel the vileness from his mouth. The last thing the man ever saw was the two boys turning their backs out of boredom to continue on their way.

~ ~ ~

"What in the hell is going on out there?" Richie said after keying the mic on his radio.

"All hell has broken loose is what. Two of your little urchins just shot a news helicopter out of the sky," Sergio replied.

"What did they shoot it down with?"

"From what I saw, and Lord knows I am struggling to believe it, one of the boys shot lightning bolts from his fingertips."

Sirens wailed in the background.

"Shit, they must know where the trumpets are too."

"Those boys are the least of your troubles. I think the girl who caused the ruckus in Morningside is heading your way and she looks pissed. You need to hustle."

"Got it," Richie said.

Cecelia watched the two boys galivanting about without a care in the world and suddenly understood why Rose Marie had sent her to watch over them. They were incompetent fools at best. Instead of heading for the zoo where the birds were, they were making their way toward a golf course with several small ponds. It was apparent Chase Jr. really enjoyed killing animals, especially ducks.

Sergio left the lights off on the car as he crept down the street two hundred feet behind the little girl. Even though it was a moonless night everything seemed to be even darker than usual as she moved due to her casting a larger-than-life shadow over everything in her path. He had no clue as to what he was going to do and he was certain if she spotted him, he would be in extreme danger, but he just couldn't let Richie and his friends face this entity alone.

"Richie, you need to put some mustard on that sandwich. She's picking up her pace and it is getting mighty black out here."

"Where is she now?"

"She's about fifty yards away from the perimeter, heading for the service entrance."

"Okay. New plan, we're going to head straight out the front of the building. Meet us in the bus parking lot. Sergio, we are going to end this, I promise you."

Just what in the hell was this? The scriptures never prepared him to face God's wrath when he wasn't deserving of it. The little girl must have anticipated their change in plans somehow and was briskly moving toward the front of the zoo. Sergio's stomach fluttered with fear and apprehension, and he harkened back to his schoolyard days when he would go out of his way to avoid bullies. He told himself back then, no more, and no more it was going to be. A blue haze began to hang over the horizon indicating the cavalry was on their way, but it didn't give Sergio any sense of relief.

Sergio saw Beverly first. She was punching in the code to unlock the exit gates. Chase was right behind her carrying a cage in each hand with Richie pulling up the rear. The ebony haired little girl stormed toward them with clinched fists tight against the sides of her thighs.

Knowing he would never make it to them on foot, Sergio slammed the car into gear, hopped the curb and ripped through the grass toward the shadow child. She was so dark in fact, she was lost within her own shadows, and he lost sight of her. Suddenly a rift appeared in front of him, and he realized what an error in judgement he had made. It wasn't that the ground was opening up into a sink hole, reality was disappearing in front of his very eyes.

"No, Serg! Turn away!" Richie screamed.

Richie heard a clamor behind him and turned to see Beverly had dropped the cages she was carrying and had shouldered the tranquilizer gun. She dropped to one knee, steadied herself and fired, all the while hoping she was in range. Cecelia turned to face the three with the angriest of scowls. She outstretched her arms and the void moved across the field until it was marching straight at them. They turned to run but knew it was no use, the darkness was speeding right at them and there was no conceivable way they would escape it.

One of the birds began to thrash about in its cage. Richie realized the animal was trying to rub its beak against the wires to abrade the duct tape off its beak. He had no clue what would happen if one of the trumpets were allowed to sound in the presence of its vessel and he wasn't about to find out. Chase saw what he was doing and dropped his cages to assist. Between the two of them they were able to subdue the bird and duct tape it to the cage with so much tape it could barely even twitch a feather.

Sergio stared at the little girl standing in front of him and was torn between which path would prove to be the right one. Even though he knew what she was and what she was capable of, he couldn't get the fact she was merely a child out of his mind. He let up on the accelerator and began turning the wheel away from the child. Cecilia turned and looked at him with a depth of hatred in her eyes he had never seen before in all his years in the military and law enforcement combined. A blackness spread across the child's face, and he knew she planned to destroy them all.

With tears streaming down his face, Sergio jerked the wheel and veered back toward the little girl who stood defiantly in front of him. The Jeep fishtailed back and forth in the wet grass several times before he was able to regain control of the vehicle. The child was engulfed in a swirling mass of nothingness and pure hatred spewed from her every pore.

"Dear Lord, forgive me for what I am about to do," Sergio said and pressed down on the accelerator as far as it would go.

Suddenly Cecelia felt strangely fatigued and dropped to her knees. Her mind swooned with a myriad of thoughts, not one of which she could grasp on to. She knew she had to get out of the way of the speeding car heading straight for her, but she didn't even have the energy to stand. All she wanted to do was sleep.

The cockpit of the Grand Wagoneer was enveloped in an icy cold and frost sparkled on the black interior. Sergio could see his breath in the frigid air. What he felt was going to be his last thoughts in this life were of his wife, his kids, and his lovely grandchildren. He smiled and braced for whatever was to come.

The brush guard bumper on the Jeep slammed into Cecilia with a thump. An ear numbing shriek emanated from within the gloom forcing everyone to cover their ears. Winds whipped all around them as the darkness churned, tearing at everything in its path. The SUV slid sideways to a stop just beyond the corpse of a little child lying dead in the grass. Sergio burst into sobs unlike he had ever cried before in his life.

The darkness swirled and twisted, growing smaller and smaller until it burst into thousands of rays of sunshine raining down on them. The sorrow was ripped from Sergio's chest, and he understood he had only done what needed to be done. He had just murdered a little girl, but he was more at peace than he had ever been in his life. He knew. He finally knew he had served a greater purpose.

Chapter Thirty-Eight

Rose Marie stormed circles around the inside perimeter of the church. Why! Why was she surrounded by such incompetence? Serafina and Samael arrived at the church just before dawn. Having not ever witnessed this side of Rose Marie, they wisely chose to make themselves scarce. They weren't sure why she was so angry, but they didn't want to find out either.

A ruckus spilled up from the catacombs below and she knew the two boys had returned from their botched mission. By the sounds of it, they didn't seem to have a shred of remorse for their catastrophic failure. Rose Marie took several deep breaths and tried to paint her best expression of motherly disappointment on her face, though deep inside, she wanted to rip their little heads off their shoulders.

Rai and Chase Jr. were laughing and pushing each other back and forth as they burst into the somber room.

"Where are my birds?" Rose Marie asked.

Chase Jr. thought about his choice of words before answering. There was no easy way out of this one. But screw her, she wasn't in charge, no one was in charge. So what, they screwed up, but it wasn't anything they couldn't fix.

"The others got to them first."

"And why didn't you just take them from the others?"

"There were police all over the place. We couldn't do anything," Rai said.

"You managed to blow a helicopter out of the sky, but you couldn't stop a few police officers?"

"There were more than just a few of them. And I got scared," Rai said.

"You got scared?" Rose Marie said, feeling her anger rise to a level she feared she would not be able to contain much longer.

"It's the woman inside of me. She makes me do things I don't want to. How do I make her stop? I don't want to do this anymore," Rai said and began to cry.

"Come on, give the kid a break. It's no big deal, we will just go get the trumpets from them tonight when everything calms back down," Chase Jr. said.

Suddenly feeling emboldened by his wing man Rai said, "Yeah, don't get your knickers in a twist." Which brought on a suppressed round of giggles from the others.

Rose Marie stormed across the room, grabbed the boy by his tuft of black hair and heaved him into the wall where he crumpled to the floor. She dropped down with her knees on his chest and began to slap him back and forth across the face until blood poured from his damaged nose. The boy let out a wounded cry and scrambled back to his feet. His fear and trepidation were quickly overruled by his anger triggering a fight over flight response. The boy took a step back, called upon the electricity coursing through him and released a bolt of lightning that caught Rose Marie squarely in the chest. The force flung her backward onto the floor. Her head cracked against the concrete not only dazing her but awakening her own ire as well.

Rose Marie shook the cobwebs off, got to her feet and dusted herself off. Cherubic faces stared back at her unsure of what to expect. But she just smiled back at the group of insubordinates.

"Cute," was all she said.

The girl closed her eyes, tilted her head back and took several deep breaths. Her hands were balled into fists at her sides as she tried to allow her anger to dissipate. But then she thought of the one who they lost due to these two boys' incompetence and blatant disregard for her authority.

A sound began to rumble in the child's belly and a guttural growl forced its way out of her mouth. Chase Jr. had to cover his ears from the deafening sound. The force of her shriek lifted Rai up into the air and slammed him against the wall. The boy felt his body temperature rising and an insatiable thirst plagued him until he coughed out a handful of sand. Rose Marie extended her arms and ripped them outward away from her body.

Chase Jr. watched in horror as his little confidant was literally torn in half from his crotch to the top of his head. His body turned to dust and settled into two piles on either side of where he had been standing creating the illusion of a dry riverbed.

"There are only six of us now, and that means you are useless to me," she screamed.

Rose Marie was both satisfied and horrified by what she had done. The room stood silent for several moments before a gust of wind blew through the open room, scattering the remnants of Rai to the wind. A darkness appeared from a split in the very air in front of them and a black mass similar to what the bird had hacked up fell to the floor at her feet. Rose Marie bent and cautiously lifted it from the ground. The twisted mass began to bristle with energy in the palms of her hands. She giggled at the sensation of a puppy's tongue licking her skin.

Suddenly the child screamed out in agony as the writhing ball of energy grew in intensity and its tendrils leeched into to her skin. The others watched in horror as her skin writhed and bulged from the invading mass. And then it was gone. Consumed. And she smiled.

The surge of electrical power surging through her was exhilarating, and she understood at once what she had to do.

"I don't need you either," she said, unleashing her wrath on Samael who was too late to turn and run. "I don't need any of you."

Chase Jr. grabbed the new little girl by the arm and ran for the catacombs. Serafina, too, recognized the danger and attempted to intervene but Rose Marie had grown too powerful to stop so she threw up a wall of flames for defense. Using the bleachers for cover, Serafina ran for the catacombs as well.

Rose Marie let loose a belly laugh that shook the very earth beneath them. She bent down, scooped up the black, snarled remnants of Samael and absorbed his essence as well. If they could not become as one, then she would become them all.

Chapter Thirty-Nine

"What in the hell was that?" Richie said.

"It felt like an earthquake to me," Chase said, peeling back the motel room curtains to see if there had been an explosion outside. "Nothing happened out here."

Sergio joined Chase in scanning the outside world. The video of him running over a little child was all over the news already. Granted, the media never saw him so they could only report *an unknown assailant* ran over a child. They did, however, get great video of Chase, Beverly and Richie running from the zoo with misappropriated rare animals. He spent most of the morning trying to run interference and getting them all to a safehouse with the least amount of exposure possible.

Chase unloaded a plastic bag filled with an assortment of gas station breakfast sandwiches that had grown cold. He put them into the small microwave and heated them up for thirty seconds at a time before passing them all around. There were a couple small tremors while they were eating but there was no mention of them on the morning news, in part because Sergio had managed to keep a lid on things for the time being under the guise of not wanting to panic the citizens of Detroit.

Wisely they had stashed the birds in lockers at Detroit Metro Airport and the Greyhound terminal downtown. Richie was fairly sure they didn't have to concern themselves with feeding the animals and hoped that duct taping them to the bottoms of the cages would keep them from making too much noise. Things were escalating and this entire ordeal was bound to be behind them sooner than later. Sergio had been reserved and had been keeping to himself. Richie wished there was something he could do or say that would comfort the man.

"Oh, daddy dearest, may I have a word with you," Chase Jr. called from in front of the motel. "You have something that belongs to us, and I must insist you return them to their rightful owners."

Chase peeked through the tiniest of slits between the curtains to see his demon spawn of a son standing in the parking lot with a small girl in tow. He shuddered at the boils and sores covering her face, and a pang of guilt stabbed at him when he thought of Janice. Richie started for the door of the motel with vengeance on his mind.

"What are you doing?" Chase hissed.

"I'm going to go spank that little shit," Richie replied.

Sergio grabbed him by the shoulder. "Have you forgotten last night already? That is not a child out there, hell, whatever he is, he's not even human."

Chase snuck a glance out the window again, this time taking in more of the surroundings. The tenant in the room next door had backed a bobtailed semi-truck into the two parking spots adjacent to their room. Away from their room, on the periphery, the reflection of a small girl glared back at him from the trucker's mirror, and she looked pissed. The fire dancing in her eyes alerted him to who she was, and an icy chill washed over him. He nearly vomited up the sausage, egg, and cheese croissant he just consumed.

"Fill the bathtub with water and throw all the bedding and towels into the water," Chase screamed as he started ripping the comforter off the bed.

All eyes fell upon him with confusion written on every face.

"I know you're in there. I'll huff and I'll puff, and I'll burn your fucking house to the ground," Serafina. screamed at them, fist clenched at her sides and her face a fiery red.

With that the others followed Chase's lead. They weren't sure what he had noticed outside the window, but they were certain it couldn't be good. Richie was disgusted with himself. He should have known better than to hole up in a place with only one exit. At the time it seemed prudent as there was only one entrance so any threat would have to come at them head on. He simply failed to remember just what it was they were dealing with.

"What's your plan?" Richie asked.

"I don't have a plan other than trying to keep us all from being burned to death."

Without warning the drapery began to smolder and thick, black smoke quickly filled the room. Sergio ripped the drapes down and stomped on them before they could burst into flames. Suddenly he began to feel warm, as if he had a fever. His skin began to blister on his forearm and Sergio screamed. Beverly quickly saturated a hand towel in the sink and wrapped it around his arm.

With the curtains now on the floor they could see the little girl standing in front of their motel room with fury adorning her face. The air rippled around her as heat vapors rose from the black tarmac.

"What the fuck is going on out here? Why is it so damned hot?" a large man hollered as he burst from his room dressed only in his underwear.

Serafina turned her attention to the fat man with a belly so rotund he looked pregnant. A tiny giggle carried across the parking lot causing Mel to catch sight of a child staring at him and was immediately self-conscious about standing in front of a little girl in his tighty whities. He turned back for the room but was staggered backward when the door burst into flames right in front of him. With his motel room ablaze, Mel sought shelter in his rig, but when he reached for the handle, he recoiled in pain due to the handle glowing red hot. The side window on the cab shattered and flames leaped out at him.

The man was rocked with heartburn so intense it knocked Mel to his knees. He rubbed his portly stomach to try and calm it down. It was just nerves after all, wasn't it? He retracted his hands as if he had touched a hot iron. It just wasn't possible for his skin to be that hot. He fought to get back to his feet and staggered for the river in search of water to cool himself down. The others watched in horror as what started out as a glowing red cherry where his navel had been began to grow and spread. The ember burned through the skin of his stomach and a small flicker of a flame escaped. Melted body fat oozed down his stomach onto the waistband of his underwear which acted as a wick and within an instant the man's entire body was ablaze, turning him into a human scented candle.

Beverly gasped and averted her eyes from the screaming trucker. Sergio drew his weapon, but the pistol was too hot to handle, and he immediately drop it on the floor. With the flaming man reduced to mere ash, Serafina once again turned her attention on the meddlers in the motel room.

"It's starting to get hot in here. What in the hell are we going to do?" Beverly shouted.

Richie saw that the paint was bubbling up on the door frame and windowsill, indicating the room would soon be engulfed in flames, trapping them inside. It was now or never. He took a long stride toward the threshold but was forced back by flames erupting from the jamb and casing. The two of them made eye contact and something odd happened, the girl's eyes glistened with tears.

Megan Holt managed to claw her way to the surface long enough to warn them. "She can't swim. And don't let the others have her," she said before Serafina was able to shove the woman back into the abyss.

"Sergio, you get behind us, and Beverly, you get behind Sergio," Richie said.

Richie nodded to Chase who dashed into the bathroom, grabbed the soaking wet comforter, and returned to the door of the motel. He handed Richie a corner of the comforter and he held up the other. Richie was struggling with the extremely heavy bedding, but it immediately began to hiss with steam prompting the men to run without a second to lose. Before Serafina knew what they were up to the men had burst through the flames surrounding the door and were charging straight for her.

Before Chase Jr. could come to her aid, Sergio broke away from the pack and tackled him hard on the tarmac. The little girl reached for him with her carbuncle encrusted hand, but he was able to kick her away and scramble back to his feet, quickly putting distance between the two of them.

Serafina turned to run but her hesitation proved to be her undoing. Chase and Richie slammed into her, forcing her to the ground. Chase quickly rolled her up in the sodden comforter and scooped the bundle up into his arms. Searing heat emanating through the blanket which was hissing due to the water rapidly evaporating. He ran for the river as fast as he possibly could while carrying a thrashing bundle of sorrow in his arms. Richie got back to his feet and chased after them.

Chase spotted a small fishing platform overlooking the river and raced for it as fast as he could. Wisps of steam swirled above the blanket making the task of running with the squirming child that much harder. He was winded and his arms were on fire, but he knew he had to keep running. Nothing was going to stop him from ending this, or at least a part of this. Acrid tendrils of smoke stung his nose and threatened to choke off whatever oxygen he could manage between gasps. By the time he hit the wooden platform the comforter was ablaze. Without hesitation he continued running until there was no more solid ground beneath his feet.

Richie, suddenly remembering he was a one-armed man stopped short of going into the water after his friend.

Both Chase and his bundle disappeared into the murky depths. Within seconds fish and other assorted river dwellers began to breech the surface and float belly up to create a bizarre apocalyptic chowder. The water in front of the dock began to roil into a full boil and Richie first became filled with grief, but then anger took charge, and he ran toward Chase Jr. with everything he had left in him. The boy turned and ran with pestilence in tow. After several minutes Richie gave up the pursuit and doubled over with his hands on his knees. Tears rolled down his cheeks as he made his way back to the dock.

Beverly blew passed Richie on a dead run as if she were on the last quarter mile of the Crim. Her foot slapped down in a gooey puddle, remnants of Trucker Mel and she nearly vomited but pushed on. She dove headfirst into the river without even stopping or giving thought the water may be boiling hot. Sergio met up with Richie on the dock, the both of them staring into the gloomy water which had calmed down considerably since the moment Chase breached the depths with Little Miss Hellfire.

"What in the hell is she doing?" Sergio asked.

"I assume she is recovering his body, though I'm not sure if she wants to see the body of a man boiled alive," Richie said.

Beverly stopped swimming and began struggling with something on the surface of the water. She tugged at the mass while trying to swim back to the shore. Once she was close enough to touch the bottom, she began dragging Chase back to shore. The men jumped in and helped her. Sergio reached down to the man's legs to dislodge a huge ball of peculiar fishing line tangled around his legs while Beverly started CPR on the man.

"Shit, that line is hot as hell," Sergio said and pulled a pocketknife from his pocket and flipped it open.

"How in the hell did you know where he was in the river?" Richie asked.

Chase coughed and expelled river water from his lungs.

"I don't really know. I just had a feeling. Now, help me roll him to the side," Beverly said.

Richie breathed a sigh of relief once he realized Chase was breathing on his own. Chase slowly opened his eyes and blinked until he got his vision back.

"I guess now I am not supposed to be here," he said and flopped over onto his back with a heavy sigh.

Sergio sported a smile of relief once he saw Chase was going to survive. But how many more encounters would they be able to endure?

Chase Jr. felt the man, Hector, struggling to break free. Having lost Samael, Serafina, Cecilia, and Rai must have weakened the rest of them. He walked back toward the commotion by the dock against his will.

"Guys, I think we may have a problem," Sergio said, pointing to Chase Jr. walking their way in one direction, the little girl with all the sores from another direction and a third girl he had yet to meet coming from yet another direction.

"What in the hell are we going to do?" Chase asked.

Richie shrugged. He was interested in the way Chase Jr. was walking, something was off about the miscreant's gait.

"You two stay here and watch over Chase," Richie said and started walking toward the boy.

He cautiously made his way over to the child but stopped a good fifty feet away, which was more than close enough for his tastes. He noticed something about the boy's eyes, they had the same glassiness to them as the girl. He took a chance.

"Hector? Hector Correa?" Richie asked.

Hector nodded while trying to find his voice.

"If you are in there, you have to fight him, Hector."

Tears streamed down the boy's cheeks, but Richie knew they were not the demon child's tears. He felt so hollow inside knowing there was nothing he could do for the man. But then again, maybe there was.

"I know you didn't kill the old woman, Hector. I know you had nothing to do with that and I promise you, I will do everything in my power to make sure he pays for what he has done to you and to everyone else."

"They both want that," he said, his hand pointing toward Chase and the others. "But you can't let him have it, and especially not her," he said, pointing at the girl heading their direction.

"They want Chase?"

He shook his head.

"Beverly? Sergio?"

He shook his head again. "They want her."

"Her?"

"The girl who was on fire. She is still alive, just in a different form," Hector explained.

Richie scoured his memory for what the child might be babbling on about. And then he remembered the object Sergio found.

"The fishing line?"

Hector forced the boy to nod.

"Thank you, Hector."

Richie sprinted back to where the others were. He looked down at Chase's legs and saw that the ball of line was indeed alive and moving, so he started ripping it away from Chase's legs. The sensation was odd, the line squirmed and struggled against his grasp. It was slippery and pulled away from him every time he tried to grip it.

"That is mine! You leave it alone!" Rose Marie screamed so thunderously it knocked them all to the ground.

When Sergio caught sight of the child's eyes he was filled with terror. "Yea, though I walk through the valley of the shadow of death, I will fear no evil."

Rose Marie laughed. "You will fear me, because you cannot even fathom the depths of my evil."

It worked once, so Richie thought *what the hell*. He stood with the black mass cupped in his hands and looked back at the girl. Behind her anger, behind her hatred he could still see the love of his life was still in there somewhere.

"Effie, I will always love you," he said.

The little girl cocked her head to the side and tried to mock him, but her odium was stifled by the woman inside her. The meddlesome bitch.

"I love you too, Richie, and I always will. You can't let her have that or she will only grow stronger."

"How can I stop her?"

"You must consume it yourself. Let it become a part of you."

"NO! Shut up you bitch!" Rose Marie screamed while pounding at the sides of her head with her fists.

Without hesitation Richie shoved the writhing black mass into his mouth. He was not sure if eating the accursed thing would accomplish anything, but he was fresh out of options. As soon as it passed his lips, he began to regret what he had done. The vileness that was the child's essence began to invade his every fiber. Tendrils of abhorrence burrowed deep into the flesh of his throat and slithered down into his stomach where they branched out into his internal organs. He felt a pure disgust for humanity seeping into his every cell.

Richie fell to his knees, shoved his fingers into his mouth, and tried to yank the beast from his gullet. He could feel the long tendrils probing and prodding at his innards as if they were searching for something. They forced their way into his veins and arteries where they traveled to his heart.

"Is Richie having a heart attack?" Chase said, struggling to get back on his feet.

While clutching at his chest he felt an evil presence invading him, trying to become him. But there was something else as well. Something good. Something wholesome but terribly sad. As suddenly as the pain started it stopped and things began to get clearer. He could sense the boy's thoughts, and the girl's as well but they were jumbled and erratic.

Rose Marie was incensed. That man had killed the others and now had stolen what rightfully belonged to her.

With her fists clenched at her sides she let loose a guttural scream that caused everyone to cover their ears. The river began to swell and surge, slapping against the dock and break wall. A thirty-two-footer heading for the lake must have seen the strange weather phenomena and turned back for the marina. Sadly, Rose Marie saw them too.

She turned her wrath toward the boat of innocent people. She breathed in as hard as she could, drawing the water and boat toward her. It looked as though a hand had reached into the water and was cradling the boat high above the river's surface on the crest of an enormous wave. With her cheeks puffed up with air, Rose Marie turned and smiled at Richie in a wicked sort of way.

"Run! All of you run," Richie called out.

"What about you?" Chase said.

"Don't worry about me," he said and started toward the girl.

Reluctantly, the others ran for the safety of the motel, grabbing the motel manager along the way and tugging him behind the building. Richie could hear the people on the boat screaming for help but had no clue how to help them. Out of frustration he stopped and screamed at the little girl. The sound that came out of him was deafening and caused Rose Marie to drop to her knees. Every time she tried to get back to her feet to finish what she had started he would bellow, once more stopping her in her tracks.

Rose Marie understood what had happened and knew she needed to flee. Discretion was always the better part of valor. Richie dropped to the ground, exhausted, and confused. The river receded back to normal levels, the pleasure boat high tailed it back to the marina and the others came out from behind the motel oblivious to what had just happened.

Chapter Forty

Richie sat in the back seat of the Wagoneer scratching at his chest which for some reason had begun to itch terribly. He could feel the mass inside of him trying to assimilate with his body. He could also sense it not only wanted to become a part of him, it wanted to control him.

Not much of anything was said between the four of them as Beverly drove them to the outskirts of town where they found a seedy, rent by the hour motel. The desk clerk sneered at them through a greasy smile as his twisted mind concocted a dozen scenarios of what they were planning with each other. Beverly definitely needed a shower, right after she made Chase check it for hidden cameras.

Once they found their motel rooms, Sergio and Chase helped Richie into the room where he immediately fell onto the bed exhausted and within two minutes the man was in a deep sleep. The others took turns cleaning up in the shower with limited conversation. Once cleaned up they headed for a diner within walking distance of the motel at the back edge of a strip mall.

"Are you sure he's going to be okay there by himself?" Beverly asked.

"Richie? He'll be fine," Chase said, not quite convinced of it himself.

The three of them picked at their plates of corned beef hash, biscuits, and gravy, for Sergio, a garden salad for Beverly, and two coneys with the works for Chase. No one came close to finishing their meals. Chase ordered several things for Richie, including a piece of homemade apple pie and hoped his friend would have an appetite.

"This is really happening, isn't it?" Sergio asked.

"I'm afraid so. But look on the bright side," Chase said.

"What bright side could there possibly be?" Beverly asked.

"We have eliminated three of them that we know of. That tells us these things can be killed."

"Chase has a point. So, what now?" Sergio asked.

"We go back to the room and see if Richie is ready to travel, and then we go find the rest of these little bastards."

"You make it sound so easy," Beverly said.

"I begged you to stay out of this, remember."

She nodded.

Sergio nodded as well while digging out his wallet. He handed his credit card to the waitress who gave them the you've *overstayed your welcome* stare and ambled toward the cash register only to return several minutes later.

"Declined," she said, shoving the card at Sergio.

"Did you try the strip instead of the chip?"

"It said it was declined, not that it wasn't working correctly."

Sergio nodded, dug through his wallet, and handed her his department issue credit card. He would find a way to explain the expenses later. Again, the waitress headed for the register only to return with an even more dour expression.

"Declined?" Sergio asked.

She nodded.

"Here, try this one," Chase said, handing her his card.

The third time was not the charm. The waitress was no longer trying to contain her frustration with the diners.

"Listen, I don't know what kind of game you're trying to run but I'm getting ready to call the cops."

Sergio was reaching for his badge, but something told him not to let on that he was a cop.

"Here, this should cover it and then some," Beverly said with a smile, handing the waitress a hundred-dollar bill from her purse. "Cash is king," she said as the woman huffed away from their table.

The waitress left the table with a more pleasant expression than when she arrived. Before the diners were able to head for the door, she had already used her counterfeit pen on the bill and was relieved she wouldn't have to make a scene. She poured a glass of water from a carafe on the counter and took a long drink. Out of a natural reflex she spewed the vile water out of her mouth and onto the floor. She peered down into the glass but saw nothing wrong. Maybe some residue from the dishwasher had gotten stuck in the bottom.

Diane was on the way back to the kitchen when all hell broke loose. Every patron in the restaurant also spit their beverages out. She opened her mouth to yell for the cook, but her throat had started to swell up and choked her airway off. Chaos erupted throughout the small diner as each and every one of the patrons, except one, dropped dead on their tables.

Chase Jr. was furious. How? How in the hell out of the three of them, not one of them took so much as a sip of anything? No coffee, no soda, no tea, not even any water. They couldn't have known he was there or surely they would have come after him. And what happened to that officious cop, Richie Black?

The boy followed them through the strip mall as they stopped to buy clothes for the woman at a small boutique. Then they moved on to the sporting goods store where he watched her purchase some ammunition, as if that would do them any good against Rose Marie. She was stronger now, too strong for even him. He needed to get Serafina's essence back from Richie, and then he needed to find the trumpets. It was clear now that only one of them was going to survive this foray, and he was going to make damned sure it was him.

The men stood at the front of the store trying not to look impatient. Beverly had assured them they would regret it if she didn't get a change of clothes soon. She was getting gamey, probably more from the stress than exertion, but the shower didn't do her any good once she put her dirty clothes back on. Besides, she needed something to comfort her, and shopping did just that.

Chase had the sensation of being watched but even with his head on a swivel he didn't spot anything out of the ordinary. He chalked it up to the events of the past several days haunting him. There was a nervousness growing in the pit of his stomach he was certain would never leave.

At Beverly's insistence they stopped at the haberdashery to get the men some clean shirts and hopefully sticks of deodorant. Sergio snuck in a pit sniff check and agreed, he definitely needed a clean shirt. By the time they got back to the motel they had been gone for more than four hours.

"Hopefully Richie is well rested and able to help us come up with a plan," Sergio said as he slid the motel key into the keyhole.

Chase put his hand over Sergio's stopping the man from turning the key. He put a finger to his lips and leaned in to put his ear to the door. Sergio followed his lead. The sounds of breaking glass and splintering wood rushed at them through the door. Beverly took a step back away from the door while Sergio slowly turned the key. They were not sure what they were going to find once the door was opened but they were bracing themselves for another battle.

What they saw when Sergio opened the motel room door took the wind right out of their sails. The room inside had been torn apart, furniture had been broken and their meager belongings had been scattered about. Beverly let loose an audible gasp when she caught sight of the man inside the room. He had shaved half of his hair off from front to back, dyed the remaining hair with jet black shoe polish he found in the dresser and had fashioned the locks into what could only be described as the feathers on the head of an ibis. He was flush from exertion, turning his face a deep crimson. She glanced over at a hardware package torn open on the bed along with his soiled bandages and then back to Richie. He had screwed a large hook intended to hang bicycles in the garage into the bone where his hand had once been.

"Richie? What the hell?" Chase blurted out, snatching the man's attention away from what he had been doing.

He turned to look at the group now gawking at him and made a strange sound. Richie started singing a song and bolted through the open door and across the parking lot into the strip mall before anyone could react. The further away he got from them the louder he sang but the song had changed.

"That was by far the most bizarre thing I have ever witnessed in my entire lifetime, and that is saying something," Sergio said.

"What in the hell was that song he was singing?" Chase asked.

Beverly gave a nervous chuckle. "I think it was Islands in the Stream."

"Kenny Rogers?"

"And Dolly Parton."

"Richie hates country."

They entered the room all the way and that was when they were able to absorb the extent of the inexplicable behavior.

"Jessop Porter," Chase said.

"What was that?" Sergio asked.

"Jessop Porter. He was the common denominator in all of this. Patient Zero if you will," Chase said.

"What does he have to do with any of this madness?"

"When Richie arrested the man, he was Loony Tunes just like this. Except the writing is different. These seem to be song lyrics, or titles to be more exact."

Island in the Stream was written in black marker all over the stark white bathroom walls, toilet tank, countertop, floor, and ceiling. There wasn't a surface, including the toilet seat itself, that was able to escape Richie's pen.

Time for Me to Fly! was scrawled over every square inch of the north facing wall.

The bedding was pulled back and *You're Not Supposed to Be Here* had been scribbled across the sheets and pillowcases at least a hundred times.

"When in the hell did he find time to do all this?" Sergio asked.

"How doesn't concern me as much as why. None of this makes sense. And while it is similar to the actions of Jessop Porter, it is also vastly different," Chase observed.

"How so?" Sergio asked.

"Porter's ramblings were pretty much a singular theme. This all seems to be much more chaotic. What in the hell does Time for Me to Fly mean anyway?" Chase said.

"Let me interject something," Beverly started. "Quite frankly this is no more bizarre than any of the events we have witnessed over the last several days. In fact, to Richie, I'm sure this was all normal and served a purpose."

"That doesn't help us much," Sergio said.

"But it would if we looked at it through Richie's eyes. We have no idea what happened out there on that river.

What he ingested. I would wager it was a living organism of some kind, most likely parasitic. Many parasites can cause mental issues and even psychosis. Maybe this entity has assumed control of most of his mind and this was all he had left to give us. This Jessop Porter you spoke of was probably hanging on to the last shred of his humanity while trying to warn someone of what was about to happen."

"All plausible, but it still doesn't explain the song titles."

"Time for Me to Fly, he's telling us that he is transforming," Beverly said.

"Transforming into what?" Sergio asked.

"My best guess would be a bird," Beverly replied.

"Or a trumpet to be more exact," Chase added while nodding in agreement.

Chase pulled out his cell phone and began taking photos of the walls, the shower stall, the bedsheets, the ceilings, and anywhere else Richie scrawled his library of song titles. He realized that while Porter appeared chaotic on the outside, he was much more organized than Richie seemed to be. The man was all over the place with song titles to the point there was no direction, no rhyme, nor any apparent reason.

"What in the hell are we supposed to do now?" Chase said as he dropped down onto the bed in frustration.

"Richie is trying to tell us something, of that I am certain. While in his mind I am sure this all made sense, but it is a puzzle for us. But it isn't unsolvable."

Beverly went out to the Jeep and brought her laptop into the room. She sat down on the bed next to Chase and fired up the computer while Sergio scanned the room from wall to wall, lost within his own thoughts.

"What are you going to do?"

"I am going to create a database of all these phrases and song titles to see if we can't find a connection."

"There has to be a connection, Richie is a smart man, a good detective, and even if his mind has been compromised, he still knows what he is doing. We just have to figure out what that is," Sergio said.

"We have to look at things in terms of the trumpets and the vials and determine which of them has been eliminated and which ones are still out there. If we know what we are up against, we might be able to anticipate their next move," Beverly said.

"I think Richie already has," Sergio said.

"What good will knowing which moves they are going to make do for us?" Chase asked out of frustration.

"Because, while these might be angels, gods, demons, or space aliens, they are still just children. Children who have shown a propensity for theatrics and also seem to enjoy spreading mayhem," Beverly said.

"We can eliminate the fifth vial, she is the girl I murdered outside of the zoo when I ran her over," Sergio said. "The fifth vial speaks of plunging the antichrist into darkness."

"Sergio, she was no child. In fact, I doubt she was even human, that any of them are human. You did what you had to do and by doing so, you saved a lot of lives," Beverly said with a comforting hand on his shoulder.

"I assume the girl I drowned in the river was the fourth vial. And then the fourth angel poured out his bowl on the sun, and it was given power to scorch the people with fire," Chase said.

Beverly nodded. "Scratch the fire starter."

"That's only two of them."

"Richie and I killed the first vial early on. The one who spreads pestilence."

"And shall we also assume that the one who came back as your son is the third vial, tainting the world's fresh water," Sergio said.

Chase nodded. "And the other child at the river, that must have been the sixth vial who dries up the Euphrates."

"Good. That only leaves two unaccounted for. The second vial, and the seventh."

"The second vial reared its ugly head in the restaurant downtown, but we haven't seen much activity from them since that incident," Chase said.

"Let us assume they are out of the picture for some reason or another," Sergio said.

"The same with the lightning bug, the seventh vial. We haven't experienced any freak storms after that night at the zoo. Maybe you put the fear of God in him," Beverly smiled weakly at her off-color humor.

"I highly doubt that, but there does seem to have been some seeds of discord sown within the little troupe of antichrists."

Sergio left the room to make a few phone calls. He needed to find out why his credit cards had been cancelled. Was it the work of his local bosses or did this come from high up on the food chain? He feared the feds were somehow involved now which would make tracking and killing these last vials that much more difficult.

"Would you like some coffee?" Beverly asked as she stepped out of the motel room to take a break from the madness inside.

Sergio nodded and she disappeared down the long building toward the motel office. He took a photograph out of his pocket and was still looking at it when she came back. Beverly took a seat on the rickety bench next to him, hoping the thing wouldn't collapse under her added weight.

"Who's that handsome dude?" she asked, handing Sergio his coffee.

"That's me, or at least a much younger version of me as seen through a time warp."

"Oh wow. You were quite the stud, weren't you?"

"It's the uniform."

"And is that your wife?"

"First wife."

"And does your current wife know you carry this photo in your pocket?"

"That will be our little secret. It's not like we would ever get back together, hell, I haven't seen or spoken to her in almost forty years."

"Then why keep the photo if you don't mind me asking."

"It's not about remembering her, or even her and I, it's about taking myself back to a simpler time. A time before life got in the way," Sergio said with glistened eyes.

"You seemed happy. What happened?"

"You know, I'd love to blame it on the military, on her, on her parents, on circumstances in general, but our failures were all my own. No matter how much I thought I was ready for marriage, I wasn't. In fact, I didn't have a clue.

I made a lot of decisions for *us*, that were actually decisions for myself without any regard for her thoughts or input on the matters."

"You were already in the military and she knew that. What decisions are you talking about?"

"When we got married, I was just a pot scrubbing jar head stationed stateside. One day as luck would have it some high-ranking cat caught wind of my shooting skills and came out to the range to watch me. Next thing I knew he was courting me for sniper school. He sure as hell dangled some golden carrots in front of my nose and I sure as hell bit on them. Long story short, I ended up overseas and under circumstances that kept me from communicating back home. In fact, it was quite similar to undercover police work. Lucy and I drifted apart and before I knew it, we were divorced. Hell, funny thing is, I can't even remember getting divorced. It's like one day we were married and the next we weren't. All water under the bridge," Sergio said and took a long sip of his coffee.

The stale coffee left a lingering bitter taste in her mouth, so Beverly reached into her pocket and pulled out a pack of cinnamon gum. She offered a stick to Sergio which he gladly accepted.

"Now, tell me about this unorthodox career path of sniper, to preacher man to cop."

"Is this something we really need to discuss?"

"Let's just say you're an enigma and I like to solve puzzles."

"I'm no puzzle. What you see is what you get."

Beverly took advantage of a long silence to walk back down to the office for something to snack on from the vending machines. She brought back two stale candy bars and handed one to Sergio.

"My last target looked me in the eye just as I pulled the trigger. Granted, from the distance I knew he was not able to see me, but it was the first time I had ever seen my target's eyes."

"And that was enough to make you quit?"

"Not that in and of itself. It's what I saw in his eyes. I saw his fear and repentance, but then gratitude as if he were thanking me. I honestly believe God spoke to the both of us that day. At the end of that tour, I did not re-enlist and moved back to Detroit where I started a church with a small congregation off Rosa Parks Boulevard. The transition to law enforcement came less than five years after burying more than a dozen of my parishioner's sons from drug overdoses and needless violence. Again, I believe God spoke to me as I held a grieving mother in my arms as her son died in front of her. I felt I could help more souls on the frontlines than I could preaching from the pulpit. I can only pray I have made a difference, even if for only one child. Do you believe?" Sergio looked over at Beverly and asked.

"Quite frankly, I have always taken the cowards approach. I have believed only because the alternative seems worse. If I spend my life believing and I am wrong, then so be it. But if I deny His existence and I am wrong, well, you know the end of that story."

"What about you two?" Sergio asked, nodded at Chase through the open door of the motel room as he pecked away at the laptop keyboard.

"It's a long, complicated story."

"It's obvious he cares for you. I can see it in his eyes. Yours too."

"Some ghosts are just impossible to get rid of," Beverly said and walked down to the ice machine, effectively putting an end to their conversation.

Sergio walked back into the motel room and scanned the walls to see if there was anything there he might have missed. There was one phrase that stood out from the others, written only one time, but it triggered a slight smile across his face and caused his eyes to glaze over.

Sergio, just pull the damned trigger!

"Does that mean something to you?" Chase asked, looking up from the laptop.

Sergio nodded. "When we were partners, Richie used to say that to me all the time. It started out as a joke, more of a prodding, when I was working up the nerve to ask Corinna to marry me. I went on and on about it for months trying to find the courage to ask her. Richie must have gotten sick of my constant hemming and hawing and said, Sergio, just pull the damned trigger. So, I did, and I have been happily married ever since," Sergio explained.

"Sounds like Richie, that's for sure."

"After that, it kind of became a thing. If I was at the soda machine trying to decide between a Vernor's or a Dr. Pepper he would pop a button and say, should have pulled the trigger. Have you come up with anything yet?" Sergio said with a head bob in the direction of the laptop screen.

"Nothing useful I'm afraid. They're just random song titles that don't seem to mean anything together. I have been trying to match them up with each of the remaining vials, but nothing seems to jive," Chase said.

"It means something to Richie."

"I plugged in the other song he was singing, Fat Bottom Girls by Queen with Islands in the Stream into the internet search engine and most of the results were porn videos from spring break," Chase said.

Beverly thought about it for a minute while singing Fat Bottom Girls in her head. She replayed the video she had taken with her phone several times. "Try island and bicycle race. He wasn't singing Islands in the Stream, he was saying island, not plural."

Even before Chase could type the information into the search engine bar Sergio blurted out, "Belle Isle. There is a charity bicycle race there tomorrow."

The room fell silent except for Chase's fingers pecking away at the laptop. The others watched impatiently as he scanned through the search results.

"Well?" Sergio asked.

"It appears this race is not the only event. It is part of a larger event. It is some sort of Eco-friendly festival as far as I can tell. And the sponsor is a company called Pure Rain," Chase said.

"Drinking water, I assume?" Sergio said.

Chases nodded. "They are planning to purify the water in the Scott fountain and are inviting people to drink from the fountain."

"That doesn't sound good," Beverly said.

"No, it doesn't. According to this there are to be well over two hundred thousand people expected from all over the world."

"It looks like we are going to be going to Belle Isle tonight," Sergio said.

~ ~ ~

Just before dark they made their way across MacArthur Bridge and parked at the Belle Isle Casino by way of Sunset Drive. There were already several out-of-state buses parked in the fountain parking lot and two large stages were set up on the greenery. A team of landscapers near a large pile of downed tree limbs were stowing their gear away and locking up their tools before knocking off for the day. The idyllic setting was peaceful and refreshingly normal.

There were still groups of people milling about so the three of them walked the perimeter of the fountain to get a lay of the land. In a moment of catharsis Chase found the gentle hiss of the spraying water kissing the reservoir washed away most of his negative thoughts. At least until he saw the Pure Rain truck setting up their equipment next to the fountain.

"People are really going to drink out of this filthy fountain?" Sergio asked.

"They certainly will," a man who appeared to be in charge of the operation answered.

"So how does this thing work? Is it simply a large water filter?" Chase asked.

"In a sense, but there is also a natural chemical and mineral purification process in which a proprietary blend of harmless chemicals are introduced, the water is then super-heated, blast chilled, then heated again before finally being cooled to the optimal drinking temperature," the man explained.

"What chemicals are used?" Beverly asked.

"I'm afraid that is proprietary. And quite frankly, even I don't know the exact chemical composition. Kind of like the Colonel's secret recipe of eleven herbs and spices," the man said with a grin.

The three of them nodded and walked away. While it would serve as the main source of the water in the fountain, the truck didn't appear to be worth the effort it would take the boy to breach.

Sergio shook his head. "If we were looking for your normal, garden variety terrorist that would make the perfect place to launch an attack. But this is no garden variety psychopath. I'm sure he merely need dip his rancid toe in the water."

"If it would even take that. You saw what the little girl was able to do without physically making contact with anything," Beverly said.

They walked around for another hour until the park started to clear out. Back at their car Beverly opened the rear of the vehicle and allowed Sergio to double check their weapons. They didn't have many, a tranquilizer gun, a nine-millimeter pistol and Sergio's personal sniper rifle he brought from home. He tried to imagine the park teeming with little kids playing in the fountain and tried to locate a shooter's nest with a high vantage point. Aside from the roof of the casino there was no high ground overlooking the fountain, not even as much as a tall, bushy tree.

They spent the next six hours sleeping in shifts and keeping an eye out for a caste of little demons. Sergio was the last to take over the watch. The lack of activity had him wondering if they had made a mistake and this event was nothing more than just a fun time for all. A caravan of vehicles with expensive bicycles in roof racks pulled into the parking lot. The bikes were quickly unloaded, and the cars disappeared back across the MacArthur Bridge.

Sergio walked over to the casino and brought back coffees for the three of them. Beverly and Chase were both awake, and it wasn't any wonder. Just in the time it took to go get coffee the island had erupted into a bustle of activity. What was once an easy surveillance task just a few minutes ago was now nearly impossible.

"When does this race start?" Sergio asked.

Chase glanced down at his phone. The bicycle race starts in just a few minutes."

"When will they finish?"

"Averaging twenty miles an hour they should complete the sixty-mile race in roughly three hours," Chase said.

"We have to watch these guys go in circles for three hours?" Beverly quipped.

Red and blue lights danced across the grass from police motorcycles as they set up barricades around the perimeter road. By seven a.m. the bicycle riders burst from the starting gate and made their way down The Strand. After the riders disappeared from their view, Chase, Beverly, and Sergio all made a mad dash for a row of portable toilets. Chase was coming out of the toilet when he caught sight of the boy.

Chase Jr. was sitting on top of a picnic table across from the Flynn pavilion on the banks of Lake Tacoma. Several kayakers with cameras around their necks were paddling toward the canal. There was some distance between them, but Chase could make out that the child was waving at him. Taunting him.

"He's over there," Chase said, tapping Sergio on the shoulder.

By the time Sergio turned to look the boy had disappeared, shielded by a wave of bicyclists making their way around the course for another lap. Chase suddenly had a bad feeling when he noticed many of the riders were being handed bottles of water with the Pure Rain logo on the reusable bottles. Before he could warn the riders, he spotted Chase Jr. standing on a pedestrian bridge watching the riders zip passed him underneath. The boy cocked his finger like a gun and began *shooting* the riders.

The entire field of riders erupted into chaos. The lead rider began to choke and fell off his bike and before he could regain his footing, he was hit by a dozen bikes, knocking him back down to his knees. The tangle of riders writhed in agony as they clutched their midsections while curled into the fetal position. Many managed to roll over onto their knees to vomit, others didn't even bother to roll over.

An EMT unit came speeding up to the pile and were immediately overwhelmed once they stepped out of their truck and saw the massive amount of injuries they were facing. Chase was trotting over to assist when he caught movement out of the corner of his eye. Richie was running toward the fountain while flapping his arms in an anomalous display.

"Shit, look," Chase said, pointing toward Chase Jr. who was making his way toward the crowd of people encircling the Scott Memorial fountain.

By the time Sergio and Beverly realized what he was talking about, Chase was on a dead run trying to outflank the boy. They scrambled to get into the Escalade so they could try to warn those at the fountain they needed to evacuate, subtle enough to not cause a stampede. Richie was yelling something, but Chase couldn't hear him over the sound of chain saws chewing their way through downed branches.

The boy stopped, turned, and wagged his finger at Richie stopping him dead in his tracks. He immediately grasped at his throat and Chase knew the little monster was poisoning his friend. Chase Jr. was having too much fun provoking the meddlesome cop and failed to notice two things, Chase bearing down on him from the flanking position and Rose Marie standing in the shadow of a piece of heavy machinery.

Chase launched himself and hit the boy with everything he had. Both of them were dazed but the boy recovered more quickly and was on his feet running for the crowd gathered at the fountain. His hold on Richie had been broken and the birdman joined in the pursuit.

Richie got to the boy first and wrestled him to the ground. He cradled him in his arms and marched the struggling lad toward the woodchipper where workers were feeding long limbs from a downed silver maple into the gaping maw. Chips of bark and slivers of leaves shot out the back into a large yellow hopper attached to the chipper.

"Hey! What in the hell do you think you are doing?" one of the men called out once he noticed Richie heading for the front of the chipper with a struggling child in his arms.

In a heroic act one of the workers swept Richie's legs out from underneath him, knocking him to the ground. Chase Jr. scampered away from the man and started running for the fountain. Again, he failed to notice Chase bearing down on him from an oblique angle. Out of the corner of his eye he saw the look on his father's face and stopped.

"Dad?" he said with a victim's expression painting his face.

Chase didn't even falter for one millisecond. He slammed into the child with full force, driving them both headlong into the woodchipper. The machine groaned in protest while the horrified workers looked on, unable to prevent the inevitable. Richie tried to scream but sand poured from his open mouth preventing him from stopping the little girl.

Rose Marie had clambered up into the hopper just before Chase leaped into the pulverizing teeth with the boy. Unsuspecting spectators were horrified when a torrent of blood, flesh and bone spewed from the rear of the mechanical beast, coating the grinning girl with viscous death.

"Ah, there you are," Rose Marie said and bent down to pick up the snarling mass of Chase Jr.'s essence which she brought to her mouth and ingested with jubilation.

Sergio watched in horror as Chase met his prophesized fate in the most gruesome manner imaginable. Richie was pleading with him, but every time the man opened his mouth sand poured from the orifice. He saw as the little girl crouched down to scoop something up from the pile of human debris and then he realized why Richie was so upset. He drew his weapon and fired at the girl several times but was too far away. She sucked the blackness through her lips like decayed spaghetti, smiled and disappeared into the crowd. Richie struggled to his feet and ran after her, oddly enough, singing a happy song as he ran by Sergio and Beverly.

"Going to the chapel, and we're going to get buried," Richie shrieked as he too disappeared into the crowd.

~ ~ ~

Sergio and Beverly spent the next several hours being interviewed by an FBI terrorist task force at an undisclosed location.

"We found the birds you stole," Agent Crawford informed Beverly.

"I stole? I didn't steal any birds. I have no idea what you are talking about."

"We have you on camera."

"I don't doubt you have someone on camera but you sure as hell have no evidence that it was me. You're fishing just like Captain White said you would."

"You being a veterinarian and all I would think you would respect the sanctity of an animal's life."

"As I have already stated, I have no idea what you are referring to. And of course, I respect the lives of animals, I do manage to save their lives on a daily basis after all," Beverly said, praying her nervousness was not showing.

"Then why would you leave birds, not only birds, but very rare, endangered birds in lockers to starve to death," the agent said, resting his palms on the table as he stood over her.

"The birds are dead?" she asked.

"So, you do know about the birds."

"I'm just concerned about the life of any animal."

"They were all dead," Agent Crawford replied, lying about there being two of them still alive.

"Good," Beverly said under her breath. She leaned back in her chair and smiled. "I think I want that lawyer now."

Chapter Forty-One

"Sergio, Tom Bancroft here."

"What's going on Tom?" Sergio asked, knowing it must be big if his longtime crosstown rival were contacting him. The two of them were on cordial terms, but rarely communicated.

"There's something going down with your man Black."

"Something like what?"

"Chatter is, he's holed up downtown in an abandoned church. The talk is he has a hostage too. A little girl."

"What kind of chatter?"

"I overheard the feds talking. They are really uptight about getting a lid on this terrorist crap."

"What terrorist crap?"

"Haven't you heard? Richie Black has been labeled a domestic terrorist. They claim he is responsible for all these recent attacks."

"That's bullshit," Sergio blurted.

"I know that. Hey, you and I may not be all that chummy, but Richie and I go way back. There is no way in hell he went rogue or dirty. I don't buy any of the bullshit the feds are spreading."

"Thanks for the head's up Tom. How long do I have?"

"Ten minutes, maybe less. Tell you what, you get your ass to that church as fast as you can, and I will try and run interference as best as I can. I've always wanted to use my new stop sticks," he said with a chuckle. "Keep your phone dialed into me so you can hear what's going down once the shit hits the fan."

"I'm already there," Sergio said and put the phone down.

He got out of the Wagoneer and began to look around. There was no suitable high ground to set up a nest. He was ready to just burst into the church guns a blazing, but he knew that wouldn't accomplish a damned thing other than getting himself and Richie both killed. And then he spotted a rickety old water tower that probably wouldn't even hold his weight, but it was his only option.

"How did you know he would be here?" Beverly asked.

"He was singing Going to the Chapel of Love when he ran by. It only stood to reason this would go full circle. This is where he first met the little girl so it makes sense it would be the last place they would face each other."

Beverly helped Sergio gather his gear and walked with him to the water tower. Sergio uncased his rifle and loaded the weapon before he dropped down to one knee and shot the padlock off the cage securing the ladder.

"So much for the element of surprise," he said.

"You're going to climb up that rickety thing?" Beverly asked.

"It's the only high ground within range."

"This looks as though it should have been torn down decades ago. Don't you have a harness or something?"

"In my gear at home, sure. Here, no. This is going to have to be free style and without a safety net."

Sergio swore he felt the water tower swaying with each rung he climbed up the rickety ladder. Once he made it to the catwalk encircling the tower he laid down and scooted himself into position. He zoomed the scope into the church between broken panes of glass until he saw footprints in the dust on the floor. He tracked the footprints until he had eyes on Richie.

"It's so nice to see you again, Detective Black," Rose Marie said, jumping up onto one of the balcony seats. It folded down with a creak of protest.

"This is over," Richie choked out after several attempts.

"No, Detective Black, this is only the beginning."

"I'm going to stop you."

Rose Marie laughed for a long minute before settling back in. "No, detective, this is what is going to happen. In just a few minutes the cavalry is going to rush in, shoot you dead and save a little girl from a maniac. Your life will end with you being nothing more than a pathetic memory, just like poor Jessop Porter. And then, then comes the real fun. The authorities will whisk me away to some unsuspecting family who will keep me safe while I become. And once I become, there will be no stopping me."

"You will be dead by then," Richie managed to say.

"No, I am destined to become a great woman, a world leader. From that position of power, I will be able to corrupt your world to the point of no return."

Sergio continued to move positions. He could see the back of the girl's head but there was a pillar in the way, as if she knew where he was and what he was planning. He tried to line up a right to left shot that would pierce the right side of her back under the shoulder blade on a trajectory for her little black heart. He had placed two mirrors, one on each side of him facing backward so he could see behind himself. If they came in silent, he wouldn't be able to hear their sirens, but he would be able to see emergency lights flashing down the streets from quite a distance at this height.

Once they were only a few blocks away Bancroft gave a few short blasts of his siren which echoed over Sergio's cell phone as a warning.

"Hear that?" Rose Marie said, cupping her ear with her tiny hand. "My knights in shining armor are on their way. And I do agree with you, Richie, this *is* over, but it is over for you."

"I love you Effie," he called out as tears raced down his face.

"Effie? That bitch is long dead, she can't help you now."

"NO!" he screamed and lunged for her, swinging his arm with a sharpened hook fastened to the bone. It whistled through the air toward her head.

Sergio managed to get himself into position where he felt confident, he could put a bullet in the kill zone. He was looking through the scope lining up his target when he noticed the finger on Richie's hand was flexing.

Sergio, just pull the damned trigger.

Sergio squeezed off a round, the gun jumped in his hand, and he settled his eye back into the scope. Rose Marie smiled and slowly raised her arms like an angel spreading her wings while leaning her body slightly to the left. Shards of glass sprayed from the stained-glass window and Richie felt a pinch in his chest. He dropped to his knees onto the cold, hard floor of the church. Richie was down on the floor in a pool of blood, the little girl craned her neck and smiled at Sergio. She had somehow anticipated his shot, causing him to kill his friend. She formed her hand in the shape of a gun and pulled the trigger as a throng of FBI vehicles swarmed the church. She had won.

"I love you Richie Black," were the very last words he heard, spat at him through Rose Marie's mocking tone.

~ ~ ~

Rose Marie's knights in shining armor rescued her from the psychopathic rogue cop and put her into the care of nuns at a local orphanage since she could not tell them who her parents were. Now months had passed and there had been no more signs of the coming apocalypse. The press conducted interview after interview with her making her the most adoptable child in the world. And Rose Marie acted the part splendidly.

"Good news, we just received word that you have been adopted by a nice, young Canadian couple from Windsor. Canadians are some of the nicest people on earth," Sister Mary Oliphant said with a smile and a tousle of the girl's hair.

"Oh, my goodness, yes. Our friends to the north don't have a mean bone in their bodies," Sister Margaret Brooks said with an added tousle of her own.

Rose Marie smiled back at them with a smile that nauseated her and turned her attention back to the doll in her lap. Under her breath she whispered, "Not for long."

Rose Marie's smile faded as they set off across the bridge into Canada. There was still a very annoying loose end she needed to take care of. She sensed there was another problem as well, something even bigger than the little girl who managed to escape her wrath. She would deal with that when the time came. She had time; in fact, she had all the time in the world.

~ ~ ~

"Hey, Richie, I'm glad to see you're awake," Beverly said.

Richie shifted positions while making an unintelligible noise.

"Damn, Black, I always considered you an ugly mug, but you have owned it this time my man."

"Shut up and quit mocking him, you know he can understand what you are saying."

"Bullshit, he's just a bird."

Richie let out a squawk that sounded like a cross between a belch and a fart.

"Damn, Bev, what have you been feeding him?" Sergio said.

She laughed and poured two coffees from a Thermos, handing one to Sergio. The remnants of a long, bleak winter lined the highway shoulder in gray piles of slush.

"Do you think they will come after us?" Beverly asked.

"For what? Stealing another bird?" Sergio replied with a smile. "Even though I burned a lot of bridges this go around, I still had a few markers I could call in. One was the coroner who was also a friend of Richie's. It was easy to convince her to let me have the body when she was done. At that point the FBI didn't care, they had tidied everything up and topped it off with a big red bow."

"I hope so."

"Turn that up," Sergio said, bobbing his head toward the radio.

"Amanda Nelson here. I am speaking with Pete Dawson with the Department of Homeland Security. Mr. Dawson, is it your belief that none of the strange events of the past several weeks had anything to do with terrorist activity?"

"None whatsoever, unless you consider the arsonist in Detroit a terrorist, but they have been caught and dealt with."

"What about the freak storms, blackouts and rising river levels."

"There has been an extensive study conducted and every event has been linked to climate change, even the eclipse over Morningside can be explained using climatology models."

"Oh, this ought to be good," Sergio said.

"Climate change? But limited to only the Detroit area?" Amanda Nelson asked.

"That is what I said. If you wish to see the data for yourself, it has been posted on the NOAA website."

"Would you care to elaborate?"

"No, I would not. It is a matter of national security and I have been advised to limit my comments to only the facts. Now, I have a meeting so there will be no further questions."

"Well, there you have it," Amanda said, turning back to face the camera. "Once again, climate change rears its ugly head," she said, trying in vain to mask her sarcasm.

Sergio reached over and turned the radio back down. He had to wonder if there wasn't a measure of sarcasm in the newscaster's last comment. Either way, he was glad to hear the story had been squashed and Richie's record had not been tarnished.

Beverly shook her head. Not a single mention of Chase or Richie in the entire broadcast. "True hero's stories are seldom told," she said with a sigh.

"Hey, I never got the chance to tell you just how sorry I am about what happened to Chase. I know you two were close."

"He told me right from the start it was his destiny. I'm okay with it, mainly because I know in my heart of hearts, he is in a much better place right now," Beverly said.

"Amen," Sergio said followed by a boisterous laugh.

Richie reverberated from the back seat.

"Where to handsome," Beverly asked, turning her head toward the ugly black bird in the cage in the back seat.

Richie stood up, ruffled his feathers, and pecked at a compass wired to the side of his cage.

"North. We're going north," she said to Sergio.

He veered the Wagoneer onto the entrance ramp heading north across the Ambassador Bridge into Canada.

"I hear the Canadians are nice people," Sergio said.

"Let's just hope they stay that way," Beverly said, looking out the window of the car hoping to spot a spring bud or two.

Chapter Forty-Two

"Welcome."

Chase recognized the voice but couldn't see who was speaking. In fact, he couldn't see much of anything. Truth be told, there was nothing to see, not even blackness. His vision was three hundred and sixty degrees as if he were looking down from a drone, but there was nothing at all to see. He tried to wiggle his fingers in front of his face, but the sensation was so bizarre he stopped.

"It will take some time getting used to."

"Used to?"

"Your new form."

"Where am I?"

"You are here of course."

"Why do you insist on being vague?" Chase asked.

"Because even if I answered every one of your questions in detail, soon, you would not recall any of it. Soon, you will only exist."

"Are you saying that I am one of you now?"

"You were always one of us, I told you that already."

"Is this heaven?"

"I don't know, it just is. In a short while you will remember nothing of who you were or where you came from. Never again will you feel, pain, sadness, frustration, or any of the myriad of sensations that caused your human self discomfort. From this point forward, you will only know eternal bliss."

Chase felt shards of himself slipping away every single second and he knew Zera was right. Painful memories were being ripped from him and replaced with a sense of peaceful wonderment that enveloped him like a mother's embrace.

"What about Richie?"

"Soon you will not remember your friend. But, for the sake of your own peace of mind at this very moment I will tell you this. Richie will be joining you soon, though you will not remember him, and he will not remember you. He has work left to do, but soon he will be brought into the fold as will the others. You have done well, Chase Coltrain, just as I suspected you would."

Chase hovered at the brink of eternity staring out into a vast nothingness. It was a void with no boundaries, no color, no sounds, nor smells, but it was absolutely magnificent. And then, Chase Coltrain was no more.

www.ingramcontent.com/pod-product-compliance
Lightning Source LLC
LaVergne TN
LVHW010556100826
845148LV00014B/2735

* 9 7 8 1 7 3 5 4 6 3 6 4 3 *